The *Nagaro* Chronicle 3

Return to Lankura

Carol Louise Wilde

Rivulus Books Trade Paperback Edition

Text, maps, and internal artwork by Carol Louise Wilde

Published in the United States of America by Rivulus Books, Arcadia, CA. The Rivulus Books name and Rivulus Books logo are trademarks of Rivulus Books.

ISBN: 978-1-944492-09-0

Cover art copyright by Cherie Foxley

Return to Lankura **is the third book of the Nagaro Chronicle**

Four years after Nagaro and his followers formed their covenant and set sail in their captured Mahuk war galley, he commands four ships and is known all the way from the coast of his native Edrovir to the Mahuk Baar. He and his men carry on a form of honorable piracy, attacking only Mahuk warships to free galley slaves, an activity that has made Nagaro a hero to the common folk of Edrovir and caused the Emperor of the Mahuk Baar to put a price on his head.

Nagaro hasn't forgotten how, at seventeen, he was forced to marry the princess by use of a will-enslaving drug and was ridiculed throughout Edrovir as the "Idiot Prince", but his former identity seems safely buried as long as he stays away from the king, the princess, and everyone who knew him in the capital city of Lankura. Nagaro is well content with his chosen work, but his activities have attracted the attention of the King of Edrovir who has instructed Kuran Kel, Edrovir's Lord of the Royal Fleet, to look for him. Nagaro's decision to boldly meet this man sets him on a course that will change his life and ultimately alter the history of his world.

To Arthur and Alex, always a part of my inspiration.
Believe in the possibility of the good and try to do what is right
to the best of your ability.

Harmoth
Edrovir
Pakoa
Chitaopa
Judaba
Tambali
Jinara
Janidi
Atadalba
Alam
Shufa
Osfaraad
Mahuk
Baar
Jaamra
Sar Tipaal
Paktaar

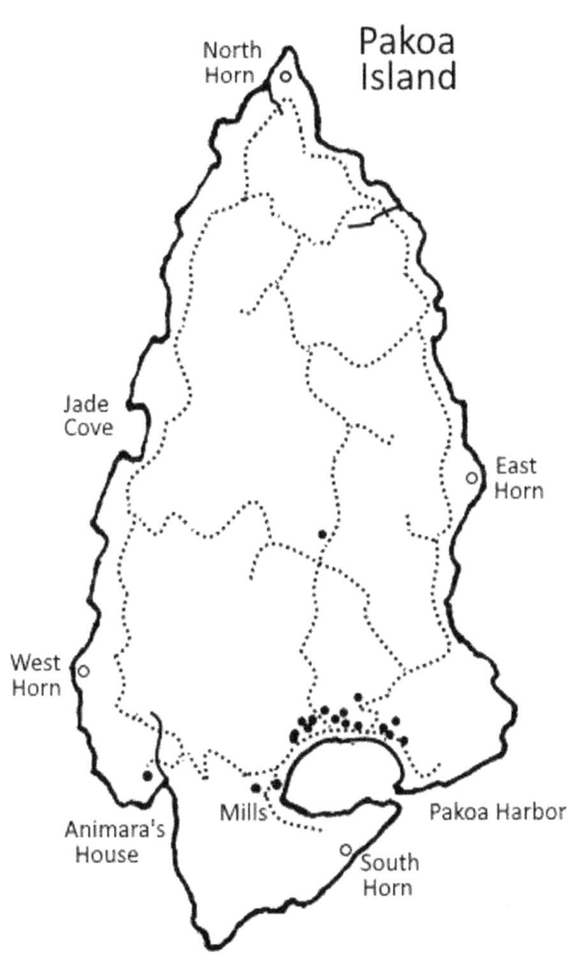

Pakoa
Island
North
Horn
Jade
Cove
East
Horn
West
Horn
Mills
Pakoa Harbor
Animara's
House
South
Horn

Edrovir
(Upper Coast)
Outer Faranos
Big Farano
Bona Farana
Long Harbor
Little Farano
Farano Channel
Inner Faranos
Koro
Tobai
Obai
Galenor
Wotana
Great Channel
Borobai
Tirobo
Lankura
Soku
Farano'sMouth
Tunapa

Lankura
Edrovir
(Lower Coast)
Tirobo
Soku
Tunapa
Farano's
Mouth
Boka
Lapoa
Omei
Oapa
Kel Tierna
Moluaro
Duani
Great
Channel
Lomoas
Kapala
Oru
Harmoth
Haru
Pakoa
(disputed border)

CONTENTS

Chapter 1

The Reason For It All

The dawn light of a bright spring morning shone obliquely across the waters of the northern coast of the Mahuk Baar, striking silver from the crests of long even swells. Later, as the sun climbed the sky, the wind would rise. Now all was calm— or it would have been, were it not for the small drama that was playing out upon that almost glassy sea.

A single Mahuk war galley, under the green and gold colors of the warlord Tuluptak, was fleeing before two pursuing ships, her oars rising and dipping in a frantic rhythm. The pursuing craft were also galleys. The steady even strokes of their oars churned the sea, and the banners flying from their mainmasts bore the image of a white sword, horizontal, on a sable field.

The commander of the Mahuk craft, Captain Taokep, understood his danger all too well. In the past four years, those white-and-black banners had become known through all the length of the Mahuk Baar. Those flags identified the ships that followed Kiraam Shaku-Tal, the "Thief of Slaves," known to his own Droviri folk as Nagaro the Pirate, or simply as Captain Nagaro.

The pirate now had four ships under his command, all captured Mahuk war galleys, and they hunted in pairs. One of the two pursuing ships bore the pattern of alternating black and white diamonds along her flanks that marked her as Kiraam Shaku-Tal's infamous flagship, the *Sword of Freedom*. If the Mahuk craft were overtaken, Captain Taokep knew he could expect, not only to be robbed of his oar deck slaves and any valuable cargo, but to find himself face to face with the feared pirate captain himself.

Tales abounded of the man, tales that claimed him to be everything from a demon incarnate to, strangely enough, a man of honor. It was said that Kiraam Shaku-Tal permitted men to keep their lives if they surrendered to him.

Among the Mautep, surrender to a manifestly superior force held no dishonor, and continued life was generally preferable to the alternative. Nevertheless, a warrior-captain who found himself obliged to go before his lord in need of forty new galley slaves couldn't expect a warm reception. And some Mautep captains had found themselves robbed of their ships as well. Therefore the captain of the fleeing craft had ordered his slave master to press the rowers to their limit while he prayed that those rowers might catch no rumor of the pursuers' identity. Slaves who sensed the possibility of freedom had an alarming tendency to suddenly become immune to the lash.

The pursuit had begun the previous evening in Jinari waters, and the two pirate craft had gained significantly on their prey before night descended, with the two moons riding up the eastern sky as the last glow of sunlight faded.

The brighter moon, Talebra, had shed her gibbous light on the chase for much of the night, allowing both hunter and hunted to observe each other's movements and leaving the Mautep captain little choice but to flee due south under sail while the wind lasted.

Necessity had required that he rest his slaves as much as possible, for they were already weary when his ship had caught the pirates' attention. Kiraam Shaku-Tal could, of course, rest his rowers whenever his quarry rested. The pirate had matched Taokep's course through the moonlit night, and the pursuers had continued to gain.

In the darkness that came when Talebra set, Captain Taokep had tried altering course, but caution had betrayed him. Not wishing to lose too much of his dwindling lead, or to stray too far from his intended course, he had turned his bow only a point to starboard, and continued so while Naru, the dark moon, had finished his westward arc and dipped into the sea.

Dawn had come, revealing the two pirate ships farther to port than they had been at last sighting, but not more distant, and they had immediately altered course to intercept their prey. The wind had died with the dawn, and the Mautep captain had been forced to put the slaves to the oars again.

So the oar deck below had been throbbing continuously since sunrise to the beat of the drum, punctuated by curses and the snap of the whip. And still the pirate ships had been steadily gaining, plying their oars as well. Already the gap between hunters and hunted had narrowed to a quarter mile.

Captain Taokep was making for the island of Osfaraad, its low shape a mile and half to the south, looming purple-gray in the dawn light. He wasn't in his own lord's territory, and it was uncertain what help he might gain from the island's fishermen inhabitants, but at least the island would offer shelter to his men if the accursed Kiraam Shaku-Tal seized his ship. The captain would have been less hopeful of a warm welcome had he known that almost a quarter of the present male population of Osfaraad were former galley slaves freed from ships like the one he now commanded, by the very man who now pursued him.

Taokep lowered his spyglass and rubbed his chin. The island still seemed disappointingly distant, while the pursuing ships had grown alarmingly close. The Mautep captain leaned over the speaking tube that communicated with the oar deck below and called for more speed. Below him on the oar deck, the slave master swore as he gave the signal to the drummer to increase the rhythm of his drumbeats. The slaves couldn't keep this up for long.

A short time later the captain also swore as, peering through his spyglass from his post atop the stern castle, he saw the rhythm of the pirate's oars increase its tempo as well. What were those sons-of-dogs made of? The two pursuing craft came on, surging forward, each hull cleaving the water like a knife. The gap between them and their prey was narrowing at a perceptibly faster rate.

Taokep made one last call for more speed, but it was already too late. The pursuers were only a few ship-lengths away and shouted words now reached the captain's ears. Men in the bows of the pursuing ships were using speaking trumpets to project their voices across the water. The words came in Droviri and in Hashti:

"Ship oars for Captain Nagaro!"

"Ship oar for Thief of Slave!"

Oars began to waver all along the flanks of the Mahuk galley, and a cheer went up from the oar deck as voices began raggedly to chant:

"Nagaro! Nagaro! Nagaro!"

"Kiraam! Kiraam! Kiraam Shaku-Tal!"

The Mahuk vessel lost way as her slave crew, ignoring the lash, began to draw the oars in through the ports. Deprived of forward propulsion, the ship was still carried forward by her momentum, but she was slowing moment by moment.

The two pirate craft came on, positioning themselves to pass close along either side of the hapless war galley. The *Sword of Freedom* took the position to starboard, and her sister ship, the *Sea Eagle,* to port. Spray plumed as the pirates' oar blades bit the water to slow them in the final stretch. Then, at the last possible moment, the pirate oars were swiftly drawn in. As the two ships came alongside their prey, teams of men arrayed along the rails flung their grapples. The iron hooks streaked out, trailing ropes like comet tails.

Beset from both sides, the Mautep crew tried desperately to hold the ships apart with fending-pikes, but they were overwhelmed as Captain

Nagaro's sea warriors left their own oar decks in force, pouring up out of the hatches to join the fray. In a matter of minutes, all three ships were lashed together, side by side, with the Mahuk galley neatly caught in the middle of the snare.

Captain Taokep stood his ground beside his ship's mainmast, facing the starboard rail. On that side lay the flagship of his terrible adversary. From that side would come Kiraam Shaku-Tal. Taokep set his teeth and gripped his sword with a sweat-slicked hand. If the tales were true, it would not be difficult to identify the Thief of Slaves.

The pirates came leaping over the rail, swords in hand, and the man who led them leapt as lightly as a deer and moved with a speed and grace like nothing Taokep had seen. The man had a close-trimmed black beard, black hair tied at the neck, and skin as brown as one of the Turowan slaves on Taokep's oar deck, though the form of his features bespoke the pale-skinned Kelorin race. He wore black pants and boots, and a leather vest the color of old blood. Just such was the description of Captain Nagaro— of Kiraam Shaku-Tal.

As the pirate captain's feet touched the deck of the Mautep ship, his gray eyes raked the faces of the warriors arrayed against him until they found and locked their gaze upon Captain Taokep. Then the man came on.

Mautep warriors who tried to defend against the pirate captain's onslaught were soon clutching at fresh wounds or seeing their swords struck from their hands by the demon swordsman. He was flanked on the right by a stocky Turowan and on the left by a tall, broad-shouldered Hashtep. The latter two men were no mean fighters in their own right, but their captain eclipsed them. Captain Nagaro came, like a wind through a field of corn, until he stood in front of Taokep. There he stopped and stood with his sword held up before him, not so much menacing as merely ready for whatever might come.

Taokep couldn't help but notice his adversary's sword as it floated before his eyes, and any doubt he might have had of the man's identity was banished instantly. He knew he was looking upon the Sword of Shofeer. The elegant weapon had a slightly curved blade, a pattern of fine gold tracery upon the curved hand guard, and a single piece of polished green stone in the pommel. According to the growing legend, Kiraam Shaku-Tal had taken this sword at the battle of Jaamra from a fallen Mautep of the House of Shofeer, and had defended his right to carry it a dozen times since in combat against some of the best swordsmen of the Mahuk Baar.

Taokep stood, scarcely daring to breathe, waiting for his adversary to strike. Waiting for the end. The idea that he might himself attack this unnatural being was out of the question. Taokep was only a moderately good swordsman, and well aware of his limitations. Swords still clashed together behind him and further fore and aft along the deck, though the fighting had stopped in his vicinity. Everyone close at hand, Mautep and pirate alike, seemed to be watching the two captains, waiting to see what they would do.

The pirate captain considered his opponent for several seconds without apparent malice. He scarcely appeared old enough to have done half the things attributed to him. Taokep hadn't expected Kiraam Shaku-Tal to be so young, but then he supposed this was not a thing men were inclined to mention when describing how the man had bested them. The smaller Turowan and the big Hashtep who flanked him were young as well. Both of these men stood with their swords ready, waiting.

Abruptly the pirate captain lowered his blade to point at the deck and spoke in accented but serviceable Hashti.

"I am Captain Nagaro. If all your man put down their sword, I swear by my honor none will be harmed."

Taokep numbly returned the other man's courtesy. "I am Captain Taokep jir-Muktaar."

He licked dry lips. Were the tales true? Could he trust the honor of a pirate? The honor of a Droviri? It struck him that, although this Thief of Slaves had disarmed half a dozen men and wounded as many more since boarding, none of the wounds appeared serious. The man— if man he truly was— had slain no one, though Taokep hadn't the slightest doubt that Kiraam Shaku-Tal could have done so if he had wished.

Some said the man who wielded the Sword of Shofeer understood honor. Some even said the man shunned bloodshed. A quick glance behind him showed Taokep that his men had already been forced together into the center of the deck, trapped between the two pirate crews. They were outnumbered two to one by the pirate warriors, and, even as he looked, his slaves came pouring from the door of the fore cabin. They were ragged and filthy, but those in the front rank were armed with long knives given to them by their rescuers, and their eyes burned with furious exultation.

Captain Taokep was not a young man. Already he had been counting the seasons until he might hang up his sword and enjoy a little peace in his declining years. Though an honorable death in battle was good, retirement after long years of service was better. Lord Tuluptak might not be happy about this loss, but Taokep reflected that the worst he might face would be the prospect starting his retirement a little sooner. He bowed his head briefly to his adversary and made his answer:

"I accept your promise." He raised his voice, then, to carry across the deck. "All man, lay down your sword! We will surrender and live!"

Captain Nagaro addressed his own men then in Droviri, the Common Speech of Edrovir. "Hold your swords! Their captain has ordered surrender. Landros, bid your men hold! And have them keep the freed-men back!"

On the other side of the deck, the captain of the other pirate ship raised his sword in salute to his commander. "Aye, Zirda," came Landros' acknowledgment. Then he turned to give instructions to the men under his command. Severaal of the pirates, some Turowan, some Hashtep, moved to check the advance of the former slaves who were stalking across the deck.

Captain Taokep maintained a stony face, concealing the relief he felt as he presented his sword to the gray-eyed, black-bearded man who stood before him.

For his part, Nagaro also heaved an inward sigh of relief. After four years of pursuing their chosen work, it was rare for his men to have to fight for very long to obtain a surrender. Still, he entered each new encounter with a knot of tension in his stomach. He bowed as he accepted the other captain's blade, then slid his own sword into its sheath. "All your slave are now free and will come with us," he explained in Hashti. "And we will take what you have that we can use." His tone was courteous but decisive. It conveyed respect for the Mautep captain, while at the same time making clear that these conditions were not open to negotiation.

The terms were only what Taokep had expected. "And my ship?" he inquired, endeavoring to conceal his apprehension.

Nagaro flashed him a quick smile, white teeth contrasting with his black beard, as he replied. "Today we do not need another ship."

All along the lines on both sides of the deck, the members of the two pirate crews began to collect the weapons of the surrendering Mautep warriors.

Suddenly there came a cry from the aft end of the deck and both captains turned in time to see one of the pirates fall, the tip of a sword, stained scarlet, protruding from his back. One of the Mautep warriors jerked his sword from the man's body and stepped away, brandishing the bloody weapon.

"*Keshaal!*" The exclamation escaped Taokep's lips. What vengeance would this bring upon them? Hurriedly he swung to face Captain Nagaro, in time to see the shadow that passed across the young man's face and hear him murmur words in Droviri: "*Vothra, guide his spirit.*" The Mautep captain didn't know the meaning of the words, but he could guess their import from the man's expression.

The shadow was gone in an instant, however. Nagaro raised his hand and cried, "*Hold!*" commandingly in his own tongue, and then, "*No man move!*" in Hashti

All along the deck, the pirates and Mautep froze. In the silence that followed there was no sound but the gentle wash and slap of waves and the cry of a distant sea bird.

Turning to Taokep, Nagaro said in Hashti, speaking low, "A moment. I must do something." He handed Taokep's sword to the young Turowan who stood beside him, saying, "You know what to do, Taru, if there's any trouble."

Taru nodded, his eyes hard.

Nagaro turned then to the young Hashtep at his other side. "Come Pavo," he said, gesturing for the tall, broad-shouldered man to follow him, and strode across the deck in the direction of the fallen man and his attacker. Though Nagaro rarely needed a translator any more, it was wise not to risk misunderstanding in a delicate situation. Silently Pavo followed.

The killer stood at bay in fighting stance, sword in hand.

Nagaro appeared to ignore the man as he came to a halt beside the body of his slain follower. He drew a painful sigh, for he remembered this young man well. The fallen man was a Hashtep, a member of the first crew of slaves they had set free the summer when first they had taken to the seas in a single captured Mahuk ship, re-christened the *Sword of Freedom*. The young man's name was Seftep. He had never mastered more than a few phrases of the Common Speech.

Nagaro turned to the nearest member of his crew and asked, "What happened here, Bouno?"

The man, a weathered Turowan was half crouching, his eyes fixed on the offending warrior, his sword held menacingly. He answered out of the side of his mouth without taking his eyes off of the Mautep. "Seftep weren't lookin' fer no trouble, Capt'n. He were just reachin' t' take the man's sword, an' the filthy rotter run 'im through!"

"Aye, Capt'n. That's how it was," one of the other pirate crewmen volunteered.

Nagaro shifted his gaze to the face of the man holding the bloody sword. "What is your name?" he inquired almost blandly in Hashti.

Surprised, the man frowned and answered him. "Hakesh."

Nagaro inclined his head very slightly, his face unreadable. "Hakesh, why did you kill this man?" he asked carefully in the killer's mother tongue.

The Mautep frowned again. He might have mistaken the levelness of Nagaro's tone for an indication of indifference to the deed. His lip curled disdainfully. "He is Hashtep. He was traitor dog, who was fighting his own people!"

Nagaro caught the hint of a movement from Pavo, who stood beside him, and he made a small, quick gesture to restrain his friend, knowing that such accusations of treason were something of a sore point with Pavo.

He addressed himself once more to the killer. "This man was named Seftep. He swore to follow me all his life because I set him free. This he has done. To me he was no traitor." Nagaro had spoken evenly, but there was now a cold edge to his words. The Mautep warrior's jaw began to go slack, and his eyes to show fear, for he was coming to understand that he had made a mistake. Indeed, Hakesh's comrades were all edging away from him.

Nagaro drew his sword in one fluid motion and held it pointing at the deck. He turned significantly to Pavo Maat. "Explain to him, Pavo," he said grimly, "that his life is forfeit for killing one of my loyal crewmen in violation of his captain's order of surrender."

There was a satisfied gleam in Pavo's eye as he translated.

The Mautep warrior jerked erect in alarm. His glance darted from Pavo, to Nagaro, to Captain Taokep. "Captain!" he cried, raising his voice to carry across the deck to where Taokep stood. "Will you let him do this for killing one little slave? You must defend me!"

There was a murmur among the ranks of the Mautep. Warriors moved farther away from Hakesh. Some of the Droviri pirates grinned expectantly.

Captain Taokep had heard his crewman's plea. For a long moment he stood frozen, feeling the tension in the air, reading it in the stance of the young Turowan who held him at sword-point. The Mautep Captain knew he couldn't hope to prevail by force of arms, and any wrong movement on his part might precipitate a bloodbath. He could try to plead for the man's life, but on what grounds? His men stood surrounded by former slaves who would have no sympathy for Hakesh, and the man had clearly violated the surrender. Were he dealing with another Mautep captain, Taokep's course would be clear: Follow the Rule of Honor.

Taokep drew a long breath. He raised his voice for all to hear and spoke the time-honored words.

"You broke surrender, Hakesh. You must defend yourself and trust in Sheptuum to protect you if your cause is just."

Almost before Taokep had finished speaking, and without any word of warning, Hakesh drove his sword at Nagaro. It was the desperate act of a man who sees his death standing before him. Quicker than thought, Nagaro's right hand came up. He turned his attacker's thrust with the guard of his sword, so that the point of the Mautep warrior's blade merely nicked his upper left arm instead of passing through his heart. Then, in a continuation of the same movement, he ran the man quickly and cleanly through the chest.

Hakesh toppled forward onto the deck, his body coming to rest beside that of his victim.

Nagaro stood over the second corpse and bowed his head. "Vothra," he said in a low voice that nevertheless carried the length of the main deck because all else was so still, "guide this spirit in its passing, as I would have you guide my spirit in the hour when my time shall come." He bent down then and slowly, almost reverently, wiped his sword clean on the dead man's tunic. He straightened and returned the blade to its sheath. Turning, he walked back across the deck, Pavo following, to where Captain Taokep still stood.

No one else moved. The first stirring of the morning breeze sighed in the rigging.

Taokep saw that there was blood on the pirate captain's arm where he had been cut. The scarlet trickle drew the Mautep's eye, for it told him that this was in fact a mortal man. And Taokep noticed also the slave brand on the man's left shoulder, above the sword-cut. The curving tracery of the pale scar, left by red hot iron, marked its bearer as the former property of Baalkir jir-Akaan, the current Emperor of the Mahuk Baar. So that part of the legend was true as well.

The legend said that Kiraam Shaku-Tal had been one of Baalkir's galley slaves until he had stolen a ship from under Baalkir's nose and led all the slaves on her oar deck to freedom. It was little wonder that the Emperor had set a price on the man's head. The name of Urchak tok-Faar, the unfortunate former captain of the re-christened *Sword of Freedom* was also known in every household of the Mahuk Baar. Known, and spoken more often with derision than with sympathy.

Nagaro regarded the other captain somberly for a moment before he spoke.

"I promise all my man that unjust death will be avenged, but I am sorry that two man are now dead."

Taokep swallowed. Captain Nagaro gave every impression of being sincere. Now the Mautep captain congratulated himself on the wisdom of his decision. This man had dealt fairly with Hakesh's treachery, and he had made the man's death mercifully quick. At the same time, it was clear that the pirate captain could have cut down any man he wished— Taokep included— as easily as a farmer cuts wheat.

Taokep raised his voice for all to hear. "It is Rule of Honor," he said, speaking words that were a ritual among the Mautep. "Dishonor was done, and with honor it has been answered."

The world seemed to breathe again. All along the deck men shifted and exchanged glances. There were murmurings among the pirates as those who understood Hashti reassured those who did not. This was justice— a death for a death. The price had been accepted and further bloodshed had been averted.

***

Two hours later, the newly-freed galley slaves and all of the Mautep ship's captured cargo had been transferred to the two pirate craft, and Captain Taokep had been allowed to go his way. Taru and Nagaro were sitting on stools in the infirmary aboard the *Sword of Freedom*. Taru was watching while Tredhold, the ship's doctor, cleaned the small cut on his friend's arm. "What was the Mautep running so hard for?" He wondered aloud. "All he had t' steal were a few silver coins, some Pakoan jade, and a pile o' rugs!"

Nagaro massaged his temples with his free hand. "Those 'rugs' are Jinari carpets, Taru," he said. "My lady guardian used to have one, and she told me once that every thread in it had to be tied by hand in just the right place to make the pattern. They're quite valuable. But it was really on account of the men— the slaves— that he was fleeing. They were worth more to him than his plunder."

"That may be," Taru grumbled, "but we've taken nothing we can sell for ourselves in Pakoa Town. There'll be no market there for those fancy carpets, or the jade. And the coins are Mahuk-minted."

Nagaro sighed. "The silver we will divide as usual among the freed Hashtep before setting them ashore. For the rest, we must trust Gedras to do the best he can for us."

Pavo Maat's imposing figure loomed in the doorway. "Two man wanted to stay on Osfaraad," he informed them. "They have both go ashore. But other Hashtep want to go to mainland. We are ready to sail now. What are your order, Nagaro?"

Nagaro considered briefly. "We'll have to make for Alam Shufa. It will take a little time to bury Seftep, and the rocky point there gives some shelter. But we don't want to arrive before nightfall. Take us due north for a while, back into Jinari waters. We'll hide among the Jinari isles, and circle back when the sun gets low."

"Aye, Zirda Captain!" Pavo saluted, his face an impassive mask. Then he grinned, completely spoiling the effect. "That is good way. Will you come out soon? Crew like to see their captain."

Nagaro weakly returned his friend's smile. "Yes, I'll come, as soon as Tred is finished with me."

Taru stood up as soon as Pavo's figure ceased to eclipse the doorway. He stretched. "I've not yet made sure that the oar deck's in order," he observed absently. "Guess I'd better get to it."

"Yes, Taru, you'd better do that."

Taru turned back at the doorway and pulled himself stiffly upright. "Aye, Zirda Captain!" He mimicked Pavo's unorthodox response and salute. Then he was gone, his laughter carrying along the passage between the stern cabins.

Tredhold paused in the act of applying a bandage to Nagaro's arm. "I don't know why ye ever went and made Taru your first mate," he said shaking his head. "He's been quite insufferable ever since."

Nagaro had smiled fleetingly at Taru's performance. Now the smile died. "He's very good at commanding the oar deck, and he was only having his fun." Then he noticed the healer's arched eyebrow. "Oh, I'm sorry," he said. "Was that a joke, Tred? I guess I'm not really in the mood for jesting."

Tredhold studied him. "Ye've been in a dark mood ever since that Mautep showed us his stern. What ails ye, man?"

Nagaro looked away. "You know I don't like it when we lose one of ours, Tred, or when I have to kill a man... that way."

Tredhold finished his bandage and let go of Nagaro's arm with a sigh. "Aye," he said, "I know. Though I thought ye'd gotten a bit hardened to it over the seasons."

Nagaro stood up, flexing his left arm experimentally. "It doesn't really get easier, Tred. Not for me anyway. Do you know that was the eighteenth man whose spirit I've sent into the void?"

"Is that it then?" Tredhold shook his head. "And ye think that's so many? I'm sure I've slain far more than that in my time, though not so many since I've been in your service. Ye do a good job o' keeping the casualties low. I'm sure I've healed more than I've slain, too. At least that's what I tell myself. And I find it doesn't do to keep count."

"But I *don't* keep count." Nagaro frowned. "I don't have to. I can remember every one— not a name or a face, perhaps, but at least the circumstances." He walked to the porthole, and stood looking out. "Too many of them have been like this one. The man knew he was as good as dead."

Tred shrugged. "He was armed, and that means he had a chance. He went for ye first, too. And he cut ye."

Nagaro sighed. "Yes, he cut me. And maybe it gave him some satisfaction in the instant before he died. I don't know, Tred. Sometimes it seems I'm not a warrior, but an executioner."

The healer sat silently on his stool for a moment. "Perhaps ye are, sometimes," he admitted at last. "Because ye have to be. But at least ye're a *just* executioner."

Nagaro laughed shortly. "That's one of the things Vothra said to me that night after Jaamra. The Spirit trusted me to choose which man to kill and which to spare." He shook his head. "Vothra also told me that I shouldn't strike the first blow. What will I do if one of them ever throws down his sword and says 'all right, then, kill me?' Then I really would be an executioner. Or else I'd be foresworn."

Tredhold had felt a little chill run along his spine at the reference to Vothra's visitation. He'd been witness to the encounter, but this was the first time Nagaro had told him any of what the Benevolent Spirit of the Kelorin had said to him that night. The healer was Leithian, not Kelorin, and out of his depth in matters of Vothrin teaching. He cast about for something to say.

"They're Mautep," he said at last. "And they're warriors. Odds are, they'll always try to fight." He paused, then added, "Ye should go out onto the deck where the freed-men are. It'll do your heart good to see them."

Nagaro sighed and nodded. "You're right about that, Tred," he said, his voice suddenly resolute. "They're the reason for it all. And it's worth it when I look into their faces. Forty men freed, and only two lives lost! If the Mautep stopped keeping slaves tomorrow, I'd be more glad than I can say. But until they do, there's work to be done."

Nagaro went out, after that, leaving Tredhold to put away his paraphernalia. The healer sighed as he picked up his basin, sponge, and strips of cotton cloth. He had given up a career as a sea warrior and ship's doctor in the Royal Fleet of Edrovir to follow this man and help him do his "work." In four years' time, he hadn't once regretted the decision.

On the deck, Nagaro walked among the freed-men, and it was indeed good to see them reveling in the open air— in sun and wind and the simple freedom to walk from one end of the deck to the other whenever they pleased.

As he went among them, Nagaro took the hand of every man who reached out to him and called each one "friend." Many of them seemed only to want to touch him— his hand, or the brand on his shoulder, or the hilt of his sword. Nagaro could only wish they wouldn't be so worshipful. Landros would always point out that the whole thing had been Nagaro's idea. He was the leader, and so it was natural that everyone should thank him personally. Still it didn't seem right that they should treat him like some kind of special being.

"You have my whole crew to thank," he told them. "I am just one man."

Pavo paused for a moment amid the routine drill of checking the direction of the wind and the fill of the sails to watch as Nagaro worked his way across the deck. The big Hashtep didn't let his pleasure show in the muscles of his face, but approval of the ritual glowed in his eyes. He didn't allow himself more than a moment, however. Pavo took his responsibilities as second mate very seriously. He had learned the art and science of it from Landros, following the grizzled Kelorin about and asking questions until the veteran sea warrior had seen the virtue of rewarding such obvious interest with more rigorous instruction. Pavo ranked third in the ship's short hierarchy of command, after Taru, but he seemed not to mind.

Now he nodded as if to himself as he turned away. "Sheptuum protect him," he said quietly, and the wind took his words. "Man who should be prince."

Chapter 2

Something Big

T he sun was sinking westward as the pair of pirate craft slipped from between two isles and set a southward course, paralleling the Jinari coast. The galleys with the black-and-white sword banners had never troubled Jinari shipping, and so the Jinari had never troubled them. Still, the long-standing border dispute between Edrovir and Jinara dictated some caution since Nagaro and his ships hailed from the island of Pakoa which was under Edrovir's dominion.

So it was that Pavo took note of a small fishing boat that altered its course shortly after the *Sword of Freedom* and the *Sea Eagle* emerged from their hiding place. One of the crew on the *Sea Eagle* saw it as well, and raised a shout and pointed. A little later, the small boat altered its course again, and Pavo went to find his captain.

"It is only very small boat," he explained to Nagaro, pointing as he leaned against the port rail of the ship's forecastle. "It does not look dangerous, but it look like it is try to meet with us."

Nagaro followed Pavo's finger, raising his spyglass to his eye to scrutinize the vessel. It did indeed look like an ordinary fishing boat, and he could only see one man on board. Then he noticed something else. Two narrow strips of cloth were tied to one of the boat's mast stays. One was white, the other black.

"It looks like one of Utabala's couriers!" he exclaimed. "And if it is, the ribbons he's flying say that I'm the one he wants to talk to."

Pavo frowned critically. "But home of Utabala is far away. We have never meet one of his boat so far south."

Nagaro nodded. "I know. And it could be someone else using the same signaling system, by chance or by design. Whatever the case, though, I think we should slow down and meet this boat, since, as you say, it doesn't look dangerous. If that man truly wants to talk to me, the mystery will be quickly solved."

Pavo went down to the main deck to give the order to slacken sail, and to shout the directive across to Landros on the *Sea Eagle*. Nagaro remained at the forecastle rail with the spyglass. Long before the little craft pulled along side, he had recognized the man at her tiller. He descended to the main deck and went to stand at the port rail to hail the seaman, just as one of the crew tossed a line across the narrowing gap between the craft.

"Well met, Matapili!" he cried. "What takes you so far from home?"

The Jinari caught the line and deftly put a turn around his bow cleat. He grinned up at Nagaro, his teeth flashing in his dark, sharp-featured face. "Ha, Cap-i-tan Nagaro! I look for *you*." His accented Common Speech came fast and staccato. "Master Utabala send out *tree* boats to look, but I find you first. Praise to de Unnamed One!"

"Three boats!" Nagaro exclaimed in dismay. "He must want to speak to me very badly."

Matapili grinned again. "Master Utabala have some-ting to show Cap-i-tan Nagaro. Some-ting big! He say to come quick."

Nagaro frowned. "What exactly does he have, Matapili?"

The Jinari shook his head. "He do not tell me, Cap-i-tan. But he say to come quick as you can!"

Nagaro's frown deepened. "We might get there tomorrow night— but only if we row."

Matapili's brow creased. "You do not need to come in de night," he offered. "Come in de day now, if you like. Dey say dere is a truce!"

The last words brought an excited murmur from the crewmen all along the rail.

"A truce!" Nagaro felt the excitement as well. "That's good news. But we can't get there any sooner than tomorrow night. We have newly-freed Hashtep to set ashore on the Mahuk coast tonight— and a comrade to bury."

Matapili grew suddenly sober. "May de Unnamed One give peace," he intoned, touching the heel of his hand to his forehead. "Dis you must do. But den you come quick!"

The pirates bade a hasty farewell to the Jinari courier and adjusted their course again, making with renewed speed for Alam Shufa. Nagaro stood brooding at the forecastle rail as the *Sword*'s iron-clad prow plowed the sea. What could Utabala possibly have to show him that was so important? In the past three years he had met surreptitiously half a dozen times with the Jinari merchant's agent. Having served together as slaves on the same oar deck, they found no personal reason to share the enmity that divided their two nations. More than that, Utabala felt himself in Nagaro's debt for his deliverance from bondage.

Utabala had first sought for Nagaro three years ago, sending a message to meet him in his home port of Tambali on the northern coast of

Jinara. That first time, the merchant's agent had shown him several scrolls containing descriptions of medicines and herb lore, remembering the interest Nagaro had shown in similar scrolls looted from a ship belonging to his Jinari master. The merchant's agent hadn't known what Nagaro feared, that those first scrolls were on their way to Dreigen, the Lore Master of the King of Edrovir. Nagaro had explained to Utabala— with some trepidation and without naming names— that his interest in herb lore stemmed from concern that such information might be used to do harm if it fell into the wrong hands. He hadn't intended to suggest that Utabala look further into the matter, but the Jinari had taken it upon himself to do so anyway, seeing it as a way to do Nagaro a service.

Utabala had begun by making a few discreet enquiries within the merchant house of his employer, Mundata Punda, and then expanded his investigation and made cautious enquiries into the dealings of a number of other Jinari merchants. Utabala had kept Nagaro appraised of each significant discovery, and over the course of three years a disturbing picture had emerged of a network of secret trade connections that converged upon the port of Tambali. The goods that moved invisibly through this network ranged from seeds and cuttings of plants, to texts of medical and botanical lore, to such paraphernalia as a distilling apparatus and the infamous bladder-thorns that were used to inject substances directly into a man's blood. In many cases the items appeared to be specifically requested and sought after. But where these secret shipments went beyond Tambali was unknown, and the identity of the person or persons who had ordered them remained obscure.

Nagaro stared moodily across the water. Evening was falling. The undulating hills of the Jinari coast were sliding quickly past, but he didn't mark them. *He has something to show you*, Matapili had said. *Something big.* Had Utabala traced the shipments to some other port? To Edrovir, even?

"What d' ye think it is this time? More scrolls? Or maybe another horse?"

Nagaro had been so rapt in his own thoughts that he hadn't noticed Taru's approach. He motioned for his friend to lower his voice, although there was no one standing near. Taru's mention of another horse was a joke, of course, though there *had* been a horse— a personal gift from Utabala to Nagaro, a graceful, spirited mare of an unusual smoky golden bay. Any thought Nagaro might have had of declining such an extravagant gift had flown right out the stable door the moment he'd set eyes on her. He had named the mare Farusia, for the white star like an opening flower on her forehead.

"It has to be more than just news of another shipment of scrolls, Taru, but I don't understand why Matapili said 'show' rather than 'tell'. And I don't understand the urgency."

Taru scratched his chin. "Aye," he said. "It's not like Utabala t' say 'hurry, hurry. Come quick.' And the men all heard it too. They're all abuzz. Ye'll have t' tell them something."

Nagaro always shared everything Utabala told him with Taru and Pavo, who alone knew the secret of what he had suffered at Dreigen's hands and why he would have liked to thwart the king's Lore Master in any way he could. The other men who sailed with them knew only that their captain occasionally did business with the merchant's agent. Nagaro always made sure there was something bought, sold, or traded when he met with Utabala, so that the story the men were told was true as far as it went.

Nagaro shrugged. "I can tell the men quite truthfully that I don't know why I was bidden to come quickly— but that I trust Utabala." He sighed. "And if this 'something big' turns out to be something I can't explain to them, I suppose I can say it was a false alarm— that Matapili misunderstood— though I don't like to lie. I prefer to be able to give the men a good reason when I ask them to row through the night." He sighed again and went back to staring moodily across the water.

***

The following night, Talebra's pale disk was already almost halfway up the sky, with Naru following close behind, when the *Sword of Freedom* and the *Sea Eagle* slipped into Tambali harbor, oars rising and falling in a slow, even cadence. The rhythm of the oars slowed and their blades were dragged briefly through the glassy swells as the two ships glided ponderously to a halt just inside the northern spur of rock that formed the harbor's mouth. There were a pair of quiet splashes as the anchors were deployed. A few minutes later, one of the *Sword's* longboats was lowered and Taru and Bouno began to ply two pairs of oars, making for a familiar landing adjacent to the buildings occupied by the merchant house of Mundata Punda. Nagaro sat in the longboat's stern, directing them. He wore a plain white shirt under a dark brown tirka. A small wooden chest lay at his feet. Across the dark waters of the harbor, the many-pillared city of Tambali slumbered under the moons.

The quay that was their destination was easily located by moonlight, and the boat was quickly made fast. Nagaro climbed lightly up the ladder and turned to receive the chest as Bouno handed it up to him.

"Ye'll be careful, won't ye Capt'n?" the seaman asked, keeping his voice low. "I still think ye should ha' brought your sword."

"I'm always careful," Nagaro assured him. "But there shouldn't be any danger— not with a truce on."

"Aye," growled Taru. "But these truces have a way o' not lasting."

Nagaro smiled wryly in the darkness. How many truces had there been with Jinara? Did anyone keep count?

"You're right, Taru," he said, "but we're not on the border here, and it takes time for word of truce-breaking to travel down the coast. In any case, you know what to do."

Taru's teeth flashed in the moonlight. "Aye. We sit here and keep our eyes open and our ears cocked. And if ye're not back in two hours, we come looking for ye."

Nagaro lifted the wooden chest to his shoulder. "Right," he said. "And now I'm off to find Tor Utabala."

He threaded his way unerringly between buildings that were the warehouses and counting houses of Mundata Punda, and knocked on a small unobtrusive door in the side of one of the latter. After allowing several long seconds to pass, he frowned a little and knocked again. He'd grown accustomed to finding Utabala at work at all hours, but it was very late. It was possible that everyone had gone home for the night. This time, however, there was a sleepy-sounding voice from inside, speaking with a questioning inflection in Jinari.

Nagaro gave the door four quick taps. It was opened then, and the yellow light of an oil lamp spilled into the night. The guard inside beckoned hastily for Nagaro to enter. Closing the door quickly, he led the way along a lamp-lit hallway, bowing repeatedly and jabbering in Jinari. Nagaro could have found his way to Utabala's study without assistance, but he allowed the guard to conduct him. He suspected the man had been dozing and was either apologizing or else inventing some excuse for his slow response. Not knowing which, Nagaro contented himself with a nod and a polite smile in response to the man's patter.

Utabala appeared at the study door at a word from the guard, whom he immediately dismissed. He smiled broadly as the guard disappeared down the hall.

"Ah, Nagaro. May I say you are well met, Captain? Dat is how your people say it I tink, is it not?" The merchant's agent was a typical Jinari, dark-skinned, hawk-featured, and black-eyed. His sleek black hair showed just a trace of gray at the temples. His Droviri was rapid and fluent, though it carried the typical Jinari accent. "And may de One We Do Not Name keep you ever in good health— as I see He has done."

Nagaro inclined his head. "Yes, thank you," he answered formally. "Well met, Utabala. May you ever prosper." Then he added, with a grin, "But don't you ever sleep?"

Utabala's strong white teeth were revealed in a sudden smile. "I was finishing with de keeping of de books," he said, motioning for Nagaro to come into his study. Indeed the large desk at one side of the room was piled with stacks of ledgers. "If you had come but a few minutes later, you would not have found me es-still here." He closed the door behind his guest, and turning, indicated with another gesture a small table flanked by a pair or chairs. "Please put down your burden, my friend, and sit."

Nagaro lowered the chest carefully onto the polished table top and dropped his own body, somewhat less gently, onto one of the cushioned chairs. It had been a long day. He had taken a turn at an oar several times himself, and he was tired.

"I might have waited until morning," he observed. "But Matapili said I should come quickly. What is this about, Utabala?"

"Ah," said the Jinari, seating himself at the desk. "It is about someting dat was more urgent before de truce— but es-still it is good dat you have come soon. I will show you dat ting in a minute, but first, since you are here, let me tell you someting dat I have learned only in de last two days."

Utabala moved a stack of ledgers aside so that he could fold his hands on the desktop. He continued, then, speaking carefully. "You know it has been difficult to tell how de tings dat interest us are leaving dis city," he began. "Dere are so many ships and so many places dey can go. I have only a few men, and dey have oder duties too. It is hard for dem to take de time to follow a ship to see where it goes and to watch and see what is done wit de tings dat are unloaded. And of course, not all de tings dat are unloaded are de tings dat interest us." Utabala paused.

"Yes, I understand. It's a very difficult problem," Nagaro ventured. "I haven't expected you to solve it."

Utabala leaned forward. "Ah, but we have," he said, and his black eyes gleamed in the light from the lamp on the desk. "We have traced some of de tings to Patamtala. Dat is a port on de island of Judaba. Dis we have known already for a little time. And den, only dis week, one of my men has found de place in Patamtala where all of de tings are being sent. It is a little warehouse at de edge of de town. De tings we have been following go from de ships to de warehouse by courier. But dey go out from de warehouse, by means of a very little dock, in little boats like dose for fishing. De boats go out wit de tings, but dey come in wit bags of gold and papers sealed wit wax."

Nagaro frowned. "Where are the boats coming from? Was your man able to tell?"

"Always they come from de north and go back to de north," Utabala replied. "And de men who sail in dem have yellow hair and es-speak Droviri."

"Leithians!" Nagaro stared at the merchant's agent, his mouth suddenly dry. He had always suspected it, but had feared to learn that it was true.

Utabala nodded in acknowledgment. "Do you want me to tell my man to make furder investigations?" he inquired.

Nagaro swallowed. "Only if he can be extremely careful. It could be very dangerous. These men may be willing to kill to keep what they are doing from being discovered."

Utabala studied Nagaro, his expression difficult to read in the lamp light. "So," he said carefully after a long moment. "I confess dat I have wondered wheder perhaps you have been banished from your home. Perhaps dese men have had someting to do wit it?"

The question took Nagaro by surprise. Though the Jinari surely must have been curious, he had never before asked for any explanation.

Nagaro didn't drop his eyes, though his mouth was dry as ash. "No one has banished me," he said carefully. Then, because he believed he could trust Utabala, he added, "There are those who think me dead, and it's better for me if they continue to think so. These men you have found are not, I think, my enemies specifically. But if they are in league with the one I fear, then there is much risk, for he is a man of considerable powers— and he has no conscience."

Utabala regarded him somberly, then inclined his head, touching his forehead with the heel of his hand. "I under-es-stand. May de One We Do Not Name protect you, Captain Nagaro," he intoned. He straightened, then, and stood up. "And now," he said, "dere is de oder ting. Follow me, please, and I will show you."

Curiously, Nagaro followed Utabala out of the room and back along the hall to a turning into a second hallway. *What could Utabala have to show him that was of greater importance than the information he had just provided?*

Near the end of the second hall, the Jinari stopped in front of a closed door. He extracted a key from somewhere about his person, fumbling a little as he turned it in the lock. He then took down a lighted lantern from a hook beside the door and held it aloft as he swung the door open. "Here it is," he said, gesturing with his head to the room that lay beyond. "Dis is de ting dat I wished you to see."

Nagaro stepped forward to get a better view. The room was not large, and apparently was ordinarily used as a storeroom. It contained several empty barrels, the remains of a dilapidated crate, two long heavy tables— *and a man.*

The man was lying on a pile of straw beside one of the tables with his feet towards the door and his head hidden in the table's shadow. He was clad in nothing but a dingy pair of pants, and the skin of his bare arms and back was of too light a color for a Jinari. He appeared to be asleep. His hands were bound in front of him at the wrists. Several loops of the rope that bound him were passed around one of the stout table legs just above a heavy cross-brace so that the rope could not be loosed by merely shifting the table.

Nagaro stood in the doorway, frowning. "Surely," he said, glancing sharply at Utabala, "this is not some-*thing*, but rather some-*one*. Why is this man bound?"

Utabala's teeth flashed briefly in a tight, uncomfortable smile. "He is bound so dat he cannot run away. He has already tried to do so two times, and he cannot be allowed to do dat."

"Why do you hold him so? What has he done? And why do you show him to me?" Nagaro was more than a little disturbed.

Utabala's expression was difficult to read. "Dis I will ex-plain," he said. He cleared his throat. "Dis man was taken in our capital city. Dey say he was creeping about de es-streets begging and es-stealing food, and trying to hide from de soldiers. As you can see, he is not one of our people." Utabala paused. "It, ah, seems by de look of him dat he is one of... *your* people..."

"You mean that he is *Kelorin?*" Nagaro frowned. "But your capital is a hundred miles from the border with Edrovir!"

Utabala nodded. "Ah, yes. Dat is true. Never-de-less, de man seems to be Kelorin. So naturally de soldiers of de city tink he must be Droviri. And de High Council of Jinara— may de Unnamed One give dem long life— dey tink he maybe is an es-spy from Edrovir."

"What? A ragged beggar-man, stealing food?"

Utabala lifted his shoulders in a gesture of helplessness. "Dey tink maybe it is very clever, ah, what you call dis-guise," he explained delicately. "No one will look at a beggar and so no one will see dat he is not Jinari."

"But how did the unfortunate man come to be *here?* And in your keeping?"

Utabala sighed. "Dis also I will ex-plain. It is dis way. When de High Council— may deir wisdom never fail— tink dey have captured a Droviri es-spy, dey have sought for a man who could es-speak de language of Edrovir. By de most es-strange fortune, I was at dat time in de capital city conducting business for my master wit one of de councilmen, and so I was summoned by de High Council so dat I might es-speak to dis man."

"I see." Nagaro nodded. It was a remarkable tale, but he imagined he was now nearly at the end of it. "And what did he tell you then? How did he come to be in your capital, and in such a condition?"

But Utabala shook his head. "Es-still I do not know," he said. "It is most es-strange ting, but it seems dat dis man does not know even one word of your Common Es-speech. It seems dat he es-speaks only Hashti."

"*Hashti?* Are you sure?"

Utabala shrugged. "I do not es-speak Hashti, of course, so perhaps I am mistaken. But to my ear it has de sound of Hashti, and den dere are a few words dat I *do* know. One word he has said many times is 'shaku'— dat I know means 'es-slave.' And dere is someting else dat he has said several times dat I tought might interest you."

Nagaro frowned. "And what was that?"

The Jinari's teeth flashed in the lamp light.

"Kiraam Shaku-Tal."

Nagaro ran a hand through his hair. "I see," he said quietly. "Do you think he was perhaps a slave or some kind of captive in the Mahuk Baar who escaped and crossed over into Jinara?"

Utabala nodded. "Yes, dat is what I tink. And dat is also what I have told de High Council— blessings of de Unnamed be upon dem. And I have told dem also dat you are a man to be trusted. So dey have decreed dat dis man be brought here to Tambali to be in my keeping until de word could be sent to *you.*"

Nagaro chewed his lip. "He must have been a captive for a very long time— ever since he was a small child— not to remember anything of the Common Speech. Does he have a slave brand?"

Utabala shook his head. "No, he does not have a brand anywhere dat I can see. But es-still I tink he must be an es-slave. I have official permission to give him to you, for you to take away, if only you will swear to see dat he never does anyting to bring harm to Jinara." Utabala paused. "I hope," he added, "dat what I have told de Council is right and dat you will take him, because if it is not so, I do not know what will happen to him. If he runs away and dey catch him again, I am very afraid dat de soldiers will kill him."

Nagaro drew a long breath and released it. "Well, he observed, "I'll take a closer look at him, if you will bring the lantern. And I'll try some of my Hashti, such as it is."

Nagaro advanced into the room, moving around the sleeping figure until he was standing a few feet in front of the man. Utabala came after him with the lantern. Even before the lantern light fell full upon the prisoner's face, Nagaro caught the smell. Accustomed as he was to dealing with newly-freed galley slaves, he recognized immediately the odor of an unwashed human body.

The man looked fairly young, certainly less than thirty. His hair was dark, dirty, and tangled. A scraggly, unkempt beard covered his chin, and it also was dark. The features of the man's face certainly appeared to be Kelorin, though his skin was darkened by a patina of grime, except on his shoulders and back where it had been burned by the sun and had recently peeled. There the paleness of it was plain to see. The man's ribs showed clearly, and Nagaro noted also that his worn and dirty pants were very crudely made, and that his back and arms bore a number of scars suggestive of beatings. There were scars that might have been left by chafing ropes on both ankles, and the condition of the man's feet suggested they had never known any proper shoes. How anyone could have imagined that this wretched being was anything other than what he appeared was beyond Nagaro's comprehension. Very likely the members of the High Council of Jinara had not actually bothered to look at the man for themselves.

Perhaps the light of the lantern shining on the man's face disturbed his slumber, or it might have been the sound of their voices or their footsteps on the flagstone floor. In any case, the man stirred as Nagaro stood over him, and opened his eyes. Instantly alert, his startled glance took in his two visitors, squinting against the brightness of the light. As Nagaro had expected, the man's eyes were gray. He didn't alter his position, but his entire body went stiff.

Nagaro frowned at this evidence of anticipated unkindness. Slowly he lowered himself to a squatting position so that he might face the man more directly. As an experiment, he addressed the prisoner first in the Common Speech.

"I am the one who is called the Thief of Slaves. What is your name?"

This utterance earned him a blank, frightened look. Obviously Utabala was correct in his assessment that the man knew none of the language of his own people. Nagaro next tried speaking in Hashti.

"I am Captain Nagaro. What is your—"

He was not even permitted to finish. The man burst into a torrent of Hashti, far too rapid for Nagaro to follow. At the same time, the captive scrambled into a squatting position beside the leg of the table to which he was tethered, his hands held awkwardly in front of him, a pleading look in his eyes.

Nagaro had caught only scattered words— "shaku" and "Kiraam Shaku-Tal" and a few others. His own Hashti vocabulary was quite adequate for discussing terms of surrender with Mautep ship's captains, but not for extensive discourse on other topics. He had the impression that the man was trying to say something that involved "going" and "seeking", but he could guess at little more than that.

"I do not understand," he said in Hashti, when the man stopped speaking. "My Hashti is not so good."

The man looked distressed, but when he spoke next, the words were fewer and slower, apparently as a result his of puzzlement. "Please, Master, what is 'Hashti'?"

Nagaro frowned. "Master" he knew was only a respectful form of address. But this man didn't even know the name of the language he spoke. This was going to be more difficult than he had thought. "These word I say now are Hashti word," he explained, struggling to find a way to express it. "Those word I said first were Droviri word. You must use few word and speak slowly."

Understanding dawned in the man's eyes. Mutely he nodded.

Nagaro tried again, "What is your name?"

"I am called... Tul—" The man had looked as if he'd been about to say more, but stopped himself.

Nagaro frowned again. The Hashti word "tul" that he knew meant "thing", which didn't seem like a name for a man. He decided to pretend not to know this. "Good," he said. "Where do you come from, Tul?"

The man named Tul frowned. "From... Tosmataak..." he ventured uncertainly.

"Tosmataak?" The name meant nothing to Nagaro. "Tosmataak is place in Mahuk Baar?"

Tul's brow furrowed in concentration. "I think... maybe..."

Nagaro frowned in frustration. He rubbed his chin and tried again. "When you came here... It was very far?"

Tul nodded emphatically. "Yes, Master! I walked very, very far!"

"You came which way? North? South?"

"From there to here, I walked north, Master. Very, very far."

Utabala had been standing patiently with the lantern, but now he spoke. "What have you learned, Nagaro? You must ask him what he was doing in Jinara. De Council— blessings be upon dem— will want to know."

Tul glanced apprehensively at the Jinari then hopefully at Nagaro. Nagaro answered the merchant's agent. "I don't think he knows very much about the world, Utabala. He doesn't seem to know where he came from, only that he walked a long way north to get here." Nagaro turned his attention back to Tul.

"Why did you come here?"

This evoked a longer utterance, but this time the man did not speak too fast and Nagaro was able to decipher the long string of Hashti.

"Please Master, I come seeking Thief of Slave. I am sorry for taking food. Only I know Thief of Slave lives in north, but I do not know where. I could not find him and I was hungry. Please Master, do you know where he is?" There was a desperate edge to the man's voice.

Nagaro sighed. He turned to Utabala. "He came looking for me. He thinks he is in trouble for stealing the food." He turned back to Tul.

"He is here, Tul." Nagaro tapped his own chest. "I am man called Thief of Slave."

The man's eyes went wide. He dropped onto his knees and bent his head down and forward as far as he could, almost to the floor. "Master, Master!" he cried. "Please, you will help me? I want to be free!"

Nagaro leaned forward to grasp the man's shoulders, and raised him gently so he could look once more into his face. "Please do not do that, friend," he said earnestly. "I will help you, if you will come with me— to my ship."

Tul's face registered gratitude and incredulity, almost equally commingled. "Daashu," he murmured. "Daashu." It meant "thank you".

Nagaro smiled. "Inan pash," he said, which was the standard polite rejoinder, roughtly equivalent to "you are welcome".

The man stared at him, apparently speechless. Nagaro wondered whether the poor fellow had ever heard anyone say "inan pash" to him before. "Thank this man, also," he added, pointing to Utabala. "He knew my name, Thief of Slave, and he told me to come."

Tul recovered himself enough to turn to the Jinari and murmur, "Daashu... daashu."

Utabala solemnly inclined his head in acknowledgment.

Nagaro addressed himself to the merchant's agent. "I don't believe there is any harm in this man, Utabala, and I will take responsibility for him. He says he will come with me."

He turned back to Tul, and, putting his hand to his belt, drew a long knife from its sheath. The man's eyes widened with apprehension when he saw the lamp light glint on the blade. As if it were an involuntary gesture, he shrank away.

Nagaro made haste to reassure him. "Do not be afraid. I will make you free now. Come with me and you will not be harmed. But if you run away, other man will harm you."

Tul nodded comprehension, and waited tensely, kneeling in the straw, while Nagaro slipped the blade of the knife between his wrists and the rope. Two careful sawing movements severed the cord and it fell away. Nagaro straightened and stood up, returning the knife to its sheath. He motioned for Tul to stand as well, and the man obeyed with some hesitance.

They all went back to Utabala's study then. Nagaro motioned for Tul to follow, and the man came padding after him, always two paces behind like a dog. In the study, Nagaro had to sign an official paper concerning the captive man. It was all in Jinari and he couldn't read it. He trusted Utabala's explanation that it contained nothing more serious than a promise that he would, to the best of his ability, ensure that Tul was never permitted to do anything to harm the sovereign state of Jinara. He carefully wrote, "Nagaro Nareyo, known as Kiraam Shaku-Tal" at the bottom of it.

The matter of the Pakoan jade was quickly dealt with after that, the chest and its contents being exchanged for a pouch of gold. Utabala was also glad to give Nagaro an estimate of what a Jinari carpet might fetch at ports outside of Jinara. Tul stood silently throughout these transactions. His eyes roamed curiously over the many commonplace wonders of Utabala's study. He seemed no more interested in the jade and the gold than in the pens and the ink.

Nagaro knew his two hours must be very nearly up, so he made haste to take his leave of the merchant's agent. The guard was clearly surprised, when he ushered them out, to see Tul in Nagaro's company, walking freely without restraint or binding. Taru and Bouno were even more surprised by the appearance of the former captive.

"Is this what Utabala meant by 'something big'?" Taru inquired archly as he gazed up at the ragged Kelorin standing on the dock above him. Tul was looking extremely apprehensive at the prospect of descending into the longboat.

Nagaro smiled crookedly. "Apparently. He goes by the name of Tul and he only speaks Hashti, so I'm not very sure of his story. He seems to have come from the Mahuk Baar and to have been looking for Kiraam Shaku-Tal. That's really all I know."

It required some cajoling to persuade Tul to get into the boat. "This is ship, Master?" he asked fearfully.

"No, this is boat," Nagaro explained. "Ship is there," and he pointed across the dark water of the harbor.

"Oh, no, no, Master! There is too much water!"

Nagaro found his Hashti vocabulary quite inadequate to deal properly with Tul's ignorance and fear. In the end, he had to resort to telling the poor man that the Jinari would kill him if he did not get into the boat. This was an exaggeration, but it had the desired effect. Once in the boat, Tul at first sat tensely in the bow, clinging to the seat with both hands. There was no wind, however, and almost no swell, and the longboat glided so smoothly over the calm water that the man soon began visibly to relax. By the time they reached the *Sword of Freedom*, the former captive was quite willing to stand up in the longboat and climb the rope ladder to the deck of the larger craft, which he happily described to Nagaro as "very big water-house."

Once on deck, Nagaro dispatched a startled member of the watch to rouse Pavo. Then, leaving Taru and Bouno to hoist the longboat aboard, he led Tul to the galley where he found smoked meat, some biscuit, and a mug of cold sothiril to offer his strange guest. Tul made a startled face when he tasted the sothiril, but drank more of it anyway. The smoked meat he attacked with an avidity that made Nagaro smile. The Jinari, he knew from personal experience, were vegetarians.

Presently Pavo found them. Tul reacted with alarm when Pavo first stepped into the galley. The former captive started to rise from his seat at the galley's trestle table.

Nagaro made haste to reassure him. "This is my friend Pavo. He speaks Hashti. He will help you understand."

This seemed to quiet Tul's concern, for his face relaxed and he sat down again and returned his attention to the meat.

Pavo had inclined his head in greeting to the ragged Kelorin and gotten the barest nod of acknowledgment. He turned to Nagaro and crooked an eyebrow. "Who is this man who look like Kelorin, but knows Hashti?" he inquired in the Common Speech.

"He seems to speak no other tongue." Nagaro quickly sketched what he knew of the former captive. "When I asked for his name, he told me he was called Tul."

Pavo frowned. "That is not name for man," he observed darkly.

Nagaro nodded seriously. "I agree, Pavo, and I hope we can persuade him to accept another— in fact, I have one to suggest. I want you to take him into your charge until we get to Pakoa. You're the best man to teach him the ways of the ship because you can speak to him and answer his questions. And you can also begin to teach him the Common Speech. There won't be any kind of life for him in Edrovir as a Kelorin who speaks only Hashti. For tonight, though, just find him a place to sleep. The hour is very late and I wish to weigh anchor an hour before dawn and be well away from Tambali before it is light. When you talk with him tomorrow, I hope you can begin to get him to tell you his life history because I'm very curious to know it."

Pavo nodded. "Yes," he said. "I can do all these thing."

"Good. Then I'll leave you with him. I'll be in my cabin if I'm needed. I still hope to get a few hours of sleep tonight."

Nagaro turned towards the door, but turned back when Pavo asked, "What name do you think to give to this man?"

Nagaro smiled a quick, tight smile. "Sindar."

Pavo made a startled movement and his dark eyes widened. "You do not think that he is maybe baby in story?" he inquired incredulously. "Baby that was son of Kelorin slave woman named Emril?"

Nagaro shook his head. "It would be very remarkable if it were so," he said. "Though his tale must be something similar if he knows none of the Common Speech. It can't be a common thing for the Mautep to take infants captive— or women who are with child. But really I chose the name because it means 'free man' in the old tongue of the Kelorin. He's obviously Kelorin, and now he is free."

"Sindar means 'free man?' This I did not know." Pavo frowned. "What does 'emril' mean?"

Nagaro shook his head. "I don't know," he said. "I've never come across it in any of my reading. Perhaps she didn't give her true name."

Whoever she had been, the woman Emril had named her son "Free Man", though the child had been born in captivity. Perhaps she had hoped it would be prophetic. Nagaro considered the name's meaning to be proof positive of the truth of the strange tale of the Kelorin lady and the Mautep Lord that Pavo had told to entertain a barn-full of slaves years ago in Sar Tipaal. The Hashtep who had told and retold that tale over the years couldn't possibly have known the meaning of the name of the infant that Lord Notep jir-Akaan had left to die beside a stream in a dark forest.

***

In his cabin, Nagaro opened one of the drawers beneath his bunk and stowed the pouch of gold he had gotten from Utabala in exchange for the jade. The drawer also contained a plain ironwood box, which he took out and set on the bed beside him just as there came a knock on the door.

"It's me, Taru."

"Come in."

Nagaro waited until Taru had closed the door behind him. "Utabala had something else to tell me," he said. "It appears that the secret trade he's been investigating is going out of Jinara by way of Patamtala on Judaba Island. It's going out in small boats manned by Leithians."

Taru gave a low whistle. "I'll wager the Kelorin Faction would like to hear about that!"

Nagaro frowned. "If those things are going to Dreigen, I'd say that King Elgurn and the Council need to hear about it. But I don't *know* that they are going to Dreigen— although it wouldn't be surprising if the Leithian Faction was helping Dreigen to get his supplies. It was the Leithian Faction that presented Dreigen to King Darion, years ago, as a kind of gift. Before that, he'd been working for Harl Sobring."

"Harl Sobring?" Taru was surprised. "Wasn't he the father of your old friend Bron?"

Nagaro winced at Taru's facetious jibe. Bron Sobring had been one of Leyel Virden's "keepers" and he had very unpleasant memories of the man. "Yes," he said darkly, then changed the subject. "The point is that nothing can be done about telling anyone in Lankura anything without more information. Not without some proof of a connection to Dreigen. And I'm in a poor position to make inquiries."

Taru grinned. "Ye're right about that," he observed. "Ye're much too famous. Ye can't set foot anywhere in the southern isles or the southern coast o' the main without it being known under every roof for five miles around by nightfall."

Nagaro scowled. "It isn't quite that bad."

But it was bad enough, he reflected gloomily. He had become the famous— and mysterious— Captain Nagaro. He detested subterfuge, and it didn't work well for him anyway because his appearance was too distinctive. He tended to draw attention even when he tried to be unobtrusive. Folk might not let on, but someone usually recognized him— or suspected they did, which was just as bad. And no matter how innocent a tale he told, folk would inevitably speculate and concoct rumors just because he was Nagaro the Pirate.

"Maybe I could try t' do it for ye," Taru suggested.

But Nagaro immediately shook his head. "I don't want you to take the risk. If Dreigen *is* involved, the danger is very real. And even if he isn't, these Leithians have obviously been trafficking with Jinara during time of war. They won't want their activities made known." He sighed resignedly. "We'll just have to keep our eyes open for any signs of suspicious Leithians in fishing boats. If anything like that turns up, I may be able to make some careful inquiries about it. Other than that, I can only hope that Utabala's people find something that can be traced— although I think that will be difficult."

"All right." Taru gave a shrug. "What I came for was t' ask about our course."

Nagaro nodded. "I want to put in at Kel Tierna before making for Pakoa to meet the *Tiger* and the *North Wind*. I can try to sell the rest of the jade and a carpet or two there, and I'll give Mendorel the news about Pavo's wedding— and our new passenger."

Taru nodded. "That's a good idea," he said. "Everyone's eager t' be home, but they can wait a little longer. Pavo said ye want to sail before dawn."

"Yes. And unless we get some wind, we'll be needing the men to row again. So I suggest you get some sleep."

Taru grinned. "Aye, Capt'n," he said easily. "I'll be sure the third watch knows when to wake us, and I shouldn't think there'll be much grumbling about it. Even with a truce on, everyone knows it's best not t' be seen in this port."

Nagaro sighed ruefully. "I know," he said. "Those Leithians aren't the only ones with something to hide. I haven't always done my business with Utabala during truce time either." He stifled a yawn. "Good night, Taru."

"Good night, Capt'n." Taru delivered an exaggerated salute and departed.

After Taru had gone, Nagaro remembered the box on the bed and opened it. The box held several small bags containing objects made of gold, mostly jewelry. The piracy practiced by Nagaro and his crew inevitably turned up things that were difficult to sell in Pakoa, things it could take months to convert into negotiable coin. The men took their shares in what coin there was, since they needed cash quickly, and entrusted the sale of the other things to Nagaro. He had always been adamant that pirate gold was "finder's gold", meaning that he and his men might use what they needed, but that any excess should be passed on to others in need rather than hoarded. His crew trusted him to see that they got what they needed, and gave him wide latitude in spending the proceeds from the sale of things like jewelry.

Nagaro untied the string on the smallest bag and dumped its contents into his palm. He quickly found the small gold ring, wrought in the likeness of a salamander with its head resting on its tail and two tiny emeralds for eyes. It was a thing he didn't intend to sell, but had put there for safekeeping. It had been given to him at Jaamra on the day that he and his fellow slaves had won their freedom, by Roheed jir-Akaan, the nephew of Lord Baalkir— who was now Emperor Baalkir, the ruler of the Mahuk Baar.

Roheed had told him that the ring had belonged to the long-dead slave woman, Emril, and had suggested that Nagaro return it to that lady's family. Nagaro had put the ring away years ago. He hadn't meant to ignore Roheed's request, but at the time he had lacked a means of pursuing the matter. In the years since, he'd nearly forgotten about it, but he realized that the situation had changed. He now had frequent occasion to call at the ports along the southern coast of Edrovir. And unlike the matter of secretive Leithian traders, there should be no risk in making inquiries regarding the ring, or Emril, or her unfortunate husband. It still wouldn't be easy, however, since he had very few clues. Other than the ring itself, there was only the woman's name and the approximate date of the ill-fated voyage that had led to her capture by the Mautep and the slaying of her husband.

Nagaro slipped the ring onto the last finger of his left hand. It barely fit, having been designed for a woman's finger. Wearing it, he reasoned, he would be less likely to forget about it again. And there was always the chance that someone for whom it had some meaning might see it and remark upon it.

Nagaro yawned. Dawn would come too soon. He turned down the lamp on its hook by the door, then pulled off his boots and his tirka and stretched himself on his bunk. Almost immediately, sleep took him.

Chapter 3

Words Of Warning

T he door of the candle shop on Kettle Street opened and closed again behind a hooded figure, giving a glimpse of deepening dusk outside. Mendorel looked up from behind the counter and marked his place in the ledger. "I was about t' close shop, Zirda," he said, addressing the cloaked man who had entered. "But I'm always happy to serve a customer if ye'll state your business."

The customer threw back his hood and smiled, the flash of white teeth contrasting with his closely trimmed black beard.

"I'd like a dozen of your best beeswax candles with the braided wicks, if you have so many left at this hour."

"Nagaro! Captain!" The shop keeper beamed. "I had heard ye were in Kel Tierna today. The gossip was that ye were selling Pakoan jade and Jinari carpets, and I'd hoped ye would pay me a visit. Though I confess I'd stopped looking for ye, with the hour being so late."

Nagaro winced at the accuracy of the gossip. "You know I always stop here if I can," he said seriously. "But I also try to be careful. I'd rather the gossip didn't follow me everywhere."

"Ah." Mendorel nodded wisely. "That's why the hood an' all. I can't say that I blame ye. And ye can bar the door if ye like— though I don't expect anyone else today. I want t' hear your news. If ye've carpets to sell, ye must have taken a ship."

Nagaro turned back to the door to drop the bar into place. Then he crossed to the counter. "Yes, we took a ship," he said. "And trying to sell jade in Pakoa is like trying to sell fish to the fisherman, as they say. But I only sold two of a dozen carpets. For the rest, I'll have to let Gedras have the trade and take his cut. Not that I mind, since he's been good to us." He paused. "But the biggest news is about Sindar."

"Sindar?" The shopkeeper's expression turned puzzled. "Wasn't that the baby that got eaten by the tiger?"

Nagaro leaned against the edge of the counter. "The tale didn't say he was eaten, Mendorel," he said quietly. "All it said was that Notep abandoned the baby by a stream in the forest. And when he changed his mind and went back, the baby was gone and there were tiger tracks along the water's edge."

Mendorel's eyes went wide. "What are ye saying, Captain?"

Nagaro met his gaze. "I think we may have found him— Sindar— grown to be a man." He quickly outlined the story of Utabala's summons and what had come of it. "Pavo finally got the man's story from him two days ago, and I've never seen Pavo so excited in all the time that I've known him."

"So what was the man's tale?"

Nagaro smiled. "It seems that this man, who called himself 'Tul,' was found in the forest as an infant, by an old man who took him home to his village for his wife to raise. The old couple treated him fairly decently, but they both died when the lad was about nine years old, and after that, the villagers made him work for them, and beat him, and tied him up when he tried to run away. After years of this— after he had grown up— Tul chanced to hear about someone called Kiraam Shaku-Tal, who freed slaves from ships. Apparently the boy who used to bring him his food told him about it."

Nagaro paused and shook his head. "Tul didn't know what a 'slave' was— or a ship, for that matter. But when he heard what the boy said, he decided that he must be a slave, and he became determined to escape and find Kiraam Shaku-Tal. Apparently he managed to cut through his rope one night with a sharp piece of flint, and he just started walking north. All he knew was that Kiraam Shaku-Tal lived in the north." Nagaro paused.

Mendorel frowned. "Well it certainly sounds as if he *could* be Sindar..."

Nagaro leaned closer. "There's more," he said, and began ticking things off on his fingers as he listed them. "The man thinks that he's twenty-four or twenty-five years old, which fits. The village he comes from was called Tosmataak— which Pavo says is the name of a forest very near to Sar Tipaal. And the name 'Tul' that he gave us was short for something longer that means '*Thing found by the water*'."

Mendorel gave a low whistle. "By the Eyes and Ears," he said in an awed voice, "I think ye *have* found Sindar!"

Nagaro straightened. "Pavo is completely convinced," he said. "And I confess that I'd like to believe it as well."

"What does the man think of it?" Mendorel asked. "Have ye told him?"

Nagaro nodded. "Yes, but I'm not sure he believes it— or else it just doesn't matter to him. He was pleased to take the name 'Sindar' even before we knew the tale, because the name means 'free man', but all I get from him now is that he wants to learn to fight with a sword and join my crew. He's all over the ship, and into everything like a boy in a blacksmith's shop. It's not that I've anything against training him and letting him try, if that's really what he wants, but he's not even considered anything else. And I'm thinking that I should try to find his family."

Mendorel nodded. "O' course ye have to try t' find them," he said. "Even if the young man doesn't care, his kinfolk surely will." His glance followed Nagaro's hand. "Is that the ring that Roheed gave to ye that ye're wearing? The one that was supposed t' belong to Sindar's mother?"

"Yes. And I'd like you to take a look at it." Nagaro slid the green-eyed salamander ring from his finger and handed it across the counter. "Have you ever seen anything like it before?"

Mendorel examined the ring, but shook his head. "I know most o' the wealthy families in Kel Tierna and their family marks, but I've never known any o' them to use a beastie like this. It wouldn't be Lord Rathgar either."

The shopkeeper handed the ring back, and Nagaro returned it to his finger with a sigh.

"How is little Narei?" Mendorel inquired.

"Growing like a new spring shoot." Nagaro smiled with genuine pleasure at the mention of his daughter. "And she's full of questions— everything from 'Why doesn't my uncle ever catch crabs in his net' to 'Where do the stars go in the daytime' and 'Where does the rain come from?'"

Mendorel chuckled. "Ah, I remember those questions, though it's been years since any o' mine were so small. Aye, those are the hard questions— like, 'What makes the rainbow?' I remember when my youngest asked me that, and I had t' say that I didn't know. Sometimes I wish I was a Leithian so I could just say it was Solbrid's hair ribbon."

Nagaro's smile had died. "*Those* aren't the hard questions," he said quietly. "The hard questions are the ones like 'Where's my Mama?' and 'Why did she go away?'" He paused uncomfortably. "Have you had any news of Jila?"

Mendorel looked sympathetic, but shook his head. "She's not with the troop of traveling players anymore. But that's all I know," he said earnestly. "Listen, Nagaro," he added. "Jila's kept herself out o' trouble, and it's clear that she's not going back t' Pakoa. It's best ye just put her out o' your mind."

"I know." Nagaro sighed. "But I can't do that. I told Jila I wished never to set eyes on her again, and from the letter she wrote to her sister I know that she means to see that I don't. But for Narei's sake I would take back those words if I could."

There was a pause.

Before it could stretch too long, Mendorel said, "Shall I get those candles ye asked for, then?" He pulled out a bin from behind the counter. "There's only half a dozen here, but I can make up the rest o' the order if I go back t' the dipping room."

Nagaro nodded, grateful for the change of subject. "Yes, of course. Please."

He stood pensively while the shopkeeper disappeared through a door that led to the candle shop's work area. Through the open doorway, Nagaro could see the older man unhooking newly-made candles from one of the long racks where they had been left hanging by their wicks to cool and harden after the final dipping. Presently Mendorel came back through the door into the shop. Laying the candles on the counter, he fetched a knife and began trimming the wicks to an appropriate length.

Presently Nagaro spoke. "How are *your* children, Mendorel? And your wife?"

"They're all doing well." Mendorel smiled musingly. "Do ye know, my eldest son is t' be married in a month? I can hardly believe it. It seems such a little time ago that he was a long-legged stripling who'd as soon pull a girl's hair as look at her." He shook his head. "They plan t' move in here, upstairs, after the wedding. And o' course my son will take over the business one day, so the shop 'll stay in the family."

"Well that's certainly good news, and I'm very glad to hear it." Nagaro suddenly grinned. "And speaking of weddings," he added "I almost forgot. There'll be one on Pakoa when we return. All four ships are to rendezvous there and I'll wager that Moraga and Timegar are there with the *Tiger*, and the *North Wind* already."

The shopkeeper's mouth had dropped open. His hand, holding the knife, hovered frozen in the air, the candles momentarily forgotten. "Is it Pavo, then, at last?"

"Yes. Pavo and Tenepti. Their new house was almost finished when we sailed, and that was the only thing they were waiting for."

"Now, by the Eyes, that's wonderful news!" Mendorel face was alight with enthusiasm. "After all this time! Tenepti's father finally saw reason, did he?"

Nagaro laughed. "I think he finally realized that no other man on the island was ever going to ask to even sit with his daughter— as long as they knew she was waiting for Pavo. Pavo's had his heart set on her since she was sixteen, after all, and she's never wanted to marry anyone but him."

"Oh, aye." Mendorel gave Nagaro a broad wink. "And ye makin' Pavo your second mate probably clinched the matter."

"Well, I suppose it didn't hurt."

The truth was that Pavo was without a doubt the most famous Hashtep on the island of Pakoa, and every bit as much a heroic figure among his own people as Nagaro was among the broader population.

Mendorel rediscovered the candles on the counter and went back to the task of wick-trimming. "*Pavo and Tenepti,*" he murmured, still smiling. "Will ye come up and join us for a cup o' hot sothiril?" he asked after a moment. "It seems we ought to celebrate such news. I think my wife has some cakes—"

Nagaro quickly shook his head. "Not this time, old friend. I'd like to, but we mean to sail tonight, as soon as I get back to the ship. Everyone's so eager to get to Pakoa that I'm afraid they'll begrudge me the time I've already spent."

Mendorel sighed. "All right then," he said, as he cut a piece of string from a spool, and began to tie up the candles into a bundle. "But ye'll give Pavo my congratulations, won't ye? And my best wishes. And tell him I'll send him two dozen candles and a pair o' brass candlesticks for a wedding present."

"He'll like that, Mendorel. And of course I'll tell him." Nagaro got out his purse and counted out the price of the candles.

The shopkeeper suddenly paused as he was picking up the coins. "There's something else I've heard that I think I ought t' tell ye," he said, frowning.

Nagaro raised an eyebrow. "Oh?"

"Maybe ye've already heard it, but there's a rumor going about that Lord Kuran is looking for ye. More than a rumor, I'd say, really. The Royal Fleet was in port here not three weeks ago, and that's when I started hearing it."

"I've heard it too." Nagaro smiled with a quick flash of teeth. "Kuran has looked for me before, but he hasn't found me."

"But this sounds serious, Nagaro," the shopkeeper insisted "This time he's got *orders*. Orders that he's to find this pirate named Nagaro and get the answers to some questions. That's what I heard."

Nagaro frowned as he picked up the bundle of candles. "If that's all that the Lord of the Fleet wants— answers to questions— perhaps I should oblige him."

"But ye don't know what *kind* o' questions, Nagaro." Mendorel looked worried.

Nagaro shot the older man a sharp look. "I've done nothing to bring harm to Edrovir," he said tightly. "I should have nothing to fear from a just man." He turned and made for the door, pausing there to raise the hood of his cloak.

Mendorel came around the counter and followed him. "Ye *will* be careful, now, won't ye, Captain?" he asked as he lifted the bar to let Nagaro out.

This time Nagaro gave him a gentler glance. "Of course I will," he said. "Trust me." As he passed out into the gathering twilight, he turned back briefly to say, "Peace, Mendorel, and good night to you."

"Good night to ye, Captain."

Mendorel stood for a moment, watching Nagaro disappear up the darkening street before he closed the door and barred it once more.

***

"Go *looking* for Lord Kuran? Nagaro, *why?*"

Nagaro, Taru, and Pavo were standing together at the stern castle rail as the *Sword of Freedom* surged forward under a cloudless sky, driven by a favorable wind. The words had come from Taru.

Nagaro shrugged. "I've thought for a while that perhaps I should talk to him," he replied calmly. "And now it seems he wants to talk to me."

Taru gaped. "Ye can't just *talk* t' Lord Kuran!" he protested.

"I don't see why not."

"*Why not?* Because he commands of the whole Royal Fleet of Edrovir! That's why not!"

At this point Pavo spoke up. "Nagaro have talk to Mautep prince," he said. "Why should not he talk to Droviri lord?"

Taru looked from one of his friends to the other and threw up his hands. "What if he decides t' clap us in irons and haul us off to prison for piracy? It's daft t' take a chance like that!"

Nagaro wasn't impressed. "There's no justification for taking such an action," he said. "We don't take Edroviran ships, nor merchant craft of any kind."

Pavo nodded decisively. "I have heard Lord Kuran is man who have honor. If he is such man, he will not do such bad thing."

"He may have all the honor in the world," Taru protested. "But what makes ye think he'll *believe* what we say?"

Nagaro frowned. "I'd expect him to give me a fair hearing, based on what I know of him from... *that time*... in Lankura. Not to mention everything I've heard about him since. He was born a commoner, a merchant's son, and he's half Turowan. He's only a lord because Elgurn wanted to make him Lord of the Fleet and—"

"—and ye have t' be a lord first to be Lord o' the Fleet," Taru finished disgustedly. "So the king made him one. I *know* that! But he got used t' bein' a lord pretty quick. He married that high-born Leithian woman—the one that died o' the plague— remember?"

Nagaro shook his head. "No, Taru. He was betrothed to her *before* Elgurn made him a lord. He'd courted her and won her all on his own."

Pavo had been listening appreciatively. "That sound like good story," he observed.

"Yes, it's a very good story," Nagaro agreed, seeing his chance to make his point. "Kuran is very popular with the common people, because they know that story— *and* the story about how he saved the day when the previous Lord of the Fleet got killed in a battle with the Mautep. And when the plague carried off Kuran's wife and his little son— his only child— the whole country grieved for his loss."

Taru gestured exasperatedly. "What has that got to do with him listening to ye, Nagaro? It just means Kuran is Elgurn's darling! Elgurn made him a lord in spite of all the Leithians making a bloody great fuss, and Elgurn's no friend o' yours!"

Nagaro flinched as if ducking a shadow. "Elgurn won't be there," he pointed out quickly. "And Kuran won't recognize me. We were only... introduced... once, for a minute or two. The *point* is that the people love Kuran and he cares about them just as I do—"

At this point the argument was interrupted by a cry from aloft.

"Boat! Boat! See! See!"

The recently christened Sindar was leaning out of the crow's seat and pointing at a small object visible at a distance off the ship's port bow.

Pavo had asked Nagaro's permission to let Sindar do lookout duty in fair weather, pointing out that the former captive knew the difference between a 'boat' and a 'ship,' and the rest of his small vocabulary of Common Speech words was more than adequate for the task. Since the young man's almost excessive keenness would actually be an advantage in this case, Nagaro had given the plan his blessing.

Pavo cupped his hands to shout a few words of praise up to the man in the crow's seat.

Nagaro shaded his eyes to study the vessel Sindar had spotted. "It looks like a fishing boat," he said. "But it's rather far out in the channel."

The *Sword* and the *Sea Eagle* were on a course for Pakoa, the southernmost island in the chain known as the Lomoas. The channel between the mainland and the Lomoas was quite wide and fishermen working out of harbors on either side of it usually didn't venture very far from land, given the risk of encountering Mautep raiders in these southern waters.

Taru frowned. "She can't be lost," he said. "Not in this weather."

Nagaro turned to Pavo. "Can you alter course and take us into hailing range?" he asked. "Perhaps her master doesn't know the danger. Or perhaps he's hurt or is ill and the boat is adrift. It will cost us a little time, but maybe we can help."

"Aye, Captain!" Pavo saluted him with a nod. Then he turned, calling an instruction to the steersman before making for the ladder that led to the main deck.

Taru drummed his fingers on the railing. "I still think we should steer clear o' Lord Kuran," he said darkly. "He might decide t' drag ye up before the king's high seat in Lankura." The sighting of the fishing boat had distracted him, but only for a moment.

Nagaro's dark brows knit together in a sharp line. "I doubt I'd be considered worthy of King Elgurn's personal attention," he said dryly. "And I don't like to have men think ill of me when I've done nothing wrong. But don't worry, I won't do it unless enough men are willing to go— enough to sail a ship."

Taru looked indignant. "Surely ye don't think the men would let ye go without the whole lot of us there t' protect ye?"

Nagaro's frown deepened. "If all four ships were to come with me, there'd be none left to see to the safety of Pakoa."

The argument continued, back and forth, until it was interrupted again by another shout, this time from the bow. By this time, the craft Sindar had sighted was considerably nearer. Nagaro raised the spyglass that was slung around his neck. "That's odd," he murmured. "I see three people aboard her, and I'd swear one of them is a woman."

At that moment, Pavo came bounding up the ladder. His face registered restrained excitement. "Can you give me spyglass, Captain?" he asked, a little breathless. "This boat have sail-rig like what is use by Hashtep fisherman!"

Nagaro promptly un-slung the strap of the spyglass and handed the tapered cylinder to his second mate. Pavo leaned tensely against the railing as he raised the spyglass to his eye. For a long moment the young Hashtep gazed through the glass in silence before uttering a string of words in awestruck Hashti. Among them Nagaro understood nothing except the name of Sheptuum, the god of the Mahuk Baar.

Before Nagaro could even frame a question, Pavo sprang away from the rail. An instant later the young Hashtep was leaping down the ladder from the stern castle. He hit the main deck running, making for the forecastle, the spyglass still clutched in his fist. Nagaro and Taru exchanged baffled glances. Then Taru bolted for the ladder. Nagaro took a quicker way, vaulting over the rail to land on the deck below and follow Pavo at a run.

***

"You remember I say I have two brother?" Pavo inquired.

The fishing boat had been brought along side of the *Sword of Freedom*, and a rope ladder and been let down to allow the boat's three occupants to be brought aboard. The two men and the woman stood on the main deck, next to the rail, hudded together, and looking entirely overwhelmed by events. Standing beside them, Pavo was beaming broadly. He had already identified Nagaro for the benefit of these guests, speaking glowingly in Hashti.

Nagaro nodded. "Yes. One older, and one younger than you, as I recall."

Pavo gestured at the older of the two men. "This is my brother Taan that is older than me," he said. "And this is his wife, Hataarti." He indicated the woman. "And this is Katuk." Pavo gripped the younger man by the shoulder. "Almost I do not know him because he was only boy when last I see him. He is brother that is younger than me." Katuk grinned uncertainly. He could almost have been Pavo's twin in face and stature. Taan was a little shorter, but if anything broader in the shoulders. The family resemblance, while still there, was less obvious.

Nagaro nodded to each of them in turn as they were introduced. Then he put out his hand to Taan. The man looked slightly stunned, but took it. Nagaro addressed him in Hashti.

"Greeting, friend Taan Maat."

Taan's mouth dropped open at hearing himself addressed in such terms by the man he understood to be Kiraam Shaku-Tal. Nagaro then bowed to Hataarti, who dropped her eyes, completely abashed. Katuk gawked in astonishment as he accepted Nagaro's proffered hand and the Hashti words, "Greeting, friend Katuk Maat."

Pavo's grin could scarcely have been any wider. "Do you know," he said with evident pride, "that they have heard of me in my old home near Sar Tipaal? They have heard that Pavo Maat sails with Kiraam Shaku-Tal and that I fight by his side. Some of Mautep in Sar Tipaal are begin to know that Taan and Katuk are my brother, and they were not safe there any more. So they decide to come and find me, and here they are! Surely it is hand of Sheptuum that have brought them to us. This is most happy day! They come just in time to see me be married!"

So the *Sword of Freedom* and the *Sea Eagle* sailed on, the *Sword* now with a Hashtep fishing boat in tow. The discussion of Nagaro's proposal to speak with Lord Kuran was quite forgotten in all the excitement.

Later that day the two ships passed the northern tip of the island of Pakoa and the men on their decks heard the horn on the north tower blare its high, clear, brassy note in sets of three short blasts that heralded the sighting of ships bearing the white sword banner. A little later, the horn on the west tower at Sand Hill Point sounded the same pattern in its more mellow tones, and later still, the horn of the south tower at the entrance to Pakoa Harbor sounded a sonorous echo of its two sisters. Not long after that, the *Sword of Freedom* and the *Sea Eagle* glided through the narrow channel into the harbor. There they found the other two galleys, the *Tiger* and the *North Wind*, already lying at anchor, rocking easily on the quiet swells.

Chapter 4

A Long-Awaited Wedding

I t was a glorious spring day. The sun was arcing towards its zenith in a sky of flawless blue. The air was balmy under the newly-leafed trees at the edge of the practice field. The bride was wearing traditional yellow— a slender sheath that enveloped her from throat to ankles— with a garland woven of white shepherd's lace and yellow heal-all in her shining black hair. The groom was in white, also traditional, with a long garland of the same two flowers draped around his shoulders and trailing down on either side.

They were standing under the traditional arch made of tree boughs tied together. Pavo had been determined that there should be no possible question that he and Tenepti were properly married, and so this wedding was to be entirely according to the established Hashtep custom. Even the hour was traditional, for the Hashtep believed that it was most auspicious for a wedding to begin an hour before noon, so that the ceremony might reach its happy conclusion just when the sun was highest in the sky.

Nagaro was thoroughly enjoying the spectacle.

Pavo had been the first to appear, stepping from some place of concealment to stand waiting under the arched branches. A tight little circle of women had then approached from another direction, walking with arms interlaced and hands clasped, accompanied by the strains of a lute, played by a musician who was carefully concealed. The women had moved to a point directly in front of the arch, where the circle had opened to reveal Tenepti standing with demurely downcast eyes. Pavo had then stepped forward to take his intended bride by the hand and draw her back to stand beside him under the arch. At the touch of Pavo's hand Tenepti had turned to him and given him a smile that mirrored the morning sunshine.

After that, there had been much standing up and speaking on the part of various male relatives who were seated in the audience. Nagaro had been gratified to see that Tenepti's father looked not merely resigned, but actually rather pleased.

The happy couple were now in the act of sharing a piece of bread and drinking from the same cup. If it were possible for any two people to look more radiantly happy, Nagaro could not imagine how.

The wedding arch stood under the trees at the edge of the field where the pirate crews normally took their sword practice, and Nagaro was seated among the invited guests on one of the benches also arrayed under those trees. Behind the seated guests, a crowd of folk who hadn't been formally uninvited spilled out onto the hard-packed earth of the practice field, all craning their necks and jostling one another to get a better view. Pavo, who was clearly basking in his celebrity, had decreed that none of them should be made to go away. Instead they were being kept at least three feet behind the last of the benches by a row of crewmen from the *Sword of Freedom*.

Nagaro was, of course, seated on the men's side, to the happy couple's right. In front of him were Pavo's brothers, Taan and Katuk, as well as all of Tenepti's male relatives. The latter consisted of her father, one grandfather and a number of assorted uncles and cousins. It had been necessary for each of these men to stand up and say a few ritual words as part of the ceremony. It all had to do, as Nagaro understood, with the proper transferring of Tenepti from one family to another. Nagaro was sitting between Taru and Sindar, and further along the same row were Tredhold, and Landros, the captain of the *Sea Eagle*. In the row behind them were Gedras the merchant, the other two pirate captains, Moraga and Timegar, as well as a number of crewmen from the ships.

The ceremony was being conducted entirely in Hashti, and Nagaro wasn't even trying to understand the words. The effort would have spoiled his enjoyment of the other details. For example, he was very much enjoying watching Pavo and Tenepti together, because they were so obviously enjoying themselves. He had never previously gotten more than a glimpse of Tenepti, but he had no difficulty now in seeing what it was that Pavo saw in her. To begin with, she was pretty and slender and almond-eyed. And although she was clearly well-versed in the art of demurely casting down her eyes whenever the script called for it, the quick, clear glances and radiant smiles that she gave at other times suggested that she was very far from being as shy and retiring as she was trying to appear to be.

This wasn't really surprising, Nagaro reflected. After all, she wasn't sixteen anymore. There had been four years for her to get used to the idea of marrying Pavo, and Pavo, for his part, was obviously thoroughly comfortable with the idea of marrying Tenepti. It was just exactly the way a wedding ought to be, Nagaro thought, and of course not the least bit like his own wedding to the princess had been all those years ago. He winced painfully at the memory, and jerked his thoughts away. *Best not to think about that, or about the fact that, after seven years, he wasn't even close to finding a woman to marry— a woman he could care for the way Pavo cared forTenepti.*

Even Taru was closer to doing that, Nagaro reflected, than he was. He glanced at Taru who was seated on his right. The young Turo was looking extremely thoughtful. Nagaro couldn't help secretly hoping that this wedding was giving him ideas. Taru always seemed to be toying with the idea of courting Tulara, the kitchen maid at the Bay Tree Inn— toying with the idea, but never quite managing to come around to taking up the pursuit. Nagaro glanced at Sindar, who was on his left. The former captive was washed, shaved, and trimmed, and was looking quite handsome in dark pants and a white shirt borrowed from Nagaro. Sindar was raptly following every word of the ceremony and judging by the expression on his face, the wedding was definitely giving the young Kelorin ideas— ideas that a Kelorin slave raised in a Hashtep village had surely never dared to entertain. Nagaro frowned. *This might pose some difficulties...*

Nagaro's train of thought was interrupted by the voice of one of his nephews, ten-year-old Pilo, speaking behind him in a stage whisper.

"Are they almost done?"

It was the third time the boy had asked the same question.

"Shh! No, not nearly!"

That would be Pilo's brother, Tavo, who was twelve, and therefore knew everything. Nagaro shook his head in mock despair. Belatedly, he heard Sudano, the boys' father, shush them both. Then, from across the aisle, on the women's side, he heard Narei's small piping voice.

"Aunty Ani, why is Uncle Pavo wearing a string of flowers?"

Nagaro heard Animara's quiet, *"Shh!"* followed by fifteen-year-old, Bahiri, explaining to her little cousin in the lowest whisper she could manage that it was the Hashtep custom for a man to wear a string of flowers when he got married. Nagaro sighed and smiled indulgently. It was a very good thing that he wasn't trying to understand the words of the ceremony.

Nagaro gave his attention back to the scene in front of him just as Tenepti's father stood up and launched into a new speech. It went on for some time and must have been very important because, when the man finally sat down, Nagaro found that all around him the heads were bobbing up and down and the eyes were shining.

Now, at last, Pavo was taking Tenepti into his arms and kissing her, an aching caress that retained just enough of chastity for the children in the audience while evoking the fire that would warm the night to come.

Nagaro thought he would always remember Pavo and Tenepti as they were in that moment: Tenepti with her yellow dress aflame in the sun and her raven hair spilling over her shoulders, stretching a little, her face turned up to Pavo who bent over her and wrapped her in a flower-draped embrace that was so perfectly comfortable and secure. It was a perfect moment, and when the newly-wedded couple stepped apart, there was a collective sigh from the women's side of the aisle, and appreciative whistles from some of the men, opposite.

And then the group of women who had escorted Tenepti appeared again, carrying baskets full of flowers, which they showered upon the happy couple and strewed about generally among the audience. The lute player, a gray-haired Hashtep man, appeared from behind a screen of bushes and struck up an energetic tune as he led the way down the aisle between the benches. Pavo and Tenepti, hand in hand, swept triumphantly after him, bringing the ceremony to its conclusion.

As the audience rose to follow the bride and groom, Nagaro felt a tug on his sleeve and turned to meet Sindar's eager gaze.

"That... I like." Sindar spoke in halting Common Speech. "I very much like! How I get one, Cap-tain?"

Sindar had given up addressing Nagaro by the Hashti word for master, and had substituted "captain" in the common speech. He had also ceased to be so much in awe of Nagaro, since Nagaro did nothing to encourage it.

Nagaro felt a little pang. "*I wish I knew...*" he murmured under his breath, but he saw that Sindar was looking puzzled. "Ask Pavo," he told the young man seriously. He had almost none of the necessary Hashti vocabulary, and he didn't want to risk trusting something like this to Sindar's very limited knowledge of the Common Speech. Then he added hastily in Hashti, "But not today. Wait some few day. Pavo has... many thing to do."

Understanding dawned in Sindar's eyes. He nodded, grinning knowingly. "Oh yes," he said. "I under-stand."

"Papa, Papa! I want a horsey ride!"

Nagaro looked down into the eager upturned face of his not quite four-year-old daughter, who seemed to have somehow escaped from both Animara and Bahiri. He laughed and scooped Narei up to place her on his shoulders, firmly holding a little ankle on either side. Looking around, he caught Animara's eye among the crowd and gave her wink, before striding off through the press of folk who were milling their way in the general direction of the Bay Tree Inn, the place where the wedding feast was to be.

"How did you like the wedding, Little One?" he asked her.

"It was so *long*, Papa. And I wanted to sit with *you!*"

Narei had an iron grip on Nagaro's hair where it was tied at the nape of his neck. "I know," he told her. "And I'm sorry you couldn't. But you know we had to do everything the Hashtep way, for Pavo."

"Uh-huh." Narei bobbed on his shoulders. "Hiri says Uncle Pavo is going to live with Tenepti in a new house now. So can I come live with you, Papa? In Uncle Pavo's room?"

From Narei's tone, Nagaro could picture the look on the little girl's face, the two little eyebrows knit together over the wide, questioning brown eyes.

"But if you did that, Bahiri would miss you. And she'd have to sleep all alone at night," he pointed out. "She might get scared."

"We-ell... yes... I guess she might." Narei's concern was completely genuine.

"And Tavo and Pilo like to play with you, and make you things," he added.

"Ye-es..." She said uncertainly.

"And Aunty Ani likes to take care of you."

But now he heard a pout in Narei's voice as she said, "all Aunty Ani ever does is say, 'Don't do that'!"

They had reached the Inn while they were talking, but there was such a crush of people on the broad front porch, and all around the front door, that Nagaro turned aside to go around to the back through the kitchen garden. There he swung Narei down from his shoulders and set her on the ground. "Do you know *why* she says that?" he asked solemnly.

Narei frowned up at him. She shook her head.

"Why, Papa?"

"Because it's her task to take care of you. If you came and stayed with *me*, then it would be *my* task, and I'd be the one who had to say, don't do that. Would you like that any better?"

Narei's frown deepened. "But you wouldn't—" she began.

"Oh yes, I'm afraid I would," he told her very seriously. "If I were taking care of you, I would *have* to."

"Oh." Narei's mouth made a little round, pink 'O,' when she said the word. She frowned thoughtfully for several seconds and then said, "I think it's better if I just come visit you, Papa."

He reached down and stroked her dark hair. "I think that's true," he said.

As he straightened, he caught an approaching movement from the corner of his eye and turned— to meet the gaze of Tira Zomora.

The island's Turowan medicine woman had halted a dozen feet from him. She was clad in what Nagaro thought of as her uniform, a light green blouse and many-pocketed yellow skirt. Her square brown face was framed by a mane of raven hair and her black-eyed stare transfixed him like an arrow shaft.

For the last four years, Zomora had given him no more than a nod of greeting on the rare occasions when their paths had crossed, and he had been perfectly content with the lack of attention. He'd felt her disapproval years ago when he had first begun the work of freeing slaves, and since she had relented, he'd assumed that she must have put that ill will aside. Zomora wasn't one to hold her tongue out of politeness. He'd suspected that his willing embrace of his illegitimate child had been responsible, at least in part, for her apparent change of heart. Yet here she was, bristling at him, in the middle of his playing the role of papa.

What could she want? There was only one way to find out. He looked quickly back down at Narei. "Go on into the kitchen," he told her. "Find Tulara or Tira Yuli, and I'll come find you as soon as I can."

Narei's eyes went to Zomora and back to her father, reading the signs of some arcane grown-up doings that would probably bore her. "All right, Papa" she said brightly, and scampered off.

Nagaro watched his daughter long enough to see her disappear safely through the kitchen's back door before returning his attention to the medicine woman. He met her stare, inclined his head to show respect, and said, "Well met, Tira Zomora."

"Captain." She clipped the word coldly, and advanced two strides to close the distance between them with a swish of skirts. All the while, her eyes impaled him. "What does the Lord of the Fleet want with ye?"

So she had gotten wind of that. It didn't surprise him. He suspected there was very little that went on anywhere in the southern Lomoas that Zomora didn't know about. He drew a breath and said carefully, "I don't know. Though I can guess that it concerns my piratical activities."

This elicited just enough of a nod to indicate that he had confirmed her suspicions. She folded her arms across her chest.

"Ye'll meet with him?"

"Yes," he said firmly, having in that instant abandoned any lingering ambivalence on the subject. "I intend to."

Zomora raised her chin and looked down her hawk's nose at him. "Not here," she said, and though her tone didn't quite make it a command, it was not a question either.

"No," he agreed, unflinching. "I will seek him by ship and let him find me in a place of my choosing."

Zomora vouchsafed him a stiff nod in response to this. "Good," she said, unfolding her arms. "Ye've done fair service to these islands up 'til now. See that ye do them no harm in serving yourself."

Nagaro stiffened. "I assure you I have no intention—" he began.

But she was finished with him. Turning her back, she walked away with surprising speed, threading her way among the lingering wedding guests who were still in the process of adjourning to the Bay Tree's common room. He stood for a long moment staring after the retreating figure, and caught a glimpse of the piebald pony she always rode, tethered to a tree on the far side of the wedding venue.

"*Bishka,*" he muttered to himself. Her final words had stung. The pointed warning in them having wiped away any satisfaction he might have derived from the praise she had bestowed on him in the preceding sentence— the first praise he had gotten from the medicine woman in the last four years.

It stung that she imagined he would place his own interests before the safety of Pakoa or the surrounding isles. For Zomora's concern was clearly that he would somehow bring the wrath of the powers of Edrovir down upon the islands and their Turowan inhabitants. They were her people, her charge, and he respected that fact. But *he* worried about them too— not only the Turo, but the Kelorin and Hashtep, as well, and not only for fear of Lord Kuran. The Lord of the Fleet had visited Pakoa a half dozen times in the past four years and Nagaro had made sure in every case that he and his captains were elsewhere. That had been for the pirates' safety primarily, of course. But there had been ample opportunity for Kuran to punish Pakoa for its association with Captain Nagaro if the man had been so inclined, and it had never happened.

In fact, Nagaro was not particularly worried about Kuran causing any harm to the inhabitants of Pakoa. It was the Mautep that worried him. Already there had been one attack on the island. Fortunately, Nagaro and the Pakoa Town Council had been prepared for possible trouble. They'd been ready that time, and it had worked. The island's official authorities clearly felt that the benefits of the pirates' presence outweighed the risks.

At least so far.

Nagaro shook his head and turned to make for the kitchen door. He worried about these things on a regular basis, and would continue to worry about them. Just not today. Today was for Pavo and Tenepti.

When he entered the kitchen, he found Yuli, the innkeeper's wife, at the table, just finishing loading up a wooden tray with honeyed seed cakes. Narei was standing on a stool and leaning over the table doing her best to "help". Her little fingers were smudged with flour. Yuli looked up as Nagaro entered, and her round brown face lit with a smile. She brushed aside a strand of graying hair that had escaped her single long braid. "Here's your papa now," she said to Narei.

The little girl straightened up and glanced over her shoulder. "I *told* you he was coming. He *said* he would."

Nagaro came up behind his daughter where she teetered on the stool and placed a steadying hand on her shoulder. "I can see you're very busy, Yuli," he said. "Where is our friend, Tulara?"

Yuli gestured with a seedcake towards the doorway leading to the common room, from which a loud babble of voices was emanating. "She's out there, getting all the food set out just right. I 'spect she'll be back in here when she's got a minute, t' get this tray o' cakes."

Narei immediately jumped down from the stool and eagerly raised her hands. "Let me take it! *Please*, Tira Yuli? I can carry it!"

"I'm afraid the tray's a little big for you, Narei," Nagaro said gently. "Why don't I carry it, and you can go ahead of me to clear the way so I don't trip."

"But *I* want to carry something!" Narei bounced up and down.

"O' course ye do! And I know just the thing." Yuli turned to a large chest of drawers and produced a handful of spoons. "Tulara will know what to do with them," she added, winking at Nagaro.

Narei delightedly took the spoons, three in each hand, and waved them triumphantly as she made for the open doorway. Nagaro hastily picked up the laden tray and hurried after her, giving Yuli a grateful grin over his shoulder.

The center of the common room had been cleared to make way for the dancing that would come later, and the tables were arrayed around the edges. Nagaro threaded his way through the mass of people milling about in the cleared space. He managed to deliver the tray of cakes to the correct table, and conducted Narei, with her spoons, to Tulara. The kitchen maid greeted Narei with her usual enthusiasm. It was with good reason that Nagaro called her "our friend, Tulara," for he had a comfortable friendship with the young Turowa, and his daughter held a special place in Tulara's heart.

"Narei, my little bird!" Tulara cried. "What have ye got for me?"

"Spoons!" Narei proudly offered up the implements.

"Tira Yuli said you'd know what to do with them," Nagaro explained hastily in answer to Tulara's questioning look.

Tulara immediately took the spoons and made a great show of arranging them around a tray of dried fruit and a bowl of sugared nuts.

"There!" she told Narei. "That's perfect. I've made up a special table for ye and the other children," she added. "It's over there in the corner, where ye can make all the mess ye want, and the big folk won't bother ye. Come along, an' I'll show ye where to sit."

"Will you sit with me, Tulara? And can I have an extra seed cake?"

"I'll sit with ye for a little while, Dearie, and ye can have all the seed cake's ye want. I made yours with extra honey." Tulara gave Nagaro a quick wink. "Do ye mind, Nagaro, if I steal her away?"

Nagaro laughed. "Not if you promise to give her back again."

He smiled as he watched Tulara lead Narei away to the children's table. If there was anyone who could rival her papa for Narei's affections, it was Tulara, but Nagaro didn't begrudge it. It wasn't surprising that Tulara felt a kind of kinship with Narei, since they both shared the stigma of having been begotten under dubious circumstances. Besides that, Tulara, like Nagaro, had no parents or siblings in the world, and so he didn't at all mind sharing his daughter with the young woman.

Nagaro noticed that Narei's young cousins, Bahiri, Tavo, and Pilo, were already at the children's table. As he watched, Tredhold's two stepchildren arrived with the older of the two children that Ilsafeth had born to the healer, a flaxen-haired boy, in tow. The younger of Tredhold's natural offspring was still a babe in arms, and doubtless with her mother. Nagaro decided to leave Narei with Tulara and these familiar playmates, and went to give his congratulations to the newlyweds.

Pavo and Tenepti were enthroned at a table by the windows and it took some time to get close enough to speak to them since nearly everyone else in the room was bent upon doing the same thing. When at last Nagaro stood before them and offered his good wishes, Pavo reached, beaming, across the table and took his hand, nearly crushing it.

Tenepti leaned forward without a trace of shyness and spoke in a voice that just carried above the din. "I want to thank ye, Tor Nagaro," she said. "Because ye didn't let Pavo give up all those years ago when my father was so set against him."

Nagaro laughed and waved her words aside. "Pavo never would have given up as easily as that," he told her. "Though, I suppose he might have suffered even greater misery if he hadn't gotten some encouragement from his friends."

Tenepti rewarded him with one of her sunshine smiles, and he made her a little bow before stepping aside to let the next guest have a chance to wish the couple well. Turning, he sought to get himself some food and find a place to sit, preferably where he could watch the show without being in the middle of it.

The food was all laid out on two tables under the windows. There were piles of fresh rolls, plates of cheese, and several kinds of sliced, spiced meats— in addition to the nuts, the dried fruit, and the traditional seed cakes. There were also pitchers of cold sothiril and two kegs of ale. Nagaro was just starting to fill a plate when Taru appeared, leading Sindar by the arm.

"Will ye look after this man for a bit, Nagaro?" the young Turo asked with more than a trace of annoyance, and without even bothering to lower his voice. "He's gotten it into his head that he wants t' talk to the Hashtep girls, and o' course it's not allowed."

Yuli had explained to Nagaro, Taru, and Pavo that one of the functions of a wedding on Pakoa was to offer an opportunity for all the young unmarried women and men to get a look at one another. Looking was all that was permitted, however, and even that was only to be done from a distance of at least a dozen feet.

When Nagaro had ventured to observe that this must make it rather complicated for a young man to walk across the room, Yuli had explained that the unmarried women would be seated at a table in a corner— well separated from everything else— and forbidden to move. Things only became slightly more interesting during the dancing, at which time the young women were permitted to dance in their own small circle off to one side. Nagaro had thought the arrangement rather unfair, since it offered the young men a great deal more freedom than the women. But then he often didn't agree with the island customs regarding male-female interactions.

"Well, of course I'll help look after Sindar," Nagaro responded to Taru's request, frowning slightly. "But why don't you both get plates and we can all sit together?"

Taru shrugged. "I'm not very hungry," he said tersely. And without giving Nagaro a chance to offer any further comment, he turned and struck off in the direction of the ale casks. Nagaro continued to frown as he stared after his friend. Taru didn't seem to be in a very good mood, and it seemed rather a shame under the circumstances.

Nagaro turned his attention back to Sindar, and he was relieved to see that, at the moment, the young Kelorin's mind appeared to be fully occupied with the subject of food. The young man had found a plate and was in the process of loading it with some of everything on the table. Nagaro hoped that the food might continue to hold Sindar's attention, at least for a while.

As soon as the young man had filled his plate, Nagaro drew him away and found a place for them to sit that was as far away as possible from the "maiden table", as it was known. He thought this would probably be safer for Sindar, and it suited him as well. Over the past four years, he'd become an expert at avoiding the gaze of young women who were trying, more or less artfully, to catch his eye, but it was a skill he preferred not to have to exercise.

Fortunately, Sindar did indeed remain focused on his food for a considerable time. It seemed that the former captive had never really had enough to eat at any time in his life, until very recently, and the variety of his diet had been severely limited as well. The wide diversity of Pakoan food was just one of the things the young man had been discovering in the week that he had been on the island, and it was one that still held much fascination. Accordingly, Nagaro found himself able to enjoy his own food in peace while unobtrusively observing the other guests from his out-of-the-way location.

Pavo and Tenepti were very much the center of attention, and it was a relief for Nagaro to find that, for once, no one seemed to be watching *him*. He noticed almost immediately that Yuli's younger daughter, Luweda, and Tenepti's older sister, Matahi, were very nearly as popular on this occasion as the bride and groom. This was fair since it had been these two women who had for years passed messages back and forth and arranged trysts between the frustrated sweethearts. They could justifiably claim a large share of the credit for the happy outcome.

Nagaro also soon concluded that weddings were an opportunity for women to show off new babies.

Tredhold's wife, Ilsafeth, appeared early with her new little baby girl, and immediately was surrounded by a circle of admiring women. A little later, Ilsafeth acquired some competition when Moraga came in with his wife Panila, who had that couple's new little baby boy in her arms. Everyone who had just been ooing and aahing over Tredhold's daughter had immediately to do the same over Moraga's son. Moraga, the new father, was hanging about at his wife's elbow grinning like a maniac and swaggering even more than usual.

Nagaro had expected Taru to join him and Sindar after a little while, but the young Turo showed no sign of doing so. Occasionally Nagaro caught a glimpse of his friend among the jostling crowd, always alone, looking moody, and carrying an ale mug in his hand. It occurred to Nagaro that Taru might be looking for an opportunity to speak to Tulara. A few times when Nagaro was able to see both of them at once in the crowd, it seemed that Taru was looking in Tulara's direction or even moving towards her, but the young woman's role as kitchen maid seemed to keep her constantly on the move and surprisingly difficult to approach.

Nagaro frowned. Taru's apparent difficulty was ironic considering that Tulara was the only marriageable woman in the room who wasn't sequestered at the maiden table. It should be the easiest thing in the world to make an excuse to get a few words with a serving woman. All one had to do was pretend to need something. *Perhaps if he were to illustrate the technique...*

He waited for an opportunity and then, seeing Tulara moving in his direction, raised a hand to get her attention. Seeing him, she smiled and came over to his table. Sindar looked up from his spiced meat, startled. Nagaro beckoned Tulara to come around to the side where he was seated, on the pretense that it was too hard to speak to her above the general babble. She came at once, bending down to say, "Is there something ye were needing, Tor Nagaro?"

He smiled at the formality. "Yes," he told her. "I need to see *you* sit down here and rest for a minute." He indicated the stool beside him, which he'd been saving for Taru.

Tulara smiled and sank down onto it gratefully. "The Spirits bless ye, Nagaro," she said. "Ye're so kind. But it can only be for a minute. I've my work t' do."

Sindar, seated on the other side of Nagaro, was looking back and forth from one of them to the other with obvious curiosity, though he didn't try to say anything.

Nagaro laughed at Tulara's words, and shook his head at her. "Surely these folk can fend for themselves for a few minutes," he observed. "They're not so helpless."

She sighed. "I know," she said. "But I want everything t' be perfect for Pavo and Tenepti. They've waited so long..." Her words trailed off, and she frowned a little.

"How are Narei and the other children getting along at their table," he asked, to change the subject.

Tulara brightened immediately. "They're getting on very nicely," she said. "I taught Narei a new string game, and she's teaching it t' all the others. She's so quick, my little bird!"

He smiled. "Well, you'll get no argument from her Papa about that."

They exchanged a few more words, but soon Tulara rose to go. As she moved away, Nagaro started to search the crowd for Taru, but suddenly Sindar spoke beside him.

"What name?" the young Kelorin asked in the Common Speech, pointing after Tulara.

Nagaro turned back to the man beside him. "What is *her* name?" he corrected, by way of instruction, then answered the question. "*Her* name is *Tulara*."

"Tu-*la*-ra," Sindar echoed. "Captain, you like... *her*... name Tulara?"

Nagaro nodded. "Yes, I like her," he said, speaking carefully. "I like Tulara very much."

An eager smile spread across Sindar's face. "You make wedding?" he asked brightly.

"With Tulara?" Nagaro was startled, and a little embarrassed, to be so misunderstood. "No, no, Sindar. I *like* Tulara, but I don't *love* her."

Sindar's brow constricted in a puzzled frown. "What is *love?*" he inquired very seriously.

Nagaro was now at a loss. "It's a... a special kind of *feeling*..." he began, but Sindar was looking completely mystified. Nagaro gave up. "I am sorry," he said in Hashti. "I do not know Hashti word for 'love.' You must ask one of Hashtep."

"Oh." Sindar nodded his acceptance. Then his gaze shifted across to the opposite corner of the long room. He pointed at the maiden table through an opening in the crowd. "Many *her* there!" He said eagerly. "I like. Go see!"

Sindar started to stand up, but Nagaro hastily pulled him back down onto his stool. There followed a rather urgent exchange in alternating and commingled Common Speech and Hashti, at the end of which Nagaro was *fairly* certain that he had made Sindar understand that it was not allowed for him to "go see" the young women up close or speak to them as he had just spoken to Tulara. Sindar was so obviously disappointed that Nagaro relented, somewhat against his better judgement, and took Sindar to a position near the tables of food from which the maiden table could be viewed from a discreet distance.

Sindar spent several minutes observing the young women at the corner table and commenting about them in Hashti. As it happened, all three of the races inhabiting Pakoa were represented there. Only two of the girls were Kelorin. One of these Nagaro didn't know. The other was Lissel, the youngest of Gedras' three daughters and the only one of them who remained unmarried. There were several Turowan girls also, but most of the young women, at least a half dozen, were Hashtep. Presumably these last were all relatives or friends of the bride, but Nagaro knew none of them.

It was the Hashtep girls who attracted Sindar's interest, almost exclusively. In his efforts to discover why, Nagaro came to deduce the meanings of two Hashtep words that hadn't previously been in his vocabulary, words that apparently corresponded more or less to "beautiful" and "ugly".

Nagaro was somewhat distressed to learn that Sindar considered the young Hashtep women "beautiful", (especially one of them), while the others, especially the two Kelorin girls, were dismissed as "ugly". This disturbed Nagaro, both because he didn't consider appearances to be so important and because he didn't agree with Sindar's assessment. While he agreed that Sindar had picked out the prettiest of the Hashtep girls, Nagaro felt that two of the Turowan girls were every bit her equal. And neither of the young Kelorin women was by any means ugly. In fact, he found Lissel quite attractive. She was looking very much more a young woman these days, he noted, since she had stopped wearing her hair in braids.

Lissel also seemed to have noticed that Nagaro and Sindar were looking at the occupants of the maiden table. At first she merely looked back at them, quite unabashed, but then she leaned over to one of the other girls, who turned to look also. At this point, Nagaro decided it was time that he and Sindar returned to their seats, so he drew the young man away.

As they re-crossed the room, Nagaro reflected that Sindar's tastes must reflect his limited experience. He had grown up surrounded only by Hashtep women in that little village in the Mahuk Baar and had no other standard for feminine beauty. Hopefully the young man's view would broaden with more experience of other races. Nagaro frowned. *If it didn't, there was likely to be trouble ahead.*

It turned out that their little excursion would have been interrupted soon in any case, for they had barely taken their seats when Tenepti's father rose and declared that it was time for the ritual consumption of the honeyed seed cakes. This, as Nagaro understood it, had something to do with wishing that the union of Pavo and Tenepti would be a fruitful one. It seemed to require a number of speeches by various guests and participants. Everything was in Hashti once again, which meant that Sindar listened with rapt attention, while Nagaro was able to scan the room in search of Taru.

He caught only one glimpse of his friend, standing off to one side, frowning into his ale. When Nagaro looked for Tulara, his gaze eventually found her at the children's table. She looked up just then, and their eyes met across the room. She smiled and waved. Narei, in Tulara's lap, waved also. Nagaro returned both gestures before someone moved to obscure his view.

And then it was time for the dancing. The lute player was there, and there were two more men with long flutes and another with a set of traditional drums. Nagaro had learned Turowan circle dances at Moraga's wedding, but most of the Hashtep dances were new to him. Sindar, on the other hand, had never had the opportunity to participate in any kind of dancing, although he managed to communicate that he had watched such things before. The former captive was very eager to learn the steps, so he and Nagaro both joined the circle, and Nagaro gave the young Kelorin as much instruction as he could, after which they both had to learn as they went along.

The task was by no means easy and it absorbed all of Nagaro's attention for some time, so that he completely forgot about following the further movements of Taru and Tulara.

Chapter 5

And The Aftermath

It was nearly three hours later and Nagaro and Sindar were resting on their stools at the out-of-the-way table by the wall. The sun was halfway down the sky. The traditional dances had all been danced— and danced— until the participants were exhausted. The celebration must have been a success, judging by all the happy and satisfied faces. The bride and groom had departed some time ago, creeping out the back door and hurrying home to the newly-finished house that awaited them. The guests were beginning to drift away as well. Ramu the innkeeper was standing by the door bidding folk good day, and basking in the general praise for a task well done.

Presently, Gedras approached the table where Nagaro and Sindar were seated. The merchant was apparently about to take his leave, for both his wife, Delmanei, and his daughter Lissel were with him. Nagaro gave Gedras and each of the two women a polite nod of acknowledgment as they approached. Thereafter he did his best not to appear to notice Lissel. Fortunately Gedras made this easy by addressing him.

The spare, middle-aged Kelorin made Nagaro a small formal bow before he spoke.

"The Town Council meeting is to be tomorrow night, Captain. There will be a discussion of the matter of increasing the number of men in the Pakoan Guard as you have suggested. I assume that you will be there?"

"Of course, Gedras." Nagaro leaned forward across the table. "Did you say anything to them about the number to be added?"

The merchant ran a hand over his sleek, graying hair. "Well, ah, *yes...*" he said a little uncomfortably. "I'm afraid you may have a bit of trouble with the idea of doubling the force. We already have the horns for warning, and two dozen spearmen and a half a dozen bowmen. And since that little affair they are pleased to call the Battle of Pakoa Town, some of them seem to believe that the Mautep only sail in small numbers and that our guard has taught them to stay away from our island."

Nagaro frowned. "The members of the guard did very well in responding to that attack," he said earnestly. "I was proud of how they used their training. But there were only two ships that time, and only one was able to set her warriors ashore before Landros and I arrived with our ships in answer to the horn. It's a lucky thing we were so close. And while the Mautep warlords have a history of working individually in the past, they've become more organized since they have a new emperor—and that emperor has put a price on my head, which gives them a strong motivation to try to find me. It would grieve me more than I can tell if any harm were to come to Pakoa because I have chosen it for my home."

"I know this very well." Gedras sighed. "And your words have proven persuasive in the past. We can only hope that they will prove so again."

Sindar had been sitting quietly on his stool during this conversation. His eyes had been traveling back and forth between the speakers, and he'd been frowning in concentration as he tried to catch familiar words of the Common Speech. Nagaro had been peripherally aware of the young man's interest, and even more vaguely aware that Lissel was watching Sindar. As Gedras spoke his last words, Lissel leaned forward to whisper something in her mother's ear, and Delmanei responded by addressing herself to Nagaro.

"We have seen you in the company of this man all afternoon, Captain," she said, indicating Sindar with a little nod of her head. "He must be some new friend of yours. Will you not introduce him?"

"I beg your pardon," Nagaro responded hastily. "I was so concerned about the matter of the Pakoan Guard that I have forgotten my courtesy. This man goes by the name of Sindar, and I'm afraid he speaks very little of the Common Speech, having been born into captivity in the Mahuk Baar."

"Oh!" Delmanei exclaimed, eyeing Sindar somewhat askance. "How dreadful for him!"

Gedras, however, extended his hand to Sindar, who was clearly aware that he was now the subject of the conversation. "Welcome to Pakoa, friend Sindar," the merchant said, with an encouraging smile. "My name is Gedras."

Sindar knew enough to take Gedras's hand. He shook it vigorously. "Good morning," he said, that being the only greeting he had learned so far.

Delmanei looked embarrassed at the young man's error, and Lissel frowned, but Gedras only smiled as he retrieved his hand.

"Yes," the merchant observed politely. "It *was* a good morning, and it is now a *good afternoon.* Allow me to present my wife, Delmanei, and my daughter Lissel."

Sindar must have noticed how Nagaro had nodded to the women when they arrived, for he now bobbed his head to each of them.

"Good... *afternoon?*" he said uncertainly. Apparently having understood Gedras well enough to take the hint.

Delmanei smiled, then, and inclined her head in response.

To Nagaro's surprise, Lissel chose to return Sindar's greeting. "Good afternoon, Tor Sindar," she said, and smiled sweetly at the young Kelorin, drawing a sharp, reproving glance from her mother.

Sindar managed only to stare at the young woman, apparently at a loss.

Gedras pointedly ignored his daughter's forwardness. Instead he cleared his throat and spoke to Nagaro.

"I will expect to see you at the meeting, then, Captain. And for now, we must bid you good day."

Nagaro nodded. "I will certainly be there." he said quickly. "Good day to you, Tor Gedras. And Zirdyns." He nodded to the two women.

He thought he should say something to Sindar about what had just transpired, but he wasn't sure what it should be. He was given no chance, in any case, because Timegar stepped up to the table as soon as Gedras moved away from it. The former Fleet warrior had approached while Nagaro was speaking to the merchant, and had been hovering in the background, apparently awaiting a chance to speak.

"Nagaro," he said earnestly, "I'm glad to find Sindar with ye. I have a proposition, and it concerns our young friend here." He nodded to Sindar, who managed a puzzled nod in return.

Nagaro frowned slightly. "What sort of proposition?" he asked.

Timegar wasted no time. "My wife and I would like t' offer him a place under our roof," he explained. "We've talked it over, and it makes some sense, now that we know that our son is dead and won't be coming back to us. We've an empty place, so to speak, and Sindar has no family."

Nagaro's face clouded. During the previous season, they had freed a slave who had shared time with Timegar's son on the oar deck of a Mahuk galley. The man had been able to describe how the boy had died, killed during a battle by a blow from a broken oar shaft. "I don't think I have told you properly how sorry I was to hear that news," Nagaro told the graying Kelorin. "I'm sure it's better to know than to go on hoping in vain, but still..."

Timegar shrugged his shoulders. "I think I always knew he was gone. Knowing how it happened makes it more real, that's all. But it came hard to my poor Kormine. She'd never given up hope. Now she's looking for something to do t' feel better again, and this seems a good way."

Nagaro glanced at Sindar, whose face was registering only blank incomprehension. "Well," he said. "It's a very good thought, and Pavo says the best thing for him is to have to speak the Common Speech as much as possible. He'd certainly have to do that, living with you, but you'd find it hard, knowing so little Hashti. There's so much he doesn't understand. You would need a lot of patience."

Timegar nodded. "I know that," he said. "But there's no one on earth more patient than Kormine." He nodded at Sindar. "Will ye ask him if he'd like t' come live with us?"

Nagaro managed, with some convolutions, to explain to Sindar in Hashti what Timegar was suggesting.

Once he understood, Sindar did not hesitate. "Yes," he said decisively to Timegar. "Yes, I come. Thank you."

A further brief exchange was needed to make the plan clear to all. Sindar would come that very day, but first he needed to collect his few belongings from the barracks room he'd been sharing with two newly-freed slaves. As soon as it was decided, Sindar stood up to go and retrieve his things. Timegar explained that he would wait for the young man outside on the inn's front porch.

Left to himself at last, Nagaro got up and looked about for Taru. The common room was now rapidly emptying and he could see no sign of his friend anywhere, nor of Tulara. He hoped this was an auspicious sign.

Tredhold was still there, talking very seriously with Moraga. The two men were comparing notes on fatherhood, and Nagaro reflected that this was probably the first time in all of their shared history that these two very different men had found a topic of mutual interest. Their two wives stood nearby, also deep in conversation. As he passed, Nagaro caught enough to tell that Ilsafeth and Panila were also comparing notes on fatherhood, from the perspective of how well they thought their husbands were handling it. Hastily he moved on.

He encountered Animara near the children's table, where she was watching with a kind of bemused resignation as her three children, together with Tredhold's oldest girl and Narei, played a game that involved setting all of the stools in two lines and chasing each other back and forth between them. It also appeared to require a certain amount of laughter and shrieking.

Animara drew him aside so they could hear one another. "I want to invite ye to a bit o' late dinner, Nagaro," she told him. "And I wanted to invite Taru as well, so he won't be left all alone tonight now that Pavo's gone from that house o' yours. But I don't see him anywhere."

"That's a kind thought, Ani," he told her. "And I expect that Taru will be glad of the offer— if he hasn't made some other plan, that is. I was just looking for him myself. I've been wondering whether he meant to speak to Tulara."

Animara arched an eyebrow. "Oh, I'd say he was thinkin' about it all right," she opined. "He's had the look all afternoon of a man that's got somethin' on his mind, and this past hour I'd say he had the look of a man that's tryin' t' find his courage in a mug of ale."

Nagaro winced, and nodded. That sort of thing could get a man into trouble, as he knew from personal experience. But *he* hadn't known what he was doing on that occasion, whereas Taru certainly ought to. "Let's wait a little longer," he suggested. "He may turn up."

Animara agreed and returned to watching the children.

Seeing that he had time to kill, Nagaro went to find Yuli in the kitchen. He enjoyed talking with Yuli in any case, but there was also a subject of secret interest to him on which he hoped he might get some news. It was a hobby of Yuli's to collect any and all news about the Princess Nevien, and she had a knack for sorting more reliable information from mere gossip and rumor. It usually wasn't hard to get the kind-hearted Turowa going on this favorite subject, and the spring should have brought at least one or two merchant ships to Pakoa during the time that he and his men had been absent.

The innkeeper's wife was sitting at the kitchen table with a cup of sothiril, taking a little well-deserved rest before clearing away the dishes and the remaining food from the common room. Nagaro found a cup, pulled up a stool, and poured himself some sothiril.

"You should take your stool out there and rest by the door, Yuli," he told her. "Ramu is getting all of the credit, and really it was you that did most of the work— you and Tulara."

Yuli laughed. "Well, t' be fair, Ramu and Habu *did* set up the wedding place and move all the tables in the common room," she said. "And as soon as everyone's gone, they'll have t' put everything back in its place."

"But Matahi and Luwela have also been getting all the credit for keeping Pavo and Tenepti's romance going by relaying messages back and forth, and you had as much hand in that as either of them. It was *your* idea, if I recall."

"Well, if *I* recall, it was *your* idea— 'cept ye were going t' use a man for it, and I told ye it was women's work if ever there was any. But it doesn't matter." Yuli swept the matter aside with a wave of her hand. "What matters is that Pavo and Tenepti are really together at last."

Nagaro raised his cup of sothiril. "I'll drink to that!"

It took him all of another half minute to work the subject around to the princess. The two new babies that had been brought to the wedding feast provided a convenient transition.

"No it doesn't seem that she's with child yet," Yuli told him in answer to his carefully casual inquiry. "Poor thing." She sighed. "Some folk are sayin' she must be barren— being childless through three marriages and all, but I think there's time yet. Her first husband wasn't but a simple-minded boy, after all, and the *second*... Well, she probably kept out o' his way as much as she could. And Prince Elyan has been away at war more than he's been at home in Lankura."

Nagaro had taken a hasty swallow of sothiril to hide his discomfort at her mention of Nevien's first husband. He knew exactly why Nevien's first marriage had been childless— and it proved nothing. He had *been* that "simple-minded boy" under the influence of a drug that had made it impossible to do anything except what he was bidden to do... *and Nevien had kept telling him to stop...*

His mind slid away from the painfully unwelcome memories.

He tried instead to focus on the *other* two marriages. Yuli might be right about the second— the one to Gillard Marchent. Though it had lasted nearly two years, it had been marred by abuse. But the third marriage, to Prince Elyan, seemed happy enough, and it had now lasted more than two years. Tredhold and Moraga had each produced a child during a similar span of time, even though they had been absent from their homes for a great deal of it.

Nagaro wasn't sure exactly why he wanted so much for Nevien to have a child. It certainly wasn't that he cared about there being a royal heir. It might have something to do with Narei. His took such delight in his daughter, and Nevien had been kind to him— as kind as could be expected. Perhaps he wanted her to have the same joy that Lokundas had sent to him.

Or perhaps the birth of a child would put the final seal upon the fact that she was married to someone else... A frown flickered across his face. Would it release him from the last vestiges of responsibility?

He had been very relieved to learn of the princess's wedding to Elyan. Lord Elyan seemed a perfect husband for her. He was said to be a fine, well-built man, very handsome, and of such a temperate nature that no one could find fault with him— not even the members of the Leithian faction, even though the man was Kelorin.

In fact, Elyan seemed to have the sense to stay out of politics. He was very popular with the common people, and he had won such respect and renown by his exploits on the battlefield that the title of "Prince" seemed to fit naturally in front of his name. No one had ever been comfortable calling Gillard by that title. Nevien's second husband had remained "Lord Gillard" to the general populace until his dying day.

Nagaro sighed and shook himself out of his reverie. He guiltily gave his attention back to Yuli.

"—I have great hopes that something 'll happen now that there's a truce," she was saying. "Prince Elyan should be back in Lankura by now, and they'll have some time together—"

She was interrupted at that point by Timegar, who put his head in at the kitchen door. "Nagaro," he said urgently, "Ye'd best come out here.

Sindar's gone and run afoul of some o' the Hashtep. It's something about one of the Hashtep girls, and the father won't listen t' me."

Nagaro groaned, and hastily gulped the last of his sothiril. He gave Yuli an apologetic look.

"Ye go on," she said. "I'll take care o' your cup."

Rising, he made for the door, following Timegar who was already well ahead of him. Just as he stepped into the doorway, however, he found his way suddenly blocked by Taru, and he came to a dead stop in startled dismay.

Taru's face was flushed, his features contorted with rage. The punch that the young Turo leveled at Nagaro would surely have struck him squarely in the face had he been any less quick. As it was, he barely managed to get his hand up in time to strike Taru's fist aside.

"Taru!" he cried. "What are you doing?"

"*Ye dirty cheat!*" Taru spat the words. "*Ye sneakin' bastard!* How long have ye been courtin' Tulara behind my back?"

For an instant Nagaro could only stare at his friend in complete astonishment. Then he found his voice.

"I've done no such thing! What's wrong with you, Taru? You're not drunk, are you?"

"Not half as drunk as I need t' be right now!" Taru's fists were still clenched, and his voice shook with fury. He took a step forward, and Nagaro retreated back into the kitchen before the sheer radiant heat of his friend's anger.

"Wait a minute, Taru—" he began.

But Taru wouldn't wait.

"Haven't I seen ye sitting with her! An' *talking!* An' *smiling,* an'... an'... *wavin'* at each other across the room! Nagaro, *I trusted you!*" Taru's voice broke on the last words. He sounded close to weeping.

Nagaro struggled between shock and outrage, trying to comprehend this assault. "Of course I talk to her, Taru," he explained desperately. "Tulara and I are *friends*. And she's very fond of Narei..."

Taru emitted a groan. "Oh, *now* I see," he said with terrible bitterness. "Ye've used Narei t' take Tulara away from me!"

"*What?*" Nagaro stared helplessly at his friend. What had happened to suddenly give Taru such ideas?

"Now see here, Taru!" Yuli had come up behind Nagaro. Up to this point, she had been a silent spectator, but she had now apparently decided to speak her mind.

Taru turned on her. "Ye be still, Yuli! This is none o' your affair!"

"I will *not* be still!" Yuli stepped closer and wagged a finger in Taru's face. "And if it's a matter o' keepin' two good friends o' mine from coming t' blows over nothing, I'll *make* it my affair!"

"*Over nothing?* Ye call this *nothing?*" Taru was quite beside himself.

"Don't ye think I would know it if there was anything goin' on 'tween Nagaro and Tulara?" Yuli snapped. "What *exactly* did Tulara say t' ye? Out with it now!"

"Ye want t' know what she said?" Taru seemed to struggle for air. "Ye really want t' know? *She said she didn't want me.*" he choked on the bitter words. "She said she wanted a man with the *right* kind o' heart! One that wouldn't let a child grow up without a father... *Someone like him!*" He jabbed an accusing finger at Nagaro. "*That treacherous, lying, cheating—*"

"Ye stop right there, Taru Nareyo! Afore ye make any more of a fool o' yourself!" Yuli stood with her arms akimbo. "Sayin' she wants somebody *like* Nagaro ain't the same as sayin' that it's Nagaro she wants!"

Taru stopped, momentarily brought up short by the diminutive Turowa's words and tone.

Nagaro had been standing very still, his face frozen. *So that was it.* Taru's overtures had been rejected, and in terms that had made reference to *him.*

He felt sick, but he spoke into the tense, brittle silence. "I'm sorry Tulara said that, Taru," he said earnestly. "I wish she'd left me out of it. Tulara and I really *are* just friends. It's never been anything more than that. You have to believe me," he added pleadingly. "You've been like a brother to me, Taru. Do you really think I'd risk letting a woman come between us?"

Taru had turned to stare hard at him. The young Turo's eyes bored into Nagaro's, but the latter's glance didn't waver. And all that Taru could read in his friend's eyes was honest pain.

Taru suddenly sagged. The anger faded from his face to be replaced by an expression of pure agony. "*Oh, bodger...*" he murmured weakly. He dropped his eyes, then turned and fled stumbling from the kitchen.

Nagaro stood frozen for several seconds, then plunged after him.

"Taru! Wait!" he cried, but he found that the young Turo had already passed out of the common room. The door leading to the inn's front porch was just swinging shut behind him. There were a few wedding guests still in the room— Animara, Tredhold, and Moraga among them. The expressions on their faces said that they had seen or heard quite enough to understand what had just occurred.

Nagaro ignored them and flung himself after Taru. Pushing the door open, he emerged onto the porch and came to a halt. Taru was already in the street, his figure rapidly retreating, but it was the scene nearer at hand that brought Nagaro up short.

Timegar was there on the porch, remonstrating with half a dozen Hashtep men. Several Hashtep women stood a little farther away in a tight knot, wearing affronted expressions. Two of the men were holding Sindar.

They had the young Kelorin's arms pinned behind him and they were not being gentle. Sindar looked utterly terrified.

Timegar glanced in Nagaro's direction. "Ah! There ye are at last, Captain!" he cried, beckoning frantically. "Can ye have a word with this lot? They mean t' give poor Sindar a thrashing!"

Animara must have quietly followed Nagaro out the door, for now she spoke at his elbow. "Ye 'd best let Taru go," she said gently. "He'll be wantin' t' be alone, I expect."

Mutely Nagaro nodded. She was probably right, and he had to see what he could do for Sindar.

***

It took a little time to get the matter sorted out, and Nagaro learned several new Hashti words in the process. The Hashtep men spoke the Common Speech much better than Nagaro spoke Hashti, so much of the discourse had to pass through them. The men were not feeling kindly disposed towards Sindar, however, and getting the young man's side of the story indirectly through them wasn't easy.

As nearly as Nagaro could reconstruct what had happened, it appeared that Sindar had returned from the barracks just as the Hashtep girl he thought was the prettiest was leaving the inn with her family. Seeing that she was now accompanied by her family and no longer at the forbidden maiden table, and having seen how Lissel had addressed him under similar circumstances, Sindar had innocently stepped up and begun to talk to her. The men's attention must have been elsewhere, because Sindar had actually managed a brief exchange— including asking whether she wished to marry— before the men had become aware of him and had intervened.

The men, all male relatives of the girl, were firmly of the opinion that a good whipping was in order. It also became apparent to Nagaro that Timegar's lack of success in diffusing the situation stemmed largely from the former Fleet officer's belligerent attitude when initially approaching the matter.

By dint of very careful and exceedingly polite diplomacy, Nagaro was eventually able to make the men understand the full extent of Sindar's ignorance of Pakoan customs. After a little further discussion, he persuaded them to concede that the suggested punishment would be excessively harsh under the circumstances. Accordingly, Sindar was let off with a very stern warning, and the assurance that a second offense would indeed earn him the promised whipping.

Sindar had ceased to look frightened rather quickly when he understood that Nagaro had come to his rescue. However, his expression of terror had been quickly replaced by one of abject misery.

The Hashtep men had released their hold on his arms once they understood that Nagaro wouldn't let Sindar run away. Thereafter, the young man had been allowed to sit on the low wall that divided the inn's front porch from the street while the negotiations continued. There he sat, looking like a beaten dog, with sagging shoulders, downcast eyes, and an air of utter dejection— all of which were taken as signs of contrition that undoubtedly aided Nagaro in securing clemency for him.

When at last the Hashtep girl's relatives were finally satisfied and had departed, Nagaro turned to Sindar to offer him what sympathy he could with his limited command of Hashti.

"This is not so bad, Sindar, " he told the young man. "They now know that you did not understand. You have many thing to learn, but this you can do."

Sindar gave him a brief doleful glance before returning his gaze to the ground. "Do you know what she said?" he asked miserably in Hashti. "She asked why I do not talk to Kelorin woman instead. When I say that Kelorin woman are ugly, she say that is all right because I am ugly too."

Nagaro winced. He sat down on the wall beside Sindar. "You are not ugly, Sindar. You are Kelorin," he said carefully, hoping that he was using all the Hashti words correctly. "She sees you only with eye of Hashtep. That eye does not see what is beautiful for Kelorin, only what is beautiful for Hashtep. To Kelorin eye you are beautiful— in Droviri, for man, we say 'handsome'."

Sindar's head came up. "I am beautiful?" he asked uncertainly in Hashti, then added in the Common Speech, *"hand-some?"*

Nagaro considered the young Kelorin critically. "Yes," he said. "I think any Kelorin will say so."

Sindar's forehead furrowed in concentration. "And Kelorin woman who say *'good afternoon'* is beautiful to you, because you are Kelorin?"

Nagaro frowned. "Yes, I think she is beautiful. But my eye have also learned to see that different kind of woman are beautiful in different way," he said as he stood up.

"Oh." Sindar stood up as well, but his gaze had become abstracted. It appeared that the afternoon's events had given him rather a lot to think about.

Timegar had been standing near at hand throughout. The older man's Hashti was much more limited than Nagaro's. Still, he seemed to have gotten the gist of what had passed. "So, then, have ye explained it all to him, mate?" he inquired, grinning.

Nagaro shook his head. "I haven't the skill for that," he said, with a wan smile. "I wish I could really have explained everything to him earlier. Then you wouldn't have had this trouble."

He heaved a final sigh as Timegar took his departure with Sindar in tow. Then he went to find Animara.

***

The first few stars were just beginning to blossom in a blue velvet sky as Nagaro wended his way homeward through the streets of Pakoa Town. He had gone to have a little soup for his dinner with Animara and her family, and with little Narei, in the house where they dwelt on the other side of the headland southwest of the town.

It had been good soup, and he had forced himself to stay until night was coming on even though he'd been preoccupied with worrying about Taru. Even watching the antics of Tavo, Pilo, and Narei as they played with straw figures on the floor, and up and down the ladder leading to the sleeping loft, hadn't been enough to fully distract him.

He would, in fact, have left sooner if Animara hadn't counseled against it. "Ye should go about your affairs as if nought were amiss, and give Taru his time," she said. "It's best ye come home just when he'd normally expect ye to, and not before."

At least it didn't appear that Taru had gone to try and drown his sorrows in drink. Nagaro had insisted on looking in at the Red Cask Tavern when their little party had set out for Animara's house, to make sure that Taru wasn't there. He had checked again on his way back through the town. The tavern keeper had assured him that Taru hadn't been in all evening. Nagaro supposed he could believe the man, though he didn't entirely trust him. Past experience had shown that the tavern keeper was willing to keep selling to a man who was drinking for the wrong reason— and one who had drunk more than was good for him.

At the first turning of the Hill Road, just past the edge of town, Nagaro came to the new house that Pavo had built for his bride. There was a warm glow behind the curtains of the front window, and Nagaro smiled a little as he passed. He and Taru had presented the young couple with a bed as a wedding gift, and he supposed it would be put to good use that night— if it hadn't been already.

His smile faded quickly, however. It would be some time before he would trouble Pavo or Tenepti with any account of the other events that had marred this, their perfect day.

From the second turning of the road, he could make out, in the gathering twilight, the shape of the house that he and Taru shared, where it stood farther up on the hillside beside the dark grove of ironwood trees. He felt the knot of apprehension in his stomach tighten when he saw that the house was dark. Even as he looked, however, a light suddenly flickered into view. It danced and wavered for a moment before it steadied and came to rest.

Nagaro felt a flood of relief. Taru was at home and was looking out for his return. As long as he, Taru, and Pavo had lived there, it had always been the custom that any of them who were at home as evening fell would hang the lamp on the porch hook to guide the steps of the others who were still abroad.

Despite his relief, however, Nagaro's feet slowed involuntarily as he drew closer to the house. He could see now that Taru was sitting on the porch seat under the hanging lantern, and he was not at all sure in what frame of mind he would find his friend.

Taru had, of course, seen him coming. As Nagaro drew close, he could tell by the tilt of the man's head that his friend was watching him, though his expression was impossible to read in the dusk. As Nagaro stepped onto the porch, Taru gestured to the seat beside him, and then looked away. Nagaro sat down and waited for the other man to speak.

When the silence began to lengthen, however, he spoke first to diffuse the awkwardness.

"Did you have some dinner, Taru?"

Taru nodded. "At the Inn," he said in a low voice, his eyes fixed on the floorboards of the porch. "I ate in the kitchen. And I... talked t' Yuli... some. She said she didn't think ye were angry, but ye've every right t' be."

There was another little pause, and then suddenly the words began to pour out of Taru in a desperate stream.

"Nagaro, I'm *sorry*! Ye're the best friend a man ever had, and I don't know how I ever could ha' thought ye'd do anything to hurt me! I want ye t' know... those things that I said..." His voice trailed off into miserable silence.

Nagaro cleared his throat. "I knew you couldn't believe any of that for long," he said, "And I expect it must have hurt— what Tulara said, I mean."

Taru gave him a grateful glance, and looked down again. "Well, aye, I guess it did," he said in a low voice. "It didn't seem t' hit me at first, but after a bit... when it came home to me that she didn't want to have anything more t' do with me... it was... as if something just broke inside." He raised his eyes, then, but kept them carefully directed straight ahead.

Nagaro could tell that he was frowning, and he doubted very much that his friend was really seeing the sweeping panorama of the harbor, or the blossoming lights in the town, spread out below them under the perfect blue arch of the evening sky.

"I can't even say I was drunk," Taru went on bitterly, though I don't expect all that ale helped matters." Abruptly he raised his hands to his face. "Ai, Nagaro! When I think o' the things I said t' ye... those things I *called* ye... There's... there's just *no excuse*—"

Nagaro ran his fingers along the edge of the porch seat, feeling the grain of the weathered wood. "Do you remember when I shouted at you, after what happened with Jila?" he asked quietly. "When you were only trying to help? I was more angry with myself, then, than I ever was with you, but I shouted at you anyway. Have you forgiven me for that?"

Taru dropped his hands and turned to face Nagaro, and the young Turo's eyes blazed. "'*Course* I have!" he said indignantly. "What d' ye think? And *that* wasn't nearly as bad, either!"

"Well, if it wasn't, that's only because I wasn't hurting as much as you were this afternoon," Nagaro put in quickly. "But it doesn't matter, anyway, Taru. I've already forgiven you, and I hope that you'll try to forget about it. Just pretend it never happened. That's what I intend to do."

Taru looked quickly away. "I think ye *are* the best friend in the world, Nagaro," he said after a moment.

There was a rather lengthy silence then, while the evening deepened around them. In the pasture behind the house, one of the horses whinnied softly.

Finally Nagaro spoke, tentatively. "Do you think there's any chance Tulara might change her mind?"

Beside him Taru immediately shook his head. "*No*," he said flatly. "Ye didn't hear her, Nagaro. She was so calm about it— cold even. She wasn't angry or anything. She just didn't care anymore—" Taru's voice caught and he broke off. "I was trying to understand why the Spirits would send me something like this," he said after a moment. "I couldn't see what I'd done t' deserve it. But Yuli knew. I kept her waitin' too long, Nagaro. That's what it was." He emitted a long heavy sigh. After another moment, he went on.

"Tulara's changed a lot since I first met her. She used to be afraid t' say 'boo'— thought of herself as dirt, 'cause that's what other folk told her she was. I felt sorry for her then. I wanted to help her, 'cause she was such a sad little thing." Taru paused, caught in a web of bittersweet memory.

"You did help her, Taru," Nagaro put in earnestly. "You helped her to get away from being a tavern woman— helped her to get the job as kitchen maid at the Bay Tree Inn."

"Oh, aye," Taru observed darkly. "And when she was more 'n a little grateful, I backed away. She wanted too much, I thought— was in too much of a hurry. And I thought she'd always be there if I wanted her." He sighed again.

Talebra was rising now, round and full over the dark harbor, and the sky was brilliantly bejeweled with stars. Nagaro couldn't help thinking that it was a breathtaking spring evening— the perfect conclusion to glorious spring day. But Taru wouldn't remember it that way.

"She's so much stronger now, Nagaro," Taru was saying. "She knows her own mind— and speaks it too. And she doesn't let anyone get away with lookin' down at her 'cause her mother was a tavern woman that couldn't even say who her father was. Ye had a hand in helping her t' see that, Nagaro."

Nagaro shifted uneasily. "It was Yuli more than me."

Taru turned to look at him. "Yuli was part of it, too," he conceded. "But ye've always treated her like she's just as good as anybody else— and ye're such a hero, Nagaro. Everyone looks up t' ye. So if ye treated her that way, how could anyone else do different?"

Nagaro had no answer for that. It always embarrassed him to be called a "hero", but he knew what Taru meant by it, and he had to concede that there was probably some truth in his friend's words.

It was Taru who interrupted the awkward silence that followed. "I want ye t' know that I won't stand in your way, Nagaro, if ye want t' court her," the young Turo said quietly.

"*What?*" Nagaro's head jerked.

Taru was looking straight at him, his expression serious, his eyes bright in the lamplight. "Ye'd have a good chance o' winning her, Nagaro," he said almost eagerly. "I mean, she thinks the world o' ye, it's clear. And she knows ye don't care about how she was gotten. The Spirits know that *ye* don't know who ye're own father was, if it comes t' that— or your mother even. And ye know she'd be a good mother to Narei."

Nagaro was caught completely off guard. "But I..." he stammered, "I've never thought of her that way—"

"Well, perhaps ye should!" Taru sounded almost indignant.

Nagaro stared at his friend. He was completely taken aback by this sudden reversal of position. Just a few hours ago, Taru had been ready to punch him for being too friendly with Tulara. "She's just a *friend*," he said desperately. "I mean... I've always thought of her as being for *you*, Taru, if she was for anyone—" Nagaro winced and mentally kicked himself.

But Taru just stuck out his chin. "Don't ye worry about *me*," he said defiantly. "I'll find another woman. And the next time I won't be waiting for years t' tell her! I've decided I'd like to see ye with Tulara. Now will ye at least promise me ye'll think about it?"

Nagaro opened and closed his mouth. "Well... all right..." he said. "I'll think about it." He supposed there was no harm in saying that much, if Taru really wanted him to, though the idea made him really quite uncomfortable.

"Good!" Taru said with forced joviality. He stood up and reached for the lamp. "Let's go in and brew some sothiril and play a few rounds o' King's Men before bed."

"All right." Nagaro rose to follow his friend, then added, "Oh, and I've definitely decided that I'm going to let Kuran find me."

Taru stopped in the doorway with the lamp in his hand. For an instant he seemed to hesitate, but then he said, "In that case, I guess he'll be finding me too."

Chapter 6

The Lord Of The Fleet

T he waters of the Lapoa Channel sparkled in the morning sun. The narrow channel separated the two islands of Lapoa, on the north, and Oapa on the south. They were rocky islands, lesser isles at the northern end of the chain known as the Lomoas. Each supported a few dozen families of goat herders, and about an equal number of fishermen and their kin. The sun being up and the weather being fair, the fishermen were all out in their boats, plying their nets within the Lapoa channel or around the headland that thrust out from the southeastern corner of the island and separated the narrow Lapoa Channel from the much wider Great Channel that ran, north to south, between the Lomoas and the mainland coast.

On this particular morning, eight sleek war galleys flying the white hawk of Edrovir on a field of blue had just finished passing south along Lapoa's eastern shore. They were clearing the headland and coming abreast of the mouth of the Lapoa Channel. Their sails were spread to a brisk breeze, and the crewmen on their decks took little heed of the fishing boats in the Great Channel that made haste to get out of the way of the much larger craft

The crewmen would normally have paid no more attention to anything in the narrow Lapoa Channel as they sailed past its entrance, but on this occasion, the lookout of the lead ship, gazing westward, spotted something that caused him to raise a cry. Shouts then went back and forth across the ship's deck and from ship to ship, and presently the fleet began to execute a wide sweeping turn to starboard that brought them into the entrance of the Lapoa Channel.

Kuran Kel, the Lord of the Royal Fleet, stood on the high forecastle deck of the lead ship. The ship's captain, Ruald, stood beside him. Below the railing where the two men stood, bold letters on their vessel's prow spelled out the name, *Pride of Lankura*. This was the flagship of the Royal Fleet of Edrovir. Ruald commanded the *Pride*, and Lord Kuran commanded Ruald— as well as the captains of the other seven craft and of all the other ships of the Royal Fleet. Lord Kuran was leaning on the rail, his spyglass to his eye.

The objects of his interest were the same ones that had caught the lookout's attention. They were four ships, sheltering in a small bay on Lapoa's southern shore.

Lord Kuran Kell was the son of a Kelorin merchant captain and a diminutive Turowa from the Farano Isles, and his physical appearance betrayed his mixed blood. It might politely be said that he favored his mother, for although he was powerfully built, he stood just five and half feet tall with his boots on. Any man who underestimated Lord Kuran, however, tended to learn his mistake rather quickly, for Kuran Kel was a man to be reckoned with. He had joined the Fleet as a common recruit and quickly distinguished himself in action against the sea warriors of the Mahuk Baar. He had risen rapidly through the ranks, and when the previous Lord of the Fleet had been killed in battle, he had stepped up to take command, thus becoming at the age of thirty-two the obvious choice to succeed his slain commander as Lord of the Royal Fleet.

Since only the son of a noble house had ever previously filled that position, King Elgurn had taken the unusual step of elevating Kuran to the ranks of the nobility, granting him lordship over a tract of land. So had been born Kel Wared and the noble House of Kel. There were some who grumbled about the propriety of this maneuver, but there were none who dared to openly challenge the king on the matter.

Kuran was quick of wit and sure of judgement, and the king valued his council. It was also said that he was as quick with his sword as he was with his wit, and as sure of his own merit as he was in his judgement of others. Whether revered or reviled, there were few who lacked an opinion regarding Kuran Kel. Yet the man was a consistent survivor. He had apparently learned the art of treading carefully among the jockeying lords of Lankura.

Captain Ruald, who stood at Kuran's side, was as tall and spare as Kuran was short and stocky. And the contrast did not end there.

Kuran stood at ease in his shirt sleeves while Ruald proudly sported the dark blue tirka of the Royal Fleet with his captain's insignia emblazoned on it. The captain was Leithian— blond, blue-eyed, fair-skinned— while Lord Kuran's eyes were as black as those of any Turo and set in a face very nearly as brown as any pure-blooded member of that race. While Ruald was clean-shaven, Kuran sported a neatly-trimmed beard. Kuran was the elder of the two by nearly a decade, a few years short of fifty, his black hair and beard lightly peppered with gray. Only in the cut of their hair were the two men identical. Both wore it clipped short after the custom favored by sea warriors of the Royal Fleet.

Presently Kuran straightened. Lowering the glass, he offered it to Ruald. "Tell me what you see there, Captain," he said.

Captain Ruald took the glass and squinted through it for a long moment. "Four ships— galleys— all flying a flag with a white sword on black," he declared. "And they must have seen us. They've put out their oars and are beginning to shake out their canvas." Captain Ruald, lowered the glass and smiled exultantly as he turned to face his commander. "It must the pirate, My Lord. We've found him at last!"

"But we haven't caught him yet," Kuran observed, acerbically. "His ships may give us a good run before we do."

"But we're fully underway, My Lord, while they have just weighed anchor! We'll close most of the distance before they can get up their speed."

Kuran had not taken his eyes from the pirate ships while the other man was speaking, and by now he was frowning. "It doesn't appear that they mean to flee," he said. "They seem to be turning this way."

"*What?*" Startled, the captain started to raise the glass again, but stopped. Even without the spyglass, it was clear that Lord Kuran was right. "What's the man about?" Ruald wondered aloud. "He can't think that he'll slip past us in this channel. Does he mean to fight?"

"I shouldn't think so," Kuran observed calmly. "From what I've heard, this Captain Nagaro is not a fool." The Lord of the Fleet stroked his beard thoughtfully. "More likely he sees that he is caught and seeks to put the best face on it that he can. We shall see soon enough in any case. When they're close enough for the speaking trumpet, Captain, hail them and order them to heave-to in the King's name. Say also that the Lord of the Fleet wishes to speak to their leader, whatever he may call himself, and commands the man to present himself on the deck of the *Pride of Lankura* without delay."

"Aye, Zirda!" Ruald saluted crisply. Then he smiled with obvious satisfaction. "That will put the man in his place, My Lord."

Kuran gave Ruald an arch glance. "I don't like to give a man an exaggerated idea of his own importance," he observed dryly. "I have a few preparations to make, but I should be back on deck before the man comes aboard. You know what to do." He started to turn away, then turned back. "And tell him he may bring his sword provided that he surrenders it to me while he is aboard this ship."

***

Half an hour later, both fleets lay at anchor a little distance apart in the shallow waters on the Lapoa side of the channel. A longboat scraped against the hull of the *Pride of Lankura*, a little forward of the stern castle. A rope ladder had been lowered there, and two armed Fleet warriors flanked the top of it, awaiting the arrival of the pirate commander.

It was not one man that ascended the ladder, however, but two.

Lord Kuran frowned when he observed this from his vantage point at the foot of the main mast. He stood with Captain Ruald amid a group of crewmen. He was still in his shirt-sleeves, but this was by design. Kuran liked to put an unknown man a bit off his footing. He had not been surprised to learn that there were two men in the longboat, but had expected one of them to stay there since only one man had been summoned. He decided, however, to ignore the presumption.

The first man came over the rail with feline grace. A handsome brown-skinned young man, he had Kelorin features but wore a neatly trimmed beard and his black hair was tied in the Turowan fashion. He was of average height and slender build, but there was hard muscle in his arms and shoulders— which were bare, not being covered by the red-brown leather vest that he wore without a shirt. The second man, who came on the heels of the first, was less striking in both movement and appearance. He was of a similar age, but half a head shorter and clearly Turowan by the features of his face.

The taller man surrendered his sword without complaint, handing over belt and scabbard when an armed crew member demanded them. He turned, then, to survey the crewmen assembled around the mainmast. His eyes swept over them and quickly fastened upon Kuran Kel. His companion gave up his sword more grudgingly and looked ill at ease. The young Turo was apparently intimidated by finding himself on the deck of the flagship of the Royal Fleet. Just as clearly, the taller man was not, for he advanced with a sure step until he stood directly in front of Kuran.

Once there, he said in a clear, confident voice, "My Lord Kuran," and executed a bow that would have done him credit in the royal court of Lankura. The shorter man performed an awkward imitation about a second out of synchrony. Straightening, the first man added, "I am Captain Nagaro, and this is Taru, my first mate."

Kuran considered the man who had addressed him with narrowed eyes. He noted again the man's apparent youth, gray eyes, and distinctly Kelorin features. Kuran's eyes narrowed further. "Have you a family name?"

Nagaro shrugged slightly. "When I have need of one I use Taru's, with his permission. It is Nareyo."

Kuran stared hard at Nagaro. "So," he said, "a sea eagle—" Here he glanced briefly at Taru. "—and a man with no name." His eyes returned to

Nagaro, boring into him. "I prefer to know the *true* name of any man with whom I am going to treat, and this is surely not the name your mother gave you."

Nagaro did not flinch. "It isn't," he replied, levelly. "But it has been good enough for my friends, and good enough for those who sail with me."

Kuran arched an eyebrow. "Meaning that it should be good enough for the likes of Kuran Kel?" he inquired, and noted that the man named Taru drew in his breath and winced visibly.

Nagaro's glance still didn't waver. "Meaning," he said politely but firmly, "that Nagaro is my name, My Lord, and I am at your service." He executed another bow as impeccable as the first. There was another intake of breath from his companion.

A tense silence followed for several heartbeats, while Lord Kuran's eyes held the other man's and no one dared to breathe. During that time, Nagaro didn't drop his gaze, and in his gray eyes Kuran read steadiness, rather than defiance. The Lord of the Fleet's glance softened fractionally.

"Then let it be good enough," he said at last.

Ruald had stood silently beside his commander throughout this exchange, frowning. Now he spoke in a challenging tone. "So you would have us believe that you are the famous Captain Nagaro?"

Nagaro turned to face Ruald. "I'm not aware of any other by that name."

Kuran gave Nagaro an apologetic smile. "My good captain has not introduced himself," he said, giving Ruald a glance of mild reproof. "This is Captain Ruald Grinard, master of this vessel, the *Pride of Lankura*."

Nagaro bowed to the captain in acknowledgment.

Ruald made a rather perfunctory bow in return and went back to looking Nagaro up and down, measuring him with an expression that suggested he was not impressed. "We have all heard that Captain Nagaro is a great swordsman," he said, still in a tone of challenge. "They say that any Mahuk warrior who sees this pirate captain before him sees his death walking."

Nagaro frowned. "The description is inaccurate," he said flatly. "I have slain fewer than twenty men, though I have faced many times that number."

Ruald smiled as if he had just caught his adversary in a false step. "You would have us believe that Nagaro the Pirate has gained his fame by being beaten more often than not?"

Nagaro's frown deepened fractionally. "I didn't say I had been beaten," he said patiently. "That has yet to happen, though it surely may. I just don't like to kill a man if it can be avoided. I prefer to prevail by other means."

Ruald's mouth dropped open. There was some murmuring, a few choking sounds, and even a little laughter from the assembled crew. Kuran remained silent. His glance had been flicking sharply back and forth between the two conversants. His eyes were narrowed but his expression was otherwise unreadable.

Ruald recovered himself. "Now this is an extraordinary claim," he said with exaggerated courtesy. "To say you have never been beaten! I'm sure you won't mind fighting a bout with me so that we may all witness your skill."

"I didn't come here to give demonstrations of swordsmanship." Nagaro spoke with obvious annoyance.

Ruald's answer dripped insinuation. "I'm *sure* you didn't."

Nagaro's thin black brows knit together sharply. "I came here," he said carefully, "to talk to My Lord Kuran." A glance at the Lord of the Fleet, at this point, elicited only a fractionally raised eyebrow. Nagaro tried again. "I will leave it to him to decide. If My Lord wishes a demonstration, he shall have one." He glanced questioningly from one Fleet officer to the other.

Ruald looked slightly smug. Kuran cleared his throat. "I think... *yes,*" he said coolly. "I would like to see this... ah... *demonstration.* Your mate can stand second for you, Zirda, and I will stand second for Captain Ruald. Will someone fetch a pair of practice swords? We don't want any injuries."

The last was addressed to the general assemblage of crewmen. The weapons were produced so promptly as to suggest that someone had anticipated this turn of events.

The two intended combatants duly received their weapons and squared off on the deck, their seconds taking their places as well. The Fleet crewmen who were present moved hurriedly to find good vantage points that were well out of the way, exchanging whispered words and significant looks. This promised to be entertaining.

Taru stood tensely in his place behind and to one side of Nagaro. His general unease with the situation was compounded by finding himself expected to play opposite to the Lord of the Fleet. One of the tasks of the second was, after all, to call out and confirm the hits.

If there should be a difference of opinion between a pirate and the commander of the Royal Fleet...

Taru shuddered at the possible consequences. He licked dry lips and tried to steady his breathing.

Nagaro weighed the practice sword in his hand. It was comparatively heavy and not very well balanced, but that was of no great concern. Nagaro always adjusted rapidly to a new weapon, and experience had shown him that he could fight effectively with very nearly anything. He raised the sword in a formal salute to his opponent. As he lowered it, he came on his guard.

Ruald did the same. An instant later he attacked. The moves were rapid and well-executed but fairly conventional. Nagaro parried them with ease.

Ruald tried again— and then again. But he could not seem to break through his opponent's guard. The pirate's sword seemed to be everywhere it needed to be upon the instant. Ruald began to sweat. This Captain Nagaro— if that were indeed who he was— moved with fluid grace, and astonishing speed. Ruald fell back, frowning and breathing heavily.

There were awed murmurs from the onlookers. Lord Kuran's face was an unreadable mask.

Nagaro stood, still on guard. He'd been studying the way the other man moved and had learned much. He had not, however, so far found the fight very challenging. Still, he was careful never to become overconfident. The Leithian might have more skill than he had as yet displayed. The best way to find out, Nagaro knew, was to press an attack. So, like lightning he moved. He was in and out before Ruald had time to react. The Leithian's involuntary wince showed that he had felt the touch of Nagaro's blade. His face registered dismay. There was a collective gasp from the little crowd of sea warriors.

Taru flung up his hand. "I saw a hit on the left shoulder," he said. "One for Nagaro!"

Standing across from the young Turo, Kuran nodded. "One hit for Captain Nagaro," he said simply, his face and voice impassive.

Nagaro moved again. This time Ruald wasn't taken by surprise. Steel rang on steel several times before the Leithian's involuntary cry revealed that he had again been hit.

Kuran spoke first this time. "A second hit for Captain Nagaro."

Taru nodded. "Two for Nagaro!"

Ruald's face had become set in lines of grim desperation. This time the Leithian moved first, and Nagaro defended himself, matching stroke for stroke with an ease that was all too apparent, until he saw his third opportunity and took it.

Taru flung up both hands. "Three hits for Nagaro!" he cried, all his trepidation forgotten in the satisfaction of a victory.

Kuran confirmed the observation with a nod. "The match goes to Captain Nagaro." His voice was still flat, but there was a glint in his eye.

The onlookers had watched the final exchange in dumbstruck silence, but now a babble of voices broke out.

Nagaro raised his sword in a salute to his opponent, a salute that flowed into a gracious bow. As he straightened, he said, "Well fought,

Captain." Then his teeth flashed in a sudden, brief smile. "Thank you for providing me this opportunity to demonstrate my skill."

Ruald's expression was a commingling of chagrin and admiration. He spun about to face his commander. "Another bout, My Lord," he cried. "I can do better! The man surprised me."

Kuran arched an eyebrow. "Oh, yes," he observed coolly. "I think he surprised us all. But I have seen enough. I wish to speak to this man and I would prefer not to be all morning about it." Then he relented a little. "You acquitted yourself admirably, Captain Ruald, but you were outmatched. There is no shame in admitting it." He turned then to Nagaro. "Your reputation is well deserved, Zirda. Will you now accompany me to my cabin so that we may talk? I can offer you some refreshment after this exertion."

Nagaro smiled as he handed the practice sword back to a crewman who had stepped forward to take it. "That would be most welcome, My Lord."

As Kuran started across the deck in the direction of the stern castle and Nagaro fell in beside him, Taru came hurrying after. "Ye'll not leave me out here, will ye?" he pleaded. Lord Kuran might have proved to be a fair judge, after all, but Taru wasn't eager to be left alone on the deck under the eyes of all of these Fleet warriors.

Kuran halted and turned to look the young Turo up and down. "No," he said after a moment with the slightest hint of a smile. "I will not leave you out. And I will have my own second as well." He called back to Ruald, who was standing, chewing his lip and looking rather somber.

"Will you attend us, Captain, please?"

It had the tone of a mild request, but Ruald started. Hastily he saluted and said, "Aye Zirda!" He came after them, then, catching up in a few strides.

Before entering the stern castle, Lord Kuran paused to beckon to the sea warrior who had charge of his guests' surrendered weapons. "I wish to see the miraculous sword of Captain Nagaro," the Lord of the Fleet observed, taking the sleek black scabbard in his hands.

Nagaro shrugged diffidently. "It is a fine sword, My Lord, but not miraculous."

Lord Kuran examined the gold filigreed hilt and the green stone set in the pommel with interest. Then he drew the blade, hefted it, and swung it experimentally. "Oh *yes*," he said with evident enthusiasm. "A fine sword indeed!"

"It's very pretty, but it's a Mahuk blade." Ruald was disdainful. "You can see by the curve of it."

Kuran gave the Leithian a sidelong glance. "The best blades made in the Mahuk Baar are better than anything we make in Edrovir," he said flatly. "And this sword is one of those, I'll wager. You don't find the curve an inconvenience?" he added, speaking to Nagaro, as he slid the sword back into its sheath and handed the weapon back to his crewman.

"It has never troubled me, My Lord."

Kuran gave Nagaro a speculative glance. "No," he said. "I suppose it wouldn't. What's that they call it?" he added as he ushered his guests through the door of the stern castle and into the narrow corridor beyond.

"The Sword of Freedom," Taru promptly volunteered, then hastily shut his mouth in response to Nagaro's look.

"The Mautep call it the Sword of Shofeer," Nagaro explained. "Because it formerly belonged to a warrior of that house."

"And you won it from him?"

Nagaro frowned. "I took it from his dead hand, My Lord. Lokundas saw fit to let the man fall into the oar deck and break his neck."

"Ah. A gift of Lokundas then." The Lord of the Fleet paused, halfway along the corridor, to consider Nagaro keenly. "But you have defended your right to carry it?"

Nagaro's frown deepened. "It seems I'm forever defending it," he said wearily. "Twice a year, at least, some man comes who wishes to take it from me, and there's nothing for it but to fight him. The first man I fought for it, I've had to fight twice. The second time he used such dishonorable tricks that I was obliged to kill him. He claimed blood of the House of Shofeer, too, but still it isn't enough. They keep coming."

"Ah, yes. I see. Most... difficult," Kuran murmured dryly as he put his hand on the handle of the door of the ship's great cabin. "Such is the price of fame." With that, he opened the door and waved the other men through.

The great cabin was a little bigger than the one Nagaro had for his use on the *Sword of Freedom*. It boasted a respectable table, set with four chairs, two on each of the longer sides. Kuran motioned for his guests to take the two chairs on one side, then went and unhooked the front of a well-secured sideboard. From its recesses he removed four glass goblets, which he placed on the table.

Ruald sat down opposite Taru. The Leithian captain's manner was subdued. He sat assiduously studying his knuckles. Taru sat round-eyed, quite astonished to find himself being waited upon by the Lord of the Fleet in the great cabin of the flagship of the Royal Fleet of Edrovir.

Kuran next went to a pair of buckets standing on the floor near the aft windows. The neck of what looked like a wine bottle protruded from one, while the other contained a silver pitcher. Kuran reached into the first bucket. "I can offer you wine," he said, holding up the dripping bottle. The buckets apparently were filled with sea water, used to cool their contents.

Nagaro answered, "Thank you, My Lord, but no. I do not drink wine or ale or anything of that kind. But if that other is a pitcher of sothiril, I'd be very glad of some."

Kuran raised an eyebrow. "So," he said, as he returned the bottle to its bucket and took up the pitcher instead, "Do you keep the ban, then, even when at sea?"

Nagaro gave a little shrug. "I've learned the wisdom of keeping it at all times and in all places, My Lord."

Kuran returned to the table. "Well then, you're a better Vothrin than I," he said easily. "I confess I've found it expedient to follow the custom of whatever company I keep, or whatever man I sit down to treat with. Since today I treat with you, it shall be sothiril."

He proceeded to fill the four glasses with a liquid as red as blood before setting the pitcher down on the table and seating himself in the remaining chair, opposite Nagaro.

Taru stared at his glass. "What's this?" he asked curiously. "I've never seen sothiril this color in my life!" Kuran's casual courtesy was beginning to put him at his ease.

It was Nagaro who answered. "I believe it's called Erantil Crimson." He picked up his glass and drank from it. "Yes," he affirmed, for he recognized the fragrant drink. "Try it, Taru. It's very good."

Taru gingerly picked up his glass and took a sip. Immediately he gave Nagaro a startled and appreciative look. Then he took a larger gulp.

Nagaro took another swallow as well. The flavor brought back poignant boyhood memories. The Lady Maramine had been accustomed to serve Erantil Crimson sothiril only on special occasions. It had been one of her few extravagances, for Erantil did not come cheaply.

He remembered sitting with her at the long table in the dining room of the house at Averwin on the evening of the Festival of the Harvest Moon. *"Erantil Crimson,"* he murmured. *"It's been a long time..."* Then he caught himself. Shaking off the coils of memory, he focused a serious glance on Kuran and said, "I believe that you have questions for me, My Lord?"

Kuran had been studying him narrowly. Ruald was watching him as well, with an expression of puzzlement.

Kuran cleared his throat. "Yes, Captain Nagaro," he said sternly. "I'm sure you can appreciate that it is a matter of some concern, to both the king and myself, to have pirates operating in these waters."

Taru stiffened and set down his glass.

Nagaro continued to meet Kuran's eyes. "Yes, My Lord, I can. But I assure you that the ships of Edrovir have nothing to fear from me or my men."

Ruald immediately sat up straighter. "Do you deny being a pirate?" he demanded."

Nagaro transferred his gaze to the ship's captain. "No," he answered calmly. "I and my men do sustain ourselves by seizing goods from captured ships. But we prey only on war galleys of the Mahuk Baar. And piracy is not the real work that we do."

"What exactly is your 'real work,' then?" Kuran inquired mildly.

"Freeing slaves, My Lord."

"Ah, yes." The Lord of the Fleet inclined his head in acknowledgment. "I have heard that said of you. But tell me, Captain, what assurance do you offer that you speak the truth when you say that the ships of Edrovir do not need to fear you?"

Nagaro regarded him levelly. "You have my word of honor, My Lord," he said simply.

Ruald leaned forward. "The honor of an admitted *pirate?*" he inquired with a smirk.

Nagaro turned to the captain. "I assure you that piracy, as I practice it, is not inconsistent with honor," he informed the man coldly. Turning back to Kuran, he added, "I swear in Vothra's name that I have spoken the truth, My Lord. Beyond that, I can only say that my actions must speak for themselves."

"I see." Lord Kuran's fingers drummed lightly on the table top. He made a gesture that seemed to dismiss the matter. "Good enough. Let us turn to the subject of... *the tax.*" He dropped the two words like stones, and when Nagaro did not flinch, he added, "I presume that you pay your tax, Captain?"

"Of course, My Lord." Nagaro spoke earnestly. "I have paid the tax on behalf of myself and my men— in the amount of one tenth of the value of what we've acquired through our activities— every year except the year of our escape. That first year we had barely enough to see ourselves through the winter and to equip a single ship to sail in the spring. I confess, also, that I hadn't begun to think of it as being our means of livelihood at that time. We made up for that omission the following year however."

"We did more'n that," Taru put in. "Pakoa came up short on the tax that year, and Nagaro paid what was wanting!"

Ruald stared in undisguised astonishment at this, and even Kuran looked surprised.

The Lord of the Fleet addressed Nagaro. "Is this true, Zirda?"

Nagaro shifted a little uncomfortably. "Yes, My Lord," he said cautiously. "It was the year after the plague, and there was an extra tax placed on the islands that had escaped the disease, in the belief that they could pay, I suppose. Many of the folk of Pakoa would have been hard-pressed to pay that extra tax, however, and by good fortune we had more than enough."

"Hmm..." Kuran considered him with a speculative expression. "In what coin did you pay?" he inquired in a casual tone.

Nagaro hesitated fractionally. "I pay in whatever coin is convenient, My Lord," he said carefully. "On that occasion it was gold."

Kuran exchanged a significant glance with Captain Ruald. "Gold in the form of small bars bearing the stamp of the Hawk of Edrovir?"

Nagaro swallowed, but nodded. "Yes, My Lord." He felt Taru's boot connect eloquently with his ankle under the table.

"And how did you come by that gold?" Kuran's tone was carefully level.

Nagaro was determined to tell the truth, and so he answered just as levelly. "We took it from a Mautep warship in Mahuk waters, My Lord. I assume that the Mahuk craft had intercepted an Edroviran gold shipment on its way from the Faranos to Lankura."

"I see." Kuran's expression was still deadpan.

Ruald was making no such effort. "Have you captured *many* such ships?" he inquired suspiciously.

Nagaro gave the captain a chilly glance. "No," he said. "We sail to rescue men, not gold. We have taken several dozen Mahuk warships, but only two of them were carrying gold marked in that way."

"Ah. I see." Lord Kuran coughed. He paused as if considering his words carefully. "Have you considered, Zirda," he asked at length, "that the Crown might wish to have this gold *returned?*"

"*Nagaro...*" Taru muttered the name under his breath and between clenched teeth, and Nagaro felt another kick under the table.

Without looking at his friend, Nagaro reached out and put a reassuring hand on Taru's arm.

"My Lord," he said, calmly addressing Kuran. "I am sure that the Crown didn't wish to have the gold stolen in the first place. But seeing that it *was* stolen, there would ordinarily have been no expectation of ever seeing it again. In these two cases, against all expectation, some quantity of that gold has actually made its way back to Lankura— something that wouldn't have happened were it not for the actions of my men. Under the circumstances, I think the Crown might account itself fortunate."

Ruald's mouth dropped open. Taru emitted a low groan.

Kuran didn't even blink. "I can see, Captain," he said carefully, "how this might seem to be a reasonable position from your point of view. *However*, to avoid incurring the king's... ah... displeasure... would you consider delivering all such gold to me as an agent of the Crown in the future? And accepting one tenth part as a fee for the service rendered? That one-tenth part would be tax free, of course."

Ruald's face had been turning red as he listened to his commander's words, and his fist now banged the table so hard that the glasses jumped. "My Lord!" he exclaimed. "Do you bargain with this *thief?* He's very likely been raiding those gold shipments himself!"

Nagaro felt Taru's restraining hand on his arm this time as he turned a decidedly frosty glance upon the Leithian. "Assuming I were a man who would do such a thing, *Zirda*," he said, in a tone that was coldly polite. "I hardly think I would pay my tax in such coin— or any other, for that matter."

He turned back to Lord Kuran, while the captain sputtered. The Lord of the Fleet' sharp black eyes were regarding him intently from a face as expressionless as a mask.

"My Lord," Nagaro said earnestly, "I have never made any effort to conceal the source of any of the goods or moneys that we have taken in our work. Nor have I made any effort to return any of it to the original owner. It would be difficult in most cases— if not impossible— to discover who the owners were. Some of it clearly has come from Jinara. I have taken it all to be 'finder's gold' and used it accordingly. If you know what I mean by that term."

Kuran inclined his head ever so slightly. "I have heard of that custom," he said evenly. "The phrase is mentioned in the Writings."

"Well *I've* never heard of it!" Ruald growled darkly.

Kuran sighed. "It's an old Kelorin custom," he said, speaking mildly while keeping his eyes on Nagaro. "If a man finds gold or any other thing of value, he may use it as he will, to serve his need. *But* if there is more than he needs for that purpose, he is obliged to seek others in need and pass the rest along. Is that not so, Captain Nagaro?"

Nagaro didn't flinch. "Yes" he said. "Exactly."

Ruald goggled at him. "You mean us to believe that you've given gold *away?*"

Nagaro inclined his head. "Whenever we have had more than we needed, Captain," he said seriously, "we've found other needs to be met."

"What sort of needs?" Kuran asked pointedly.

Nagaro hesitated then. It embarrassed him to speak of the many projects he and his men had undertaken.

Taru suffered from no such compunction. "Oh, there's been *lots* o' things, Zirda, and not just on Pakoa either," he explained eagerly, and he began to tick things off on his fingers. "There's the new Council Hall we built, and the guard house, and the new wing for the Bay Tree Inn. Those were on Pakoa. And roads and channels and cisterns for water on several islands. And there's a school for the children—"

"That's quite enough, Taru." Nagaro put a hand on his friend's shoulder. "Lord Kuran doesn't need the entire catalogue."

Lord Kuran coughed into his fist. "I see. Well, if some of the gold of Edrovir has been used in this way, I suppose there's no harm in it. But surely you understand, Zirda, that finder's gold ceases to be finder's gold when the owner comes asking after it?"

Once more Nagaro inclined his head. "That is true, My Lord," he said calmly. "But who truly owns the gold from out of the earth? Is it the man who sweats and bends his back to dig it out of the ground? Is it the man who puts his mark upon it? To my mind, simple justice dictates that once the men who dug it have been fairly paid for their labor, the rest should be used to serve all the people of the land."

Kuran frowned. "I'm not sure I follow you..."

Nagaro leaned forward, ignoring the grip of Taru's fingers on his arm. "Consider this, My Lord," he said carefully. "Some of the wealth we have seized has been used to do good works on Pakoa and other Lomoan islands, as Taru has just told you. And some of that wealth has come from gold dug out of the Faranos— what you are pleased to call 'Edroviran gold.' Now, these Lomoan Isles are part of Edrovir, are they not?" Nagaro made a sweeping gesture, broad enough to include the entire island chain that now surrounded Lord Kuran's fleet. "But before we began to do our work, how much 'Edroviran gold' did the folk of the Lomoas ever see?"

Kuran's eyes had narrowed as he listened. "I think I understand your meaning, Zirda," he said quietly.

"I hope so, My Lord, but there is more," Nagaro continued, ignoring Taru's tightening grip, and another kick under the table. "Another part of what we have taken has been used to support our continued efforts. May I assume, My Lord, that the Crown does not object to the freeing of galley slaves?"

Lord Kuran frowned. "Certainly not. The freeing of Edroviran citizens captured and enslaved by the Mahuk is entirely commendable."

Nagaro nodded his acknowledgment and plunged on. "Then I should tell you that the remainder of what we take is used to help those we have freed to rebuild their lives. They come from all parts of the coast— from the Lomoas, the Faranos, the mainland. Most of them have lost everything and have nothing to go back to. Freedom alone isn't enough when a man has no money to buy a house or a fishing boat or a little land and a flock of goats. Does the Crown begrudge them these things? Especially when these men were taken from homes on Edroviran shores? Shores that are under *your* protection, My Lord, as commander of the Royal Fleet of Edrovir?"

One could have heard a feather drop in the silence that followed Nagaro's speech. For a long moment there was no sound but the creak of the ship's timbers. Kuran sat, frowning darkly, while Ruald face registered outrage. Taru's fingers dug painfully into Nagaro's arm.

At length Kuran reached for his glass. Raising it, he took a swallow without taking his eyes from Nagaro's face.

"You're a bold man, Captain Nagaro," he said evenly as he set the glass down. "You argue your points well, and they are well taken. If, in the future, you take more gold bearing the stamp of Edrovir, I will expect you to deliver *half* of it to me. The other half is to be used to the benefit of freed slaves and of the folk of the Lomoas— free of the tax— and with one tenth part for your own activities, as I said before. Failure to comply with this to the best of your ability will certainly earn you the king's displeasure, and I assure you that there *will* be consequences. Have I made myself clear, Zirda?"

Taru's fingers relaxed their grip even as a little gasp escaped him. Ruald looked positively stunned.

Nagaro bowed from the waist where he sat. "Yes, My Lord," he said earnestly. "Perfectly clear. And thank you."

Kuran took a long, leisurely drink of his Erantil Crimson. "Good," he said as he set his glass down with a satisfied clink. "That settles the king's business. Now to the other matter."

Chapter 7

Other Matters

Nagaro felt a touch of unease. "What other matter, My Lord?"

When Kuran answered, his tone was stern, though the glance of his bright black eyes was perceptibly less so. "I am worried about the safety of the island of Pakoa, where you've chosen to winter. Eventually the Mahuk must learn the location of your headquarters. If they attack while you are in port, your men would, I assume, come to the defense of the island. But, if you are absent when the attack comes, innocent folk may come to harm. If any ships of the Fleet were near at hand, we would render assistance, but the Fleet has many charges and a whole coast to defend."

Nagaro had listened with a gathering frown, and he spoke as soon as Kuran paused. "The safety of Pakoa has concerned me ever since we began our work," he said seriously. "And my concern has increased since Emperor Baalkir set a price upon my head a year ago. With that incentive, Mautep captains may come specifically seeking me. While I have expected— even hoped— that the Mautep would become aware of our activities, there is this undesirable consequence. Already there has been one attack on Pakoa Town—"

"An attack?" Kuran spoke with alarm. "When was this?"

"Last summer—" Nagaro began.

Taru interrupted. "Ye've not heard o' the Battle of Pakoa Harbor?"

"No," was Kuran's acerbic response. "I've heard nothing of this."

"There's no reason that you should have, My Lord," Nagaro put in quickly, giving Taru a reproachful glance. "It was a very limited exchange, although the men of Pakoa who successfully defended their town are justly proud of it."

Kuran's eyes narrowed. "Describe this *limited exchange*."

Nagaro cleared his throat. "Two Mautep warships entered Pakoa Harbor on the third of last Oteyin, My Lord," he said. "One of them sailed up to the dock and about two dozen sea warriors came over the side onto the wharf. Our archers met them with several flights of arrows, killing one and wounding several. There followed an assault by our spearmen, who killed another man and did enough harm to convince the rest to return to their ship. At that point, my ships sailed into the harbor, my men joined the fray and—"

Kuran raised his hand. "Hold a moment, Zirda," he said. "If you and your men arrived so belatedly, who were the archers and spearmen that you spoke of?"

"The men of the Pakoan Guard, o' course!" Taru interjected before Nagaro could say anything.

Kuran's glance flicked to Taru and back to Nagaro again. "But you called them *'your'* archers—"

"Well, yes..." Nagaro was uncomfortable. "We trained them, you see—"

"*Nagaro* trained them. And the spearmen, as well!" Taru wasn't about to let his friend escape with less than full credit. "It was his idea t' have a Pakoan Guard in the first place too. And it's a lucky thing the Town Council saw the wisdom of it!"

"Taru!" Nagaro exclaimed in exasperation. He turned back to Kuran. "It doesn't matter, My Lord, who did the training or whose idea it was. What matters is that they did their work well that day."

Kuran inclined his head. "Yes. Quite so," he observed blandly. "And your ships arrived when they did, perhaps, because you heard one of the horns?"

Nagaro nodded. "Yes, My Lord. We were fortunately just off the northern tip of the island when we heard the south horn signaling the sighting of a Mautep war galley. We headed south, at once, but we heard the horn signal an approach, and then an attack just as we came abreast of Fishhead Point."

Kuran raised his hand again. "How can you learn so much from the sounding of a horn?" he inquired keenly. "How did you know it was the south horn? There seem to be four of them."

Nagaro looked startled. "I thought you would have taken note of these things," he said, frowning. "The watch towers and the horns have been there for three years now."

Kuran smiled tightly. "Let us say that I've had other things requiring my attention. Please enlighten me."

Nagaro bowed his head briefly. "Your pardon, My Lord. We knew it was the south horn by the tone. Each horn sounds a different note, with the north horn the highest in pitch and the south the lowest. The rest is only a matter of knowing the code of the horn blasts."

Kuran had leaned forward in his chair, comprehension dawning in his dark eyes. "*Different notes!*" he murmured. "*Clever.* We have signal towers with flags running all along Big Farano Island, but they only serve when the weather is fair. Who would have thought of using horns with different notes?"

"That'd be Nagaro, again," Taru informed him smugly.

"What?" Kuran's eyebrows shot up as he addressed Nagaro. "The folk of Pakoa have you to thank, Captain, for the horns and watch towers as well?"

"Ah, yes, My Lord," Nagaro answered quickly, and this time it was he who kicked Taru under the table. "But I should explain the code. It could aid the Fleet ships when they're in Pakoan waters."

Kuran's eyebrows descended again. "Proceed."

Nagaro took a swallow of sothiril and cleared his throat. "It's fairly simple," he said. "Sighting of a merchant ship is signaled by a single long blast, two long blasts means a Mahuk galley, and three long blasts a Fleet warship. A ship flying my banner is welcomed by two short blasts. The signal is repeated at intervals if need be, and with increasing frequency to warn of a dangerous ship approaching the island rather than passing by. An attack is signaled by a continuous series of short blasts. That signal would be sounded if any Mautep tried to land anywhere on the island. So you see, My Lord, that we had a fair idea of what we would find when we entered the harbor that day."

"Ah. Yes." Lord Kuran was regarding him speculatively. "It seems a good system. I wonder, though, why you felt the need to have a different signal for vessels of the Fleet than for your own ships. Wouldn't a single signal for all friendly craft be sufficient?"

Nagaro's teeth flashed in a brief smile. "We've found it useful to know when your ships were about, My Lord, not being sure how our activities might be viewed."

Kuran looked thoughtful. "A fair answer," he conceded.

Ruald had been listening for some time with an expression of mingled curiosity and distrust. Now he spoke up. "You haven't told us the end of your great 'Battle of Pakoa.' If the island men had already routed the sea warriors, it seems there wasn't much left for you to do," he said ungraciously.

Nagaro frowned without malice. "I suppose that the Mautep on the first ship might have had enough," he replied. "But they had left two of their men dead on the wharf— struck down by arrows and spear. We may think that those are fair weapons for defense against a pack of sea raiders, but the Mautep consider them dishonorable weapons. So they were angry and looking for blood. *And* there was a second ship, besides. If both crews had decided to go ashore in force it would have gone hard with our defenders. There were just twenty spearmen and six archers at the time, though I have recently persuaded the Town Council to double those numbers."

Kuran nodded understanding. "I see, Captain. Is there any more to your tale?"

Nagaro took a quick swallow of sothiril. "Not much," he said. "We had four ships, so we had them outnumbered— and trapped like flies in a bottle because the harbor entrance is so narrow. It wasn't hard to talk them into surrendering without further bloodshed."

Ruald looked shocked.

Kuran was clearly surprised as well. "You persuaded Mahuk sea warriors to surrender?"

"I know it sounds daft," Taru put in quickly. "But that's what Nagaro does."

"But they were *Mahuk raiders!*" Ruald protested. "Making an attack on Edroviran soil. You should have slain them all!"

Nagaro sighed. "It wasn't necessary."

Ruald gaped. "I don't believe this!" Scowling, he turned to Lord Kuran. "I've never known Mahuk to surrender, My Lord. This man is telling us a crooked tale!"

Kuran pointedly ignored his captain. He was studying Nagaro with an expression that was impossible to read. "Tell me, Captain," he said almost casually. "What were your terms?"

"That they surrender their slaves to us as well as anything of value they had on board. In return they were allowed to keep their lives and to claim their dead. We then escorted the two ships out of Edroviran waters."

"*And* they had t' promise never to land on Edroviran shores again," Taru put in. "Or they'd face Nagaro's sword!"

Kuran crooked an eyebrow. "They accepted these terms?"

Nagaro nodded. "They did, My Lord."

"Yet that promise may mean little," Kuran observed dryly. "Made under threat of violence."

Nagaro shook his head. "There was no threat, My Lord," he said earnestly. "They swore on their honor that they would not return. It was only *after* they had sworn that I mentioned what the consequence would be if they ever were foresworn."

The Lord of the Fleet stared a Nagaro for several seconds and then threw back his head and laughed.

Ruald threw up his hands. "This is absurd!" he cried. "*If* it ever happened. Such an oath from a Mahuk is worthless! They have no honor!"

Nagaro turned his earnest gaze upon the captain of the *Pride of Lankura*. "On the contrary, Captain. The *Mautep*— that is to say, the warrior class of the Mahuk Baar— have a very well-developed sense of honor that they practice among themselves. What they *don't* have is an appreciation that there could be honor among folk of any other kind. These past four years, I have tried to teach them by my example that such a thing is possible. I think I'm beginning to have some success. Whether those two captains keep their oaths will depend partly on whether they believe their oaths were sworn to a man of honor, but it will also depend on how much honor each of them personally has. Men of any kind are not all equally to be trusted, as I'm sure you are aware. I am therefore waiting to see what the outcome will be. And if either of those captains breaks his oath, I'll have to see what lesson can be taught with a sword."

Captain Ruald sat dumbstruck at the end of this speech.

Lord Kuran had contained his earlier laughter, and all mirth died in his eyes as he drained his glass. Picking up the pitcher, he refilled it and reached across to Nagaro's, which was nearly empty as well.

"By the Eyes, Captain," he said, after setting the pitcher down and taking a sip from his own glass, "You are a very strange pirate. First you tell us that you give gold away, and now it seems that you're in the habit of letting your enemies keep their lives and making them swear oaths of honor."

Nagaro did not drop his eyes, but they clouded. " The word 'pirate' may be an apt description of what we do, but it's not a title that pleases me, My Lord," he said.

Kuran considered him. "Do you swear that everything you have told me here today is the truth?"

Nagaro sat up straight. "On my honor and in Vothra's name, I swear it."

"It will go hard with you if I should ever discover otherwise."

"Of course. I understand."

Kuran sighed. "In that case, I find my questions well answered," he said. "And I am content to let you continue as you have, at least for the present."

"Thank you, My Lord." Nagaro made a little bow of acknowledgment where he sat. Then he said, "If you have no more questions for me, My Lord, perhaps we might turn to *my* reason for seeking this meeting."

Kuran raised an eyebrow. "*Your* reason? I was under the impression that it was I who sought to find *you*."

"I know that, My Lord," Nagaro responded earnestly. "I had heard that you were looking for me, and that *is* one reason why I sought you out, but—"

"What fantasy is this?" demanded Ruald. "Pretending that you chose to be here, when we caught you with your oars shipped and your sails furled!"

Nagaro turned to face him. "You may be forgiven the error, Captain," he said almost gently, "since that was all you saw. We had been watching you since daybreak from the crest of the headland, which provides a view of Lapoa's eastern shore from one end to the other. We were waiting for you. But if we hadn't been, you wouldn't have caught us if we had chosen to flee."

Taru had been rather inadequately suppressing his mirth for some time, and there had been the hint of a twinkle in Kuran's eyes when Nagaro had started speaking. At the last words, however, the twinkle died, and the Fleet Lord frowned. "That seems an ill-considered boast, Captain," he said. "What makes you think you could outrun my ships?"

Nagaro answered without hesitation. "Our ships are of Mautep construction and they are faster by virtue of their design. We also know how to get the best speed from them, since speed is necessary for the work we do."

Kuran's face darkened. "Faster by virtue of their design? How so? It seems to me we're able to overtake Mahuk warships as often as not."

Nagaro shrugged. "You fare as well as you do, My Lord, because you can carry fewer men, which means less weight. The Mautep must carry two full crews, one to row and one to fight. But the superiority of construction of the Mautep ships is in the shape of the hull. The Mautep galleys, at bow and stern, are shaped like *this*." He held up his hands to illustrate his words, making a V with them. "Edroviran ships are shaped more like *this*." He cupped his hands a little to make a narrow U. "Some ships of either manufacture are faster than others, but the best ships built on the Mahuk Baar are faster than anything out of the shipyards of Lankura, and the four ships we have are among the best."

Kuran was studying Nagaro intently. "You seem to have made a study of this," he observed.

Nagaro shrugged. "I've taken some interest in the matter, and have made some observations," he replied diffidently. "And I have information from reliable sources. There are men sailing with me who have seen the shipyards in Lankura, and the Mautep set their slaves to work in their shipyards during the winter. But this isn't what I wished to talk about—"

"Now, see here!" Ruald interrupted. "You claim you were watching from that headland, but how could you have known that we were coming this way in the first place?"

Nagaro turned his gray eyes upon the Leithian. "I had word that Lord Kuran was on his way south from Lankura with eight ships, sailing in the Great Channel, skirting the islands."

"*Word from whom?*" This time it was Kuran who spoke, and there was a distinct edge to his voice.

Nagaro didn't flinch as he turned back to the Lord of the Fleet. "From the fishermen, My Lord," he answered calmly. "They see things and they hear things. And they're good at passing news from one to another. They also count me as a friend, so I have only to put out the word when there's something I wish to know."

Kuran's brow darkened. "Fishermen sail only short distances, out into the channel and back to shore, while we sail the entire length of the channel— and more swiftly. How can the news reach you ahead of our ships?"

Nagaro shrugged. "It doesn't always," he said mildly. "But in this case, it did. The fishermen trade news at sea by day and on shore by night. Men can cross from one side of an island to the other while ships must go around. And in this case, you anchored at Tirobo in the southern Faranos for most of a day, and the word got quite some distance ahead of you during that time."

"*Hah!*" Kuran barked a mirthless laugh. "We did, in fact. Did your fishermen friends tell you anything *else?*"

"Just that you have been traveling only under sail, because two of your ships aren't carrying crews of oarsmen," Nagaro responded matter-of-factly. "They say that you're escorting them to Harmoth— possibly to base them there where they can help defend the southern coast. If that is true, it would be most welcome."

Now Ruald's mouth opened and closed wordlessly as he began to rise from his seat. "*What treachery is this?*" he sputtered. "*What treason—*"

Lord Kuran put out a hand to grasp the Leithian's arm and pulled him back down onto his chair. "There's no need to speak of treason," he said coolly, though his black eyes glittered. "It is only the wagging of our crewmen's tongues in some place where fishermen could overhear. And Captain Nagaro is not an enemy of Edrovir." He sighed.

"I have sometimes sought information from merchant captains," he went on, addressing Nagaro. "Some of their families have been friends of my father's family for generations. But the fishermen are not known to me. And as I said, they sail only short distances. Of course there are so many *more* of them, aren't there?"

Nagaro inclined his head. "Yes, My Lord. They could tell you a great deal about the movements of Mahuk warships."

"Or about the whereabouts of *your* ships, Captain," Kuran pointed out.

Nagaro's teeth flashed. "Yes, My Lord. But first you must convince them that you mean me no harm."

"Ah. Yes. Quite so." Kuran smiled tightly. He took a sip from his glass, looking thoughtful. When he set the glass down, he asked, "What was the matter you wished to discuss with me, Captain?"

Nagaro instantly turned serious. "The fact that you sink ships, My Lord."

Kuran frowned. "Yes... *Mahuk warships—*"

"With oar decks full of slaves." Nagaro's gray eyes were locked onto Kuran's, and the emotional edge to his voice was unmistakable. "Every time one of those ships goes down, between thirty and forty men die... helplessly... chained to their benches."

Kuran did not immediately answer, but a shadow crossed his face as he toyed with the stem of his goblet. "This is a thing that has troubled me for some time," he said quietly. "It didn't concern me greatly in the beginning. They were only Mahuk, after all. Enemies, I thought. But as time has gone by, I have heard more and more tales of Edroviran men— merchant seamen and fishermen— being taken captive. I can no longer pretend that only Mahuk die when one of their galleys goes down. I know that some portion of the oar deck slaves are citizens of Edrovir, and their loss grieves me greatly."

Nagaro spoke earnestly. "That portion, My Lord, is somewhat more than half—"

"*What?*" Kuran recoiled as if struck. "Can there be so many?"

Grimly Nagaro nodded. "The proportion varies from warlord to warlord, and from ship to ship. The captains don't all have the same enthusiasm for taking slaves in this way. But those who come most often into these waters are likely to have taken the most captive oarsmen— and their ships are also the most likely to be sunk by ships of the Fleet."

Kuran sat mute, clearly stricken by these words.

Even the skeptical Ruald looked uncomfortable. "But how can you know this for a certainty—" the Leithian began.

Nagaro turned to him. "The Mautep call me 'Kiraam Shaku-Tal,'" Captain," he replied. "It means 'Thief of Slaves'. Together with my men, we have subdued dozens of Mahuk ships, and freed hundreds of slaves from their oar decks, so I have only to count. I can tell you that the ship on which Taru and I were forced to serve was quite typical. Only a little more than a third of the men chained on the oar deck of that ship were common folk of the Mahuk Baar— Hastep is what they call themselves, not Mautep. Of the remaining two thirds, the greater number were Turowan."

"*Vothra, Lord of my choosing!*" Kuran bowed his head and put a hand to his brow, covering his eyes as the agonized words broke from his lips. When he looked up, his dark eyes were clouded with pain. "I wish you hadn't told me this, Captain Nagaro," he said in a voice that shook. "This is a heavy burden to bear, though bear it I must, since I am charged with the defense of Edrovir. The Mahuk will go on sinking our ships, and I must go on sinking theirs—"

"But *why*, My Lord?" Nagaro cut across Lord Kuran's words, equally impassioned. "Where is it written that if a man strike you in the face, you must strike him back in the same way?"

"Nagaro!" Taru cried in dismay. "*He's the Lord of the Fleet!*"

Nagaro turned a startled glance upon his friend. "Yes, Taru," he answered patiently. "*That's* why I'm telling him this. He's the only one who can do anything about it!"

"Yes, but what exactly would you have me *do*, Captain?" Kuran demanded. "Ask them to surrender as you do? And what would you have me do if they *refuse?*"

Nagaro turned back to face Lord Kuran's burning gaze. His sighed. "I am sorry, My Lord," he said with genuine contrition. "I'm sorry that I seem to take you to task, and sorry also to have brought you such painful knowledge— though I think it is better to know the truth. I don't know whether the way I have found would work for you. For one thing, it requires some knowledge of Hashti. I thought perhaps you could capture ships instead of sinking them— or overwhelm the crews long enough to get the slaves safely off. After that, you could take the ships if you like, or sink them, or let them go as we do. They're crippled without any men to row them."

"Surely the warriors can row!" Ruald objected.

Nagaro shook his head. "They have no experience, Captain. And they believe the work of slaves is beneath them besides."

Kuran had recovered some of his composure. "*Keep the ships...*" he murmured. "These ships that you say are faster because their hulls have a different shape? If we could take one or two back to Lankura to study how they are made..."

Nagaro was momentarily startled, but then he nodded. "Yes, My Lord. You certainly could do that," he said. "But you would want the very best examples— ships designed by Baalkir's master shipbuilder at Sar Tipaal, or else ships from Lord Angkat's shipyards. You would know them by the shipbuilder's marks on their keels. If you have paper and pen, I can draw the marks for you."

Kuran was studying him narrowly now. "Of course," he said carefully. "I would appreciate that. And please write labels to tell me which is which." He rose and went again to unhook the sideboard. This time he brought back paper, pen, and ink to the table and pushed them across to Nagaro.

Nagaro reached for the writing materials. He unstopped the ink bottle, dipped the pen, and carefully sketched two strange marks on the paper. Then he quickly wrote out the explanations of what each one represented in his fine, bold hand and passed the paper to Lord Kuran. "You'll find the marks on the keel," he said, "as I've written. Generally in three places— fore, aft, and amidships."

Kuran took the paper and inspected it with keen interest before folding it and slipping it inside his shirt. "Thank you," he said. "That may be of some use." He sat for a moment, apparently lost in somber introspection. Presently, however, he shook himself and returned his attention to Nagaro. "I will give thought to what you have told me," he said gravely. "I'll consider whether it is possible to do something that won't result in there being more lives lost among my sea warriors than would be saved among the slaves."

Nagaro bowed his head. "I can ask no more than that."

Kuran rose, and gestured for his guests to do likewise. "Since we are finished, you may return to your vessel and go your way," he said. "Your swords will, of course, be returned to you."

Nagaro stood up. Moving away from his chair, he performed another of his elegant bows. "Thank you, My Lord."

Kuran ushered them from the cabin. As they passed along the corridor, he spoke to Nagaro again. "How long were you held a slave, Captain?"

"A year and a half, My Lord."

"So long? It must have been a terrible ordeal."

Nagaro sighed. "There are many who have endured longer, My Lord. It was made easier by friendships both old and new. The worst was when we rammed another ship. Ours was never struck, but its ram sank several, and I'll never forget the screams of those other men. I have to live with the knowledge that my hands were on one of the oars that drove the ram home."

Kuran gave Nagaro a sympathetic glance. "I begin to understand why you take such an interest in the plight of these poor wretches," he said seriously.

They had reached the end of the corridor. Lord Kuran opened the outer door and they all stepped blinking into the sunlight. More than a dozen sea warriors were there, trying to appear busy or simply lounging about the main deck. Most of them looked up and many exchanged glances when the Lord of the Fleet emerged with Captain Ruald and the two guests.

Kuran paused outside the door of the stern castle. "I confess I am curious to know how you deal with the slaves that are... *Hashep*, did you call them?" he continued. "Don't they take the part of their fellows, the sea warriors, and fight against you?"

Nagaro shook his head. "They're every bit as much victims as the Edrovirans," he replied. "They are men sentenced to life in the galleys for minor crimes that would earn them no more than six months labor in Edrovir. Most of them we put ashore wherever they wish on the coast of the Baar. Some have chosen to dwell on Pakoa. A few sail with us."

Kuran raised an eyebrow at this, yet he nodded. Turning, then, he led the way to the place by the rail where Nagaro and Taru had come aboard.

The sea warrior who held the two swords was there, and Kuran directed the man to return the blades to their owners. The seaman handed Nagaro his weapon with a show of deference. Taru's was returned to him almost as an afterthought.

Kuran dismissed his crewman. "Do, you consider yourself an honest man, Captain?" he inquired as Nagaro was buckling the sword belt about his waist.

Nagaro's black brows came together. "I try to be," he replied. "But there are times when it's ill-advised to tell the entire truth."

Lord Kuran's teeth flashed. "I grant you that," he said. "But still it pleases me to put your honesty to a test. Tell me how you picked me out so easily when first you came aboard. I am wearing no badge or sign to indicate my rank."

Nagaro wished that Kuran had chosen a different question. Still he had given some thought to how he would answer such a query. "I've heard descriptions of your appearance, My Lord," he said.

It was a true statement, if not the true answer to the question. The truth was that Nagaro had seen the Lord of the Fleet on several occasions, years before, during that terrible time he had spent in Lankura. He had even been introduced to the man as 'Prince Leyel,' very briefly. The prospect of meeting Lord Kuran now, seven years later, had given him only the very slightest concern, however, since it was unlikely that Kuran would recognize him. Not only was his appearance greatly altered, but his manner was entirely different than it had been under the influence of the drug, heskial. He knew he must seem an entirely different person.

Kuran gave a brisk nod in response to Nagaro's words, suggesting that the answer was what he had expected, but he evidently wasn't finished, for he thrust out his chin and fixed Nagaro with a penetrating gaze. "Then tell me, Captain," he said smoothly, "what the words were that so well described me." ·

Nagaro swallowed. This was, of course, the real test, and it was much more difficult. The physical descriptions Nagaro had heard of Kuran Kel had often not been very complimentary.

He hesitated a fraction of a second before replying. "A man of mixed Kelorin and Turowan blood, small in stature, but not in any other respect," he said. "There were also some details of hair and beard that were accurate, My Lord."

Lord Kuran gave a short, satisfied laugh. "'Small in stature, but not in any other respect!' I like that! Who was it that gave this description, I'm wondering?"

Nagaro held the older man's gaze. "A perceptive man, I think," he answered. The words had, in fact, been his own, spoken to Taru that very morning.

"A clever man, as well, I would say," Kuran observed archly. "And now tell me, Captain, *on your honor—* is what you have just told me the entire truth?"

"No, My Lord," Nagaro answered with perfect candor and without the slightest hesitation.

This time Kuran threw back his head and laughed long and loud. Abruptly, then, he turned around and spoke a few words in a low voice to Captain Ruald, who had been standing, a bit warily, behind him the whole while and frowning as usual.

The tall Leithian looked surprised at whatever his commander had said, but he saluted. "As you wish, My Lord," he said, with a hint of resignation, and turned to retrace his steps in the direction of the stern castle.

Turning back, Kuran addressed himself to Nagaro. "I have in mind a little gift for you, Captain— nothing of any consequence— but I've sent Ruald to fetch it, and it will take him a few minutes." He turned to Taru, who had been standing tensely in the background throughout the entire exchange. "Taru Nareyo," he said in a tone that was at once polite and quite firm, "I would ask you now to go down to your boat and wait there. And I assure you there is no need for that look, Zirda. I truly mean no harm to your captain."

The look in question vanished instantly from Taru's face, to be replaced by one of shock at being so addressed by the Lord of the Fleet. "Ah... ah... yes, My Lord," he managed. Then he gave Nagaro one final glance, like a plea for forgiveness, and made for the rope ladder, leaving Nagaro and Kuran alone together, standing side by side at the ship's rail.

Kuran waited until Taru had reached the boat below before saying in a conversational tone: "Is he a good first mate?"

Nagaro was startled, but nodded. "Yes, My Lord. When he commands the oar deck, the oarsmen respond to my every word upon the instant. He could be a captain, so far as his ability is concerned, but he has so far shown no such ambition."

"Ah. I see. He seemed a little... out of his depth... at this meeting. I wondered why you brought him."

Nagaro sighed. "He insisted on coming. The truth is, My Lord, that Taru more than half expected that I would end the day in irons. And if such was to be my fate, he was determined to share it rather than leave me to face it alone."

The intensity of Lord Kuran's gaze softened a little. "A good friend then?"

"More like a brother."

"Tries to keep you out of trouble, does he?" There was a hint of a twinkle.

Nagaro smiled faintly. "Always, My Lord. Occasionally he succeeds. And what of Ruald? Is he a good captain?"

Kuran crooked an eyebrow. "You are thinking perhaps that he hasn't the sharpest wit and is not very diplomatic?"

Nagaro frowned slightly. "I wouldn't have put it quite so bluntly, but yes."

Kuran sighed. "Ruald is a fine captain— courageous and steady in battle, efficient, and devoted to duty. He does very well as captain of my flagship, where he is under my direct command, but he lacks... shall we say... *imagination?*" Here Kuran gave Nagaro a sly glance. "Nevertheless, he has his uses in a meeting such as this one."

Nagaro paused fractionally, trying to digest the implications of the last remark, and uncertain whether he ought to be worried or flattered by the apparent confidence. At length he gave it up and said: "He is not, then, your second in command?"

"No, that would be Commander Geldoran, who is in the Faranos at present. Which brings me to the reason why I sent our two friends away."

Nagaro was startled. "My Lord?"

Lord Kuran bent close. "There are many miles of sea and shore between Harmoth and the Faranos," he said in a low voice. "I'd be obliged, Captain, if you would keep an eye on my back garden while I make the delivery of those two ships."

Nagaro attempted to cover his astonishment at this unexpected request. He hardly knew what to think of it, except that it seemed he could not very well refuse. "We have our own work to do, My Lord," he said cautiously. "But we certainly can search for Mautep raiders in the northern Lomoas for a week or so. And if we see anything that is more than we can deal with, we will alert the fishermen. So... if one of them attempts to hail you—"

"—we should stop long enough to hear what he has to say." Kuran finished the sentence with a smile of obvious satisfaction.

"That would be wise, My Lord." Abruptly Nagaro stiffened. "But here comes Captain Ruald—"

The Leithian had emerged from the stern castle and was fast approaching. He had a small packet in his hand, wrapped in linen cloth and tied with string, which he handed to Lord Kuran as soon as he reached the place where the other two men were standing. He bowed a little stiffly to his commander as he did so.

Kuran took the packet and promptly presented it Nagaro. "As I said, Captain, a small gift. With my compliments." His tone was carefully formal.

Nagaro accepted the packet, bowing rather more graciously than Ruald had done. "Thank you, My Lord," he said with matching formality. The contents of the packet had the knobbly feel of dried sothiril berries.

He moved towards the rail and the rope ladder, then, but Kuran detained him yet again by speaking. "One thing more, Captain."

"My Lord?"

"As your ships depart, would you please show us your best speed so that we may see if we can match it with the *Pride* and with the *Tempest*, there." Lord Kuran indicated one of the other Fleet ships that rode the nearby swells.

Nagaro raised his eyebrows. "Another demonstration, My Lord?"

The Lord of the Fleet smiled a tight smile. "Let's say I like to see things for myself."

Nagaro smiled his best pirate smile at that, a feral flash of white teeth in his black beard. "Good enough, My Lord," he said, and went over the rail.

***

Lord Kuran watched the longboat as it made its way back to the *Sword of Freedom*, propelled by the oars in the hands of both of its occupants.

Captain Ruald stood beside him. Presently the Leithian spoke. "Will you tell me now, My Lord, what you *really* think of him?"

"What do I think of him?" Kuran spoke without turning. "I find him a remarkable young man— intelligent, bold, and wise beyond his years. Well beyond, I should say, for he is at least ten years younger than I imagined he would be. When first I saw him, I confess I thought that perhaps the real Captain Nagaro had sent over some young whip to play the part and tweak us. He soon convinced me otherwise however."

"You're quite sure of that?" Ruald sounded disappointed.

Lord Kuran gave him a slightly exasperated glance. "Even if there weren't the quality of his swordsmanship and the brand on his shoulder, he displayed too detailed a knowledge on too many subjects to have learned it by rote. He seems to know his adversary very well for example. So yes, I believe he is quite genuine."

Kuran's gaze grew abstracted. "He shows his youth in some ways: his brashness— and his optimism. There's an innocence in the way he approaches the world, yet then he turns around and discourses astutely on the limits of men's honor and on oath-breaking. And he shows uncommon restraint. Most men who had suffered as he has at the hands of the Mahuk would be set on killing as many of them as they could.

Instead, we see a man who persuades Mahuk to surrender whenever killing them isn't necessary."

Ruald sniffed. "I might question the courage of a man who is so reluctant to kill his enemies."

This time, Kuran gave the captain a hard look. "A man so skilled with a sword that he could likely kill any man he wishes doesn't need to have courage for killing," he observed. "And to win without bloodshed is always a blessing."

"He *is* good with a blade," Ruald conceded. "But *you* should have gone a bout with him, My Lord. You'd have shown him something!"

Kuran laughed without mirth. "I think not, Captain. It's not a good thing for men to see their commander bested. Speed is my greatest virtue— it must be, since nearly every man outreaches me. But this man had superior reach *and* superior speed. I saw to it that he had the worst of our practice blades, and still you couldn't touch him. No, Captain, I am quite content to have left the honor to you."

There was an uncomfortable pause while Ruald chewed his lip. At length he said, "Do you believe everything he said? Much of it was hard to credit."

Kuran's brow furrowed. "I never believe everything a man says without testing the truth of at least some of it. But if I'm any judge at all, Captain Nagaro is one of the most honest men I've ever met. Either that, or he's one of the most artful deceivers— which I simply do not credit. I tested him regarding what he'd heard about me, and was able to press him to dissemble for the sake of courtesy. He did so moderately well, but his discomfort was evident. He clearly prefers the truth. And he seemed willing to answer anything I asked."

"Except his real name!"

"True." Kuran chewed his lip. "But Vothra permits a man to put his past behind him, provided the purpose is to take a better course, rather than to avoid the consequences of misdeeds. Besides, if his intention had been to deceive me, he could have easily made up a more credible name and I would have been none the wiser."

"So you *do* think he has something to hide?" Now Ruald sounded hopeful.

"Undoubtedly." Kuran gazed at the *Sword of Freedom*, whose crew were in the act of hoisting up the longboat. "And therein lies the great mystery: Who is he? Where did he come from? And what could there be that so young a man wishes to hide from the world?"

Kuran frowned "One who is as fair-spoken as you or I," he continued musingly. "Who bows like a courtier. Who fondly remembers Erantil Crimson. And who writes with the ease of a man who has known his letters since childhood. This is no fisherman's son. He comes from one of the educated classes— merchant, or noble. And as for the talk of his being half Turowan, I'd be surprised if it were more than a quarter— though if he's wearing kuma stain, it is artfully applied. I could find no flaw in it." Kuran heaved a sigh. "But don't you think you had best give the order to weigh anchor, Captain?" he added. "They're beginning to let out sail."

Ruald jumped, suppressing an exclamation, and spun about to rake the pirate ships with his eyes before snapping a hasty salute and striking off across the deck.

As the captain hurried away to give the order to sail, the Lord of the Fleet continued to stand at the rail, lost in thought. *It is ill grace to pry,* he thought. *Still I think I might make a few inquiries. That emerald-eyed salamander ring on his little finger seems like a design I may have seen somewhere. Perhaps some merchant family of the coast has misplaced one of its sons...*

Chapter 8

Minding The Garden

The last of the four pirate ships rounded the northern tip of the isle of Oapa, bearing south between that island and a pair of more seaward isles. Nagaro leaned forward to put his mouth to the speaking tube. "Ship oars, Taru. They can't see us anymore."

"Aye, Capt'n!" came Taru's cheerful rejoinder.

Two minutes later, the young Turo joined his friend at the forward rail of the *Sword of Freedom's* stern castle. "Well," he said with satisfaction, "I guess we showed 'em."

Nagaro nodded. "Yes," he said soberly. "Lord Kuran has seen for himself what we can do."

The *Pride of Lankura*, and the *Tempest* had pursued them the length of the Lapoa channel, but the four pirate craft had taken the lead as they left their anchorage, and the gap between them and the two Fleet ships had immediately begun to widen. At first, all of the ships had proceeded under the power of sails alone, but halfway along the course, the Fleet vessels had unshipped their oars and had begun to reduce the pirates' lead until Nagaro had ordered the *Sword's* oars out as well. The captains of the *Tiger*, the *Sea Eagle*, and the *North Wind*, had immediately followed their leader's example, and the gap between them and Lord Kuran's ships had begun to widen again, more rapidly than before.

Only as the end of the channel approached, had the captains of the *Pride* and the *Tempest* at last given up the effort. Apparently acknowledging themselves beaten, they had turned their vessels back to rejoin the other ships of the Royal Fleet.

Pavo came bounding up the ladder from the main deck. "This is heading you wish to keep, Captain?" he asked as he joined his two friends at the stern castle rail.

Nagaro was gazing broodingly ahead. "Yes," he said. "For now."

Taru turned to the massive Hashtep. "Ye should ha' seen him, Pavo. He argued with Lord Kuran over the gold! I swear it by Hakura Kili! He *argued* with the Lord of the Fleet! And then he told him t' stop sinking ships!" I tell ye, my heart kept jumping into my mouth every other minute. I can still hardly believe we came safely back!"

Pavo's broad, impassive face registered just the slightest hint of a smile. "Did not I say it would be so?"

Taru opened his mouth and shut it again. He looked fit to burst.

Nagaro shook himself out of his thoughts. "I didn't tell Lord Kuran to stop sinking ships," he said with mild annoyance. "I only suggested that he try to find another way of accomplishing his ends. And I told you before we started that we would be all right as long as we were honest."

"Honest is all well an good," Taru retorted. "But did ye have t' be honest about *everything?* And when *I* tried to be honest, ye kept telling me t' hush!"

Nagaro sighed. "You were bragging about things, Taru," he said. "And I don't like to brag. But for the rest of it, I think it was wisest to answer everything as honestly as I could. Lord Kuran is a very clever man— much cleverer than I, I'm sure. If I'd tried to pick and choose when to tell the truth, he would have known it. As it is, I'm sure he learned a good deal more than the answers to his questions. But they say that Kuran likes a bold man, as long as he's honest."

Taru dropped his anger like a piece of old fish. "Well I guess that's what ye are, Nagaro," he declared. "Bold and honest just about sums ye up in two words. And Lord Kuran *did* seem to take a liking to ye, at that. What did he say t' ye after he'd sent me away? Or was it too private t' be telling us?"

Nagaro's brows came together. Part of what had passed between him and Lord Kuran had concerned Taru and did not bear repeating in his company. The other part, however, was the thing he'd been thinking about when Pavo had interrupted him.

"He asked me to watch his back garden," he said quietly. "While he was away south, going to Harmoth."

"*Watch his back garden?*" Taru gaped. "What d' ye mean? Look after the coast for him?"

Pavo's normally impassive face registered surprise as well. "He must think very good thing about you, Nagaro, if he ask you to do that."

Nagaro chewed his lip, still frowning. "I don't know," he said. "It would be very flattering to think that Lord Kuran trusted me enough to ask for my help after just one meeting, but I can't help thinking he has some other motive. As I said, he's a very clever man."

Taru's expression turned instantly wary. "Ai, Nagaro! What d' ye think he's up to?"

Nagaro laughed. "I don't think he means us any harm, Taru. He may just have wanted to see what I would say— or see whether I would actually *do* it. Something of that sort."

"Ye told him we would?"

Nagaro nodded. "At least I gave that impression, and I said I would send word by the fishermen if we saw anything seriously amiss. It means we're bound to stay well north of Pakoa, in the Lomoas, until we hear that Kuran is sailing back this way. I'd rather be able to sail where we choose, but I think I have to do what Kuran asked of me. And I think the men will understand."

"What about Pakoa?" Taru asked. "We brought all four ships on this venture because the men wouldn't hear o' doing anything else. But now it's safely done and we've left Pakoa unguarded in the meantime."

"You're right." Nagaro nodded, frowning. "But we don't have to stay together to do this watchman's work. The *Sword* and the *Sea Eagle* should be enough for it. We can all sail south together for the first part of the way, going slowly and keeping our eyes open. Then Landros and I will turn back and take our crews north again while Moraga and Timegar take the *Tiger* and the *North Wind* the rest of the way to Pakoa."

***

Three days later, the four pirate craft lay anchored in the shelter of a little cove at the southern tip of the large island of Moluaro in the middle Lomoas. It was a blustery afternoon, and Nagaro had called his three captains together in the great cabin aboard the *Sword of Freedom* for a final council before the little fleet would divide itself in two.

Moraga, the master of the *Tiger*, came aboard fuming, his scarred face hot with anger. The former Turowan merchant seaman scarcely allowed any of them to settle in their chairs before launching into a tirade on a subject that had nothing to do with the matter at hand and everything to do with the state of his own temper.

"So, now— after they've been seen at it— Nanu and Chaheel *admits* t' bein' crossed men! After pretendin' t' be straight-sailors all these years! An' what're ye two lookin' like that for?"

The last words were directed at Landros and Timegar, who had just exchanged suffering glances across the table. The two Kelorin sea warriors turned their wary and expectant eyes to Nagaro.

Nagaro had listened silently to Moraga's outburst. Now he sighed. "I wouldn't say they've been pretending they weren't crossed," he observed reasonably. "They just haven't said one way or the other, and that has let everyone think whatever they were inclined to think. It's hardly their fault if you made the wrong assumption."

"What, then, didn't ye think the same?" Moraga demanded.

Nagaro inclined his head. "Of course I did," he replied mildly. "In the beginning. And I'd probably still be thinking it if Simion hadn't told me about Nanu and Chaheel before he left."

At this, Landros and Timegar looked surprised.

Moraga nearly choked. "Ye *knew?* And ye didn't *tell anyone?*

Nagaro drew another long sigh. "I couldn't think of any good that would come from telling," he said seriously. "And I could imagine a great deal of harm, considering how badly Simion was treated."

"So ye put em' on *my ship?*"

Nagaro massaged his temples. "Each ship needs someone who can translate Hashti," he said patiently. "Chaheel is the best we have— after Pavo, who is *my* second mate— so I wanted Chaheel with either you or Timegar, since you two work together. Timegar has picked up some Hashti, himself, so I gave him Haofa, and put Chaheel on the *Tiger*. And of course Nanu goes with Chaheel. But really, Moraga, I don't know why you're so upset about this. Haven't they proven themselves good fighters, good oarsmen, and good comrades in every way? They've done no harm to anyone, and they're so devoted to each other that there's no reason they should look at any other man."

Moraga's mouth worked silently. He wiped his split lip with the back of his hand, and turned to Timegar. "Well?" he demanded at length. "Haven't ye got so much as a word t' say?"

The veteran sea warrior stroked the narrow salt-and-pepper beard on his chin and glanced at Nagaro before answering. "If ye don't want them on your ship, Moraga, I'll take them on mine. Ye can have Haofa and any other man ye choose— but I'll be getting the better end of it. It's just as the captain says. Nanu and Chaheel are good men, and they've done no harm."

Moraga was clearly beginning to feel outnumbered. He turned desperately to the captain of the *Sea Eagle*. "Landros...?" he pleaded.

The former Fleet officer ran a hand through his grizzled hair. "My old mother used to say that there's all manner o' folk in the world, and no cause to make trouble for any man that makes none. I'd say ye're making a tempest out of a rain-squall."

Moraga's shoulders sagged. Nagaro gave the discomfited man a sympathetic look. "It's Vothrin teaching, Moraga," he said, almost gently. "You're one lone Turo in a room full of Kelorin."

The one lone Turo frowned truculently. "Ye of all people, Capt'n," he blurted, "Goin' on about doin' no harm, after Simion took a shine t' ye, and ye had t' go lie wi' that Jila woman, to prove..."

His voice trailed off as the change in the quality of the other men's silence became apparent. A glance at the faces of Timegar and Landros told him that the two older Kelorin wouldn't have put the matter so bluntly.

But Nagaro spoke mildly when he broke the uncomfortable silence. "Simion never hurt me, Moraga, only himself. It was my mistake to let the sting of other men's disapproval push me into doing something that I shouldn't have."

At that moment there was an urgent knocking at the door, and Taru's excited voice came through the planking.

"Nagaro! Captain! There's a fisherman that's come wi' some news ye'd better hear!"

Four heads turned towards the door.

Nagaro raised his voice. "Open and enter!"

The door fairly burst open. Taru stood in the doorway. Pavo was behind him, and hovering beyond the big Hashtep was Sindar, who had become Pavo's ever-present shadow whenever he wasn't in the crow's seat. The former captive's face wore its usual expression of eager bewilderment.

Taru spoke breathlessly. "There's a man here that says he saw ships... galleys... and they're northbound—"

Four sets of chair legs scraped the floor as the captains all leaped to their feet. There was a general movement towards the door and a chorus of questions.

"When?"

"Where?"

"How many ships?"

"What were their banners?"

Somehow Taru managed to sort out the cacophony, or perhaps he merely guessed what the other men wanted to know. "It was yesterday. He saw six at least— but he couldn't tell for certain. Couldn't make out their banners, either. They were taking the Sea Passage, as far out as they dared t' go!

Timegar had reached the doorway first, being the closest. There he paused. "Six would be more than just a raiding party, if they're Mahuk," he said. "Could it be Lord Kuran's ships, heading north again?"

Moraga shook his head. "He'd ha' never got so far already. Not if he was going t' Harmoth."

"Maybe he wasn't," said Landros, grimly. "All we know from the fishermen is that Kuran's fleet crossed over to the mainland side o' the Great Channel after we parted, and headed south. Kuran's an old fox. Maybe going to Harmoth was just a ruse. Or maybe he made new plans after he learned that the old ones had been found out."

Nagaro stood frowning in concentration. He had risen with the rest, but still stood beside his chair. "We haven't been moving very fast," he said thoughtfully. "If they made all speed and left those two ships at Kel Tierna, then crossed over to the island side and rounded Moluaro at night, they just might have been able to get to the Sea Passage south of us without our hearing of it." He frowned harder. "But there shouldn't be more than six ships, if it's Kuran. And that's assuming that he left the two ships at Kel Tierna, or let them sail on to Harmoth unescorted."

He sought Landros' eyes. "I would swear that Captain Ruald believed they were escorting those ships to Harmoth, but Kuran never actually admitted it— not in so many words. Would he tell a false tale to his own men? Is he really that devious, Landros?"

The former Fleet officer smiled tightly. "He *can* be, but that doesn't mean he's doing it this time. I'd say ye had best begin by guessing that these are Mahuk craft."

Nagaro nodded. "I agree," he said. "And since I told Kuran we would watch this part of the coast, we have to go after them to at least find out what they are." He shook his head. "Six ships, or more! I had planned to head north with just two, but even with all four it would prove too much for us in a fight—"

"We have to go after them with all four ships!" Landros eyes were hard and his jaw set.

"Aye, Capt'n!" Timegar nodded decisively.

Nagaro turned to the one of his three captains who hadn't spoken. "What do you say, Moraga? Landros and Timegar are old Fleet warriors, and old loyalties linger— but you and I have never been Fleet men. Should we leave Pakoa to whatever chance may send?"

Moraga was frowning darkly. "I don't much like it," he growled. "But it seems we've got no choice. Six ships at least? That's a fleet, that is! They must mean t' make a real attack— *if* they're Mautep. But if it's Lord Kuran playin' games with us, I'll have a word for 'im, I will— an' it won't be a pretty one!"

Nagaro smiled a small tight smile. "If it's Kuran playing games, I'll have a few words for him myself, especially if any harm comes to Pakoa while we're off chasing him! But I'm glad we are at least in agreement." He turned to Taru. "Is the fisherman still out there?"

"Aye, Capt'n. I thought ye'd want t' question him."

Nagaro nodded and made for the door. "Let's see if there's anything more he can tell us." The other three moved to follow him.

In the corridor, Nagaro slowed to address Moraga. "If it bothers you too much having Nanu and Chaheel aboard the *Tiger*, I won't object if you want to trade them to Timegar since he offered. But I'd prefer that you talk to your other men first to see how they feel."

Moraga gave him a sideways glance. "This don't seem like the time t' worry about it," he said gruffly. "Truth is, it seems a bit foolish when I come t' think of it. They *haven't* done any harm. And they *are* good men, an' I always thought well o' them up 'til now. I don't suppose they can help bein' crossed."

Nagaro smiled ruefully. "No," he said. "It's not your way or my way, Moraga, but it's how they were made."

Moraga rolled his eyes, but he nodded. "Leave 'em be for now," he said with a shrug.

The fisherman was a middle-aged Turowan man who gave his name as Muwabei. Standing at the tiller of his little boat as it bumped against the *Sword's* side, he was clearly in awe at first to find himself talking to Captain Nagaro.

"They was makin' good speed, Capt'n. I saw 'em yesterday from the North Kapala Channel." The weathered Turo pointed across the water of the Inside Passage. The northern tip of the island of Kapala lay to the west, directly across it. The North Kapala Channel opened there to reveal a glimpse of the open sea and the distant horizon. "I was trying me luck in the channel, Capt'n, when I looked up an' saw 'em. Six for sure, but I didn't stay any longer'n it took t' count so many. If they's Fleet ships, there's no harm in runnin'. And if they ain't, there's no good in stayin,' if ye follow my drift."

"I do, friend Muabei." Nagaro smiled sympathetically, leaning over the ship's rail. "What hour was it when you saw them? Did you happen to mark it?"

The man blinked at him. He was having some difficulty getting used to being called 'friend' by someone who was famous from one end of the Lomoas to the other. "It were about an hour past noon, Zirda. And this morning I run into me wife's cousin, Tibo. An' he says he saw ships yesterday too— an' hour afore sunset— when he was lookin' out t' sea from the South Duani Channel. So they was makin' good speed, if they was the same ships. *He* said there was eight o' them, but Tibo's been known t' see things what ain't quite there when he gets excited, if ye know what I mean."

Nagaro chewed his lip. "Could Tibo make out their banners?"

The fisherman shook his head. "They was too far away, Zirda, an' they had the sun behind 'em."

"Is there anything else?"

"No, Capt'n. That's the long and the short of it. An' the Spirits know what deviltry they're about, if they're raiders."

Nagaro nodded agreement. "There's one thing more I'll ask of you, Muwabei. Could you put the word out among the fishermen to tell this tale to Lord Kuran? He should be somewhere in the Great Channel."

The fisherman looked doubtful. "I can put the word out, Capt'n, but Lord Kuran don't stop to talk t' the likes of us."

"He will now." Nagaro gave the man his best pirate smile. "I've explained to him how useful you can be."

Muwabei's eyes went wide. "Ye *explained* it to him? Oh, aye, Capt'n! Ye can count on me. I'll tell 'im!"

Nagaro dropped his smile. "And tell them also that we mean to follow these ships. Eight, or even six, is too many for us to take on, but if they attack anyone, on land or at sea, we may be able to lend a hand."

After Muwabei had gone, Timegar spoke up. "How shall we follow these ships, Capt'n? If we take the Sea Passage, they'll be able to see that we're following them from miles away."

"And they know our banners," Taru put in. "And don't forget, Nagaro, that there's a price on your head."

Nagaro frowned. "I doubt these Mautep would consider that price to be worth taking on four ships when they surely have some other mission. But I think we will go back up the Inside Passage. That will keep the islands between them and us, at least until we get to the northern end of the Lomoas. Whatever these Mautep are about, they'll have to turn in among the islands to do it. There's nothing worth their interest on the seaward side. And the fishermen should be able to tell us something of their movements."

This plan met with approval from the other three captains. The additional facts they had gleaned from questioning Muwabei had only served to increase the sense of urgency. So they filled their waterskins without further delay, weighed anchor, and turned their bows north.

***

Two days later, Nagaro had begun to doubt the wisdom of his choice, for they had gotten no further word of the fleet of ships. The seaward-facing shores of the islands were sparsely populated, being unsheltered from the fury of the gales that swept in off of the open sea. There were neither towns nor gold mines on the seaward side of the Lomoas. There were also very few fishermen who dwelt there, and those who frequented the calmer, more sheltered waters among the isles had caught no glimpse of the rapidly moving war galleys.

Unfavorable winds had hindered their speed but could also have affected their quarry, and Nagaro hoped they had shortened the lead of the fleet they were following. During the day they had rowed as much as they could, and they had continued through part of each night by the light of Talebra's waxing disk. Still, it was undeniable that their path was slightly longer than that of the unknown ships, as they angled this way and that to follow the Inside Passage as it wended its way between the islands. The presumed Mautep fleet would have been able to sail a more nearly straight course, out there in the open ocean. In addition, the unsheltered Sea Passage was blessed— or cursed— with stronger winds that might drive a ship more swiftly if they didn't force her to seek a safe haven.

It was early in the afternoon of that second day when they finally got news of their quarry. The wind had been rising since noon and was scouring the ships' decks and picking whitecaps from the choppy swells. Ominous storm clouds were massing to the west, over the open sea. Landros spotted a small craft bearing a pair of fishermen, and hailed the men with his speaking trumpet. Once the boat got within shouting range, a call came back from one of the two men aboard her.

"Aye, Zirda, we saw ships out there this morning! Seven or eight o' them!"

A few minutes later, the news of Landros' conversation with the two fishermen was being shouted from ship to ship. The fishermen had described the galleys' banners as "yellow and black or maybe brown." They'd been quite emphatic that the banners were *not* Edroviran blue. They were also very clear as to the hour of the sighting and the ships' position.

Nagaro received the news on the stern castle deck of the *Sword of Freedom*. From the time and place of the sighting, he calculated that the *Sword* and her companions had shortened the Mautep's lead considerably. The Mautep fleet had been nearly two days ahead of them, but now was less than half a day in the lead. That was much better than he had expected. The Mautep must have stopped to take on water or to forage. There were places along the seaward coasts of the isles where even eight ships could have done so without being seen by a living soul.

Nagaro took the speaking trumpet from Pavo, who had been calling his questions across to Landros, and directly addressed the captain of the *Sea Eagle*. He had to raise his voice to a shout so that the wind wouldn't carry it away.

"I want to make Boka Omei before the storm hits! Lie up in one of her harbors. If we can't make that, we'll stop at Lapoa!"

"Aye, Capt'n! Tell Pavo t' watch your canvas!" A gust of wind snatched at Landros' words. "If they're making for the Faranos, they could ha' already crossed the Mouth!"

Nagaro raised his trumpet again. "Only if the wind wasn't too bad when they got there! I want speed, Landros! We need to row!"

The "Mouth" meant the strait called Farano's Mouth. It separated the northernmost isles of the Lomoas from the southernmost of the Inner and Outer Faranos. It was only a few miles across at its seaward end because the chain of the Outer Faranos straggled southward, while the inner island chain was almost a dozed miles shorter than the outer one. To leeward, the Mouth opened to several times that width, becoming as wide as the Great Channel with which it became confluent.

The strait was a natural place for ships coming north along the seaward side of the Lomoas to cut in among the islands or enter the Farano Passage, which separated the Outer from the Inner Faranos. Half a dozen years ago when Nagaro and Pavo had been captured at Wotana Bay on the mainland coast by Mautep raiders, they had doubtless been carried out through Farano's Mouth, out into the open sea and thence south to the waters of the Mahuk Baar. The Mouth was a dangerous passage in a gale because it was shallow and there were vicious rocks— "Farano's teeth"— at several places, that were more or less covered by water depending on the tide. In a storm, the tell-tale signs of their presence could easily be missed by unwary seamen among the general froth of wind-whipped waves.

An hour later, they were passing to the west of Oapa. Nagaro paced the deck of the stern castle as the *Sword of Freedom* surged ahead under the power of her oars. He had been alternately gazing keenly ahead and glancing worriedly at the lowering clouds that were looming ever closer beyond the low spine of the island that lay to windward. Now a few towering pillars of cloud outpaced the larger mass, their blue-gray underbellies dark with rain. It had the look more of a late winter storm than an early spring one.

Reluctantly, he gave the order to ship oars. The men needed to rest.

Less than an hour later he ordered the oars out again. They had just left the southern tip of Lapoa behind them, deciding not to stop in the Lapoa Channel. It wasn't much farther to Boka Omei's twin harbors and Landros believed they could make it. Still, the ships had all been heeling so severely under the force of the wind that Pavo and the other second mates had decided to shorten sail. They would have to row to keep up their speed and pray they could keep their oar ports open. The entire western sky was now a mass of purple-black cloud.

The westering sun had disappeared behind that threatening wall. As a premature dusk settled over the Lomoas, the grumble of thunder could be heard over the rush of the wind. The fishermen, being sensible men, had all made for shore. There wasn't a small sail in sight.

Half an hour later still, as they were passing to leeward of the southern end of the large island known as Boka Omei, they had to furl the sails completely as wind-driven rain began to spatter the deck. Very soon they would be obliged to close the oar ports as well, and Nagaro gave the order to make for the Bay of Omei, the more southerly, and therefore closer, of Boka Omei's two harbors. Within minutes, the four ships were passing through its entrance and the Bay of Omei opened before them.

It was deep and well-sheltered, enclosed on the north, west, and south sides by shoulders of land. The southern and western shores sported several wharfs and a number of small piers to which were moored an impressive array of fishing boats. The town, of the same name as the bay, partially encircled it and climbed the gentler slope on the southern shore. All of this could be made out in the gloom of the storm-darkened afternoon during the time it took the four pirate ships to glide to a halt within the shelter of the harbor, ship their oars, close their oar ports, and drop anchor.

The last of these actions had scarcely been accomplished, however, when the sky was sliced in half by a sheet of lightning and there came a deafening roll of thunder. The echoes of that thunderclap had scarcely died away when the clouds above opened their vaporous floodgates and the rain came sheeting down.

***

The storm raged and howled through the night, but the dawn came clear as crystal.

The little world of island and bay glittered like a green-and-blue jewel in the early morning sunlight as four men made their way up the steeply zig-zagging path that started at the northwest corner of the harbor and worked its way to the top of the ridge of land that bounded the northern side of the bay. Farther to the north, on the other side of that ridge, the land descended in more gentle undulations to the island's other principal harbor, Boka Bay. To the west of where the men labored, the rocky ridge they were scaling merged with the island's rolling green highlands. To the east, it thrust out into the sea, ending in a near hundred-foot cliff that sprang straight out of the surf. This impressive headland was known as the Stone Head, and even at the lowest tide, it was impossible to pass safely around the base of it on foot. Thus Boka Omei's twin ports had grown up as worlds apart, though separated by only a few miles as a gull might fly.

Nagaro paused just short of the ridge crest to catch his breath and to let the other three men catch up. Pavo was the first to join him. The big Hashtep seemed scarcely winded and grinned when Nagaro gasped a greeting.

"I do not hurry so much as you," Pavo observed laconically. "And I do not waste breath like those two." He gestured at the two stragglers, Taru and Landros. From their gesticulations, it appeared the young Turo and the grizzled Kelorin were arguing over something as they climbed the rocky path.

While he waited, Nagaro took in the view. The four pirate ships rode peacefully at anchor in the bay below. Even without employing the ship's spyglass, which was slung about his neck, he could see people moving on the wharfs and along the streets of the town. Fishing boats were already venturing forth from the harbor and he could see other small sails, here and there away into the distance, scattered along the channel.

He and Taru and Pavo had all risen at first light and eaten a hurried breakfast, being eager to complete their reconnaissance expedition as early as possible. As soon as they emerged on deck, Landros had hailed them from the *Sea Eagle* and so had joined the party. They had all been here before and knew the value of the vantage point they were approaching.

Boka Omei was the northernmost island of any size in the Lomoan archipelago, and on a clear day like this one, the top of the Stone Head offered a view of the entire northern end of the Inside Passage from just south of Oapa to Farano's Mouth and beyond it to the southernmost isles of the Outer and Inner Faranos. The Mouth would not of course be visible until they actually crossed the crest of the ridge and were able to look north. From this side, however, Nagaro could see a long way south, back along the path they had traveled the previous day, as far as the first place where the passage angled and an island blocked his view.

The Passage was a ribbon of stunning silver in the morning sunlight. There was nothing untoward to be seen moving on it— but there was also no sign of Kuran's ships. Nagaro frowned. Where, he wondered, was Lord Kuran right now? Had the man received his message? Of course, he reminded himself, the Lord f the Fleet might be bringing his ships north on the landward side of the Lomoas, via the Great Channel.

As he stood watching, a large two-masted craft emerged from the narrow Lapoa Channel, moving into the wider channel of the Inside Passage. A quick deployment of his spyglass confirmed that it was a merchant ship, not a war galley. He pointed it out to Pavo.

The Hashtep nodded. "That one comes probably here," he observed. "See how it have turned this way?"

At that moment, Taru's voice reached their ears, breathless, but argumentative. "I still think they could ha' passed... clean by the Mouth t' seaward. They could ha' made it that far yesterday morning. Before there were any clouds t' see. Before the wind came up so strong..."

"Aye, sure... of course they *could* have. But they *wouldn't*... ye see," came Landros' patient but gasping rejoinder. "I've sailed that way... and there's no safe harbors along the seaward side o' the Faranos. Not for miles, there ain't. Storm or calm."

Both men had come around the last switchback in the trail, and as Landros finished speaking, they came puffing to a halt beside Nagaro and Pavo. Pavo promptly shook his head at them and set off up the last curve of the path. "You will make us late with all your talk," he said over his shoulder in mock disapproval.

Taru assumed a wounded expression. "Here now!" he said. "*Ye've* had a chance t' rest!"

Nagaro laughed. "You can rest here if you like," he said, turning to follow Pavo. "But we're almost at the top in any case. A few more steps and you can rest up there."

Indeed, it was only two dozen paces to the point where the trail topped the rise and Pavo was half way there already. Beyond that point, the ridge-top was broad and flat, and it was an easy walk of another twenty paces or so to where one could look down the other side.

Landros shrugged and followed Nagaro. Taru gave a little growl of protest, but started after them both. "Landros seems t' think... the Mautep must ha' crossed the Mouth," he puffed. "That they're making... for the Farano Passage. I think they might ha' stayed t' seaward."

"Not if they knew what they were doing!" Landros growled.

"They could ha' been planning t' turn east somewhere.... between the isles... once they got past the Mouth—"

"Not in a storm! There's no safe passage in a storm. Not this side o' Big Farano!

"What if they didn't know the storm was coming!

Nagaro had just crested the rise and stepped onto more level ground, but now he stopped and turned around, drawn into the argument. "Either course would have been possible," he said. "It would have depended on what the weather looked like when they had to make the choice."

Landros came to a halt two paces from Nagaro. "But seeing as how... ye never know... what the weather is *going* to be," he panted, "they wouldn't ha' kept to the Seaward Passage. *Not if they knew what they were doing!*" He stopped, somewhat red in the face but looking triumphant. Then suddenly his gaze shifted and refocused, looking past Nagaro. "What's this?" he exclaimed. "Here comes Pavo!"

Nagaro spun around. Pavo was indeed coming back towards them, striding purposefully across the ridge top. The tautness of his expression suggested suppressed excitement— or alarm. As soon as he got close enough, he raised his voice in a shout.

"They are down there!"

"*What?*" Nagaro and Landros chorused, and then Taru joined them with, "*Who?*" and "*Where?*"

Pavo closed the remaining gap in a few strides and halted. He drew a shuddering breath. "There are six war galley," he gasped. "In Boka Bay!"

All other talk was forgotten in the rush that followed. Soon they were all standing on the farther edge of the ridge, looking down the long slope to the hamlet and harbor of Boka Bay. Nagaro and Landros were using their spyglasses to good effect. Six war galleys were certainly there, riding at anchor in the bay.

"They're Lord Angkat's ships," Landros muttered. "The banners are brown and gold. So they must be the same ships we've been following—"

"But there's only six o' them," Taru pointed out. "There's more than one man counted eight in the fleet we've been chasing—"

"Down! All get down!" Pavo abruptly grabbed Nagaro's arm on one side and Taru's on the other, and pulled them down among the tall grass in which they had been standing. Landros flung himself down as well. Pavo pointed urgently to three figures that had just appeared on top of an outcropping of rock a few hundred yards down the slope.

"*Sea warriors!*" hissed Landros.

Nagaro trained his spyglass on the figures, confirming as he had expected that the men wore uniforms of brown and gold. They also appeared to be passing a spyglass back and forth, but they were pointing it to the north.

"They must have come all the way up from the harbor," he said. "For the same reason we've come— to spy out the Mouth."

"We're lucky they didn't decide to come all the way up here," Landros observed. "There's no cover here but this grass."

Nagaro nodded. "And lucky we didn't try to make for Boka Bay last night. We'd have sailed right into them!" A sudden thought struck him. He raised the angle of his own spyglass, scanning the broad expanse to the north in the direction the Mautep seemed to be looking.

Boka Omei lay very nearly at the northern end of the Inside Passage. Beyond it on this side of the channel lay only the tiny islet of Soku, visible beyond the spit of land that formed the farther side of Boka Bay. To his right, on the farther side of the Inside Passage, was the low, rocky island of Tunapa. Directly in front of him, in the middle distance, lay the broad expanse of Farano's Mouth. Irregular patches of white foam marked the positions of several of the more prominent "teeth". Beginning off to Nagaro's left, at the seaward end of the Mouth, the silhouettes of the nearest isles of the Outer Faranos marched away into the distance like overlapping paper cutouts in ever paler shades of misty blue. A bit to the right, almost too pale to see, were the low shapes of the Inner Farano islands of Tirobo and Borobai.

The slow sweep of Nagaro's spyglass suddenly halted. "I think I see the other two ships," he said quietly.

"*Where?*" asked Taru in a breathless whisper.

"Over there." Nagaro pointed to the left. "Just on the other side of the Mouth, near the tip of the second of the outer islands." He handed his spyglass to Taru. "I can't make out the banners at this distance. But they're war galleys, and there are two of them."

"Ha!" said Landros. "They must ha' tried to make for the Faranos as the wind was comin' up— just as I thought— and two o' them made it that far, but the other six were forced to turn east, hugging the coast o' Boka Omei."

Nagaro nodded. "Very likely. Boka Bay would be the nearest safe anchorage to ride out a storm. And there's not another ship in sight— neither merchant nor galley. And once these other six have got across, they'll have a clear run up the Farano Channel!"

Below them, one of the Mautep warriors unfurled a signal flag and waved it. Then, having apparently finished their reconnaissance, the three sea warriors began descending from their rocky perch. A moment later their figures could be seen moving off down the slope in the direction of the harbor and its adjoining town.

Taru was following them with the spyglass. "I don't see any o' the townsfolk," he said.

"They've likely fled to the caves," observed Landros. He turned his own glass in a new direction, training it upon a hillside not far away on their left. "Aye," he said after a moment, with evident satisfaction. "I can make out someone hiding in the rocks by the cave's mouth. By the look of him, it could be Doren, the Town Chief."

"Look!" cried Pavo. "All of ship are letting down their sail. They are making ready to go!"

Nagaro took the spyglass back from Taru and saw that it was true. He could see the men on the yardarms. "That signal flag probably meant that all was clear along their intended heading," he said. "And now the ships are only waiting for those men to get back aboard."

"What we do now?" Pavo asked.

Nagaro frowned. "I don't know," he said. "We can't stop them. We can't follow them directly because we'd be seen. And the same would be true if we go east around Tunapa into the Great Channel. It's all open water and a clear view from there all the way to the Inner Faranos."

"We should warn the fishermen back in Omei Bay—" Taru began urgently.

"Can't, mate," put in Landros. "By the time we get back down to Omei, those ships 'll be well out o' the harbor. But fishermen have sharp eyes," he added, seeing Taru's look. "Ye can trust them to look out for themselves."

Nagaro continued to frown intently. "I have an idea," he said. "But we can't get our own ships safely out of the bay until the Mautep fleet has cleared Soku Island. Which means we have a little time.

Landros cocked his head. "What's your plan, mate?"

Nagaro shifted uncomfortably. "You may tell me it's daft, Landros," he said. "But I was thinking we could sail around the south end of Boka Omei and take the seaward passage north past the Mouth— if the weather stays favorable. Then we could cut back in between the islands at the first opportunity and try to find those ships again. Ask the local fishermen for news or find a hill to climb and see what we could see. It seems sound to me, but you know that part of the Outer Faranos better than I do."

Landros furrowed his brow and nodded sagely. "Aye, that could work."

"Now wait a minute, Landros, ye slippery eel!" Taru protested. "Didn't ye tell me that nobody would try that if they knew what they were doing?"

Landros grinned wickedly. "I said the *Mautep* wouldn't," he drawled. "Cause they don't know that coast the way *I* know it, from my Fleet days. I wouldn't ha' tried it *yesterday*, and that's a fact. But if the weather is as fair as it is right now when we get to the near side o' the Mouth, and if we take Sawtooth Bite— that's the first safe passage on the other side— when the tide is running high, then it should be safe enough. Ye can make that run in an hour and a half, easy, and the weather don't change *that* fast— at least not in the normal course o' things."

"*Hmmph!*" Taru was not mollified. "It sounds t' me as if the Mautep might ha' done that, just as I said— if they'd got there in the morning before the wind was well up!"

Landros gave the young Turo a level stare. "They might ha' tried it," he conceded, "if they knew only a very little bit about that coast. But yesterday morning was already blustery, and the outside o' the Faranos is a bad place to be if there's any kind o' wind off the sea. It drives ye right on shore, and that coast has more rocks than a shark has teeth. It's one o' those things a man'll try if he don't know any better— and likely come to grief. And a man that knows a *little* more 'n that will know better than to try it. That's the Mautep. They'd play it safe. But a man that *really* knows that coast..." and here Landros indicated his own chest with his thumb, "knows what he can get away with in any kind o' weather! And there's something to be said for doin' what the other man doesn't expect."

Nagaro cleared his throat. "Well, I'll put it before all of the captains," he said. "And it will have to go to the men as well. Apart from the risk of that passage, I'm not sure how fair it is to ask them to keep chasing those ships. The Faranos will be under the eye of Kuran's second in command. How many ships might Geldoran have, Landros?"

Landros squinted speculatively. "Eight, at least. Maybe as many as ten or eleven, but I'm guessing. And he wouldn't keep them all together. The Faranos are a big territory to patrol."

Nagaro nodded. "Well, we'll talk it out back at the bay. Right now I want to go down and talk with Doren to see how the townsfolk here have fared. Taru can come with me," he added, seeing his friend's look of alarm. "But Landros and Pavo should head back over the ridge at once. Pavo can take word out to the ships, and Landros can let the Omei Town Council know what's afoot."

So the little party split in half. Landros and Pavo took the path back the way they had come while Nagaro and Taru set off across the hillside in the direction of the caves, moving stealthily from bush to bush like stalking hunters.

Chapter 9

Into The Faranos

A s it turned out, the townsfolk of Boka Bay had suffered nothing worse than being frightened out of their homes and having some of their livestock taken, for which Nagaro compensated them out of his own purse. When he returned to the ships, he found his captains in agreement with his plan. The rest of the pirate crews agreed as well. No one liked the idea of seeing the Mautep slip away after having followed them so far and finally gotten so close.

Less than an hour later, the four ships set sail, turning south out of the harbor's mouth. They sailed with all haste, slowing only to ask several local fishermen to pass the word around to look for Kuran and tell him where the Mautep ships had gone— and that Nagaro's ships meant to follow them.

Fortunately, Landros' confidence proved well founded. The four pirate craft rounded Boka Omei and safely passed the outer opening of the Mouth. They successfully slipped between the second and third islands of the Outer Faranos, traversing Sawtooth Bite when the tide was just past its crest.

Over the two days that followed, they made two more similar maneuvers, slipping back out to sea, sailing north a cautious distance, then cutting back in between a pair of islands through some channel known to Landros. This "skipping and hopping", as Landros called it, slowed them down. And it was complicated on the second day when the weather turned stormy, with intermittent gusty winds and squalls of rain. Their only consolation was that the rain, which greatly reduced the visibility, must be hampering the Mautep as well.

Based on the news they got from local fishermen, and the few glimpses they were granted, the Mautep fleet was about half a day's sail ahead of them, and at least the distance didn't seem to be increasing. Indeed, the Mautep seemed to be trying to make a cautious run up the

Farano Passage, anchoring out of easy sight at night, and pausing only briefly to do a little mischief along the way.

Nagaro's men got news of one merchant ship being plundered by the raiders. Its crew had fortunately escaped, saving themselves by taking to the longboats. Several fishermen in small boats had not been so fortunate, however, and the news of their capture roused the righteous anger of the pirate crewmen, making them more willing to continue the pursuit.

***

At almost mid morning of the third day, the four pirate ships lay anchored in the narrow channel at the south end of the island of Little Farano. There had been rain during the night and into the morning, and the clouds had only just broken and moved off to the east a little, offering the hope that the lookouts they had sent to the top of a nearby headland might at last get a view to the north up the Farano Channel.

The four captains were gathered in the *Sword's* great cabin to discuss their situation as they waited for the two lookouts— Tredhold and Taru— to return and make their report. The discussion was more contentious than those of the past two days had been. There were two reasons for this. First, they had now come well up into the territory that was protected by Geldoran and were getting very close to the first of the gold ports. And second, they would have to change their strategy of forward movement if they wished to continue followings their quarry.

The small channel they had come in through the previous evening, known as the "Back Gate", had been deep, fairly wide, and relatively free of dangerous rocks. It could have been traversed even in a moderately strong wind, but there were no more such passages for a very long way to the north along the outside of the Outer Faranos. Little Farano Island was only "little" by comparison to Big Farano. It was nearly twenty miles long, and Big Farano was more than forty. And the passage between them wasn't passable by anything as large as a galley, at any time, under any conditions. The truth was that Big and Little Farano were only separate islands when the tide was in.

Nagaro was sitting quietly on one of the four chairs at the cabin's small table listening to the other three men's conversation. If he gave them enough time, he knew they would cover all the options in their own way, and he would hear all of their opinions aired as well.

"We've come as far north as we can go, and this here is Geldoran's back garden, not Kuran's," Moraga was saying.

"We haven't gone as far as we can go," Landros countered. "We can cross to the other side o' the Farano Passage, slip through the Inner Faranos into the Great Channel, and go north that way between the Inner Faranos and the mainland. Or we can go straight up the Farano Passage—"

"And be bobbin' there like pelicans? *We* can't fly— in case ye hadn't noticed— an' there's no place t' hide in the Farano Passage!"

"We can hide between the isles of the Inner Faranos," Landros explained patiently. "And when the Mautep meet Geldoran in the channel—"

Moraga's fist banged the table. "When *that* happens, we'd best be miles away! The first time we set eyes on any o' Geldoran's ships— and see that he's got things in hand— we should be turning 'round an' going back t' the Lomoas! Nagaro never promised Kuran he'd mind the Faranos. And Geldoran's got no way o' knowin' that Kuran ever asked him to mind *anything!*"

"That's true, mate," Timegar put in. "Kuran surely didn't expect us to come this far north just to do him a favor. But he surely never expected there t' be a bloody Mautep fleet the size o' this one sailin' up his skirts, either. He'd have chased them himself if he'd known. And *he* wouldn't be talking about stopping now, or turning back!"

Moraga scowled. "That's fine for *him!*" he retorted. "It's his work. But I ain't noticed Lord Kuran payin' our wages, an' I don't care t' risk me skin protectin' the king's gold! Where is Geldoran, anyway?" he added. "The only reason I agreed t' come this far is 'cause we ain't seen mast nor sail o' the Fleet."

Timegar turned to Landros. "Aye, where *is* Geldoran?" he echoed. "Here we are, nearly to the first gold port— Long Harbor is just at the other end o' Little Farano— and there's been no sign of any of his ships!"

Landros frowned. "Commander Geldoran is a good man," he said seriously. "Kuran has him picked for the next Lord o' the Fleet, and Kuran's no fool. He knows quality when he sees it. So ye may be sure that Geldoran is no fool either. His job is to guard the gold ports, and I'm sure that's what he's doing, but there's four gold ports and he's likely got fewer 'n a dozen ships."

Timegar turned thoughtful. "We could hole-up here, where we are, 'til the fight's over," he ventured. "After they tangle with Geldoran at Long Harbor, the Mautep 'll likely run back this way— whatever's left o' them— and we could take some o' the leavings."

Landros frowned again. "Ye're assuming that Geldoran's got ships at Long Harbor— and that he'll get the best o' the fight," he said. "Neither of those is certain. If Geldoran's ships are all farther north, the Mautep 'll be able to raid Long Harbor and run back this way with their loot afore word can get to Geldoran by way o' the signal towers. And if there's only a *few* Fleet ships at Long Harbor, the Mautep 'll trounce 'em! And if Geldoran just happens to be there with too many ships for the Mautep to handle, they'll likely try to sneak past and strike Bona Farana instead!

There was a pause while the other two men digested the implications of Landros' assessment, and it was just then that there came the sounds of booted feet and voices in the passage outside, followed by a crisp, loud knock on the cabin door.

Nagaro responded immediately. "Enter!"

The door opened to reveal Tredhold and Taru., both men radiating excitement.

"There's something afoot up the Passage—" Tredhold began.

"Aye!" Taru cut across the Leithian's words. "Something's scaring the fishermen! We saw a few little boats go out when the clouds cleared off— into the channel just north of us. Ye wouldn't think they'd be such fools," he added. "They must ha' seen the ships go by yesterday. I guess there's always a few that'll chance anything in hopes of a catch."

When Taru paused for breath, Tredhold immediately picked up the thread. "They'd scarcely been out a quarter of an hour, when the ones way up the Passage— as far north as we could see with the glass— started heading back in! We thought we saw some bigger sails then too, way up north. Maybe as far as Long Harbor—"

"Right!" Taru cut in. "And then the closer boats started making for shore too. Or heading south. Something's got 'em panicked!"

"We couldn't see a battle," Tredhold finished. "But I can't think what else it could be."

Landros stood up, his face set. "It'll be *in* Long Harbor," he said with calm certainty. "That blind passage is big enough t' hold three sea battles, and ye'd never be able to see any of it from here." He turned to Nagaro. "So, what'll it be, Captain? We'll all do whatever ye decide." He turned back to the other two men. "Isn't that right, mates?"

Timegar simply nodded in response. Moraga muttered, "Ye know we will."

Nagaro sighed. Over time he'd grown used to being the one to decide. He was still called just "Captain", since he had taken no other title. Landros, Timegar, and Moraga were captains too, yet he remained "The Captain", the one who had established the covenant four years ago at Pakoa Harbor, in the common room of the Bay Tree Inn.

"I think," he said carefully. "That we should go up there, as close as we need to get to see what can be seen." He caught Moraga's look. "But I agree with Moraga about one thing," he added. "I won't ask any man to risk his life just to protect the king's gold. That's Geldoran's work, not ours. But there may be lives that can be saved, or a chance to set some slaves free. And if a battle has already begun, we may well get there too late for anything but dealing with the 'leavings,' as Timegar put it."

He drew a breath. "As for *how* we should go, it should be right up the Farano Passage, for the best speed. But we'll keep a sharp lookout and go up the eastern side where we have a chance to hide among the Inner Faranos. Geldoran doesn't know we're his friends, and we don't know what we might meet, so we'll have to be ready for anything. We'll fight if the cause is right, and trust to vigilance and our speed for the rest."

His gaze swept their faces. "What do you say?"

"Aye Captain!" Landros snapped a Fleet salute.

Timegar inclined his head. "I'd say that's good council," he said.

Moraga rose to his feet. "I swore four years ago that I'd follow ye wherever ye led, Capt'n," he said soberly. "An' I ain't goin' back on me word now."

***

In the end it was the weather that frustrated them. There was a brief, brilliant interlude of sunshine just as they set off, but within half an hour of their crossing the Farano Passage and striking north along the farther side of it, the sun was completely obscured again and rain was threatening.

The weather was typical of a spring storm, not violent like the one that had driven them into Omei Bay. The wind, while gusty and changeable, wasn't blowing so hard as to be dangerous, but the rain, when it came, was heavy enough to make it impossible to see very far in front of them. They could perhaps have proceeded very slowly, but the wind was so changeable, and the clouds were so low to the water that, if the rain stopped suddenly, there was danger of the clouds lifting and revealing everything to all eyes.

The prospect of suddenly finding the Mautep fleet a hundred yards in front of them didn't appeal to anyone, so Nagaro decided there was no choice but to get the ships out of the open water of the Farano Channel. They backtracked southward into the narrower channel separating the Inner Farano isles of Obai and Tobai. There they waited at anchor, floating on a rain-spattered gray sea under clouds so low that they formed drifting draperies of mist, intermittently obscuring the green-gray shapes of the islands on either side. The place where they were anchored was familiar to both Nagaro and Taru, since Obai and Tobai were the islands nearest to Taru's former home on Wotana Bay.

While they waited, Nagaro sought news from the local fishermen, some of whom were sheltering in the same channel. Unfortunately, the news was conflicting and of doubtful accuracy. These fishermen hadn't actually seen the warships. They were reporting second- or third-hand news— shouted over the water by badly frightened men. It was clear that ships of both the Edroviran and the Mautep fleets had been seen in the vicinity of Long Harbor, and it was fairly certain that a battle had been joined. It was not at all clear, however, exactly where that battle was, how many ships were involved, and whether it was still going on. Or, if it were over, what the outcome had been.

After an hour of this, the wind settled some. The rain turned to a steadier drizzle, with the clouds lifting enough so that they dared to leave the narrow channel and turn north again.

At first the Farano Passage was a gray expanse of water under a low-hanging leaden blanket of cloud. The shore of Little Farano could be made out dimly on the farther side. Ahead, to the north, sea and sky came together, merging into gray obscurity. There was no sign of any other ship. The wind was out of the west and the clouds were being driven before it. After a time, however, there came some breaks in the clouds, splashing brilliant patches of sunlight onto the green slopes of Little Farano.

A little later, the clouds parted immediately in front of them and radiant light poured down onto the nearby waters of the Passage, wakening hues of deep blue and green, flecked with snowy foam. In contrast, the sea and sky farther up the Passage seemed almost black where the sun didn't penetrate the masses of drifting cloud.

Anything might be lurking in that gloom. Nagaro would rather not have sailed their ships out into the bright patch of light where they would be revealed to anyone watching from that shadow, but the appearance of the sun was so sudden and so close that there was no other choice, short of turning back. So they swept forward out of the misty cloud-shadow and into the sunlight.

All around them, the sea glittered green as the clouds opened directly overhead to make a window filled with sapphire sky and framed by billows of snow. Standing at his place at the forward rail of the stern castle, Nagaro shook the rain out of his hair and laughed aloud in spite of himself. It was moments like this that reminded him of how much he loved being out on the sea in anything with sails.

He surveyed the glorious scene as the clouds continued to drift. More and more of the northern end of the island of Little Farano came into view, and he saw the southernmost of the signal towers visible in the distance. He frowned at that because it meant that anyone in the tower could also see their ships. He hadn't long to think about this, however, because the clouds continued to move, and a long black plume of smoke came into view.

Sindar, aloft in the crow's seat, must have seen it at almost the same instant that Nagaro did. The former captive hadn't yet learned the word for "smoke", but he did his best.

"Fire! Fire cloud! See! There, to port!"

Cries of "Where?" and "Are ye sure?" arose from across the deck, but anyone had only to look to have the answer. The plume was unmistakably smoke— thick and black and fanning out on the wind— not to be confused with any of the billowing masses of cloud. It was also very clearly issuing from the north end of the island of Little Farano.

"It's Long Harbor! They're burning Long Harbor!" The words sprang from a dozen throats.

Nagaro cupped his hands to his mouth. "To the oars. We'll row while we can!"

"Aye, Capt'n!" Taru's shout came from amidships.

The men scrambled for the ladders, and soon the *Sword* surged forward under the power of her oars. *Tiger, North Wind,* and *Sea Eagle* sprouted oars moments later and surged ahead as well.

For a little while, they made good speed, but it couldn't last. The moving clouds soon obscured the smoke plume again, and not long after that, the four ships passed out of sunlight into cloud-shadow. By necessity, they slowed the pace of their oar strokes, and soon the oars had to be pulled in again as rain once more descended.

Cursing their luck, the pirates gingerly edged their way around a point and into an anchorage at the northern tip of Obai. There they dropped their anchors and waited, chafing at the delay, while wild talk spread among the crew concerning the fate of Long Harbor and Geldoran's ships. Had there been any fishing boats about, Nagaro could have questioned their skippers and perhaps have gotten some reliable news. The local fishermen must have been frightened off by the nearby battle, however, and the crews of the four pirate vessels were left to their speculations.

To their immense frustration, it was nearly two hours before the weather improved enough for the ships to proceed. Even then, they had to go cautiously because the drifting clouds were so low that the tops of their masts and sails were intermittently obscured by shrouds of mist.

Once back around the northern tip of Obai, they struck out into open water, seeking to cross the Passage and pick up the shore of Little Farano. The sea faded to gray about a hundred yards from the ships in all directions. Accordingly, the four ships moved forward at a painfully slow pace, keeping close together to avoid losing one another in the fog.

To make matters worse, the afternoon was now waning. Above the clouds, the sun was sinking westward. Its light would have been diminishing even without any clouds to block its rays. So it was that everyone's spirits lifted when, at last, the clouds began to open to the west over Little Farano, and the slanting rays of the westering sun lanced across the waters of the Farano Passage. A little at a time, over a matter of minutes, the channel ahead was revealed to them.

Then, all of a sudden, as the shadow retreated, there were ships.

"Sail! Ship! Five ship ahead!" Sindar's cry rang out from the crow's seat, even as other voices were raised by crewmen on the deck, making the same observation.

The ships were perhaps a quarter mile distant. They were one point to starboard and bearing directly down upon the little pirate fleet. Nagaro hastily raised his spyglass to confirm what he thought his eyes had told him. The banners of the five ships bore Edrvir's white hawk on a field of blue.

"They're Geldoran's!" he cried, and his brows knit in a frown. It was a relief to find that the ships were not Mautep craft— so close at hand and revealed so suddenly— but Nagaro was not at all sure what to expect from them. He had made a habit of staying out of the way of ships of the Royal Fleet. There was no way that Kuran could have communicated the results of his meeting with Nagaro to Geldoran, and the warriors aboard these craft had surely identified his banners as quickly as he had identified theirs.

Pavo Maat, looked up from the main deck below. He raised his voice to call out, "What we should do, Captain?"

"Hold steady!" Nagaro called back. "See what they do."

They had not long to wait. Nagaro heard the shouts of men borne over the water, though he couldn't make out the words. Then the five ships sprouted oars, and Nagaro read their intent all too clearly in the rapid cadence of their oar strokes.

The Fleet ships were going for ramming speed.

Cupping his hands to his mouth, Nagaro shouted: "Hard turn to port. Pivot on the oars! Make for the south Obai channel!" Snatching up the speaking trumpet from the place where it was secured under the rail, he shouted more orders across the water to the *North Wind*, immediately to stern, knowing that Landros would pass the word to the *Tiger* and *Sea Eagle* in turn.

There were shouts and thudding feet as men scrambled to their appointed tasks. Within a minute, the *Sword of Freedom* was making a tight turn, her port oars dragging the water while her starboard oars reached and pulled in unison. One after the other, the four ships turned to port, , pivoting on their oars, to finish in a tight grouping with the *Sword* in the lead.

The race then began in earnest.

Even as the pirate craft had turned, the pursuing ships had narrowed the intervening gap alarmingly. Nagaro's little fleet now made use of its speed— and needed it.

There followed a very tense half hour, but by the time the four pirate ships turned eastward into the channel at the south end of the isle of Obai, the Fleet vessels had fallen well to stern and were fading into the gloom. Nevertheless, Nagaro gave orders to sail right through the channel and turn north along the eastern shore of Obai without slowing to see whether they were still being followed.

Only when they had reached the secluded anchorage known as Otter Cove, partway up Obai's eastern shore, did he at last call for a halt. They were clearly no longer being pursued. Dusk was falling in any case, and it would soon be too dark to sail— at least until Talebra rose, and that wouldn't be until nearly midnight.

***

The following morning dawned bright and clear, the storm having completely passed. While the ships' cooks were making breakfast, the four captains gathered for counsel in Nagaro's cabin aboard the *Sword* as the ship rode easily at anchor in the little cove.

The night had been uneventful and, with the coming of the morning light, Nagaro and Taru had gone ashore and made inquiries among the fishermen who dwelt in the huts that ringed the cove. They had learned enough to piece together the previous day's events involving the confrontation between the Mautep and the ships of the Royal Fleet.

The Mautep had apparently sailed into Long Harbor in the morning and found it unguarded. They had, however, also found that there was little gold to be carried off because the first spring shipment had already gone out, and this discovery had put the sea raiders very much out of temper. The Mautep had set about plundering the town instead, but before they had time to wreak very much havoc, five of Geldoran's ships had appeared in response to messages sent out by way of the signal towers. A battle had ensued— partly at sea and partly on shore— that would have likely gone badly for the Edrovirans if Geldoran himself hadn't arrived with the other ships under his command.

The Mautep had then managed to gather themselves together and flee, though not before setting fire to some of the buildings along the water front out of spite. One of the buildings, used for storing grain, had gone up like a torch, and it was presumably the smoke from this fire that the pirates had seen as their little fleet had come up the Farano Passage in the middle of the afternoon.

From what the fishermen knew, the fleeing Mautep had sailed down the Farano Passage and passed through the south Obai channel round midday, turning southward into the Great Channel. The Mahuk craft must have been sailing south down the western shore of Obai while Nagaro and his men were sheltering at the island's northern tip, so that the two fleets had missed each other completely. By the time the pirates had later fled south and passed into the Great Channel through the same escape passage the Mahuk ships had used, the enemy ships had been somewhere to the south and out of sight in the fog.

Nagaro told this tale to the other three captains and then sat with his elbows on the table and his head in his hands while the other men's talk flowed around him. He was feeling rather chagrined. It seemed that his choices had been proving ill of late. They were more than three weeks out of Pakoa without freeing a single slave. They had come a long way north only to be run off by Geldoran, and on top of everything else, they had arrived too late to be of any assistance.

Moraga, predictably, was fuming. He' had been angry when they had dropped anchor the previous evening, and the night hadn't improved his temper.

"It's fine gratitude, for ye!" he ranted. "Tryin' t' ram us after we chased those Mautep all the way up from the Lomoas!"

Nagaro raised his head. "They had no way of knowing how we came to be there," he pointed out, wearily. "Or why. And we *are* called pirates, you will recall."

Timegar rubbed his narrow beard. "It's likely they thought we had come t' see if the Mautep had left any loot behind."

Landros nodded soberly. "I'll warrant they would have been more friendly if we'd come in the midst o' the battle and brought our swords to their aid," he observed.

"Very probably." Nagaro tried to put more conviction into the words than he felt. He was more stung by Geldoran's reception than he was willing to openly admit. It hadn't troubled him to confess to Kuran that he practiced piracy, or to endure the Lord of the Fleet's pointed questions. At least the man had listened to his explanations— even seemed to accept them. But to be chased off by Geldoran's ships like a band of sea raiders— when they'd never done anything to harm the interests of Edrvir— was a hard thing to bear.

Nagaro heaved a sigh. "It's clear that we've done as much as we can in the Faranos. Geldoran has fought off the Mautep fleet, and I suppose he has matters in hand. It's time we headed south— back to our own back garden."

"I'm with ye there!" Moraga was emphatic.

"Well, aye," Landros put in. "That Mautep fleet is headed south again, anyway—" He stopped, cocking an ear. "What are they shouting about out on deck?"

All four men paused to listen to the rising jumble of sound, but it was impossible to make out words, until Sindar's voice rose momentarily above the rest, crying, "So-moke! *So-moke!*"

"Smoke?" Timegar wondered aloud. "Sindar's learned a new word since yesterday, and he's showing it off, I reckon. He can't really have seen more smoke—"

Nagaro frowned. "I don't think he would do that. He takes the lookout task too seriously."

The four men exchanged glances. Then, as one, they were out of their seats and making for the door. In the passageway, they collided with Taru, coming the other way.

The young Turo was breathless with excitement. "Sindar's spotted more smoke! Ye can just make it out t' the south! South by southeast, above the headland!"

The captains crowded past him without waiting to hear more.

On the deck, the men were all crowding the rails and craning their necks. Some were even climbing the rigging. Nagaro bounded up the ladder leading to the stern castle deck and shouldered his way through a group of crewmen to get a place at the port rail, facing south. Even from this vantage point, the highest on the ship except for the masts and rigging, the southern arm of land that encircled the cove prevented him from seeing the water of the Great Channel in that direction. But the smoke could be plainly seen above the crest of the headland. The plume was more gray than black this time, and broader, though it was more distant. It rose in the air to a considerable height before spreading and fanning out to the east.

Taru had come up the ladder with the other three captains behind him, and they were all standing at the rail, shading their eyes. Nagaro turned to look up at the crow's seat where Sindar still stood, pointing triumphantly at the smoke plume. Nagaro cupped his hands to his mouth.

"Where is the fire, Sindar?" he called. "Can you see?"

Sindar shouted back immediately. "On land! Not sea. Not island. On big land!"

Nagaro felt a sinking sensation in the pit of his stomach. His mouth had suddenly gone very dry. Landros dropped his hand from his eyes and his glance met Nagaro's.

They spoke their thought in unison:

"Lankura!"

A babble of voices erupted, then, but Nagaro stood frozen, a stream of thoughts pouring through his mind.

Lankura... He had been seventeen, his will enslaved... his words and actions not his own. He'd been the object of ridicule, a laughing stock... trotted about the court, paraded through the streets... surrounded by laughter, jibes, mockery. The idiot prince... the Princess Nevien's pathetic, simple-minded husband. And there had seemed to be no way out. He had wanted only to die...

Caught in that overwhelming flood, he was only distantly aware of the voices around him.

"Is it the same lot that Geldoran ran out o' Long Harbor, d' ye think?" *That was Moraga.*

Landros' voice answered: "I'll wager it is. Geldoran spoiled their fun, and they got no gold, so they went looking for easier pickings—"

"Lankura's not easy." *That was Timegar.*

"Not the city, but maybe the palace—" *Landros again.* "That's the weak spot. When it was built, in Darion's day, no one looked for trouble from the sea."

"Maybe we should go to help—"

"An' get run off again?"

"What do ye think, Captain?"

Nagaro was staring, unseeing. *Lankura... He had all but sworn that he would never go back there. The things he had endured in that place...*

He shuddered, trying to push the thoughts back down into the depths from which they had arisen. Lankura held painful memories, yes— quite possibly danger for him, as well. Still, Kuran Kel hadn't recognized him... and that place might also hold some answers...

With an effort, he dragged his mind back to the stern castle deck, where the men were waiting for his answer. Landros, the last man who had spoken, was looking at him keenly, expectantly.

Nagaro focused on the question: What should they do? Sail on by, pretending that an attack on Edrovir's capital was no concern of theirs? That was a coward's course. Go back into the Farano Passage and try to alert Geldoran? If yesterday was any indication, that would be folly. He ran a hand through his hair. There really was only one choice.

He heard himself say, "We should go see if we are needed. See if there's anything we can do." He became aware of Moraga's frowning look. "We were going to head south in any case, Moraga," he pointed out. "If there are no Fleet ships at Lankura, there will be no one to run us off. And if there *are* Fleet ships there, they'll be Kuran's."

Moraga suddenly grinned. "Ye're right, Capt'n!"

Nagaro turned to Landros. "How long do you think it will take us to get there?"

Landros considered. "There's not much wind yet, but it'll likely rise as the sun gets higher. Now that it's finally clear, I'd say maybe two hours. Less if we row hard."

So, what else could they do? Nagaro turned to address the other men, raising his voice and hoping it sounded steadier than he felt.

"See to your breakfasts, men, and make ready to sail. As soon as the cooks have banked their fires, we'll weigh anchor and make for Lankura. Once we get there and see how things stand, we'll know what we must do." He paused, drawing breath. "And if we do go ashore to fight, it won't be for Lord Kuran, or for gold, or even for men's freedom. It will be for Edrvir!"

His eyes swept the ring of eager, resolute faces, and he felt a sudden surge of pride in these men who sailed with him. "What do you say, men?" he cried. "Are you willing? Shall we see if we can show them that we're men of Edrvir, even if they call us pirates?"

All around, the voices rose in chorus.

"Aye, Capt'n! We're with ye!"

Moraga was grinning broadly now. "Aye, mate! We didn't chase that pack o' dogs all this way for nothing! I say we show 'em a bit o' steel for all the trouble they've put us to!"

Nagaro stood watching as the men scattered to attend to their duties. Their cries echoed in his ears, and he wondered what he had just done.

Landros and Timegar saluted him smartly and made for the ladder to the deck below. They had their own ships to see to. As they moved away, Taru approached wearing a worried look.

"I hope ye know what ye're doing, Nagaro," he said, keeping his voice low. "Have ye thought o' the danger?"

Nagaro swallowed. "Of course I have," he said. "But it's been seven years, Taru. It's likely no one will even remember what I looked like then, and I've changed a lot." He was confident of his disguise: the bound hair, the beard, the kuma stain. That, and the effects of the passage of time... *and most of all, the absence of the effects of heskial.*

"Aye, ye have changed a lot at that," Taru said, though he sounded only half convinced. "I hope ye're right," he added with a shake of his head. Then he smiled guiltily, and raised his hand in a salute. "Most likely ye are," he said. "And I'd best see that everything's shipshape on the oar deck."

As Taru went down the ladder, Nagaro noticed Tredhold for the first time, standing a little distance away at the port rail, watching him. The healer must have been among the crowd and had lagged behind on purpose. Tredhold knew that Nagaro had suffered in some way, though he didn't know the details, and Nagaro had once confided to the healer his reluctance to go to Lankura.

Now the sandy-haired Leithian raised an eyebrow as their eyes met, but he said nothing. Then he gave Nagaro a quick smile of encouragement and punched the air in a gesture of support before turning to follow Taru, leaving Nagaro alone with the tangle of his thoughts.

Half an hour later, the four ships had slipped out of Otter Cove and turned into the Great Channel on a southeast heading. Dead ahead, the smoke was still rising and spreading ominously on the morning air. Presently, the oars were brought out and began to rise and fall to the steady beat of the oar deck drums.

Nagaro stood on the captain's platform at the stern castle rail, his eyes fixed on the pillar of smoke, his face set in determined lines. He'd already had his spyglass to his eye and had scoured the view for ships, both ahead and astern. He had seen two merchant craft a considerable distance to the north, astern of them. There were also a number of distant sails dotting the channel, a long way off to the south. They were most likely merchant ships as well, though too far away to be sure.

Nowhere was there any sign of the Mautep fleet that they'd been following, nor of the ships commanded by Kuran Kell.

As he stood watching the source of the smoke grow ever nearer, Nagaro felt, more than heard, Pavo Maat come to stand at his side.

"So you will go back again to Lankura, Nagaro?" The big Hashtep asked quietly. "To place where those bad man hurt you so much? Are you afraid?"

Nagaro glanced at his friend. "Yes, a little," he confessed, then quickly added, "But it was seven years ago. You probably have more to fear than I do if you go ashore to fight. The folk of Lankura don't know a Hashtep from a Mautep. There will be men there who will look at your face and think they see an enemy. Are *you* afraid, Pavo?"

But Pavo shook his great head. "I will be with you."

Nagaro winced. Pavo's unswerving confidence in him was often unnerving. "That may not help very much, since men may look at me and see a pirate," he pointed out ruefully. "You don't have to go ashore, Pavo. We'll need some men to stay aboard the ships."

Again Pavo shook his head. "I will go where you go," he declared unperturbedly.

Nagaro sighed. "At least promise me that you'll explain the danger to the other Hashtep."

This time Pavo nodded. "Oh yes. I will explain. Most will stay on ship. But I will go where you go. I want to walk in place where Nevrath have walked with Minowei. I want to see palace built by great King Darion. Do you mean to sail up River Edro?"

Nagaro frowned. He had all but forgotten Pavo's fascination with the old tale of Edrvir's beginnings. "We probably won't sail up the river," he said. "The river's mouth is the harbor for Lankura, and I think it's likely the Mautep fleet will be there. I was hoping to go ashore at the little cove that lies just to the north of Castle Rock."

Pavo's brow wrinkled. "I do not know place," he said. "Where is Castle Rock?"

"There's a small cape that sticks out into the sea just north of the river's mouth," Nagaro explained. "And Castle Rock makes the tip of it. The cove is just on the north side of the cape."

"Oh." Pavo nodded. "Where is city of Lankura? And palace?"

"The city is on the river's north shore, filling the space between the river and a low mountain called Kel Lankura. The palace and its gardens are on the cape. The palace is on the southern side of it— the flatter part of the cape beside the river. The garden is on the north side, which rises into a long hill that runs from Kel Lankura to Castle Rock."

Pavo nodded again. "Is there wall around it?"

"Yes. Except where the wall joins Castle Rock. Castle Rock is as good as a wall. There's a wall around the city too. There's a stretch of wall about a hundred yards long, where they come together, that has city on one side and palace grounds on the other."

Pavo's brow furrowed with the effort of visualizing what Nagaro had described. "Then if we anchor in cove," he ventured at length, "what we must do is go over wall of palace garden?"

Nagaro smiled faintly. "That's right," he said. "That's believed to be how Angkat's men got into the palace when they raided it seven years ago."

"That is also when you got away from palace?"

Nagaro's smile died. "Yes," he said. "But I don't remember anything about it. Not the raid... or... how I got away." He turned his gaze back to the sea before them.

Several seconds passed before Pavo spoke again. "Do you not think," he asked, "that king will have made it more hard to get in?"

Nagaro was grateful for the change of subject. "I expect so," he said seriously. "That's why I hope the Mautep won't have tried the cove. Also the cove isn't big enough for eight ships. I hope we can find defenders on the wall to help us. Assuming they see us as friends... I hope we can surprise the Mautep by doing what they think can't be done."

Pavo regarded him with his narrow dark eyes. "I think this is good plan," he said. Then, after a pause, he reached out and put his large brown hand on Nagaro's shoulder. "Do not worry, Nagaro," he said calmly. "It is sure that Sheptuum guide your feet. You have not come so far, and done so many thing, only to die at Lankura." The big Hashtep flashed him a sudden, bright smile of trust and encouragement as he withdrew his hand. Then he turned and strode off in the direction of the ladder that led to the main deck.

Nagaro closed his eyes. It must, he thought, be tremendously comforting to have faith that there were benign powers that moved the world. But dying was not what he was most afraid of. He sighed as he opened his eyes and picked up his spyglass. The smoke was nearer, and still rising. Through the glass, he could make out the cape he had spoken of, and Castle Rock. There weren't any ships visible anywhere along that distant stretch of shore.

So far, it appeared that Lokundas smiled. But then, it was said that when Lokundas smiled, it meant that the Turner of Worlds was laughing.

Chapter 10

The Back Gate

"Well, if the Mautep went over that wall to get into the palace seven years ago, ye can see why they didn't try it *this* time!"

That was Timegar's succinct assessment. And as Nagaro gazed up at the wall that enclosed the palace grounds, he could only agree.

He was crouching with the other three captains, along with Taru, Tredhold, and several other men, in the concealment of a large clump of bushes near the top of the steep slope that rose from the shore to the foot of the wall. It was quite clear where the older, more weathered stonework of the wall ended and a four-foot-high course of newer masonry had been added to the top. The original wall had been about eight feet high. The augmented version was close to twelve.

Just as Nagaro had described it to Pavo, the wall ran along a crest of high ground that connected the mountain of Kel Lankura, whose summit lay some distance away on their left, to Castle Rock which was somewhat less far away to their right. The ridge bearing the wall dipped to its lowest point immediately above them, but that didn't help much.

Nagaro turned to peer over the bushes at the cove below, where the four ships lay at anchor with furled sails. Most of the men were gathered near the ships on the shore beside the mouth of a stream that cascaded down from the heights of Kel Lankura. Beyond the stream lay the edge of a dense forest— a forest that stretched uninterrupted all the way to Wotana, twenty miles to the north.

Seven years ago, Taru had found him lying, unconscious, nameless, where that forest met the shore of Wotana Bay...

Nagaro shook himself free of the useless thought. He had dared to hope that coming to this place might evoke some memories that had eluded him, but so far that hadn't happened. The place— with the wall, the cove, and the forest— was very much as he'd *imagined* it would be, but still he had no memory of it.

And right now, there were more important matters to attend to. A hundred and twenty men waited below, armed and ready. Amazingly, they were prepared to follow him into a fight for the defense of Edrovir. Some of his followers, including most of the Hashtep, had volunteered to stay with the ships and longboats, to guard them, but it had been necessary for each of the captains to choose a few men to complete the number needed for that duty.

One of those reluctant men had been Sindar. The young Kelorin had been visibly disappointed when Nagaro had told him to stay behind. The former captive had already learned some swordsmanship. In fact, he displayed considerable talent for it, but Nagaro had judged him not ready for what could be the most serious battle any of them had ever faced.

"The lads *could* get over it, mind ye," Moraga offered. "Given a couple o' hours, t' splice a few ladders together and get the whole lot of us over a bit at a time... But yer battle'd likely be over afore we was all on the other side."

Nagaro turned back to gaze up at the wall and sighed. Moraga could always be counted on to see the difficulties in a situation. The bit about splicing together rope ladders was as close as the man had ever come to making a positive suggestion.

"I don't think it would take very long to do the splicing," he ventured. "But we have only enough rope ladders to make about two of the length we would need. That would be one to go up the outside and another to go down on the inside. I'm not sure how long it would take to get a hundred and twenty men over that, one at a time." He frowned. "It might be better to sail around to the river mouth, but that will take time as well. And we'd lose the advantage of surprise."

"Where do ye suppose the guards have got to?" Taru wondered aloud.

"Gone to the fight, I'll wager," was Landros' prompt response. "It's not a good sign either. Well-trained men don't go leaving their posts unless they're needed badly elsewhere."

Nagaro chewed his lip. There were several watchtowers spaced along the wall. One of them was scarcely a dozen yards to their left. The fact that they hadn't been hailed was a pretty clear indication that the towers were unmanned, since both the ships and the men standing on the shore were plainly visible. He could almost hear Lokundas laughing. And he was also afraid that things were going badly for the defenders.

Although he and his men couldn't see the palace, nor any part of the city, from where they lay hidden, the smoke was still very much in evidence. It wasn't rising so thickly now, but it had spread out widely in the upper air and hung above them like a pall, dimming the sunlight. They could smell it too, and they could hear shouting, and other sounds that suggested battle, coming from the direction of the city.

Nagaro frowned. "There must be another way," he murmured. "Something quicker. Something *easier…*"

He stared at the wall.

The popular tales had it that the Mautep sea raiders had gained access to the palace by going over this wall on that fateful night seven years ago. But when he thought about it, there seemed to be something wrong with the idea.

On that night, several ship-loads of Angkat's warriors had made a lightning quick raid on the palace and succeeded in taking quite a number of hostages— highborn men and women— whom they had ransomed for a considerable quantity of gold. Somehow the Mautep had gotten the hostages back to their ships. Had they really taken their captives over this wall? Even if it were four feet lower, it wouldn't be an easy climb for women in skirts.

Nagaro's frown deepened. *If only he could remember…*

As far as he knew, he had somehow made his escape from the palace during the attack— from the palace where he had been held for months under the sway of the will-enslaving drug, heskial. Had he been among the hostages?

Had he come over this wall, and once on the outside, broken free and made a run for the forest? It seemed possible, even probable, though it didn't explain how he had avoided perishing from the effects of heskial withdrawal…

Nagaro jerked his mind back to the problem at hand and swept his eyes over the entire scene once more. From this vantage point, on the outside in broad daylight, the place seemed entirely unfamiliar. He closed his eyes, trying to picture the scene at night… *lit by the light of Talebra's disk and seen from inside the wall…*

His eyes snapped open.

"*There!*" he said, pointing. "Where the wall meets Castle Rock. There must be a way up from this side."

He stopped speaking and found that the other men were staring at him. Taru looked as if he were seeing a ghost.

"Now how do ye know that?" Landros asked, voicing what the other men were surely thinking. His tone wasn't accusing, merely curious.

"I don't," Nagaro said quickly and quite truthfully. What had come to him in a flash hadn't been memory, but insight— an insight of such convincing plausibility that it carried the force of certainty. "But don't you see?" he went on, taking refuge in logical argument. "They took some of the queen's women. Those women could never have gotten over an eight-foot wall. Castle Rock may be steep, but not as steep as a wall."

The truth was that he knew for a fact that there was a path leading up onto Castle Rock on the inside. He had seen it many times, though he'd never climbed it and didn't know where it led…

At least he didn't think he'd ever climbed it...

All eyes except Taru's had turned towards Castle Rock.

"*We-ll*," Moraga drawled. "I suppose it don't do no harm t' look."

"Aye, lads. Come on then!" Timegar rose and moved off through the bushes in the direction of the rock. The other men followed.

Nagaro trailed after them, frowning. Taru nudged his shoulder. "Did ye remember something?" he hissed.

Nagaro sighed. "Nothing new," he said. "There *is* a path leading up on the inside. The rest just seems... obvious..." His words trailed. The other men had already arrived at the rock face and were examining the part nearest the wall. Moraga and Tredhold were even trying to climb the rough, steep surface, with limited success.

Nagaro was studying the rock with narrowed eyes. "They're not looking in the right place," he murmured. "Do you see that line? That starts way up *there?*" He pointed towards the crest of the rock. "See how it runs all the way down, to over *there*... almost to the shore..."

Taru stared at him, wide eyed. "Don't *do* that, Nagaro," he said. "Ye give me shivers!"

"Do what?" Nagaro asked vaguely. "It looks like the edge of a crack, that's all. Like the crack I use to get up and down to my 'stone seat' on the rocks near our house on Pakoa. Come on!" he added, and strode off down the slope towards the bottom end of the line he had just pointed to. Taru followed, leaving the rest of the men poking about other parts of the rock's base, or trying to climb its weathered face.

Moments later, he and Taru were standing very nearly in the sea, looking up a narrow, irregular gash in the rock. It was half a crude ramp, half a natural stair, and it ran all the way up and disappeared over the crest of the rock, high above their heads.

Taru shook his head. "*Hamanei mata noa*," he breathed. "*Please* say that ye remember this, Nagaro. Otherwise I'm starting t' believe that the Spirits are *telling* ye things!"

Nagaro laughed outright at the expression on his friend's face. "Neither the one nor the other," he said. "It just made sense that there ought to be a way up. Now, I'm going to go up there and have a look."

"Not alone, ye're not," muttered Taru. "Lead on. I'll be right behind ye."

The bottom of the crack was the hardest. The way became wider and less steep as it curved up over the top. At the last minute, it took a sharp bend to the left. Nagaro slowed his steps out of caution as he approached the turn and peered around it. Hastily, he ducked back behind the shoulder of the rock. He turned, and spoke in answer to Taru's questioning look.

"There's a big wooden gate that's blocking the way," he explained, frowning. "It must be four feet wide and eight feet tall, and it's about a dozen paces past the turning."

Taru actually grinned. "Oh well," he said brightly. "That's nothing a man with a rope and a grapple can't get over! And once one man is over, it's up with the bar and the fox is in with the chickens!"

Nagaro continued to frown. "There's also a guardhouse, up at the level of the top of the gate. It's made to look almost like the rest of the rock, but I saw the roof beams sticking out and a narrow window. I didn't see any guard though."

Taru waved this aside with a dismissive gesture. "It'll be empty like all the rest, I expect. The guard will ha' gone t' the fight."

Nagaro nodded, still frowning. "Probably," he said. "And one way or another, I think we'll get in. Let's go down and get some grapples and the rest of the men."

***

Ten minutes later, Nagaro was approaching the bend in the narrow path for the second time. He had a grappling hook and a coil of rope slung over his shoulder, and there were a hundred and twenty men behind him climbing up the crack, one or two abreast as the width of the path would allow. Several of them carried ropes and grappling hooks as well.

This time Nagaro stepped boldly around the corner— and got four paces before a voice brought him to a dead stop.

"*Halt in the name o' King Elgurn!* Who are ye, and what are ye doing in this place?"

The speaker was trying to sound bold and confident, but the voice had a youthful pitch and a noticeable quaver.

Nagaro raised his eyes to the guardhouse window, a long horizontal slot about eight inches high. It had been empty when he rounded the bend in the path, but now he found himself staring at the sharp end of crossbow bolt, pointed straight at his chest. The face behind the crossbow, what he could see of it, was pale and framed by dark hair.

Nagaro carefully spread his hands, hoping the guardsman wouldn't shoot out of sheer nervousness. "I'm Captain Nagaro," he said in a steady voice. "I've brought some men. We saw the smoke and came to see if we could help."

The crossbow wavered. Its aim shifted a little lower, but not enough to remove the risk to Nagaro's person. A bit more of the guardsman's face came into view.

"*Captain Nagaro?*" The voice was now frankly incredulous. "Captain Nagaro, the pirate? The one that sails up and down the coast, killing Mahuk and stealing back our gold?"

Nagaro winced inwardly. "Well, sometimes," he admitted. "Mostly what we do is free galley slaves—"

Abruptly, Landros stepped up beside Nagaro, shading his eyes with his hand as he squinted up at the guardhouse window. "Delvin!" he cried jovially. "By the Eyes! Is that you, lad? How's your father, and that brother o' yours? Still both alive, I hope?"

"*Uncle Landros?*" The crossbow abruptly vanished, fully revealing the face of the beardless Kelorin youth who had been wielding it. "What are ye doing here?"

Landros smiled broadly. "Following this man," he declared, clapping Nagaro on the back. "Best captain I ever had! Now are ye going to let us in, or aren't ye?"

"Of course! Right away!" The young man's face instantly disappeared from the window and they heard boots on wooden stairs.

Nagaro turned to the grizzled sea warrior beside him. "*Uncle Landros?*" he inquired with a raised eyebrow. "Is he really your nephew?"

Landros dismissed the question with a wave of his hand. "Just the son of an old friend from my days in the Fleet," he explained. "I've got quite a few old friends, though, and a fair number o' them have sons. Some are in the City Guard or the Palace Guard. I thought I might meet one before this day was over, but I have to say that this was a rare bit o' luck."

There was a clank and a creak, and the gate swung slowly open. Delvin stared wide-eyed at them as the long line of pirates began to file through. Nagaro inclined his head soberly to the young man as he stepped past. He couldn't help noticing that the youth appeared to be on the young side of eighteen.

There was a small staging area just on the other side of the gate, apparently cut out of the rock. The men were too many to all fit within that limited space however. Some pushed their way through the open door at the bottom of the guard tower and began to fill its lower room as well. When no more could fit there, the rest moved a little way down a path and the stairs that led from the tower to the top of the wall.

While the men were taking their positions, Landros and Nagaro began questioning Delvin regarding the Mautep attack. It turned out that the youth could give them very few details. He had been on duty in the guard tower since sunset the previous evening, an hour before the attack began. He could tell them definitely that the Mautep had come at the hour when most folk were at their dinners.

The palace must have been assaulted from the river side, since the guardsmen on the rear wall had seen nothing at first. They had eventually heard shouts and a commotion, however, and their commander had sent two men to investigate. One of these had returned with the news that a large force of Mahuk sea raiders had overrun all or part of the palace.

"Is that when all the other guardsmen left the wall?" Nagaro asked when Delvin got to this point in his story. "To help with the fight?"

Delvin looked vaguely worried. "Captain Worling took most o' the men away to the fight before dawn, Zirda," he replied. "But I thought he left a few, like me, to watch. Didn't anyone hale ye from the wall?"

Landros shot Nagaro a look and gave a slight shake of his head. "Perhaps those in the nearest towers have gone, lad," he said lightly. "But if ye were told to stay, ye did right to stay."

Delvin looked relieved. "Captain Worling told me to stay and guard the gate," he said earnestly. "He took Oran, that was here with me, but he told me to stay 'til I was relieved, or slain, or the palace burned down. That's not going t' happen is it, Uncle Landros? I wouldn't want to have to tell folk that I stayed here and just did nothing while the palace got burned."

Landros confidently shook his head. "Not a chance, lad," he said. "Can ye tell us anything about how the fight's been going?"

Delvin looked uncertain. "There's been some loud shouting, several times, from over by the Common Wall. That's the bit that's part o' the city wall, Zirda," he added, addressing Nagaro. "I thought maybe the men o' the City Guard were trying to take back the palace."

Landros nodded. "That sounds likely."

Nagaro frowned. "If the Mautep took control of the palace," he said, "why haven't they gone back to their ships with their hostages to ask for ransom? Why would they stay and let the City Garrison attack them? Something must have gone wrong for them. Maybe they don't hold the entire palace. Or they're cut off from their ships."

Landros frowned in his turn. "I think ye've got something there, Captain," he said. "But it looks like we'll have to go in t' find out."

Nagaro turned to Delvin. "Will you come with us?" he asked. "To help us find our way?"

Delvin looked startled. "Captain Worling told me to stay—"

"—'til ye were relieved," Landros finished for him. "And that's just what's happening. We'll leave two or three men here to keep watch. But Nagaro is right. We don't know our way around the palace. We need ye, lad."

Delvin's brows knit together in a frown, but he nodded. "Well... all right then."

Nagaro murmured his thanks to the young man. He was relieved by the young Kelorin's willingness, since it solved an awkward problem for him. The truth was that he probably knew parts of the palace better than

Delvin did, but he couldn't let anyone know that. He turned to address the men.

"Friends, this is it," he said, speaking loudly enough for his voice to carry to all ears. "This time it seems that we're not too late, and I expect we'll be going into a real fight— worse than anything we've seen before. This is going beyond the covenant, and if there's any man who wants to turn back now, I'll not think any the less of him."

There was dead silence from the group of men that lasted for several heartbeats. Then someone towards the back spoke up. "Lead on, Capt'n. We're with ye!" The cry was immediately echoed on every side.

Nagaro heaved a mental sigh. These men were determined to follow him. He raised his voice again. "I need two or three volunteers to stand watch here at this guard tower."

Again there was silence, and this time it stretched. He sought out the face of Chaheel, one of two Hashtep in the group. He found him, as usual, next to Nanu. "Chaheel," he said gravely, "You know there's an extra risk here for you."

But Chaheel shook his head. "I am go with you," he declared flatly.

Nagaro sought again. "Pavo?"

The big Hashtep met his gaze unflinchingly. "I will go where you go. I have already said it."

"Anyone?"

More silence.

"All right, then." Nagaro pointed to the three men standing closest to him. "Kunoa, Haruda, and Tomo, you will stay. The rest, follow me."

As he strode to the top of the path that led downwards, Pavo Maat stepped to his side. Nagaro noticed as he passed Delvin that the young guardsman was staring at Pavo in astonishment. Evidently the youth hadn't noticed at first that there were Hashtep among Nagaro's followers. Nagaro saw Landros bend close to the young Kelorin's ear and caught part of the older man's muttered words. "...*used t' be a slave. What they call Hashtep. Not the same as the warrior class that comes raiding our coast...*"

Nagaro strode on at the head of his men, following the path that zigzagged in three switchbacks down the inner face of Castle Rock, ending in a grove of birches at the bottom. This path, he noted, had clearly been cut from the rock by men. As he went, it occurred to him to wonder again whether he had been marched up this path on that night seven years ago. He resisted the urge to stop and turn around to look back up the path. Once he reached the bottom, he stopped to wait for the men to assemble in the little grove of trees.

There, turning to watch the men's descent, he caught his breath. In a flash, there came into his mind an image of the rock and the path, bathed in moonlight, with a line of armed Mautep and their prisoners— men and women— marching upward. The image was gone as quickly as it had come, however, and he had no chance to try to recover it, for he knew that he needed to give his attention to what they should do next.

The palace loomed at a distance across the garden. The building was an impressive sight, being faced with snow-white marble, elegantly highlighted with courses of green and black stone. There were wisps of smoke issuing from it in several places, all at the farther end, closest to the city.

Taru, standing beside Nagaro and seeing the building for the first time, gave a low whistle. Pavo Maat stood silently drinking in the sight, aware that he was looking upon a building that had been built for Darion the Great, the first king of a united Edrovir.

The palace was quite large, standing three stories high, with a number of wings and several little turret-like towers rising from various points. It was the royal residence, but only a portion of the third floor was given over to the living quarters of the royal family. The larger function of the building had always been to serve as a complete seat of government. There was the king's Audience Chamber, the Great Hall, and the royal kitchens of course. And there were also meeting rooms of various sorts, offices, record-keeping rooms, and the like. There was even an entire wing made up of guest quarters for visiting lords and their families.

Nagaro was intimately, indeed painfully, familiar with some parts of the palace, while there were other parts into which he had never been permitted to venture. Now, of course, he had to feign complete ignorance of all of it.

Delvin, on the other hand, was eager to show off his knowledge. "Most o' this side, facing the garden, is taken up by the Great Hall," the youth told them. "It's past that kind o' three-sided courtyard ye can see over there. There's three or four big doors going into the Hall from there, but we'd never get in that way without anyone seeing us. The Guard's quarters are down at the other end, across from the stable— that low building there. Ye can make out the roof of it over the trees. Ye don't suppose there 'd be any help from the rest o' the Guard, do ye?" he added hopefully.

Landros coughed. "I don't think so, lad," he said gently. "They'd have been called out, first thing. I reckon they'll have been in the thick o' the fighting."

"What about this end of the building?" Nagaro asked quickly, before Delvin had time to think about the implications of Landros' words.

The youth frowned. "Well, on the ground floor it's the kitchens on this side. And I think the other side's the bath house for the guests."

Nagaro looked to Landros. "Is there any reason why we shouldn't try the kitchen?"

Landros shook his head. "Can't think of any," he said. "It's the closest, and that makes it the best, really. There *is* a separate door going in, Delvin, isn't there?"

Delvin nodded. "Oh, aye. Right off o' the kitchen garden."

They crossed the palace gardens as quickly as they could, Nagaro pressing for speed. He knew how clearly visible the garden was from the second and third floor windows. A hundred and twenty men couldn't exactly hide themselves by skulking among the bushes. So if anyone was watching from those windows, the pirates would lose the element of surprise, but there was no help for that.

Nagaro knew every inch of the garden, since the princess had been very fond of it and had often taken him out walking there. It wasn't easy to give the appearance that Delvin was leading, but he hoped he managed it.

When they reached the kitchen garden, they found the door into the scullery standing open, which made both Landros and Nagaro uneasy. Inside, both the scullery and the kitchen beyond it were dark and appeared deserted. The kitchen room into which the men filed was, in fact, only the first of three kitchens, joined together in a row by large arched doorways.

The pirates nearly filled two of these large rooms, and as their eyes adjusted to the light, the men gazed about them in humble astonishment. There were huge fireplaces and ovens along the inside wall, and all around there were tables, counters, and wash basins. It seemed that every flat surface was littered with assorted cooking utensils and the debris resulting from the preparation of a meal.

"*Hakura!* Did ye ever see so many pots, an' spoons, an' dishes?" one of the Turo in the front rank exclaimed in a stage whisper. "If my old mother could be here an' see this, she'd think she was in Hanuroa. Just think what a dinner they must ha' cooked in here!"

At that, a voice suddenly spoke out of the darkness.

"Well, bless your old mother, then, lad, and it's a pleasure to make her son's acquaintance."

They all jumped at the unexpected sound. The voice was clearly female, and not young, and it came from the direction of the doorway leading to the last kitchen. Presently the speaker appeared in that doorway, emerging from the gloom. She was a tall, spare Kelorin woman with a sharp jaw, a nose like a knife, pale gray eyes, and silver hair neatly braided and coiled atop her head. She held a very large kitchen knife in her hand in a very purposeful way.

Nagaro stepped up to stand before her. He was relieved to find her here. She was presumably one of the kitchen staff, and her presence suggested that the Mautep had paid the kitchens little attention. "Good morning, Zirdyn," he said with a bow. "I am Captain Nagaro, and these are my men. We've come to help in the fight against the Mautep. Are these, then, your kitchens?"

The woman drilled him with her eyes. "They're the dear queen's kitchens, bless her, though I am queen *in* them," she said tartly. "I am Tira Filora, Mistress of the Royal Kitchens. I've heard of Captain Nagaro," she added, looking down her nose at him. "And they say he's a pirate. Now, you and your lot *do* look a bit like pirates, but ye're awfully fair-spoken, Zirda, for a man that doesn't see fit to wear a shirt."

Nagaro sighed, even as he winced. "Well met, Tira Filora," he said. He touched his leather vest. "This is my battle dress. Folk expect it. Most especially, the *Mautep* expect it," he added with a quick flash of teeth. "We would be very much obliged, Zirdyn, if you'd tell us anything you know about what we might find in there." He gestured towards one of the doors leading from the kitchen into the corridor beyond.

"Of course ye would," she said curtly. "And I will tell ye what I can, though I've been in here the whole time— according to my duty— and didn't see any of it with my own eyes." She paused to reposition a hairpin with her free hand, then continued.

"The lords and ladies were all at table— just finishing their dinner— when it started. We heard a great deal o' screaming and shouting, and the serving girls came running in here crying that we were being attacked. As near as I can tell, the raiders got all the way 'round to the courtyard and came into the Great Hall by the doors on that side. The doors were open on account of it being a fine spring night. So the lords took the ladies and ran out the other side o' the Hall, looking for a better place to make a stand. It was something about the Great Hall having too many doors..." She paused again. "Then there's what Captain Worling said—"

At this, Delvin pressed forward. "Captain Worling is here?" he cried. "Where?"

Tira Filora gave him a sympathetic look. "He *was* here, lad," she said gently. "Hours ago, before dawn. He came in the same way your lot did, with about a dozen guardsmen. He asked the same question," she added, turning back to Nagaro. "And I gave him the same answer. I told him I didn't reckon he could do much with that little troop o' his, but he just had to go and see anyway. They'd not been gone more than two minutes, when about eight o' them came back, running like the hounds were at their heels. They didn't stop to talk. Captain Worling shouted, '*They're barricaded in the Audience Chamber!*' and then he was gone, out by the way he'd first come in, and all the rest with him." She shook her head. "I expect he meant that the lords and ladies were barricaded," she added.

Nagaro nodded. "I'm sure you're right."

"Captain Worling wouldn't run away!" Delvin protested, looking distressed.

Landros made haste to explain: "It's called a 'retreat', lad," he said. "A good commander doesn't throw lives away to no purpose. When he saw he couldn't do any good here, he likely went to join the force on the Common Wall."

Nagaro rubbed his chin. "Well, at least we know where to look, assuming nothing has changed.." He paused. A thought had been nagging at him, and now he voiced it. "Where have all the serving girls and the other cooks gone?" he asked. "Are they somewhere safe?"

The woman gave him an appreciative look. "Bless ye for asking, Zirda. I sent them upstairs to their quarters— where I expect they're all hiding under their beds, poor dears. I stayed here to guard the stairs," she added, with a steely glint in her eye. "If they want to make sport in my kitchens, they'll have to deal with me!"

She raised the knife significantly. Several of the nearest men stepped back a pace.

Nagaro stood his ground and bowed to the woman a second time. "Well met indeed, Zirdyn, he said gravely. I'm glad you decided we were friends, not foes."

Filora gave him a curt little nod that suggested this praise was no more than her due, and turned to survey the assembled pirate force. "At least ye brought enough men to maybe do some good," she said approvingly.

"Well, I hope so," Nagaro agreed. "We have more than a hundred. But the Mautep could have at least three times that many. Of course, we can hope that a lot of them are out on the wall. And being inside a building like this will limit how many men can face each other at a time. Unless it's in the Great Hall—" He checked himself. "—I would imagine," he added hastily, since he wasn't supposed to know exactly how big the Great Hall was. He covered himself further by asking an obvious question, to which he very well knew the answer. "How can we get to the Audience Chamber from here?"

Both Delvin and Tira Filora immediately launched into competing explanations. There were, in fact, two ways.

One was to go left along the corridor onto which the kitchens opened, to the Great Hall, through it, and across a large room known as the Compass Room because its floor featured a large compass rose worked in different colors of marble. Approached by this route, entering the Compass Room from the north side, the main public entrance of the Audience Chamber would be directly opposite.

The other way was to turn right along the corridor outside the kitchens and follow it to its intersection with the long central hallway, which in turn could be followed to the Compass Room, entering it from the west. From the cental hallway, it was also possible to take a path through several minor hallways around to the Audience Chamber's rear door.

Nagaro knew almost all of this layout, although he'd never actually been in the kitchens before. He let the discussion go on long enough to make it convincing that he should have been able to master the arrangement of the rooms. When at length there came an appropriate pause, he spoke into it.

"Yes, I think I understand," he said. "And I think we should divide our force into two parties— one for each door of the Audience Chamber. It doesn't make sense to make more elaborate plans since we don't know what we'll find— though we'll likely find most of their force in either the Great Hall or the Compass Room. How many men can fight among the lords who are here, Filora? How many might there be defending the Audience Chamber?"

The Mistress of the Royal Kitchens looked thoughtful. "It was a small company for dinner last night," she said. "Only three tables, so I'd guess a dozen, perhaps, at most, counting a few guardsmen."

"But we can't have two parties if we've only got one guide," protested Moraga, predictably seeing the difficulty.

Nagaro frowned. "Delvin can guide the party to the back door. It sounds like the more difficult path. You and Timegar can lead that party. I and Landros will lead the larger force through the Great Hall. I think we can find the way—"

To his dismay, Filora drew herself up. "I can show ye the way to either door," she declared. "All I ask is that ye leave a man or two to guard my kitchen."

Nagaro opened and closed his mouth. "I'm afraid it's likely to be quite dangerous, Zirdyn. Most Mautep do consider it dishonorable to kill a woman— on purpose— but you could easily be hurt or killed by accident in a melee."

She waved a hand dismissively. "Oh, tush!" she said. "I'm still spry enough to get out o' the way. And if any o' them does come at me..." She waggled her knife under his nose rather alarmingly. "I've been hanging about in the kitchen for hours, not being of any use."

Nagaro backed up a foot to get clear of the knife. He didn't like this at all, but the woman seemed determined and she was certainly old enough to make her own choices. He sighed. "Do you think you can keep her safe?" he inquired, turning to Timegar.

The former fleet warrior shrugged his shoulders. "*Well...*" he said, scratching his head. "I expect she knows every side room and hall she can duck into— and she does seem a game lass." He gave the woman a wink, and she actually blushed.

Nagaro sighed, but he nodded. He thought the way through the Great Hall would likely involve the most serious fighting, and didn't want to take Filora that way. "All right," he told the woman. "Delvin can guide us through the Great Hall, and you can guide the party to the back door. And thank you, Tira Filora." He turned to the general assembly. "And now I don't think we should waste any more time."

They quickly divided the men. About two thirds of the number would follow Nagaro and Landros, and the remainder would be led by Moraga and Timegar. Two men were chosen to stay and watch the kitchens and the door by which they had entered from the garden. Nagaro had Taru, Pavo, and Tredhold, as well as Landros, in his company.

"We'll probably meet the Mautep before you do," he told Timegar and Moraga. "And I expect to make a direct assault. So keep your ears alert for the sounds of battle."

Each of the kitchens opened separately onto the corridor. Timegar and Moraga made their exit from the first kitchen by way of the first door, turning right.

Nagaro and Landros led the larger company out through the third kitchen by its door, since it was closest to the Great Hall. They crept cautiously out into the corridor, and turned left. The men filed silently after them and formed up ranks, five abreast.

Several of the lamps along the hallway had burned out for want of tending, and the passageway was quite dim. Their immediate goal lay a short distance ahead along the corridor where an open doorway in the right hand wall spilled light from the room beyond. It was the first of two doors that entered the west end of the Great Hall, one on either side of a raised dais where the royal family would be seated on feast days. Nagaro could have deduced this from his own knowledge, even had Filora not described it to them.

A pale shape was visible, lying in the hallway a few steps from the kitchen door. It turned out to be a man wearing a white tirka, the uniform of the Palace Guard. He was lying face down, with his head toward the kitchen, a dark stain running down the left side of his body and more blood on the smooth stone floor. Tredhold turned the man over. "One of Captain Worling's party, I expect," he said quietly. "From the trail of blood, I'd say he was wounded in a fight somewhere up ahead and managed to get back this far before—"

"*Oran!*"

Delvin had come up close enough to see the dead man's face in the dim light, and was staring, stricken. "*Oh, no... Oh, Vothra!*"

Landros put a hand on the youth's shoulder. "Steady, lad," he said quietly.

Tredhold gently turned the dead man back over so his face was towards the floor and stood up. "There's nothing ye can do for him now, son," he said gently. "And he'll ride with Kronig tonight. But there may be others we can still help."

Delvin was still staring, blankly, fixedly. He didn't appear to have heard the healer's words. "His spirit will live again, won't it?" he asked on a note of rising desperation. "It'll go into some little baby somewhere, and—"

Tredhold was out of his depth in such matters of Vothrin belief. Instinctively he turned to Nagaro.

Nagaro stepped quickly in front of Delvin, placing his own face in line with the young man's blank stare. He took both of the youth's shoulders in his hands. "Yes," he said with conviction, looking directly into the young Kelorin's eyes. "His spirit will go on to another life. Vothra is in the world again, and will make sure that it is so. There's nothing left to do for Oran but to grieve, and now isn't the time for that. There's work to be done."

Delvin's gaze came back into focus on Nagaro's earnest face, and his expression passed from anguished shock to angry determination. "*Aye, Zirda!*" he said with sudden fierceness. As Nagaro released his shoulders, the youth saluted him, with feeling, and made as if to stride off up the corridor.

Tredhold caught the young man's arm. "*Wait, Delvin!*" he hissed.

Nagaro sighed. "Why don't you two go ahead and take a look through that lighted door," he said quietly to Tredhold. "But be careful. There'll surely be Mautep guards, and quite possibly a large company of them. Try not to be seen, and come straight back."

The healer nodded and moved off, beckoning Delvin to follow him, which the youth readily did. Nagaro turned and spoke in a low voice to Landros. "I'm not sure we should have brought Delvin with us, Landros—even if we do need a guide. He's terribly young, and I don't think he's had any battle experience."

Landros met his eyes with a steady gaze. "Ye're right," he said quietly. "He would only have joined the Guard last fall, I think, and ye don't usually see much action in the Palace Guard. I'd wager money Captain Worling left him at his post to keep him out o' the fight. But he's in good hands with us, and there's a first time for everyone—" Landros broke off as Trehold and Delvin came hurrying back.

The healer's voice, when he spoke, was tense with excitement. "There's Mautep in there all right," he said. "But I only counted ten— and they're all together near this end of the room, where the tables are laid. I'd guess that they were supposed to be guarding all the doors o' the Great

Hall, but they got hungry and came to see what pickings they could find from last night's dinner."

Delvin was scowling. "Aye," he muttered indignantly. "They're all at the tables, and they're eating the king's meat!"

"Ha!" Landros kept the exclamation low. "We should attack them and slay them all swiftly, so they can't carry a warning to their fellows. Ye do see that it's the best way, Capt'n?" he added, giving Nagaro a probing look.

Nagaro was aware that Tredhold was also eyeing him closely. Both former Fleet warriors knew his distaste for butchery. "Yes," he admitted, because the merit of plan was obvious. Taking Mautep captives when his men had no rope to bind them wasn't feasible. "But we shouldn't all rush out there at once," he added. "If they see such a force coming at them, they'll bolt, and we'll never catch them all. We should send out a smaller number— few enough that they'll think they can prevail— with other men ready to leap out and join the fight as soon as they're needed."

Landros permitted himself a quiet chuckle. "Trust ye to make it a fair fight, Capt'n," he said, shaking his head. "But ye do have a point."

Nagaro knew he had to lead the attack. However little he liked killing, he couldn't ask others to do what he wouldn't do himself. He chose Taru, Pavo, Landros, and Tredhold for the sortie. These four men had been at the core of his original front line when he had first taken to the sea four years ago. He trusted their skill.

Delvin begged to be included, but Nagaro firmly told him no. "You can be in the second wave," he told the youth, with some reservations.

The entire company crept stealthily along the corridor towards the lighted door. Even before they reached it, they could hear the voices of the Mautep in the Great Hall, sounding jovial and at ease.

Nagaro stopped just short of the door jam, a restraining hand held out to keep the others behind him. Taking a deep breath, he stepped forward and peered around the edge of the doorframe.

Chapter 11

The Fight For The Palace

Nagaro had thought he was prepared to look into that room— a room in which he had endured countless public humiliations— but the emotions evoked by the sight of it hit him almost like a physical blow.

The space was huge, long and high, with the two rows of slender pillars running the length of it. There was the vaulted ceiling and the great arched windows along the north wall, aglow with spring sunshine. The dozens of long tables, with their elegantly carved wooden chairs, were arrayed around the edges of the room. The center of the floor between the pillars was clear for dancing. The memories conjured by that familiar sight made Nagaro shudder, and he inadvertently drew in his breath, even as he jerked back into the shelter of the hallway.

How many excruciating hours had he spent in that room, a helpless puppet, subject to the will of those who had enslaved him... or at the unwitting mercy of anyone who chanced to make the most casual suggestion...

Stop it!

He thrust the memories from his mind. There was work to be done, and he mustn't falter.

Even in his distraction he had seen what he needed to see. The room was about eighty feet long and forty feet wide, and the three tables of which Filora had spoken, laden with plates, glasses, platters, and the remaining food, were close to the doorway where he and his men waited in concealment. The Mautep were there, just as Tredhold had said. They were standing or sitting at their ease around one of the tables, about fifteen feet from the door, talking among themselves and laughing as they enjoyed the cold remains of the previous night's repast.

Nagaro drew a steadying breath and turned around. His eyes swept the faces of his four comrades. Each indicated by a nod that he was ready. Beyond them stood the rank of men who would follow them when bidden, with Gurd, Landros' first mate, commanding them.

Nagaro took another breath, raised his hand, and gave the silent signal to advance, followed by a gesture indicating in which direction their quarry lay in the room beyond. He then stepped to the doorway, where he paused for a heartbeat while his friends came up beside him. Then, as one, the five men stepped through the doorway and flung themselves at the invaders.

Though caught off guard, the Mautep warriors responded swiftly. Those facing the door cried alarm as soon as they saw movement, and those who had their backs to the intruders immediately sprang to their feet and spun about, sending chairs clattering. All of the men drew their swords, and in that moment Nagaro forgot about everything else that had ever happened in that room.

As he went for the man nearest to him, one of the others pointed at him and cried, "*Kiraam Shaku-Tal!*" Two-to-one odds in their favor undoubtedly looked good to the Mautep sea warriors, and the price that Emperor Baalkir had placed on Nagaro's head was substantial. So it wasn't surprising that none of the Mautep thought to turn and flee or summon help. Instead, they all converged on the five unexpected attackers, their eyes agleam with avarice.

Nagaro met the nearest man, sword to sword, and heard the sound of clashing steel on either side and behind him as his friends hastily formed a defensive circle, back to back. His first opponent lived just long enough to regret having so hastily answered the call of greed. Nagaro drew his bloody sword from the man's chest and found himself facing two new assailants who promptly sprang at him, hoping, no doubt, to do better than their compatriot.

The men were well-trained, and Nagaro found himself hard-pressed until Taru drew one of the men off. Nagaro promptly dispatched the other, offering a silent prayer for the man's departing spirit. He was moving to help Taru finish the third man, when there came a cry from Landros, behind him.

"*Delvin, look out!*"

Nagaro spun about to find that Delvin was standing over a dead Mautep, his sword running blood, and a look of astonished horror on his young face.

Nagaro had barely time to register the fact that Gurd had ordered out the second wave of pirates before he realized that a Mautep raider was in the act of lunging at the distracted Delvin. This had been the reason for the warning cry from Landros, who had his own hands full with another man. Swift as a striking snake, Nagaro leaped in to turn the Mautep's sword aside and run the man through, all in a single motion. The body toppled and fell sprawled on top of the man Delvin had slain.

Delvin blinked and started. He looked up into Nagaro's face, the realization of his close escape dawning in his eyes. His mouth opened, but before he could say anything, shouts rang out.

"That one's escaping!"

"After him!"

As pirates stampeded past him, Nagaro spun around again, just in time to see one of the Mautep warriors sprinting toward the door that led from the Great Hall to the Compass Room. A massive table in Nagaro's path barred him from immediately giving chase.

In the next instant, the three Mautep who were still standing managed to break away from Pavo, Taru, and Tredhold and tried to follow their fellow. Those three didn't get far because their attackers sprang after them, and some of the other pirates moved to help, even as their comrads closed in on the first fleeing Mautep. But the man had too great a lead to be overtaken and he darted through the distant doorway, which was slammed shut behind him.

Landros, who had been one of the man's pursuers, swore roundly. Then he rallied the other nearby pirates to him and turned them back towards Nagaro.

Nagaro shook his head, frowning at the Mautep's escape. Still, he reflected, at least they had suffered no casualties. He became aware of Delvin at his elbow.

"I... thank you, Zirda..." the youth stammered. "I'm sorry I didn't wait for Gurd's signal. I... I... wanted to kill one— for Oran. But I don't think he even saw me coming... And it's my first time..." Delvin's words ran out.

Nagaro gave the young Kelorin a sympathetic look. "Anger often makes for poor choices, but it's very natural," he said. "And the first time I killed a man, it felt as if the world had stopped. It's gotten easier, but I still try not to think about it."

Delvin looked down. "Did... did that man get away because of me? Because ye and Uncle Landros were distracted?"

Nagaro sighed. "I don't know," he said truthfully. "It probably would have happened anyway. And their main force would have become aware of us sooner or later. Come on, now," he added, turning to circle around the table that blocked his way. He raised his voice enough so that all the men could hear him.

"To me!" he cried. "Form up!" And then, as the remaining men poured out of the corridor to join him, and Landros and the other scattered pirates fell in beside him, he spoke in a lower voice. "Since they now know that we're here, the best thing we can do is give them as little time as possible to plan what they're going to do about it."

Landros nodded grimly. "Aye, Captain. Ye're right."

Not surprisingly, they discovered that the pair of heavy oak doors separating the Great Hall from the Compass Room resisted being opened, though damage to the wood suggested that the locks were broken. Most likely the damage had been done when the lords, fleeing that way with the ladies, had attempted unsuccessfully to hold the doors against the Mautep in the first minutes of the attack. The broken locks meant that the doors were now only being held shut by men's bodies, or barricaded with furniture— of which the Compass Room contained very little.

Nagaro quickly sketched out a number of possible tactics he thought the Mautep on the other side might use, and how to counter each of them. Then he set Pavo and several others of the largest and strongest to put their shoulders against the doors. On the third concerted heave, the doors gave— opening first only a hand's breadth, then a foot, while the sound of Hashti curses could be heard from the other side. There followed a hasty pelting of feet, and the great oak panels swung suddenly wide.

Crying, "forward!" Nagaro leaped into the gap, with his followers advancing on either side, or behind him, according to his instructions. The doorway was wide enough for six grown men to comfortably pass through it abreast under normal circumstances, but the pirates essayed it in close ranks, eight abreast and ten deep.

The Compass Room beyond was a scene of chaos. The air reeked of smoke, and scorched remnants of furnishings and wall hangings littered the floor, together with shards of glass from shattered windows high overhead. Here and there were piles of what appeared to be intended loot— chests, jewelry boxes, and various items of gold, silver, porcelain, or rare woods.

Directly opposite their entry point, the doorway of the Audience Chamber was obstructed by a barricade made from the charred remains of its two huge doors. They had been torn from their hinges and set on their long edges, one in front of the other, across the opening. Above this barrier, swords bristled in the hands of haggard, grim-faced men, both lords and members of the Palace Guard.

Of more concern than any of this, however, was the fact that between the pirates and the beleaguered defenders there were standing about forty armed Mautep. They were arrayed in an arc that was centered on the doorway through which the pirates were attempting to pass.

Nagaro took all of this in within the instant that he crossed the threshold. At the same time, his peripheral vision caught the presence of massed men to right and left of the doorway. "*Flanks!*" he shouted, to alert the men behind him to the presence of one of the threats he had anticipated.

He heard the shouts on either side of him and then the clash of steel as some of his men turned sharply to right or left to take on the flanking raiders. Immediately, there came a shouted order from among the semi-circle of Mautep and they charged, all together, swords flashing in their hands.

Nagaro and the rest of his front line sprang into action. The exchange that followed was intense, though bloodless, and ended as quickly as it had begun when the Mautep fell back to regroup. Apparently the sea raiders had hoped to gain the upper hand by having half of their number lying in ambush on either side of the door. Nagaro's foresight and alertness had foiled their plan, however, and produced a standoff. The entire pirate force had succeeded in passing through the doorway, and they stood fanned out before it in a tight grouping. The Mautep raiders faced them in a wider arc. Though roughly equal in number to their foes, the line of Mautep warriors had to cover a greater distance and were therefore more thinly spread.

Standing at the center of his front rank, flanked by Taru and Pavo, Nagaro ran his eyes over the Mautep arrayed against them. He raised his voice, then, and spoke the first Hashti phrase he had ever learned.

"*Kia kaar hanuk-tak!*"

It meant, "put down your swords", and Nagaro had little hope that it would gain him anything this day. The odds were presently too even, and there were very likely more Mautep close enough at hand to be brought in as reenforcements. Already he thought he had seen some of the Mautep raiders slip out of the Compass Room through the east door that led to the outer entrance of the palace.

A man to Nagaro's left, one of the Mautep officers identified by gold insignia on the collar of his tunic, stepped in front of the line and moved to face him.

"*Shaku raal!*" The man's tone was derisive. The Hashti words meant "slave dog", and were a less complimentary name for the man widely known among the Mautep as the Thief of Slaves. The officer continued in Hashti, which Nagaro was able to understand. "Too easily I surrendered to you at Pakoa!"

Nagaro recognized the man then as one of the two captains who had accepted his terms after the "Battle of Pakoa" the previous summer. He gave the Mautep captain a cold stare. "You swore to me on your honor," he said in Hashti, "not to put your foot again on land of Edrovir."

Behind him, he could hear Pavo translating the exchange in a low voice for the benefit of those among the pirate ranks who knew no Hashti.

The Mautep raised his chin. "What is oath to slave dog?" he asked contemptuously. "Always you stand and talk. I think it is true, what they say. You have no heart in you for killing."

Nagaro heaved an inward sigh. To say that he had no love for killing was accurate, but it was not the same as saying he wasn't willing to do it when circumstances demanded. There was a time for second chances—for leaving a man his life so that he might learn from his mistake— but that time was not now.

He raised his sword and sighted down the length of the blade to look the Mautep squarely in the eyes. Then he smiled a feral smile— his best pirate smile— a flash of white teeth in the midst of his neatly trimmed black beard. "No more surrender," he said in a voice that rang across the room for all the Mautep to hear. "Man without honor. Breaker of oath. Defend yourself!"

Nagaro advanced upon the dishonorable captain with deliberate steps. The man hesitated, the contemptuous expression beginning to lose its grip on his features. Then he took a step back, and another. Words in Hashti broke from his own men, arrayed behind him:

"Kill him! Kill him!"

The Mautep captain found himself caught by his own bravado. Seeing that he must otherwise lose face among his men, he made up his mind to act. He lunged, coming in low, under his opponent's sword— or it would have been under it if Nagaro's blade had still been where it was an instant before. Steel rang on steel exactly once as Nagaro parried, and an instant later, the Mautep captain fell dead at his feet, pierced through the heart.

For perhaps two seconds, no one moved while Nagaro stood with his bloody sword in his hand, two paces in front of the rest of his own front line. Then one of the other Mautep officers saw the opportunity and barked an order.

Several of the men in the line in front of Nagaro leaped forward, intending to fall upon the Thief of Slaves from both sides. Two things happened then in rapid succession. First, Nagaro moved swiftly to engage one of the men, and felled him so quickly that the others hesitated. And then Landros shouted an order of his own, and the pirate line leaped forward to flank their threatened captain.

It was likely that nothing could have prevented the battle that followed. The movement of the pirates had brought them into sword range of the Mautep, and many of the raiders jumped to the attack before the order came from their commander's lips. The pirates, who found themselves attacked, responded even before they heard Nagaro's answering order. They didn't need to hear him add, "Don't hold back! We must win this fight!"

On his left Nagaro heard Landros say, presumably to Delvin, "Ye watch, now, lad, and ye'll see some swordsmanship!"

This time the fight was neither brief nor bloodless, and Nagaro was literally in the middle of it. He moved forward, and the line moved with him, but he was careful not to move too fast. He must not drive the center of the line in advance of the flanks. Instead, he had to let those flanks, led by Landros on the left and Gurd on the right, gain ground more rapidly than the center, straightening the line.

Slowly, relentlessly, the pirates drove the Mautep raiders back. Nagaro saw a number of his men go down around him, and each of those losses cut a raw, red gash across his soul. The pain was in no way diminished by the knowledge that Mautep were also falling, a number of them struck down by his own hand. Later he would count the cost. For now, he grasped and held the thought that always served him in such circumstances: *Don't think about it. There is a task to be done.*

Nagaro was moving with swift and elegant precision. As if from a distance he heard the bold cries of his followers and the shouts of encouragement from the weary men behind the barricade. His sword sang in his hand and the wild refrain found a resonant chord within him, at once thrilling and terrible. He had felt it before. It was *power*— but power under his control. There was a task to be done, and he was equal to it— equal to the choices that must be made, second by second.

A wrong would be put right... He and his followers would stem the tide of greed and violence that had carried the Mautep raiders here to violate this place— to break, and burn, and send helpless women fleeing in terror.

The Mautep had been pushed just past the center of the room when new sounds penetrated Nagaro's concentration. They were the sounds of shouts and running feet coming from beyond the doorway to his right, the western doorway, the one leading to the central hallway.

That door had been left standing open, and now a company of between twenty and thirty Mautep burst through it in apparent flight. Some of them turned around and tried to close the heavy oak doors, but the pursuit was too close behind them, and they were too late to prevent the first of the pirates that were on their heels from pushing through.

First among these came Moraga, whooping and swinging his sword like a scythe. The Mautep at the doors momentarily scattered before him. When Moraga's fighting blood was up, the former merchant seaman was capable of a berserk ferocity that tended to unnerve anyone confronted by it.

Unfortunately, roused as he was on this occasion, Moraga had outdistanced all but a half dozen of his own vanguard, and only these few managed to come through the door behind him before the Mautep rallied and made a second— this time successful— effort to swing the doors shut. Moraga and his handful or crewmen immediately formed a tight circle, back to back. Nanu and Chaheel, the two massive lone men, were among them, towering above the rest.

The Mautep who had already been in the room rallied at the sight of more of their kind coming to swell their numbers, and redoubled their efforts. Nagaro thus found himself hard pressed just as he became aware of the plight of Moraga's little band.

"Gurd!" he cried. "To Moraga!"

Gurd and the other men on the right flank had already seen the need. They leaped forward.

Almost at the same instant, the door from the central hallway burst open again, and Timegar and the rest of the men under his command came charging through.

There followed a brief scrambling chaos, during which Mautep and pirates sorted themselves out— each to their own kind— while simultaneously doing as much damage as possible to the other. The sorting process ended with the pirates under Nagaro and Landros still holding the north side of the room, but now flanked by those under Moraga and Timegar who held the room's west end, all the way to the barricaded entrance of the Audience Chamber. The Mautep raiders had regained a little ground in the center, but were mostly squeezed into the room's southeast corner and the area around the east door.

There came a pregnant pause as both sides caught their breath and took stock of the situation. Nagaro took advantage of the moment to assess his opponents. It was hard to tell with Mautep, who prided themselves on stoicism, but is seemed to him that quite a number of the men facing him showed signs of fear.

Tensely Nagaro wiped the sweat from his own brow. His hand came away bloody, but he wasn't aware of any pain so he paid it no heed. He caught a movement near the east door and frowned. He thought he had seen two men slip in through that door, from the palace's front entry-hall beyond, and they were now pressing their way forward through the Mautep line.

A sudden shout from off to his right took his attention. He turned, to see that four men had come from the Audience Chamber, over the barricade, and were coming in his direction. The ranks of the pirates parted to let them pass.

Three of the men were guardsmen in white uniform tirkas— one of them an officer by his insignia. The fourth man, who had taken the lead, was plainly a lord. He was a tall, handsome Kelorin of athletic build who looked to be in his early thirties. His finely tailored royal blue velvet britches and elegant silk shirt of a dark gold color were both cut in places and stained with blood and soot, but the man carried himself in a way that said unmistakably that neither the fineness of his clothing nor its current condition were of the slightest concern to him. He walked like a warrior upon the field of battle, sword in hand, and there was steel in his gray eyes.

Taru, staring awestruck, stepped aside to yield the man his place at Nagaro's right-hand side. The glance the Kelorin lord turned on Nagaro as he came to stand beside him held respect, and there was evident sincerity in his voice when he spoke.

"Well met, Zirda," he said simply. "I am Elyan." And he temporarily transferred his blade to his left hand so that he might extend his right.

Nagaro similarly juggled his own weapon and gripped the proffered hand. "Well met indeed, My Lord Prince," he said. "I am Nagaro." Under other circumstances, he would have bowed to the princess's husband, but at that moment, such a gesture seemed superfluous.

Prince Elyan released Nagaro's hand. "Captain," he said simply, nodding his acknowledgment. Then he transferred his gaze to the ranks of Mautep facing him across an intervening width of battle-stained marble floor. "Their commander has gotten bad news, I think," he continued, with evident satisfaction. "See the look on his face after speaking to those two men."

Nagaro nodded. "They came in through the east door, I think. And there were several who went out that way earlier when we began our attack. Perhaps their reinforcements aren't coming?"

"Perhaps." Again there was measured satisfaction in the prince's voice, and his eyes remained on the Mautep. "That could be good news, if it means that Lord Korenthos and the City Garrison are having some success upon the wall. We should attack now," he added matter-of-factly. "While they're still weighing their options."

Nagaro frowned, his eyes also on the Mautep. "You may give that order, My Lord," he said. "And I will follow you. But I've been advised not to strike the first blow if I don't wish to become a butcher."

The prince turned and raised an eyebrow. "Who gives a man such advice?"

Nagaro was still watching the Mautep, and therefore missed the other man's expression. "Vothra," he said simply, and an instant later he cried, "*Stand ready, men! They're coming!*" as he saw the enemy begin to move.

The startled look that had appeared on the prince's face when Nagaro mentioned the Benevolent Spirit vanished in an instant as he turned back to face the oncoming foe.

The new Mautep assault was swift and initially so furious that the pirate line was pushed back in several places. Standing side by side at the center of the line, Nagaro and Prince Elyan could have advanced, but held their ground instead, marking time, waiting for the men on their flanks to recover.

The enemy warriors seemed almost to melt away before Nagaro's blade. Elyan was also a superbly skilled swordsman. The tall Kelorin fought with focused concentration and an almost serene smile on his face that seemed to say that this was work he'd been born to do.

As the pirate forces rallied, Nagaro gave the signal to advance, and this time the Mautep were pushed back, slowly, all along the line. One step. Two steps. Three steps. The enemy gave ground, and there were renewed cheers from the remaining men behind the barricade.

Then, suddenly, the enemy commander shouted something.

The entire Mautep line broke and made a dash for the east door, which swung instantly open to let men pour through it into the room beyond. The pirates charged after them, only to be checked as the best Mautep fighters turned to defend the doorway. These desperate Mautep fought long enough for the rest of their fellows to escape through the door, then turned, ducking through it themselves, and slammed it shut behind them.

Nagaro immediately ordered a small force of his men under Rubo, Moraga's first mate, to go back and help guard the barricaded doorway of the Audience Chamber. Then he directed half a dozen of his strongest men to put their shoulders to the east door.

"And don't forget," he added. "They may be lying in wait for us on the other side."

Elyan nodded. "Yes. We can't pass more than eight men abreast through that door, and they know it," he said grimly.

The prince had made it quite clear that he intended to go through the door himself and be part of whatever fight was happening on the other side. The three members of the Palace Guard who had come with him were of the same mind. The officer among them was Commander Harthred, chief of all the Palace Guard. A middle-aged Leithian with a scar on his chin, Harthred was heard to mutter something about being stuck in a bloody hole all night while the real fight was out there.

Nagaro now remembered the man from his earlier time in Lankura. Fortunately, it didn't appear that Commander Harthred remembered him.

Indeed, Nagaro had to pretend ignorance of what lay beyond the door that his men were heaving at. Fortunately, Delvin, Elyan, and Harthred were all able to offer enough description so that anyone might form a detailed mental picture. Beyond the door lay the palace's entry hall, a room less than half the size of the Compass Room in which they were standing. Its farther wall contained the palace's front door, which was set in a high portico at the top of a wide flight steps that descended to a broad courtyard spread out in front of the palace. On the farther side of the courtyard was the city wall, with a gate that gave passage into the city of Lankura.

When the door finally gave way, the pirates and their new allies were well prepared. Nagaro had assembled his best fighters to lead the charge through the door, and he added Elyan and Harthred to that front line, where they stood on his right hand. He was glad to have the prince there, and well aware that neither of these men would have been pleased to be anywhere else. Flanking them were Taru, Pavo, and Landros.

All together, they were a formidable force. The Mautep, about twenty of whom were waiting in ambush behind the door, quickly fell back before their onslaught, allowing additional ranks of pirates to pour through the doorway and fan out to either side.

Prince Elyan laughed outright. "See their commander's face!" he cried. "He thought to have held us longer!" So saying, the prince waded forward into the entry hall, his sword moving with a terrible precision.

Nagaro allowed himself the faintest hint of a smile at the Mautep commander's discomfiture as he also pressed forward, beating blades aside. After several seconds, however, during which the pirates advanced slowly but steadily across the entry hall while the Mautep raiders retreated, he frowned. *This was too easy.*

"They're only fighting to slow us down!" he shouted.

"Ha!" Elyan barked, "Come then, Captain! Commander!" And he redoubled the speed and forcefulness of his attack.

Crying, "Forward!" Nagaro moved swiftly to flank the prince. Harthred and the other men in the front line leaped forward as well. There followed an intense and violent exchange that was as bloody as any Nagaro had seen that day. He was holding nothing back now, and was moving a little ahead of the line, so when Elyan stumbled and fell back a pace, he found himself suddenly beset from three sides at once.

Keshaal! He swore mentally. There was a limit to how many men he could deal with at once. Desperately he dodged one stroke, parried another, and ran a man through almost as an extension of the same movement. Whirling, he parried again, dodged again and felled another man. Turning once again, he faced a man who unexpectedly backed off.

"*Judili hanuktar!*" The Mautep was staring at him in dismay.

The cry was taken up and echoed on every side, and those raiders who found themselves closest to Nagaro simply turned and ran. In doing so, they very nearly impaled themselves on the swords of the rank of men behind them, who in their turn also turned and fled. Seeing his front line dissolving around him, the Mautep commander yielded to discretion and ordered a full retreat.

Prince Elyan stood, sword upraised, chest heaving from the exertion. He was also staring at Nagaro. "What were they saying?" he gasped.

Nagaro frowned ruefully. "It means 'demon swordsman.' They seem to think there's something unnatural about my skill."

Elyan raised an eyebrow. "Well, I pray that I never have need to fight against you," was all he said.

Nagaro sighed. "You won't— as long as you fight for Edrovir," he said. "Come on!"

The fleeing Mautep were disappearing through the open doorway at the other end of the entry hall. The doorway framed a blaze of sunlight. It was ten feet wide, and the doors opened inward. The raiders made no effort to hold this doorway, not even bothering to swing the doors shut as the last of them passed through.

Nagaro led his company across the hall at a run, slowing only out of caution as they neared the open doorway. A glance told him that the design of the portico didn't offer any place for men to lie in concealment on the farther side. There were perhaps ten feet of level polished stone with pillars on either side before the steps began their descent. The entire space was clear of enemy warriors.

Nagaro, Elyan, and the rest of the front line came to a halt at the top of the steps, surveying the scene laid out before them. Below them was the courtyard, or parade ground, flanked by the river and the River Wall to the right, and by the royal stables and some other outbuildings to the left. The stretch of city wall known as the Common Wall formed the courtyard's farther side.

Directly opposite the front door of the palace, the gate that allowed passage through the Common Wall into the city was flanked by massive double guard towers. Other similar guard towers stood at intervals along the wall, stretching away to the left towards the long flank of Kel Lankura. On the right, there were only two towers, one at the corner of the courtyard where the Common Wall joined the River Wall, and the other where the River Wall abutted the palace. The River Wall was not as high as the Common Wall, and it contained a pair of arched openings leading to the river and the quay that served as a landing point for supplies being delivered to the palace by water.

The details of the layout were familiar to Nagaro and he needed no time to review them. What did require his attention was the disposition of the armed men within that space. These were everywhere, and the colors of their uniforms told much about how events had fallen out.

The courtyard was in the hands of the Mautep. All that could be seen there were the brown-and-gold uniforms of Lord Angkat. Similarly, Lord Angkat's men held a long stretch of the Common Wall, including the first tower to the left of the city gate and all of the wall that he could see stretching north towards the mountain, Kel Lankura. But the actual gate towers and everything to the right of them, including the River Wall with its two flanking towers, were all manned by men in the blue uniform of the

City Garrison, with here and there a little group of men in white tirkas—the remnants of the Palace Guard.

Nagaro realized that he was looking at a standoff. The city gate, of course, was closed, and the Mautep were thus unable to enter the city by that route. Presumably, the defenders within the city were preventing them from issuing, on the city side, from the doors at the bases of the towers that they held. And the Mautep were cut off from reaching their ships through the openings in the River Wall. The City Garrison, on the other hand, was cut off from the palace, because there was no way to enter the palace directly from the River Wall.

That the Mautep raiders were not presently in the city was apparent because there was very little smoke rising from beyond the wall. What smoke could be seen was thin and pale, suggesting fires nearly extinguished, and all of it came from points close to the gate and to the river. This suggested that there might have been a foray through the gate, or perhaps the use of fire-arrows.

It was while taking note of the smoke nearest to the river that Nagaro noticed a thin wisp a little nearer at hand, rising from beyond the River Wall— from the river itself. The tip of a charred mast was just visible above the wall where the smoke originated, jutting at an odd angle. There was another one as well. The masts of the other remaining Mautep craft stood higher above the wall, and straight, moving slightly with the undulation of the water.

His heart grew sick within him. "They've sunk two of the ships," he said woodenly. "I hope they got the slaves off—"

"I shouldn't think so," Elyan began easily, then stopped as he noted Nagaro's expression and the light of understanding dawned. "I'm sorry," he added hastily, realizing he was speaking to a man who had once been a galley slave.

Nagaro was still staring at those two mast tips. *The water of the river mouth wasn't deep. The ships didn't need to sink very far to rest on the bottom. But that wouldn't have mattered to men chained to benches on the oar deck, only a few feet above the water line. And before the rising water, there would have been the smoke... the flames...*

He jerked his mind away. *Don't think about it. There is work to be done...*

He shook himself. Only seconds had passed since he and his men had emerged from the palace. The company of Mautep they had been pursuing had crossed the courtyard to join another force that was preparing to mount an assault on the River Wall. Even as Nagaro watched, another group of warriors clad in brown-and-gold launched an attack against the towers of the city gate, while yet another group was moving purposefully towards the next tower to the left along the Common Wall.

He glanced again at the Mautep masts. If he could do whatever he wished, he would take his men to the River Wall and try to rescue the slaves from those ships that were still afloat. But that wasn't what was needed most.

Nagaro turned decisively to Elyan. "How may we be of service to you, My Lord?" he asked, his voice level and steady.

The prince considered, studying the scene before them. "Best not to try to kill them all," he said. "There are too many, and we would suffer heavy losses, as well. We must drive them off— back to their ships."

He turned back to Nagaro. "I say we divide into three. Leave one of your captains here with a crew to secure and defend the palace— there could still be Mahuk in there. Then, if you'll trust me with some of your men, I will lead them against those who are making for the gate towers and the Common Wall. You lead a contingent down to the River Wall to tell the Garrison men there of our plan. Once that's done, go wherever you're most needed. What do you say?"

Nagaro took approximately one second to decide. This was Elyan's territory, and the need was immediate. "Aye, Zirda," he said.

He turned to the men who were massed behind him, some inside the palace and some already outside standing in the portico. "Moraga and Landros," he said. "Take your men and follow Prince Elyan. He knows the wall and will lead you well. Timegar, you and your men secure the palace. Taru and the rest of my crew are with me."

"Aye, Zirda!" Timegar saluted. Moraga growled, "Whatever ye say, Capt'n!" and Landros nodded decisively.

A moment later, those who were to descend the steps plunged down them and charged out across the courtyard to right and left, their swords held ready in their hands.

Chapter 12

The Queen's Request

The battle had ended only an hour before, with the surviving Mautep taking whatever booty they had in hand and fleeing in their remaining ships. The defenders of Lankura had begun to pick up the pieces and assess the damage in the aftermath of what had been the costliest conflict the city had ever known.

Nagaro and Delvin waited at the door of the Audience Chamber while their names were announced by one of Timegar's men who was doing his painful best in a role usually performed by one of the Palace Guard. Presently, they passed through the ruined doorway and began to approach the high seat upon which sat Elgurn, the King of Edrovir.

Some effort had been made to put the room in order following the events of the previous night and of the morning, but the effect only served to accentuate the fact that the situation was far from normal. Though the barricade had been moved aside, the doors were too badly burned for repair and would take some time to be replaced. The air was still tainted with smoke. Glass shards from shattered windows in the clear-story high above their heads had been swept only as far as the edges of the room. Only two of the eight huge tapestries that normally adorned the walls were presently in their places.

Besides King Elgurn, who was seated on the dais at the end of the room opposite the door, a number of lords were present, watching from some of the seats in one of the two panel-enclosed seating galleries that ran along either side of the room. Nagaro avoided even looking at the lords in the gallery. If the king didn't recognize him, the others weren't likely to, and he preferred not to know whether he recognized any of them.

Beyond the left-hand gallery, a row of doors interrupted the east wall of the chamber. Nagaro knew that these doors led to a number of small rooms accessible only from the Audience Chamber. On this day, the doors were guarded by several men whose dress proclaimed them to be of the noble class.

Nagaro noted that several of the doors were ajar, and that curious faces— female faces— were peering out. Above the voices speaking in hushed tones from the gallery, he could hear a few giggles from the direction of those not-quite-closed doors. He studiously ignored them. The princess would be there somewhere, no doubt. He hoped she wasn't one of those peeking out at him. While she had never known him as anything other than simple-minded, and he knew that he must now seem completely different, still he had spent more time in her company than anyone else's during his time as the "idiot prince."

If he had thought about it, he would have realized that he must at present look very much a pirate. The fighting was not long over, and he'd been far too busy to give any thought to his appearance in the short time since it had ended. He still wore his leather vest, without a shirt, and his sword at his hip. Besides that, there was blood crusting the wound on his left temple, and he had somewhere received a sword cut on his right forearm that was still oozing scarlet.

None of this was in Nagaro's mind, however, as he walked down the aisle of the Audience Chamber, a pace behind Delvin and to the young man's left. This was properly Delvin's audience, but the youth had literally begged for Nagaro's company. Considering the subject to be discussed, Nagaro had to concede that there was a good deal of sense to his inclusion. He and his men would figure prominently in any report on the current disposition of the palace and the forces securing it.

As recently as a few hours ago, he would have sought some way to decline Delvin's request. King Elgurn was one of the few people left in the world who had known the truth about Leyel Virden— that the princess's hapless first husband had appeared simple-minded only because he had been drugged to obtain his submission.

Not only had Elgurn known him as a youth with a sound mind, but the king had surely also known that young Leyel had a talent for swordsmanship. Still, Elgurn had every reason to believe that Leyel Virden was dead. Nagaro had heard the king's Lore Master, the dreaded Dreigen, assure the king that a victim of repeated heskial administration couldn't survive without continued doses of the drug.

How he *had* survived remained, in fact, a mystery. But Nagaro felt quite sure, as he approached the dais, that Elgurn would be unable to see the truth of his identity simply because the man wasn't expecting ever to see Leyel Virden alive again under the sun.

The events of the last several hours had, in fact, raised Nagaro's confidence in his disguise to an unprecedented level. He had been moving freely about the courtyard, the walls, the palace— often finding himself in the presence of men that he knew had been in the palace, or in the city, during that horrible time seven years ago. They had looked him in the face today, even shaken his hand, and they had all acted as if they were meeting him for the first time. They had shown him respect, gratitude, even admiration. It all felt very good, and it served to make him feel secure in his new persona.

So it was that Nagaro was moving with his usual bold assurance as he and Delvin reached the rectangle of black marble in the floor in front of the dais where they had been told to stop, stand, and wait to be addressed. There were four impressively carved wooden chairs mounted on the dais in a row, and King Elgurn was seated on the largest of them, just to the right of center. The other three chairs were empty.

Nagaro had been studying the king, and he hadn't missed the fact that Elgurn had been measuring both him and Delvin throughout their approach to the dais. The man's eyes had been flicking sharply back and forth between them.

The king was richly but somberly clad in black silk and dark brown velvet with only a very modest amount of gold embroidery. He sat in the high seat easily, as one long accustomed to it. He held his back as straight as ever, but he looked thinner and grayer— older than Nagaro remembered him, by more than the seven years that had passed since Nagaro had seen him last. His blond hair was so nearly white that the narrow gold circlet he wore about his brow stood out in contrast against it. His close-trimmed beard, quite plainly red before, now showed only traces of that color amid the gray.

The eyes that now studied Nagaro were the same, however— sharp, shrewd, and cold as ice. Nagaro returned the king's stare, unperturbed. He read keen curiosity in those eyes, and a certain amount of disapproval, but not the shock and disbelief that would have accompanied recognition. Nagaro felt his dislike for this man rear itself— but it was only dislike. The murderous rage the king had once evoked in him was not, at the moment, being rekindled.

Delvin bowed as they came to a halt, and added a salute. Nagaro saw no reason why he should give Elgurn quite so much homage. He executed a bow, not his deepest or most elegant, and straightened to stand again at his ease.

"Guardsman Delvin reporting, My Lord King!"

Delvin was trembling visibly under the monarch's probing gaze. The young man had been through a great deal that day. Although he had often been in the thick of things, he had somehow managed to escape with only a few minor cuts and bruises. His nerves, however, were another matter. He had witnessed more violence and death in the space of a few hours than in all of his previous life— by a wide margin —and he was clearly in danger of being overwhelmed by finding himself pressed into service to present the official report of the Palace Guard to the King of Edrovir.

It didn't help that the king was skewering the young man mercilessly with his pale blue gaze.

"Where is Commander Harthred?" the king inquired sharply.

Delvin flinched. "C-Commander Harthred is d-dead, My Lord," he stammered.

"*Dead?*" The king could not conceal his dismay. His glance traveled quickly to Nagaro and back to Delvin. "Where, then, are Captains Perenil and Worling?"

Delvin licked pale lips. "Captain Perenil is dead... too... My Lord. And Captain Worling is wounded."

"Wounded too badly to stand before me?" Again the pale blue eyes flicked to Nagaro and back.

"I-I'm afraid so, My Lord. He couldn't sit or stand when I saw him. He... he told me to make the report, My Lord."

"I see." Elgurn's glance returned to Nagaro. He seemed to expect Nagaro to speak.

Nagaro, however, merely returned the king's gaze and kept his silence. He was doing his best to keep his expression neutral as well. He preferred to let Delvin tell what he knew. There was so much bad news, and it seemed that it shouldn't come from him. The worst was yet to be told. The slightest of frowns flickered across Nagaro's face. It had been a bloody day. The cost of this victory was high. *And he had lost his count...*

The king's eyes narrowed slightly, watching Nagaro's face, but he returned his attention to Delvin.

"Very well, Guardsman, let's have your report." The words were cool and clipped.

Delvin shuffled his feet nervously. "We've lost a lot of men, My Lord. Besides Commander Harthred, and Captain Perenil, there's Oran and Morberk that I knew from the night shift— and another man I didn't know. And from the morning shift there's—"

The king interrupted. "Just tell me the number, Guardsman."

A glance at Delvin's face told Nagaro plainly that the young man had felt the rebuke.

Delvin tried again. "More than half of the force, My Lord," he said, anguish plain in his voice. "There's only fourteen that's able-bodied... and eight more that the healer is seeing to. He says at least six o' them will... recover... but they'll not be fit to man their posts for days... or weeks. I... I'm sorry, My Lord..." Delvin's voice died.

In the silence that followed, there was audible murmuring among the lords in the galleries.

Elgurn leaned forward slightly, eyeing the young Kelorin narrowly. "You know all this for a fact?"

Delvin looked startled. "Aye, My Lord!"

The king straightened, frowning. "And how is the palace being held secure, with so few of the Guard fit for duty?" His tone suggested to Nagaro that he thought he knew the answer.

Delvin evidently did not read the subtle signs, for he brightened visibly. "Captain Nagaro and his men are doing that, My Lord."

The muscles of the king's face tightened in bitter satisfaction. "Ah," he said, in a voice that was hard and flat. "Then you've come to report that the palace has been delivered from the Mahuk sea raiders into the hands of a band of pirates. Is that how it is?"

Nagaro stiffened. He felt his anger begin to rise.

The king's glance slid over to him again, but snapped back to Delvin when the young man burst out with, "No, My Lord! They came to help us! And Prince Elyan *asked* Captain Nagaro to secure the palace. I heard him do it!"

There were muted exclamations, at this news, from among the watching lords.

Elgurn sat a little stiffer. His face darkened. "And where is Prince Elyan now?

Delvin jumped. "He... he's wounded, My Lord—" he began in a wrenching voice. "The healer says it's bad—"

"*Elyan wounded!*" Distressed whispers ran along the gallery.

"How did this happen?" Elgurn asked sharply.

"He... he was fighting on the Common Wall, Zirda. They said he was struck from behind. But I didn't see it, My Lord. I was with Captain Nagaro at the city gate."

Elgurn turned instantly upon Nagaro. "How very *convenient* for you, Captain," he said sourly. "Shall we end this charade? You've obviously played skillfully upon this boy's innocence, but we should, perhaps, dismiss him now so that you and I may come to an *understanding*."

Nagaro had gotten a grip on his anger and was holding onto it with both hands. He felt sure that he understood Elgurn quite well, but he did his best to appear to misunderstand, hoping the king might ascertain his own error. He disliked the man too much, however, to keep the chill out of his voice.

"My Lord King," he said, "Prince Elyan may very well be mortally wounded. This is most grievous, and not at all convenient for anyone. As for guardsman Delvin, he is young but he has done very good service this day, and there is nothing I have to say to you that I'm not willing to say in his presence."

There was an intake of breath from Delvin, and a rustling along the gallery.

Elgurn's eyes registered surprise for the space of an instant before annoyance displaced it. The educated manner of Nagaro's speech was obviously not what the king had expected, but the manner was only a momentary distraction from the meaning. "What, then?" he inquired coldly, "Does it please you to stand here in front of him and discuss the price or your... *assistance?*"

Nagaro didn't move for the space of several full seconds. His anger was increasing again, and his grip on it was slipping. He'd heard Delvin gasp outright, and he could feel the young man's eyes on him.

"My assistance has no price," he said at last. His voice was deceptively calm, though there was an edge to it.

Elgurn stared hard at him. "Would you have us believe that a *pirate* does anything without the expectation that there is gold to be had?"

This was too much. Nagaro's eyes flashed. "We are pirates to the Mautep sea raiders, only, My Lord King, and it is slaves that we are chiefly known for stealing. My men followed me here for the defense of Edrovir. Our assistance was freely given, and if it has a *price*, it is nothing more than we've gotten from every man we have met this day— save you— and that is common courtesy and simple respect!"

Even as he finished speaking, Nagaro suspected he had let his anger carry him too far. There were shocked gasps from all along the gallery this time, followed by a breathless, pregnant silence.

"*Ai! Captain Nagaro!*" Delvin's pleading whisper sounded loud in the still room.

Elgurn had not taken his eyes from Nagaro's face, and his own face had gone livid. The king's jaw worked silently for a moment, and when at last he spoke, it was in a voice that shook with suppressed anger.

"Do you presume to rebuke me, Zirda? You would never dare to speak to me in such a manner, I think, were you not in control of my palace!"

Nagaro drew a long breath, fighting to master himself.

As much as he disliked Elgurn, and as grossly unjust as the man's words might be, this man was still the King of Edrovir, and picking a fight with him could have unpleasant consequences. Besides, there were others who might suffer for it. Delvin, for example, who had unlocked the back gate and let the pirates in. Clearly, he must try somehow to throw a bridge across this rift before it widened any further, but he couldn't make himself say that he'd been in the wrong in the face of Elgurn's insulting assumptions.

He drew another breath, and in letting it out, he tried to let his anger run out with it. He succeeded well enough to be able to speak in a voice that was at least superficially calm, though there was a tension underneath that a perceptive man might have read.

"I apologize for my tone, My Lord," he said evenly. "And I should perhaps have found other words to say that you are... *mistaken.* But my words needed saying. Has it not been said that there is nothing worse for a kingdom than to have a king who can't be told that he is wrong?'"

It was King Darion who had said those words, and everyone in the room very likely knew it. It seemed that Elgurn flinched at them, for his face stiffened and his glance faltered for an instant. Yet, surprisingly, he made no verbal response.

Nagaro continued, speaking over the murmurs that ran along the gallery.

"As for my men being in control of the palace, My Lord," he said, this time managing an approximation of a conciliatory tone, "We have only secured it against further attack. You and your people may come and go as you wish. My men will not hinder you. They're here to guard you from harm, not make you prisoners."

The king was studying Nagaro closely now. His face had relaxed fractionally, and the shrewdness of his glance had reasserted itself. He inclined his head when Nagaro ceased speaking, and smiled in a way that moved the muscles his face without extending to his eyes.

"I accept your apology, Captain," he said in a voice that was carefully controlled, though noticeably cool. "And I regret it if I may have... *misjudged*... you. Please understand that appearances have been against you. We all look forward to witnessing the proof of your words."

Nagaro had to bite down on the retort that suggested itself. The king's insincerity appalled him. The last bit was no better than saying, "We'll believe it when we see it". Did anyone present *not* see through this artfully qualified concession?

Yet Delvin, beside him, had relaxed and was looking greatly relieved. Not trusting himself to answer with words, Nagaro managed to convey his acceptance of the king's utterance with a bow. He supposed he had gotten the best he could expect from Elgurn. It appeared they had a truce.

"There are some further details to report, My Lord." he ventured, taking refuge in the mundane. He was determined now to give better than he had received. "Perhaps Guardsman Delvin would care to continue."

The king gave him that same stiff smile. "By all means." He turned to Delvin. "Guardsman?"

Delvin licked his lips. "Captain Nagaro should tell it, My Lord," he said quickly. "He'll do it better than I could."

Nagaro suppressed a groan. He would much rather that Delvin had at least made an effort, but he didn't like to push the youth further than he was willing to go. He therefore simply turned back to address himself to the king.

"With your leave, I will do so, My Lord," he said earnestly. "I was present when Captain Worling charged Delvin with making this report. The Captain was near fainting from loss of blood, and Guardsman Delvin asked me to accompany him here, knowing that there might be some details of the situation with which I would be more familiar."

In fact, "near fainting" was putting it mildly. Nagaro could see clearly in his mind's eye the stricken look on Captain Worling's ashen face when Delvin had told him that he was the only remaining officer of the Palace Guard. The man, a lanky Leithian in his mid forties, had gasped out his instructions to a trembling Delvin and promptly lapsed into unconsciousness. Fortunately, Captain Worling was one of those that Tred believed would fully recover.

The king's pale blue eyes were now regarding Nagaro keenly from a face that was otherwise carefully expressionless. "Proceed," was all he said.

Nagaro drew breath and plunged ahead. "As guardsman Delvin has told you, My Lord," he began, "my men have secured all of the entrances to the palace. They are even now going through all of the rooms to be sure there are no more Mautep raiders anywhere within these walls— other than the six who have surrendered. Of those who were outside, we believe that all have been either slain or driven to their ships, and the ships have taken to the sea and fled— the six remaining ships, that is. Two were burned and sunk—"

The king raised his hand. "Did you say that six of the raiders have surrendered?" he asked with a raised eyebrow.

"Yes, My Lord. They were guarding some prisoners in the palace dungeon," Nagaro explained. "They weren't inclined to fight to the death over the two wounded guardsmen and handful of gardeners and servants that they were holding in the cells, so they surrendered. We set their prisoners free and locked them in the cells instead."

The king frowned. "What do you expect us to do with them, may I ask?"

Nagaro sighed. "I promised them their lives, on my honor, My Lord, so I would not have you slay them. I might suggest that you see what ransom you can get for them."

"I see." The blue eyes regarded him shrewdly. "Perhaps we will do that. Go on."

Nagaro's face clouded. "There is not much more to tell, My Lord, save that it's been a bloody day. Delvin has told you the worst of it— the wounding of Prince Elyan and the decimation of the Palace Guard. I'm not certain how many men the City Garrison has lost, but Commander Korenthos looked rather grim. Among my own men, there are fourteen who will never see Pakoa again. And when those two Mautep ships went down they must have taken at least seventy slaves to their deaths."

Pain had been audible in Nagaro's voice, and he now paused and bowed his head. These were things he'd been pushing out of his mind all day. Speaking of them forced him to think about them again.

And I've lost my count of the men that I have slain...

The king spoke, in a hard voice. "When you have lived as long as I have, Captain," he observed tersely, "you will come to understand that everything one does that is worth doing— or needs doing— has a cost. A man who cannot bear that cost isn't fit to lead."

Nagaro's head came up. *Have you the nerve to speak of what things cost, Elgurn?* he thought. *With all that you have done?*

He met the king's cool stare unflinchingly. "I have learned enough about the cost of things," he said in a voice that carried throughout the room, "to know that it makes a difference whether it's paid out of your own purse, or that of another man."

Nagaro thought he caught the faintest flicker of something, then, that might have been pain, behind the king's blue eyes. If it had been there, however, it was gone in an instant, and there was no hint of it when the king spoke. "Enough!" he snapped. "Zirda, you have leave to go. The Guardsman will remain. I have more to say to him."

Nagaro stared at the man seated in the high seat. He was scarcely able to believe that he was being so summarily dismissed when men under his command had fought and died to help deliver the palace from the Mautep invaders. Angered afresh, he made no immediate move to depart. Instead he spoke, unbidden.

"I said you were all free to come and go as you please, My Lord King," he said. "But I think you might do best to keep your people within these chambers for the present— especially the ladies. We've scarcely begun to take up all the bodies, and it will require some time to do so with appropriate honor. Also, there are a number of piles of intended loot that the Mautep left behind when they fled. These we don't intend to touch. We leave them to you."

He turned on his heel, then, to go without waiting for a response, though the king's expression, which he glimpsed as he turned, spoke volumes. He had not gone more than half a dozen strides in the direction of the door, however, when a voice stopped him in his tracks.

"Captain Nagaro, wait!"

It was a woman's voice, gentle yet commanding, and very like that of the Lady Marmine who had raised him from infancy. Such were the patterns of courtesy engraved upon Nagaro's soul that he would have answered that voice even had he not known to whom it belonged. As it was, he turned about on the instant and came back to stand on the rectangle of black marble before the king's high seat.

Delvin hadn't moved from there, but stood gaping at the regal, dark-haired woman who had come to stand just in front of the left-hand end of the dais. She must have come from one of the side rooms. Perhaps the wooden structure of the spectators' gallery on that side of the room had concealed her entrance and she had only moved into view after Nagaro had turned his back.

Nagaro came to halt in front of the woman and executed a bow that was, this time, his deepest and most elegant. "My Lady Queen," he said as he straightened. "How may I serve you?"

Queen Semorel wore no circlet. Instead, her own dark brown hair, lightly interspersed with strands of silver, was wound crown-like about her head. She had always been a tall, slender woman. Nagaro remembered her so, but now she seemed thinner still, and somehow insubstantial, ethereal, in a shimmering gown of pale blue silk. She had been beautiful, but now her face appeared almost waxen, the skin stretched to translucency over the underlying bones.

Her gray eyes, though, were the same as ever— gentle, but reserved. Kind, yet distant.

She inclined her head to him in acknowledgment of his show of respect. "First," she said, "you may do so by accepting our thanks for this deliverance."

Nagaro was surprised by this, though he knew that kindness had ever been the queen's way. He inclined his head also, and said, "This is surely light duty, My Lady."

As he raised his eyes, his glance was drawn for an instant to Elgurn, who had risen from his seat. The king was standing rigidly at the edge of the dais, his gaze fixed upon his queen. The expression on his face was a curious commingling of admiration, exasperation, and pain. Nagaro had no time to wonder at this, however, for his attention was drawn back to the queen, who was speaking to him again.

"Such gallantry deserves reward, Captain. How may we show our gratitude?" She smiled at him benevolently. There were shocked murmurs among the lords seated in the gallery.

Nagaro was caught off guard. He had never considered any sort of reward, nor had he expected the queen to diverge so far from the stance her husband had taken. He glanced at Elgurn, more than half expecting an explosion.

In fact the king was frowning, "*Semorel—*" he began upon a rising note.

But the queen waved her husband's warning aside with a frail hand. "Should we not be gracious, Elgurn?" she asked him in a tone that was gently chiding.

To Nagaro's surprise, the king appeared to yield. "Of course, my dear," he said in an unexpectedly mild tone. But then he added, "Let us see how he reveals himself by his request." The glance he gave Nagaro contained both a challenge and a silent warning, as if he expected Nagaro to take advantage of the queen's natural generosity.

The pause had given Nagaro time to consider what he would say. He first returned the king a look of injured innocence. Then, turning back to the queen, he bowed low again before her.

"I ask only to be allowed to bury my dead with honor, among the others who have fallen in Edrovir's defense, My Lady," he said in voice that he made sure could be heard among the gallery. "And, if it is possible to raise the sunken Mahuk ships, I beg that the bodies of the drowned slaves aboard them may be laid to rest in proper graves. Their names may never be known, but at least their bones should not lie lost and forgotten at the bottom of the river."

The queen smiled again, ever so gently and a little sadly. "The first is easily granted," she said. "And the second shall be granted also, if as you say, it is possible."

Then, looking at him, she seemed to notice something, and she frowned. "You are wounded, Captain," she said. "And your hurts are untended."

Nagaro glanced at the oozing gash on his arm. "I'll have it tended in good time," he said. "There are others in far more need, and the healers are busy."

"Then you must send for Master Ambras, my physician," she said. "I will write out the summons myself, and this young guardsman can deliver it." She turned to Delvin. "Do you know how to find the Street of the Brass Lantern, young man?"

Delvin bobbed his head and managed to say, "Aye, My Lady."

The queen returned her gaze to Nagaro. "I hope that will be of some help."

Nagaro inclined his head to her. "It will be most welcome, My Lady. I have my own ship's doctor, and there is a healer employed by the Guard, but they are overtaxed, and they will need to rest."

"Yes, of course—" The queen abruptly stopped speaking. Her eyes fluttered closed and a spasm of pain crossed her face.

The king was at her side in an instant, catching her elbow to support her. "My dear," he murmured solicitously. "You shouldn't tax yourself so."

But the queen opened her eyes again and smiled faintly. She patted her husband's arm. "I am quite all right, Elgurn," she said in a voice that was surprisingly firm. "And I must yet ask the Captain a favor." She turned her gray eyes back to Nagaro.

He swallowed past a sudden tightness in his throat. The queen was plainly not well. "Anything, My Lady Queen," he said huskily. "Only name it."

"Will you have your men seek for my daughter?" There was, perhaps, just the slightest catch in the queen's voice.

Nagaro felt as if a stone had been dropped into his stomach. "The princess?" he said in dismay. "But... isn't she *here?*"

The queen's gray eyes held him. Very gently she shook her head. "Nevien complained of a headache last night, Captain, and left the table a few minutes before the raiders burst in upon us. We have seen nothing of her since, nor heard any word..." The Queen's voice trailed as emotion overtook her.

"*Vothra!*"

Nagaro's mind reeled. He ran a hand distractedly through his hair. *Nevien missing! Nevien in the hands of the Mautep...* With an effort he brought his focus back to the queen's face. He wasn't even aware of Elgurn's look of annoyance.

"We can find her ourselves—"the king began, but Nagaro paid him no heed, cutting across his words.

"We will look for the princess at once, My Lady," he said earnestly. "If she is anywhere within the palace or about the grounds, you may be sure that we will find her and bring her to you."

And if she isn't there...

But he couldn't bring himself to voice that thought— not to the queen. He made one final hurried bow to the royal lady. He could read the gratitude in her eyes, though she seemed too much overcome to speak. Then he spun about, without waiting to be dismissed, and strode from the Audience Chamber, oblivious to the king's thunderous look and the babble of excited voices that rose behind him.

***

Taru waylaid his friend in the Compass Room outside the Audience Chamber's wide open doorway.

"Are ye daft, Nagaro? What were ye *thinking?* Telling the king he should have more courtesy. Ye're lucky he didn't throw ye in the dungeon for that! I tell ye, I couldn't bear to watch!"

Nagaro brushed past his friend impatiently. "Not now, Taru," he said distractedly. "The princess is missing, and we have to find her! Where is Pavo?"

Taru gaped at him. "The princess? Missing...?" he asked in confusion.

"Yes— Hoy, Pavo! Over here!"

The massive Hashtep had just entered the room. In answer to Nagaro's call, he altered his course and came directly to where the other two men stood. He listened impassively to Nagaro's news and immediately responded to his friend's request for a report on the progress of the search for any remaining sea raiders.

"We have gone through all of room, upstair and downstair," he explained. "We have not find any more Mautep warrior. Also we have not find any young woman who looks like lady. Maybe Mautep have taken her away in one of their ship."

Nagaro frowned, but he had already thought about this. "They were cut off from their ships very early in the attack," he said seriously. "Unless they caught her very quickly, and took her to a ship immediately, I don't think they can have taken her away with them."

"But if they have," he added, with rather more heat, "we'll have to go after them and fetch her back!"

Taru looked taken aback. "Well, *someone* ought to," he conceded. "But I don't see why it need be *us*."

Nagaro checked himself. There were quite a number of the other crewmen in the room, and some of those closest were obviously listening.

"We have the ships to do it," he said in as easy a tone as he could manage, and with an effort at a careless shrug. "But most likely she's hidden somewhere in the palace— or perhaps in the garden, or about the grounds. She might have been fainting or unconscious, and so not heard our men when they passed through making their search."

Fortunately, this statement seemed to have satisfied most of the men who were listening, although Taru still regarded him with suspicion. Pavo Maat also gave him a glance with his enigmatic eyes.

The truth was that Nagaro would have been hard put to explain exactly why he felt such a strong protective impulse towards Princess Nevien. He had told Taru long ago that he didn't consider his marriage to the princess to be valid— since it had been made without his true consent— and he had meant it.

It's just that I knew her, he told himself. *And she was kind... gentle... innocent...*

He issued orders, then, trying to suppress his urgency. A contingent of men would be sent to go back through the palace, searching room by room, looking for places a woman might hide. A second contingent would go out to search the gardens and all around the palace on the outside. He made sure not to cast prudence aside, however, making sure that there were still men left to guard all the palace entrances.

Pavo, he directed to lead the first party, and Taru the second, as much so that they would have to stop looking at him as for any other reason.

Nagaro pointedly did not include himself in either search party, thinking it would be better if he turned to other things. He didn't want to appear too interested in the matter. Once the searchers had gone, he tried to busy himself, but his mind kept running over the various possible fates that might have befallen the princess.

It didn't help that he wasn't clearly needed anywhere. He checked with each of his work details and found everything proceeding apace.

Timegar and Moraga were very capably overseeing the security of the building. Delvin had been dispatched to fetch the queen's healer, and in the meantime, Tredhold and the Palace Guard's physician had Nanu and Chaheel helping them with the wounded. The Guard's infirmary was filled to capacity and the hall outside of it was being pressed into service as well.

Tredhold gave Nagaro a hollow look when asked about the prince's condition. "No worse, but no better," was all the answer that he gave.

Landros was directing the grim work of gathering up the bodies of the fallen. They were using the Great Hall as their morgue, laying the bodies out in rows with the Edroviran casualties— guards and pirates— on one side and the Mautep on the other. Landros gave a satisfied nod upon hearing the news that their slain brethren would be buried with the same honor as the fallen guardsmen.

"It's no more than fair," he said gruffly. "It's the least they could do for these brave lads."

Nagaro walked along the row of his fallen comrades, fixing the face of each in his memory. That sad duty served temporarily to take his mind off of the princess's fate.

As he moved away from the row of bodies, however, he found himself near the kitchen end of the Great Hall. A door there, on the side opposite the windows, opened into a kind of atrium that led to the central hallway. Looking at that door, Nagaro recalled that the atrium also housed the foot of a staircase leading up to the second and third floors. The thought sprang into his mind that this was almost certainly the way the princess would have gone when she left the hall the previous evening.

He knew the way— excruciatingly well— for he had walked it many times, though not under the power of his own will. He hadn't meant to involve himself in the search, but the door stood provocatively ajar, and he found himself thinking, *why not?*

He knew the way to the royal apartments and knew his way around them as well. Who could search them better than he? He frowned. Should he tell anyone what he meant to do? After a moment's hesitation, he decided not to. One of the advantages of being the commander was that he wasn't directly accountable to anyone.

Taking a deep breath, he walked decisively to the door and set his hand on the handle to swing it wide. Stepping through into the room beyond, he made for the stairs.

Chapter 13

The Royal Chambers

I t was not until he reached the final flight and stepped out at the crossroads of hallways at the top of the stairs that the memories descended in force.

He had trodden in many familiar places already that day without suffering much trouble of mind. Attention to the task at hand had driven him forward, and the exhilaration of feeling the power of his gift bend to his will had carried him along. Now, however, the battle no longer pressed and his sword hung inert at his side as he stood in that terribly familiar place, so close to the rooms of the royal living quarters.

He had seen a great deal of this corridor— far more than he had wanted to. And he remembered, oh yes, he remembered... *the unshakable grip of the will-enslaving drug, heskial, more cruel than any iron chain... Dreigen, the king's sinister Lore Master— dark, gaunt, and hungry-eyed— like some pitiless vulture bending over him... The three Leithian lords, Kale, Bron, and Gillard, who had been his keepers— one painfully kind, one smugly mocking, one purposefully and casually cruel...*

...And Nevien...

His steps had slowed involuntarily, even as his heart began to race and his breath came more quickly while the wave of memories washed over him. But the rising panic receded a little when he focused on the princess. Instinctively he grasped at that one thread out of the tangled skein and held it. By forcing himself to breathe slowly and deeply, as Tredhold had once taught him, he was able to slow the hammering of his heart.

There were also uncomfortable memories involving the princess, to be sure— moments of excruciating embarrassment over something the drug-bound puppet part of him had said or done... how he had been made to press himself upon her in the bedchamber... or the agony of lying helplessly immobile beside her on the bed while she tried to hide the fact that she was weeping.

Still, in spite of all that, Nevien had been the one bright spot in that dark time, because of her kindness to him, her sweetness, and more than anything else, perhaps, her innocence. It was these thoughts that brought him firmly back to the present and the matter at hand.

Where was the princess?

Nagaro looked carefully around him at the third floor hallways. They appeared to be completely deserted. All was still, although there were clear signs that the Mautep had been here. Doors stood ajar, and various items lay scattered on the floor as if carelessly discarded. Most were articles of clothing or other personal effects. In one case, a large chest had been moved out into the hallway and abandoned.

There was a balustrade around the open top of the stairwell, and it was possible to walk all the way around it to reach any of four hallways that branched out to the four points of the compass.

To Nagaro's left, the south hall led past suites of rooms he had never been allowed to enter, the function of which he didn't know, to a pair of doors with windows set in them through which streamed the light of the mid-afternoon sun. Those doors, Nagaro knew, opened onto one end of a long balcony with a view of the sea to the southward.

To the west, directly in front of him, was a short hall leading to one of the palace's little towers. The lower room of this tower was sealed with a heavy oak door. He could see from where he stood that the door was closed, as always, and he knew that beyond that door lay Dreigen's sanctum... two chambers, one above the other... *where the Lore Master lurked.*

His breath caught in his throat as the image of Dreigen's dark, leering countenance rose in his mind. "*Oh, Vothra!*" He gasped as a sudden thought seized him. *What if Dreigen were in one of those rooms right now?*

Almost at once, a calming sigh seemed to breathe through his mind, and words formed themselves:

The one you fear most is not here, Spirit called Nagaro. He is below. The one called Elgurn thought to use him for defense, but no opportunity presented itself, and besides, he fears to play with fire.

"Well he might," Nagaro muttered, under his breath as relief flooded through him. Silently, he added, *thank you.* There was no response.

Fleetingly, he thought of asking the Benevolent Spirit's help in finding Nevien, but that wasn't what Vothra was for. The Spirit had given him only the information needed to steady him, so that he could carry out his own search of this fraught place.

She wouldn't be hiding in Dreigen's rooms in any case, he told himself. No one would willingly enter those two tower rooms— and nothing could have induced him to search them, even knowing that Dreigen wasn't there.

The short north hall also led to a tower, but its lower chamber was open to the hallway. It was a sun room, its outer wall pierced by a number of windows.

And finally, there was the east hallway. The longest of the four, it led to the suites of private rooms belonging to the royal family. That was the way the princess would have gone after leaving dinner the previous evening, and so it was the way that Nagaro meant to go as well.

As he followed the balustrade around the top of the stairs, however, he was brought up short by a sound: a series of three faint, muffled thumps. If it hadn't been otherwise so quiet, he might have missed them, for they were barely audible. He stood still, listening, trying to decide whence they had come.

Finally, there came one more thump, and the direction seemed to be from the north tower. Frowning, he turned and walked as quickly and silently as he could in that direction. He drew his sword, just in case. It was true, as he had told the king, that there could still be sea raiders lurking in these halls.

Upon reaching the sunroom, he peered cautiously in through the doorway, then stood, perplexed. The room was very plainly empty. Its only furnishings were several seats spaced around the walls, a pair of tapestries, and two small carved tables on each of which had stood a porcelain vase. One of the tables had been knocked over and its vase lay smashed upon the floor. The sound of it falling could not have been what he had heard, however. The breaking vase would have made a very different and much louder sound.

It took a moment for the answer to occur to him. The thumping must have come from the room above. But where was the door leading to the stairs?

Nagaro stepped forward into the center of the room, closed his eyes, and turned silently around, trying to picture the room from memory. Though he had never been in the upper tower room, he had been in this lower one a number of times. It seemed to him that there had been a door... *and it was...*

His eyes flicked open... *There*, in the wall to the left of the entrance— where one of the tapestries now hung...

He tightened his fingers on the leather handgrip of his sword and cautiously approached the wall hanging. *Was the princess hiding there? Or was it one of the Mautep?*

To find out, he would have to give away his presence. There was no help for it. He drew a breath and spoke aloud, beginning with the more optimistic possibility.

"If someone is there, you needn't be afraid. The sea raiders have been driven from the palace."

He waited for several seconds, but there was only silence. Finally, he spoke again, this time in Hashti.

"I know where you are. Put down your sword and come out."

Still there was only silence. After several more seconds, Nagaro moved. Stepping swiftly forward, sword held ready, he seized the edge of the tapestry with his left hand and flung it aside. He found himself staring at a closed door there in the wall, just where he had remembered it.

Shaking his head in perplexity, he put his hand on the door handle. If there was anyone here, they must be just beyond the door, or on the stairs, or in the room above. *And they had surely heard his voice.*

Gritting his teeth, he turned the handle and opened the door in a single quick movement. Again, there was no one visible on the other side. There was only a little vestibule at the foot of a flight of stairs that led up and to the left.

He stepped quickly through the doorway, sword ready, but there was clearly no one in the vestibule. The light from a tiny window at the top of the stairs revealed that there was also no one on the stairs, nor on the landing at the top. There was only another door, there at the top beside the window. It was closed.

Nagaro was beginning to wonder if he had been mistaken about the source of the thumping noise. He had heard no more sounds since entering the tower. Still, he thought he should complete his search, since he had come so far.

So, with his sword before him, he stealthily ascended the steps. The door at the top looked very thick and solid. It also had a prominent keyhole, though not the sort through which it was possible to see anything.

He took a deep breath. "If anyone is there, you have nothing to fear from me—" he began, and stepped back, startled, when a muffled voice answered him from the room behind the door.

"Mercy! Mercy on the old man—"

It was a man's voice coming through the wood. It didn't sound exactly old, though it was rather indistinct, which made it hard to be certain. Instinctively, Nagaro grasped the doorhandle but found that it wouldn't turn. He supposed it might be locked from the inside if the occupant were trying to escape the Mautep.

"It's all right to come out," he said, raising his voice so that he might be heard. "The sea raiders have been driven off." Who was it, he wondered? A servant, perhaps?

The voice came indistinctly from inside again.

"Mercy on the old man, his hair is white as snow—"

That was what it sounded like. Nagaro frowned. Abruptly then, the doorhandle rattled, though the door remained firmly closed. This was followed a second later by a resounding *thump* that made the whole door shake. Nagaro guessed that the man must have flung himself against the other side of the door.

"*Alas! Alas!*" came the wailing voice. "*They have locked him away and the key is in the river—*"

That was as much as Nagaro thought he understood before the rest was drowned out by a barrage of smaller thumps, suggesting that the man was beating on the door with his fists.

"Stop! Stop!" Nagaro cried urgently. "You'll only hurt yourself!"

There was silence for several seconds. Then, very muffled, as if the man had moved away, came the words, "*Mercy on the old man—*"

And that was all, though Nagaro called several more times to the man, asking how he had gotten locked in, whether he was hurt, and how long he had been there. In the end there was nothing he could do but give up the effort.

"Take courage! I will find help for you," were the last words he shouted through the door before turning around and descending the stairs. He wondered whether the man were hard of hearing and hadn't understood him, or whether being locked in the room for hours had made him a bit hysterical. The man hadn't seemed entirely coherent, but he was at least probably safe where he was.

In any case, his rescue would have to wait. Nagaro had to finish his search for Princess Nevien.

Passing out through the tapestry-covered lower door, he went back through the sun room and along the short hall to the space at the top of the balustrade-encircled stairwell. There he turned left and entered the long east hallway that contained the royal apartments.

Nagaro knew the princess's room was near the farther end of the hallway, on the left. He had meant to begin his detailed search there, but as he moved along the hall, his feet slowed again. He knew what rooms lay behind almost ever door along this corridor. He'd been in many of them, and they held unpleasant memories. The princess's bedchamber was not the worst in that respect, but it was a close second, and he had to pass the worst room to get to it.

And another thought was nagging at him.

It was a natural thing to call out to the princess as he looked for her, but what if she recognized his voice? His appearance might be greatly altered, but his voice surely wasn't. If she saw him first, before she heard him speak, his secret would probably be safe, but if she *heard* him first...

Regretfully he came to the conclusion that he must search silently.

To set his mind on a different path, or perhaps to delay having to enter the worst rooms, he took a detour into the first of the large bedchambers along the lefthand side of the hall. He knew it belonged to the king, though he had never before been inside it.

The room was deserted, and it had been ransacked. The doors of the wardrobe were flung wide, and the contents strewn about. The blankets had been pulled from the bed, and even the long window curtains had been pulled down. Nagaro did not stay long, but passed into the queen's chamber through an internal door that linked it with the king's. This second bedroom was in a similar condition, and Nagaro's heart began to sink. If the princess had tried to hide somewhere in these rooms, it seemed she would surely have been discovered by the sea raiders.

He went back into the hallway and from there to the queen's sitting room. This room also had its curtains down, and clearly contained no other hiding place. After that came two small closet-rooms used for storing linens and the like— also quite unpopulated— and then he was approaching the room he had been dreading the most.

It was a small room, next to the one that would be Prince Elyan's, and it was where he had been kept during the time he had spent in Lankura as Prince Leyel.

The room could be entered only from the hallway, and he could see as he approached that its door was wide open. Once again his steps slowed. He remembered the room being bleakly furnished, with a pallet bed, a tiny bedside table, a washstand, and a larger table with a chair, all very drab. It had usually been dimly lit, the heavy, dark draperies on the window being used to block out the light.

He'd come to loathe everything about that room.

He had endured countless "experiments" there devised by Dreigen, and been forced to sit— or stand, or lie— for hours, listening to the scratching of Dreigen's pen as the Lore Master filled the pages of his accursed notebooks with accounts of those experiments. It was there that he had been commanded, more times than he could count, to drink the next dose of the drug that had kept him enslaved. He'd been unable to do anything other than comply.

On occasions when the drug had begun to wear off when he had been elsewhere in the palace, he had found himself briefly in control of his limbs. At such times he had tried to run away, but he had always been overtaken when the shaking and the pain of heskial withdrawal had come upon him. Then one or more of his keepers would catch him, fling him to the ground, and hold him until Dreigen came to stick one of the abominable bladder-thorns into his arm and inject the heskial directly into his blood.

Afterwards, he had invariably awakened back on the narrow bed in that terrible little room, fully conscious but bound by the paralyzing "deep trance" of heskial. So far as he knew, he had spent every one of his nights there. He was sweating as he took the last few steps to the room's open doorway. He drew a steadying breath and forced himself to look inside.

It was absurd to imagine that the room would be as he remembered it. Still, he must have been expecting it to be. Instead, what he saw when he looked was so startling that he drew his breath in sharply.

The room had been transformed into a small sitting room, furnished with a bookcase, several comfortable-looking seats, and a low table, all in dark wood. The cushions of the seats and the carpet on the floor were in hues of blue and green, while the plaster walls, which he remembered as being a dull gray, had been repainted in a clean shade of white. There were pictures on those formerly bare walls— two pictures of sunny green hills with trees and flowers. The curtains that framed the window were snowy white, and parted, allowing light to bathe the room. A potted ivy plant graced the windowsill.

Nagaro stood quite still in the doorway for several long seconds, drinking in the blue-and-green vision, like a man athirst in the desert who has stumbled upon an oasis. The sight had a remarkable effect on his spirit, like a soothing poultice applied to an open sore. It gave him a different picture, a new image that he could hold in his mind whenever he thought of this place.

He stepped forward into the room, instinctively seeking to bathe himself in its healing. It was only then that it occurred to him to be grateful for the fact that the room had not been disturbed by the Mautep. Presumably they had seen at a glance that it contained nothing of value to them.

It also contained no place for anyone to hide. The curtains were short, not the floor-length draperies as he had seen in the bedchambers.

Nagaro frowned, remembering his mission. Nevien could not be here, and he shouldn't linger.

Before leaving, however, he crossed to the window, swung it open, and looked out. There'd been a time when he had been left standing facing that window when the draperies had been parted. He had been left there forgotten for the better part of an hour while his muscles had screamed and knotted from standing rigidly in one position. It had been the first time in his life that he had seen the sea— or at least a little bit of it.

He could see it now as he looked out across the garden, past the saddle in the long ridge that joined Kel Lankura's shoulder to Castle Rock. Even after the wall on the ridge's crest had been made higher, there was still a bit of flat blue-gray to be seen there, extending to the horizon.

But today there was something more. The tips of four masts could also be seen poking up above the wall, four masts from which fluttered the black-and-white sword banners of his own devising. A little smile curled his lips. What changes the past seven years had wrought!

He also could see and hear his own men moving about down below, searching in the garden. They obviously hadn't yet found the princess. But neither had he, and it seemed to him less and less likely that he would with every room he entered.

Grimly, he turned away from the window and went back to the hall, where he stood for a moment, uncertain.

None of the rooms along this hallway offered much in the way of concealment, and it looked as if the Mautep had been through them all. If Nevien had fled ahead of the raiders to some area where they had searched less thoroughly, she could be anywhere. He had already nearly reached the end of the hall. There was another stairway at that end, he knew. Though physically closer to the front of the building than the stair by which he had ascended, the royal family had always referred to it as the "back stair" because it was narrower and less grand than the other, and it ended in a hallway beside the quarters of the Palace Guard, near an exit leading to the stable.

If the princess had tried to descend that way, she would have run right into the fight.

Nagaro frowned, not wanting to think about that. The sea raiders probably wouldn't have harmed the princess. They would have meant to ransom her. But since they had been forced to flee with little to show for their efforts, they might decide to keep her as a kind of prize— carry her away to be a slave or concubine as had happened to the lady named Emril in Pavo's tale.

Nagaro shivered. He knew that as long as there was life in him, he couldn't allow the Princess Nevien to suffer such a fate.

He shook his head to banish the unwelcome train of thought and turned back to his task. He hadn't yet looked in any of the rooms on the other side of the hall, but he decided to finish on this side first and work his way back along the other.

He passed rather hurriedly through the prince's room. Though it had nominally been his room when he'd been married to the princess, he had never actually used it— had never even lain on the bed, much less slept in it. Still, it felt awkward being there, knowing that it was now Elyan's room.

That thought led to another one— of the prince now clinging to life— which Nagaro tried to shake off as well. The room had been disturbed somewhat less than the other bedchambers. The draperies were still in place, and Nagaro had his sword ready as he made certain there was no one behind them. Since there were no other obvious hiding places in the room, he headed for the interior door joining Elyan's room to Nevien's.

The door was nearly closed, open no more than a crack, which allowed him to move it without making a sound. He swung it open and paused on the threshold, struck immediately by the changes. The bed was still the same bed, but it had been moved across the room to the wall between the windows. The table at which he had been sitting when the princess had given him the glass of wine to drink was gone, and the pair of chairs with it. Instead there was a small writing desk. The changes helped to keep him steady by anchoring him firmly in the present.

He noticed that the drapery on the nearer window were still in place. As he approached this window to check it, his boots crunched on some shards of broken pottery. The washstand had been knocked over, and the finely wrought china basin, pitcher, and drinking cup lay smashed in pieces on the floor.

He quickly determined that there was no one hiding behind the long curtain, probing it cautiously at arm's length with the flat of his sword. As he turned around, an object on the dressing table caught his eye and nearly stopped his breath.

It was a woman's decorative hair comb, carved from cream-colored ivory with the shapes of three delicately unfolding rose blossoms along its spine. Nagaro recognized it. It was one of a matching pair, and he could picture exactly how Nevien had been accustomed to wear them in her honey-colored hair, one on either side. The comb was lying on the dressing table beside her hairbrush and comb, just where the princess would have put it down after removing it while she reached for the other one.

But where was the other one? Was it still in her hair? Or lost somewhere in the palace along whatever way she had fled— or whichever way she had been taken?

The tale that single comb seemed to tell of an action interrupted brought Nagaro's heart into his mouth. He stooped, hastily searching the floor around the dressing table for the missing comb. The second comb, however, was nowhere to be seen.

As Nagaro straightened, he thought he heard a small noise— a slight creak of wood, perhaps? He froze, listening, but there was no further sound, if sound there had been.

He searched the room with his eyes, and noticed that there were two large wardrobes against the farther wall, on the other side of the bed and flanking a chest of drawers. One of the wardrobes was standing open, and half of its contents had been pulled from the hangers and lay in a heap on the floor in front of it.

But the doors of the other wardrobe were closed!

Nagaro's heart began to hammer against his ribs. Cautiously, stealthily, he moved across the floor, avoiding bits of broken china. He rounded the foot end of the bed and approached the closed wardrobe. As he did so, he saw what the bed had previously hidden from view. There was part of a garment— blue, the skirt of a gown, perhaps— protruding from under the bottom edge of one of the closed wardrobe doors. It was as if the wardrobe had been opened, the contents disarranged, and the doors hastily closed again.

And it was too obvious. Surely the princess couldn't have concealed herself there and been missed by both the Mautep and the pirates making their earlier sweep of the building? Nagaro's fellow crewmen most likely had been moving fast, looking for men in plain sight. They might well have missed this possible hiding place. But the Mautep would have had time to look for potential hostages.

Nagaro's hand tightened on the hilt of his sword. When he got to within a dozen feet of the wardrobe doors, he noticed something even more telling. There was the faint, dusty outline of a footprint on the protruding blue cloth. The dimensions of the mark were clearly those of a man's boot, and the toe end was pointing toward the inside of the wardrobe.

Nagaro took a step back, his sword held ready, and spoke in Hashti.

"I am Thief of Slaves, and I know you are there. Put down your sword and come out! You will not be harmed."

There was silence, while the seconds ticked by: *One... two... three... four...*

And then the doors of the wardrobe exploded outward. The Mautep warrior who leaped out drove his own blade straight at Nagaro's chest in a lightning-quick lunge.

"Kill me, slave dog," he snarled. "Or I will kill you!"

The clash of steel on steel sounded horribly loud in the still room as Nagaro parried. Three times he turned the Mautep's blade aside before he was able to oblige the man by finding his heart and stilling its beat forever.

Stooping, Nagaro wiped his sword on the man's gold-colored tunic, then stood with bowed head as he murmured the prayer used by hunters and executioners:

"Vothra, guide this spirit in its passing, as I would have you guide my spirit in the hour when my time shall come."

As he raised his head, he thought for the second time since entering the room that he heard a very small sound. This time it seemed it was just the slightest rustle of movement and it seemed to come from somewhere *behind him*, fairly close at hand.

The hair rose on his neck as he spun about, his sword up and ready.

There was no one there.

The room behind him appeared as empty as when he had entered. *But it hadn't been empty then, had it?* Nagaro moistened dry lips and stood very still, considering. He might have imagined that second sound, but then he hadn't imagined the first. Was there any possible place of concealment that he had missed?

The drapery of the second window was down on the floor in a flattened heap. The wardrobe, now open behind him, clearly held no one else. The bedclothes on the bed in front of him were smooth and flat. There was no space under the bed either. Like all the beds he had seem in the palace, it was built on a solid-sided platform of wood… He sucked in his breath as his thoughts spun suddenly to a halt.

The canopy of the bed was also built of wood!

He knew this very well, having lain so many times under it, helplessly staring up at the carvings on the canopy's underside. Yes, the canopy was of solid wood, with just a decorative fringe of fabric around it. Though it surely wasn't strong enough to bear the weight of an average man, it would very probably support that of a slender woman.

Hastily, he thrust his sword back into its sheath. Three quick steps took him around to the foot end of the bed. There he raised his foot and set it on the footboard. At the same time, he reached up and grasped the edge of the canopy, feeling for the wooden frame under the fabric. He pulled himself up, straightening his legs until his head was thrust above the canopy edge.

He found himself staring into the frightened face of a young woman, not three feet from his own.

Chapter 14

Nevien

S he had been lying on top of the canopy, but had reared back, raising herself with her hands as he made his sudden appearance. Her hair, the color of dark honey, hung loose on the right side of her face, while on the left it was still twisted up and held by an ivory comb, a twin to the one on the dressing table. Her eyes held no trace of recognition. They were wide and startled, and every bit as green as he remembered them.

"*Nevien...*" he breathed, as relief washed over him. Then he hastily corrected himself. "I mean, My Lady Princess?" He managed to twist the end of it into a question, although he knew the answer.

"*Ye-es...*" she said uncertainly. Then she added, heartfelt relief sounding in her voice as well, "Sweet Lady Lissafel! You gave me such a turn!"

Nagaro straightened his arms to put himself at a little more distance from her. "I'm sorry I surprised you," he said seriously.

He was a bit startled to hear her swear, though she *would* swear by the Lady of course. Lissafel, the maiden goddess, was a favorite among Leithian women. He just didn't remember that she had previously been inclined to swear at all.

"There's no more need to fear," he went on. "The sea raider who was here is dead, and I believe the others have been driven from the palace. My men are making sure that all is safe and secure."

The princess gathered her legs under her and maneuvered herself into a kneeling position. She was studying him now, her delicate brows coming together in a little frown.

"But who are *you*, and where did you come from?" she asked, fear having evidently given way to curiosity. "You're not one of the Palace Guard, or the City Garrison. That's plain."

Nagaro dropped down to the floor and stepped back away from the bed so that he was fully in her field of view. He gave her his very best bow. "I am called Nagaro," he said simply. "My men and I saw smoke rising from Lankura early this morning, and we came to see what the trouble was and whether we could help."

Her brows shot up. "Nagaro the Pirate?" she asked. There was surprise in her voice, but not a trace of apprehension.

Nagaro winced, but shrugged. "I have been called that," he said, as lightly as he was able. "I prefer 'Captain Nagaro'. We've been seeking for you, My Lady. The queen, your mother, has been very worried."

A shadow instantly crossed the princess's face. "Oh dear," she said with a sigh. "Mother *would* worry, of course. And Father would too, though he wouldn't show it."

"Can you get down?" he asked.

"Yes, I can." Nevien backed carefully, on hands and knees, towards the head end of the canopy on the side farther from the wardrobes.

Nagaro moved around to that side, frowning a little.

He wondered how she had gotten up onto her perch and whether she might need assistance getting down, but the princess seemed to know what she was doing. She dropped onto her stomach again at the edge of the canopy and confidently swung her legs over the side. The skirt of her dark green gown caught a little on the canopy edge, briefly revealing slender calves clad in cream-colored stockings. Then she got one foot on the headboard of the bed, slid down a little until her other foot found the top of the night stand, and a little more to reach the edge of the mattress. From there, it was an easy drop to the floor.

She landed lightly, shook out her skirts with a shrug of her body, and gave them a perfunctory dusting with her hands. As she straightened, she reached up and pulled the ivory comb from her hair. Shaking out the loosened tresses, she quickly ran her fingers through them in an un-self-conscious gesture that left the hair smoother, but still a bit disheveled.

"I've been wanting to do that for *hours*," she murmured.

Treading gingerly among the shards of china on the floor, she moved to the dressing table and laid the second comb next to the first. She turned, then, to give Nagaro a wan smile. "And I'm perishing of thirst."

Nagaro had been studying the princess with mingled surprise and admiration. He'd found her quite attractive when she was sixteen, but he realized now that she'd been little more than a girl then, though very fair in face and figure. Now she was in the full flower of young womanhood.

The dark green gown she wore, accented with gold embroidery, was very becoming, as it echoed the color of her eyes. It had a very modest neckline, but the bodice was tailored so precisely to the contours of her body as to make any further revelation quite superfluous. He couldn't help noticing that her figure was a bit fuller than he remembered—everywhere except the waist.

Her coloring and features were as he remembered them, a striking mix of Kelorin and Leithian. Her hair was several shades lighter than that of any Kelorin, a rich, light brown with golden highlights. The green of her eyes was rare among Leithians and unheard of among the Kelorin, but her brows and lashes were dark, not the Leithian's pale gold. Her face was neither of the rounder Leithian form nor as narrow as that of most Kelorin. She had a Kelorin's high cheekbones, though, with just enough of the strong Kelorin chin to be pleasing, and her delicately sculpted nose was just ever so slightly elevated at the bridge.

He had heard that she had a scar— the work of her abusive second husband, Gillard Marchent. He saw it now, on the left side of her face. It was a thin, pale line about an inch long, starting just below the temple. It didn't much mar her beauty, though it made him angry to think of anyone having hurt her.

All of these physical features Nagaro had noticed when he first saw her, or in the first few seconds after she had descended from the bed canopy. But what struck him most forcefully was the difference in her manner from what he had seen in her seven years before.

There was a somberness about her now that he didn't remember, and there was also the way she had sworn by the goddess Lissafel. She had the same directness and openness— it showed in the easy way that she spoke to him, despite the fact that she must think him a complete stranger— and one who had invaded her bedchamber at that. But the sweetness— the girlish innocence he remembered so well— was gone, as if burned away by the things that she had experienced during those intervening years.

It should have been obvious that she wouldn't be unchanged by the passing of seven years, especially when he had changed in so many ways. Yet, irrationally, he found himself thinking that those changes should have been prevented.

A guilty thought suddenly nagged at him— that he had run away, escaping from this place of dark machinations, and left her here, unprotected.

So it was that although the princess had spoken lightly of her thirst, Nagaro responded as if stung. "I'll find you some water," he said quickly. "Wait here while I look in the other room."

He set about it, too, before she could make any answer, striding away through the doorway that led to Prince Elyan's room. It was a very little thing to fetch her water, but at that moment, it was all that he could do.

There was indeed still water in the pitcher on the wash stand in the prince's room. Nagaro filled the heavy glass tumbler that was there, and came quickly back into the princess's chamber.

He found that Nevien hadn't stayed where he had left her. She was on the other side of the bed, staring down at the body of the Mautep raider. The man had fallen face down, and Nagaro noticed guiltily that there was blood staining the fine old carpet on which he lay.

Thinking it was hardly a sight for the princess's eyes, Nagaro moved hastily to join her. "Come, My Lady, he said, thinking to draw her away. "I'll have some of my men remove the body— and the carpet. I'm sorry," he added, "about the carpet."

"The carpet isn't important." The princess raised her eyes, and spoke with surprising steadiness. "We always can get another."

She paused, then said, "I got up onto the canopy last night as soon as I heard the sounds of battle. And I hadn't dared to move from there all this time because I kept hearing them come in and out— searching for things to steal. Then, this morning, there was some shouting and one of them knocked over the wash stand. This man, here—" she indicated the dead Mautep— "came in soon after. He poked around at first, and hid when he heard men speaking the Common Speech. *They* scarcely did more than look in at the door, though, and were gone before I could make up my mind to call to them. Then *he* came out again, and was moving about— until someone came into Elyan's room. I suppose it was you."

She looked at him, frowning. "I thought there was another Mahuk though. I heard two different voices speaking their tongue."

Nagaro made haste to explain. "One of the voices was mine."

He found the calmness she displayed in the presence of a corpse somewhat disconcerting. And the matter-of-fact way in which she had recounted her ordeal bespoke a toughness that was new to him. He held out the glass to her.

She took it, but paused with it halfway to her lips. "You speak their language?"

"Only a little. It's called Hashti. I have to be able to speak to then if I'm going to deal with them."

"You *deal* with them?" This finally surprised her. "Whatever did you say to him, anyway?"

"I told him to put down his sword and he wouldn't be harmed."

Her eyebrows shot up. "You expected him to surrender?"

Nagaro sighed. "I thought he might, but he preferred an honorable death, so I gave him one."

She frowned a little, and then seemed to remember the glass in her hand. She raised it and drained it, scarcely pausing for breath a she drank. A little of the water trickled down her chin and she wiped it away with the sleeve of her gown. She seemed not the least concerned about displaying such a lack of daintiness.

"Thank you for fetching the water," she said simply, and went to put the glass on the nearer night stand. As she turned back, she asked, "Do you always say prayers over the men you kill?"

"Only when circumstances permit," he confessed. "In the press of battle, I rarely have time."

She gave him a sidelong glance. "Do you know, Captain," she said, "I think you're a very strange pirate."

He bowed to her, gratified, and flashed her a quick smile. "Others have called me that as well. But we should go, My Lady. I can take you to where your mother is— downstairs— and I must tell my men that they need search no further. I would offer you my arm," he added. "But I've spent the morning fighting sea warriors, and I fear I'm in no fit state for such duty." He lifted his bloody right forearm.

He had expected her simply to accept this, since she was so little given to formality, but she gave him a look of simulated aggrievement.

"I am not such a delicate flower," she told him firmly. "And I've just spent a whole night and most of a day on top of a bed canopy. So I'm hardly in a fit state for polite company either. I think I would like to have a man's arm to lean on just now, and I am not inclined to be put off by trivialities."

So saying, she stepped up to Nagaro's left side and tucked her right hand around his bare arm just below the elbow, effectively capturing him. It would have been impossibly rude to have refused her.

He automatically flexed his elbow to make a right angle, having been taught how to walk with a lady on his arm. At the same time he went tense all over.

Up until this moment he had been rather pleased by this opportunity to speak to the princess with his own words. For some reason, it had pleased Lokundas to give him that rarest of opportunities— a second chance to make a first impression— and Nagaro had been relishing it. But the Turner of Worlds had turned again, and sent him the very last thing that he wanted— to have to walk the halls of this palace with *this* woman on his arm.

Though the Lady Maramine had taught him how to escort a lady, he had only had occasion to demonstrate the skill with one woman in his entire life, and that one woman was the very one who now held him captive. How many times had he walked the halls of the palace with the sixteen-year-old Nevien on his arm, moving like a puppet on strings, hearing the little snickers and whispered words of derision? This moment brought all of those memories flooding back.

He cursed himself for having brought the matter up— though the princess might well have suggested it even if he hadn't. He was learning that he couldn't expect her to be as he remembered her— or to behave very much like a princess, for that matter.

He flinched slightly at the touch of her fingers on his skin, resting lightly there where the bladder-thorn scars clustered most thickly. She wouldn't have noticed them of course. They were very faint. Only someone who knew what to look for, like Tredhold the healer, would see them.

"I should at least be wearing a shirt for this work," he muttered, hoping to explain his discomfort, if not to change her mind.

"It's all right. Really," she said., the words spoken firmly, though not unkindly.

He sighed, seeing that his fate was sealed, and started forward, making for the door that led to the hallway. He moved a little stiffly, trying not to think about her hand on his arm.

Nevien seemed determined to make conversation. "However did you think to look on top of the bed canopy?" she asked. "No one has ever found me there before."

"It was the only place left," he answered distractedly, "after the wardrobe." Then the second half of what she had said penetrated his distraction. He frowned and asked, "Do you hide there often, then?" He was finding it difficult to remember to call her "My Lady".

They had stepped into the hallway, and he had to decide which way to go. The back stair would be quickest, but the halls at the bottom were full of wounded Palace Guards. *Better the main stair. They would only meet his own men there.* He turned right.

"I've done it before a few times." She glanced at him sideways. "Actually, I would rather that you didn't tell anyone where you found me, Captain."

This was odd enough that he stopped to glance at her in surprise. She was studying his face with apparently genuine concern for what she might read there.

"I won't if you don't wish it, My Lady," he said with earnest courtesy.

She looked relieved. "Thank you," she said. "If anyone asks, you can say I was hiding in the wardrobe."

He nodded. He thought he understood. A princess must not have many places to hide— or ways to be alone. He started forward again, escorting her along the hallway.

They went several paces before she spoke again.

"What is this mark on your shoulder, Captain? I thought at first it was some kind of decoration— the way the lines curve— but it looks like a scar."

Nagaro smiled tightly. "It's a slave brand. It marks me as the former property of Lord Baalkir jir-Akaan, who is now the Emperor of the Mahuk Baar."

"Oh! How dreadful!" she exclaimed. "And I do beg your pardon. I'm surprised you don't cover it. I shouldn't think you would want it to be seen."

"Why not? The shame of slavery lies with the slaver, not with the slave."

"Ye-es... I suppose so... But I wouldn't think you would wish to be reminded."

At this, he actually laughed. "I'm not likely to forget it, My Lady. Besides, it's part of how I'm known when I go about my work. To the Mautep, I am Kiraam Shaku-Tal, the 'Thief of Slaves'. Although, 'Man Who Sets Slaves Free' would be better, since that's what I and my men do. It's why we turned to piracy and why we only prey on Mautep warships—"

He stopped abruptly in the middle of his explanation, quite heedless of the princess's wide-eyed stare. They had reached the balustrade at the top of the stairs where the hallways met, and speaking of setting men free had suddenly reminded him of his earlier discovery.

"I almost forgot," he said. "There's a man trapped in the upper room of the north tower. I told him I would send help—"

He realized that Nevien had stiffened. "Oh Gods!" she murmured. "*Kale!*" Then she let go of his arm as both her hands flew to her mouth in dismay at what she had just let slip, and she cried, "Sweet Lissafel!"

"*That was Kale?*" he exclaimed in his turn, gaping at her. "*Kale Fendred?*"

He read the truth of it in her eyes, even as she shook her head as if trying to deny it. Then, fearing he had revealed too much interest, he sought to cover himself. "I... I thought I heard he was dead... that's all," he stammered. "Several years ago. He and his wife... something about a carriage accident."

He stopped. The princess had dropped her hands and was avoiding his eyes. He could sense her indecision. For several seconds, he feared that she was going to try to dissemble, but then she straightened her shoulders and returned him a direct glance.

"I may as well tell you," she said. "Since you know so much already. But I beg you to keep this in close confidence."

He swallowed. "You may be sure I will, My Lady."

She gave him a curt little nod. "Father made up the story of the carriage accident because it's kinder than the truth," she said, speaking quickly, as if that made it easier. "Kale Fendred isn't dead, but he's quite mad— and has been ever since the day he was found in his own house, standing over the strangled body of his wife, staring at his hands and talking in verse—"

Nagaro suppressed a cry of dismay, and the princess caught his startled movement.

"I know," she said, anguish in her eyes. "It's quite horrible. My father told my mother that Kale must have been driven mad when he found his wife murdered— he did adore her so..." She looked down at her own hands, biting her lip. "But I know what Father really thinks. He thinks that Kale somehow went mad and killed her— as if madness alone weren't enough."

Nevien had started wringing her hands, and she now stopped, very deliberately, then looked up at him, her eyes full of pain. "He was such a gentle man, Captain. But now he's dangerous... violent. He's gotten loose twice, and both times he tried to strangle someone..." Her voice died.

Nagaro stood staring at her, caught somewhere between hope and horror. A man he had thought dead— whose kindness he had hoped one day to repay— was alive! But now it seemed that Kale was beyond his help for a reason that was, if anything, worse. Involuntarily he took a step in the direction of the north tower.

Instantly Nevien caught his arm. "No!" She held him back. "There's nothing you can do. Though it's good of you to wish to help him. Father will attend to him as soon as he can, you may be sure. He keeps Kale here because he wouldn't have anyone else do that duty— or take that risk. Kale was his friend since they were children, and he says that Kale has never tried to harm him. So perhaps some part of the man remembers."

Her eyes were shining, now, even through her pain.

Nagaro frowned, struck by the realization that Nevien admired her father. It was to be expected, he supposed, and he had to admit, grudgingly, that the king's loyalty and care for his friend did appear admirable. It left him, however, still wondering what the the king might really know about the cause of Kale's madness.

"It isn't natural," he murmured, thinking aloud. "Men don't go mad suddenly for no reason."

Her hand tightened on his arm. "He was a good man!" she cried, almost defiantly. "I don't believe it's a curse from the Gods!"

"No more do I—" he began, and bit off his words. He hadn't been thinking of the Leithian gods at all. He didn't believe they existed. He had been thinking of Dreigen— of the sudden madness that had overtaken Gillard Marchent.

Though the two men's madness had taken different forms, the differences only suggested that different agents had been used. Nagaro had no difficulty imagining that Dreigen might know more than one potion that could drive a mind to madness. But he dared not say these things. He feared he had shown too much interest already. So he began to move again towards the head of the stairs, circling the balustrade.

Nevien moved beside him, and her fingers on his arm relaxed a little. "How did you happen to find him?" she asked. "The room is well-concealed."

Nagaro winced inwardly, but shrugged as easily as he could. "I heard thumping, and followed the sound," he said, hoping that would satisfy her. "I think he was throwing himself against the door."

Now she winced. "It's our best-kept secret," she said. "Scarcely anyone knows. The guards and servants on this floor have been sworn to secrecy. His children know, of course— they were nearly grown when it happened. But you see, don't you, that it's better if folk believe that he is dead?"

Mutely Nagaro nodded.

He began to escort the princess down the stairs, and he was so distracted by the news about Kale that he quite forgot to feel awkward at having her on his arm. When he felt her leaning on him a little to steady her descent of the steps, he was a bit surprised. On reflection, however, he realized that she had probably eaten little dinner the night before because of her headache, and nothing since. Besides that, she had probably slept very little, if at all. All of this she had suffered, but she had spoken no word of complaint— save to ask for water.

***

At the second floor landing they encountered Pavo, leading the others of his search detail.

It was hard to say who was more stunned, the princess or Pavo, and there were curious glances from the other crewmen as well. Nagaro could think of nothing else but to ignore all the wide-eyed looks. He spoke in as level a voice as he could manage.

"My Lady Princess, this is Pavo Maat, my second mate," he said, then turned to Pavo. "As you can see, Pavo, the princess has been found, so the men may cease their search for her. But tell them to continue going through the rooms with great care. I found a Mautep warrior hiding in a wardrobe and there could still be others. The body," he added as an afterthought, "is in the second room from the end, on the left side of the east corridor."

Pavo had recovered himself and his dark eyes had narrowed once more. "Aye, Captain," he said calmly, and saluted. Then, puzzled, he asked, "But what is wardrobe?" The faces of several of the men behind him mirrored his curiosity.

"It's a big wooden box— as tall as a man, with two doors in front." Nagaro gestured with his free hand. "To hang clothes in."

"Oh." Pavo's expression suggested that he was having difficulty digesting the concept of having so much clothing as to need such a thing.

At length, emboldened perhaps by Nagaro's introduction, he turned to Nevien. He didn't know how to bow, having never been taught, but he ducked his head to her and said, "Good afternoon, Lady Princess."

Nevien had recovered as well. Her expression was mildly amused. She rose to the occasion with fine courtesy, saying, "Good afternoon, Zirda," and giving Pavo a bright, warm smile and a little nod of acknowledgment.

This earned her one of Pavo's rare and incongruously shy smiles in return.

It was not until Nagaro had conducted her halfway down the next flight that she asked hesitantly, "Have you... many Mahuk among your men?"

Nagaro kept his eyes on the steps of the stairs as he answered.

"The word *Mahuk* refers to the country, not the people, My Lady. Pavo Maat is of the *Hashtep* class, the common folk of the Mahuk Baar. The warrior class, who plague our coast, are called *Mautep*. Pavo is a fisherman's son who had the ill fortune to be made a galley slave for the crime of killing two of the lord's rabbits to feed himself and his brothers. He and I were chained at the same oar for several months. He's not only my second mate, but a very good friend as well."

He glanced at her quickly. "To answer your question, there are a few other Hashtep who sail with us. Most of them chose to stay with the ships. They weren't sure how they would be received, but Pavo seems always to choose to go where I go."

The princess simply nodded thoughtfully, apparently absorbing this information. They reached the first floor before she spoke again, and then it was on quite another subject. "The wound on your temple," she said, "looks rather bad— worse than the one on your arm."

Nagaro shook his head. "Scalp wounds always bleed out of all proportion. It's only a scratch. The other is of greater concern, but still not serious."

He turned to escort her across the atrium to the central hallway, not wishing to take her through the Great Hall, past the bodies of the dead.

"Really?" she said with apparent interest, leaning across to examine the wound on his arm more closely. "Does it hurt?"

"Only when I think about it."

"Oh!" She straightened hastily. "I'm sorry." Then, as if to change the subject, she asked, "Where are all of the Palace Guard? I've not seen a single one."

Nagaro frowned painfully. "I'm afraid that a great many of them were slain."

"Was the fighting very bad, then?"

He swallowed. "Yes, what I saw of it."

"All of the other palace folk— the women, the servants— are they safe?"

"I think so. We've found none dead at least."

"And Elyan? If there was fighting, I know he would want to be in the thick of it."

Nagaro stiffened, and his heart sank. It was the first time that the princess had spoken of her husband. And what could he tell her? He felt suddenly guilty for enjoying his conversation with her when her husband lay nearby, probably dying. But it didn't feel right that Nevien should learn of the prince's plight from him, a stranger.

They had reached the door of the Compass Room, and he stopped, searching for words that might serve to turn her question aside or to delay his answering it.

"Prince Elyan led the battle on the wall," he said carefully, "where the fighting was fiercest. There were many men wounded in that fight."

Nevien must have felt his tension or read something in his voice.

"He's been wounded, hasn't he." She sounded, not alarmed, but oddly certain.

At that moment Nagaro would have given anything to be as good a liar as Taru, but all he could do was say, "Yes." He couldn't look at her, and his stomach felt as if it were full of lead.

"Badly?" Still she didn't sound greatly distressed, and it was barely a question.

"I'm afraid it may be so... I... I'm sorry, My Lady..."

He risked a glance, for she seemed to be taking it very calmly. He saw that she was staring straight ahead, frowning slightly. She must have felt his gaze then, for she looked at him, and her eyes were clear and very bright.

"Well, I'm sure I shall learn all about it soon enough," she said briskly, and then it was she who moved forward into the Compass Room, drawing him by the arm that her hand still rested upon.

The Compass Room was full of men, most of whom were pirates going about various tasks. Quite a number of them stopped to stare unabashedly as their commander crossed the room with a richly clad young woman on his arm. Murmurs ran behind them.

"Is that the princess?"

"Yes, the princess... the princess and the Captain..."

The pirate who was currently on duty at the door to the Audience Hall gawked at them in astonishment, and Nagaro didn't bother to wait for the man to recover enough to announce him or his charge.

He stepped past the man into the Audience Chamber and escorted the princess halfway down the aisle, but then came to a halt.

A quick sweep of his eyes had taken in the scene. The queen had been seated on one of the chairs on the dais when they entered, but started up with a cry of joy when she caught sight of her daughter.

Elgurn had been hovering over his wife, but he turned immediately when Semorel rose. Even from that distance, Nagaro was able to read the expression of intense relief that crossed the man's face upon seeing Nevien. Nor could he miss the look of annoyance that followed, as the king took note of the manner of his daughter's return.

There were other murmurs and whispers along the galleries and from the direction of the doors leading to the side rooms.

Nagaro tried to ignore all the attention. He had been feeling far too many eyes on him to be comfortable even while crossing the Compass Room. Now his only wish was to be done and to get away. He had no desire to have to speak further to the king.

He turned to the princess. "I must bid you good day now, My Lady," he said with almost stiff formality. "It's time that my wounds were tended."

She took her hand from his arm at last and stepped away, moving to face him. "By all means," she said seriously. "Good day, Captain Nagaro, and thank you."

Then she smiled at him, one of those warm, winning smiles that he remembered so well, and abruptly she extended her hand to him in a gesture that was unmistakable.

He hesitated for a second, caught off guard because he would never have expected this from her. Still, he had been properly schooled and he knew what to do. He took her hand and bowed over it, carrying it to his lips, which he allowed to lightly brush her fingers.

He straightened and released her hand. "You are very welcome, My Lady," he said.

She was looking at him with that direct gaze of hers. "Tell me, Captain," she said, as if on an impulse. "What were you before you became a pirate?"

He flinched inwardly. "A slave, of course." That at least was true.

She frowned slightly. "I meant *before* that," she chided.

This time he actually smiled. "Before that, My Lady Princess, I was a fisherman."

But she shook her head at him. "That I will never believe."

And now the game had gone far enough. Wishing only to get away, he gave her his best pirate smile, a feral flash of teeth contrasting vividly with his black beard. "You may believe what you will, My Lady," he said politely, but firmly. "Now good day, and farewell."

Turning, he strode from the room before she had a chance to think of any response.

Behind him, there rose a startled murmur of voices.

Chapter 15

The Victors And The Fallen

Nevien did not stand for long looking after the pirate captain. She was puzzled that, after all his plain speech, he had become evasive when she had asked him a rather harmless question. But she had other things to worry about, not the least being that she was both exhausted and hungry. First, however, she knew she must go and embrace her mother.

The queen clung to her, murmuring expressions of thankfulness until Nevien said, "Mother, I am quite well, but you are not, and you're going to overtire yourself. You should sit down."

She was relieved when her mother didn't argue, but nodded and sank down again into her chair, leaning her head against the high back and closing her eyes.

Nevien was surprised when her father stepped forward next to enfold her in his arms. The king wasn't generally given to public displays of affection. His motive became clear, however, a moment later when he drew her a little away, out of her mother's hearing.

"Did Captain Nagaro's men find you then?" he asked, speaking low and with obvious disapproval. "I would rather have sent our own men, and spared you that, but the pirate wouldn't listen. Nor would he wait."

Nevien was taken aback by her father's tone. "*He* found me, Father," she informed him, keeping her voice low. "And I needed no sparing from it."

The king frowned. "He wasn't forward with you?"

"No. He was a perfect gentleman. If anyone was forward, it was me. He was reluctant to offer his arm because he was bloody and unwashed from the battle, and wearing no shirt— but I insisted." She studied her father's face.

"Why, Father?" she asked. "Is there something about him that disturbs you?"

The king's frown deepened. "We are entirely in his hands, Nevien," he said. "The Palace Guard is in ruins— there's only a handful left alive that aren't wounded. He's letting us come and go from this room freely, but there are armed men of his at every doorway. You've had an opportunity to speak with him and to observe him. Tell me honestly what you think of the man."

Nevien frowned in her turn as she considered how to answer. She felt instinctively that her father's concerns were unjustified, but she knew her father wouldn't be swayed by intuition.

"I think," she said, "that we are in good hands. I was frightened when I first saw him, but only until he began to speak. He looks like a pirate, but he doesn't speak or act like one. He told me he only became a pirate to free slaves from Mahuk war galleys."

Her father's expression did not improve. "Was he properly respectful to you? To me, he seemed very brazen."

Nevien suppressed a smile. "He was as respectful as I wished him to be," she said. "But then I prefer to speak freely, and be spoken to the same way. I would guess that he doesn't care for formality any more than I do, but he was certainly polite enough."

The king's mouth twitched. "A smooth-tongued manipulator then," he muttered, glancing quickly at the queen. "He charmed your mother— acted quite the courtier with her."

"Perhaps Mother charmed *him*," Nevien suggested. "She does that. With her Vothrin ways. And he is a Vothrin too."

"*Him?*" Her father gave her a sharp look. "Vothrin? Are you sure?"

"Yes. I heard him kill one of the sea raiders, and he said a Vothrin prayer for the man's spirit. That was before he could have known that I was there, too, so it couldn't have been for my benefit. I don't think we have anything to fear from a man who follows the Vothrin Path."

The king listened to this explanation, still frowning, his only other response a raised eyebrow at mention of the prayer.

"I see," he said when she had finished. He rubbed his chin while his pale blue eyes probed her face. "Thank you for your words, daughter."

The last was spoken gravely, even sternly. And Nevien had to be content with it.

She wondered what had happened to make her father so suspicious of a man who had impressed her so favorably. But from his tone, she knew that her father considered the matter closed. He wasn't easy to read when he didn't wish to be, and he clearly wasn't going to reveal any more of his thoughts.

"What has happened to Elyan, Father?" she asked instead. "The captain told me he was badly wounded."

This time the king didn't even try to dissemble. His face turned gray.

"Yes, it's true," he said. "I had hoped that Ambras would give us a different report than what that pirate's doctor said, but the Master has only just left this room to go back to his patient after confirming the unhappy tale. Elyan took a sword thrust, fighting on the wall. He's breathing very badly and has been spitting blood."

The king's eyes held genuine pain. "Ambras is certain we will lose him, Nevien. I'm sorry. I've asked to have him moved to one of the officer's quarters, away from the other wounded, so he can have individual attention and appropriate honor. But that's all I can do."

Nevien bowed her head, closing her eyes. *So it has come*, she thought. *A little sooner than I thought it would. He's still so young...* She opened her eyes again and raised them to meet her father's. "How long?"she asked. "Could Ambras tell you?"

"It takes some time to die of this kind of wound." The king's voice was tight. "It will be hours at least, perhaps even several days."

Nevien grimaced, but nodded. She knew she must play the proper royal wife— dutiful and strong— although she knew that Elyan didn't need her to help him play out this final scene in his life's drama.

"I must be ready to see him when he asks for me," she said. "To say farewell. But it seems there is a little time yet, and he won't want me to sit there and watch him die slowly. I will rest first, and eat something, so I'll be stronger for the task."

Her father accepted this with a nod. "Come," he said, "and help me persuade your mother to lie down again. Then you can take your rest among your ladies. There's food remaining from what was brought to us, and I'll see that some of it is sent in to you."

The queen did not protest the suggestion that she should rest— a sure sign that she was feeling very unwell. Semorel leaned heavily on the arms of her husband and her daughter, one on either side, as they escorted her the short distance to the closest of the small rooms adjoining the Audience Chamber. There they were met by several of the queen's ladies, a group of older noblewomen who rustled and murmured and took Semorel away to a couch that had been made into a makeshift bed for her.

Nevien turned away with a pang as the door was closed. She met her father's eyes, and felt his arm around her shoulders— another unaccustomed gesture.

"When Master Ambras can be spared from Elyan's side," he said quietly, "I will see that he looks in on her as well."

***

There was no couch in the room that was being used to shelter the princess's ladies. Nevien had noticed the bare walls of the Audience Chamber and had also noted several great folded heaps of fabric on the floor in the room that her mother had entered, but she hadn't bothered to ask what they were. Now she knew.

She sat cross-legged with her skirts tucked about her on one of the Audience Chamber's great tapestries. It had been folded several times and laid on the floor to serve as a sleeping mat. The room— normally a utilitarian office— held two more of the folded tapestries, taking up most of the floor between the various desks and cabinets that lined the walls. It was on these rude beds that the young women who served as Nevien's companions had spent the night.

The current number of the princess's ladies was six, and it happened that three of them were Leithian and three were Kelorin. The Leithian maidens were named Brendet, Alisset, and Clarimel. The Kelorin ones were Tulevien, Rianine, and Kendira, the last being the youngest and the most recent addition to the group.

They had crowded eagerly around Nevien when she entered and then had settled, two of them on chairs— of which there were only two, of plain hard wood— and the other four on the folded tapestries. Their eager requests for the tale of her adventure had almost immediately been interrupted by the coming of Lady Meriel, one of the queen's ladies who served as a guardian and chaperon to these younger women.

Meriel was a diminutive Leithian woman of about forty with a sweet, kind face framed by hair that was still undiluted gold. She had come with a pitcher and a basket, and she had pulled the room's low table close to Nevien's seat, where she knelt, cutting pieces of bread and cheese and then pouring cold sothiril into a cup that came out of the basket.

"Now then," she said, as she handed Nevien the cup. "Please do tell us about what happened to you."

Nevien had been secretly glad of the interruption caused by Lady Meriel's arrival, since it had given her time to think about how to answer the other women's questions. She had no intention of telling many of the details of her adventure to this audience, and had decided to make her tale as brief and uninteresting as possible— with a bit of outright deception regarding her hiding place.

"There isn't much to tell," she said lightly. "If I hadn't been so afraid that one of the Mahuk would find me, it would have been very dull. The worst is that I didn't sleep all night. You've no idea how uncomfortable it is inside a wardrobe."

The last was based on personal experience. She had tried hiding in one once, years ago.

Her gambit was quite effective. It set the other young women off on descriptions of how they had passed *their* night, to which she listened with half an ear.

"It was quite dreadful in here," Brendet was saying. "First there was a lump under my hip, and when I moved, then there was one under my shoulder. I tossed and turned all night!"

"*And* there was the smoke," complained Clarimel. "Some of it got in before the door was closed, and once it was *in* there was absolutely no way of getting it *out*. We smelled it all night! And everything still reeks of it! The tapestry... my gown—"

There was more in a similar vein as the other young women chimed in, enumerating their sufferings. Nevien hurriedly ate her bread and cheese while she could do so uninterrupted.

Lady Meriel had cut an apple into slices and now offered them. "Take this, dear," the older woman said, ignoring the chatter. "And when you've finished, you can lie down and get some rest. I must go back to your mother, but if Elyan asks for you I'll come wake you at once."

"Thank you, Meriel." Nevien gave her a wan but grateful smile.

The chaperon had no sooner left than Brendet turned to Nevien and said eagerly, "Now that she's gone, tell us about *him!*"

"Oh, yes!" the others exclaimed in breathless excitement. "Tell us!" "What's he like?"

"Who do you mean?" Nevien feigned innocence, though she could guess perfectly well and knew she hadn't much hope of avoiding giving some sort of answer. Her question was greeted with another chorus.

"The pirate, of course! Captain Nagaro!"

Nevien sighed. Rumors about the pirate captain had first reached Lankura more than two years ago, and the list of his exploits had been growing ever since. His popularity among the common people was so great that his tale had begun to acquire the quality of legend. The question of what he was *really* like had been a topic of speculation among the princess's ladies for months.

Nevien stalled by biting into a slice of apple. She wasn't in the mood for frivolous gossip, not with Elyan on his deathbed and her mother lying ill in the next room. Besides that, she thought the question was rather rude.

"He's rather different than I expected," she ventured. "Not much like a pirate. More of a gentleman—"

"A *gentleman?*" exclaimed Alisset. "How could he be a gentleman?"

"Well, he *did* kiss her hand," Tulevien put in. "Whatever made you give him your hand?" she added, turning to Nevien. "You never do that!"

Nevien had finished the apple. She washed it down with a swallow of sothiril and proceeded to empty the cup before answering.

"I just wanted to see what he would do," she said with a shrug. *He did it quite perfectly too,* she thought, *and a man surely doesn't learn that in the islands.*

Aloud, she said., "I think I would like to lie down now, and try to get some sleep."

"Of course, dear." Tulevien was immediately solicitous.

Brendet, however, acted as if she hadn't heard Nevien's words. "Whatever did you talk about?" she asked curiously.

Nevien frowned. She really was tired, and this was not a simple question. Most of it, in fact, she had no intention of divulging. She chose something harmless.

"He said he only became a pirate so that he could free slaves from Mahuk ships," she said. "He and his men only attack Mahuk war galleys."

"*Really?*" Tulevien's eyebrows shot up. "I suppose that would explain why he got so out of temper when your father asked him what his price was for helping us."

"Father thought he wanted *payment?*" Nevien was so surprised that she asked the question before she could stop herself.

"Oh *yes.*" Clarimel spoke in that supercilious way of hers that Nevien always found so off-putting. "And Captain Nagaro was *so* impudent. He as much as told your father to be more respectful! I mean, *really!* The King of Edrovir should be respectful to a pirate!"

Nevien winced. She thought that probably explained a lot. If the pirate captain had spoken to the her father as freely as he had to her, her father might well have taken it amiss. And her father's reaction could have offended the pirate in turn. She sighed and massaged her temples with her fingertips. Her head was beginning to hurt.

Sweet Lissafel, I'm tired! she thought, stifling a yawn.

The other young women were still prattling on, but they seemed to have lost interest in Nevien's story, and she was glad of it. She lay down on the folded tapestry and tried not to listen. She could hardly help hearing, however, the room being so small.

"He's much younger than I thought." Brendet was saying. "And did you see the muscles in his shoulders? If only he weren't so dark, he might be handsome—"

"*Handsome!*" Clarimel sniffed. "*I* found his looks quite outlandish."

"Oh, yes!" Alisset chimed in. "That black beard— and his hair tied like that—"

"*I* think he looks splendidly barbaric." That was Rianine, who was never happier than when she was saying something outrageous.

"*Splendidly barbaric?*" Clarimel's voice dripped scorn. "I mean, *barbaric,* certainly. But hardly *splendid!* What did he mean by coming in with his bare arms, and blood all over him?"

"He'd been in the battle, and I don't suppose he'd had time to wash," Rianine countered.

"What did you think of him, Tulevien?" Alisset asked.

"Don't ask *her!*" Brendet interjected. "She's engaged to be married. She's not supposed to look at another man. We should ask Kendira. She hasn't said a word."

Kendira spoke in a small, hesitant voice. "I think he's very handsome just the way he is."

Nevien could almost hear the girl blush.

"What about you, Nevien?" Brendet suddenly inquired. "You got a much closer look at him than we did. *You* don't think he's handsome, do you?"

Nevien opened her eyes and rather pointedly covered a yawn. "I really couldn't say," she said rather cooly.

There were times when she was grateful for the company of her ladies, but this wasn't one of them. They were all younger than she was in years— except Rianine, who was the same age. In terms of worldly experience most of them often seemed to her to be virtual infants.

Alisset giggled and said, "You *know* she won't say, Brendet, because she can't compare anyone to Elyan—" She stopped and her hand flew to her mouth as she turned scarlet.

The other young women exchanged guilty glances. It had finally occurred to them to think of the prince's plight.

Nevien didn't bother with a reproach. "Would you turn down the lamp, please, Tulevien?" she asked, trying to make herself as comfortable as possible on the makeshift bed. "Then, if you would all just talk softly, I think I might be able to sleep."

"Hush now, all of you!" Tulevien scolded. "I think I shall take a nap too," she added as she went to the lamp that was burning on a side table, and turned down the wick until it was barely lit. The room became quite dim, the only natural light being what found its way down a ventilation shaft that entered high up on one of the walls.

Nevien sighed and closed her eyes again. She heard rustling and some murmuring as the other young women rearranged themselves.

She tried to relax her body for sleep, and her mind began to drift a little. But her companions could not seem to keep still. Several of them began to talk again in hushed whispers, and they soon forgot themselves and their voices began to rise until Nevien couldn't help hearing every word. She found herself listening in spite of herself, identifying each speaker by voice.

"But why must he tie his hair and wear a beard?" (That was Alisset.)

"It's a Turowan fashion." (Rianine, always the expert.) "He must be part Turowan."

"*Half* Turowan— or he wouldn't be so brown." (That was Brendet.)

"At *least* half." (Clarimel, trying to sound scornful and bored at the same time.)

"But his face looks Kelorin— not like Lord Kuran's." (That was Kendira, sounding puzzled.) "Maybe he's only brown from the sun."

"The sun doesn't make Kelorin people that brown." (Rianine, again.) "I tell you, he must be part Turowan."

"Let's ask Nevien." (Alisset.)

"Shhh! She's asleep!" (Brendet.) "I hear her snoring."

This was too much for Nevien. "I'm not asleep, and I'm *not* snoring," she said. "You're hearing Tulevien. And Captain Nagaro can't be half Turowan because his eyes are gray. It's not possible for a half-Turowan to have gray eyes."

"I don't see why not!" Brendet protested.

Nevien sighed. "It just doesn't happen. I've known a fair number of half-Turowan people, and their eyes are always brown or black, like Kuran's."

There was a little silence. Then Rianine said teasingly, "So you noticed the color of his *eyes*, Nevien?"

Nevien was glad that they couldn't see her expression in the gloom. "He appeared suddenly right in front of me, and I was afraid for an instant that he was a Mahuk," she said tartly. "So of course I noticed his eyes! Now if you can all just be still for five minutes, I will surely be asleep, and then you can whisper as much as you like."

Silence reigned at last.

Nevien re-settled herself, and attempted once more to quiet her mind for slumber. This time it worked quite quickly, for she was truly exhausted. As she drifted towards sleep, a last thought fluttered through her mind.

Eyes dark gray with little flecks of blue and green...

She had seen eyes like those somewhere before... though it couldn't have been him, of course. If she had ever met *that* man before, surely she would remember...

***

Nevien was awakened from a dream— in which her three husbands had been passing before her in silent procession— by Lady Meriel gently shaking her shoulder.

"I'm sorry to wake you, dear," the older woman said softly as she bent over her. "But at least you've had a few hours of sleep. And Elyan has asked for you."

As Nevien sat up, two things immediately struck her. The first was that the sun must have set because, although the lamp had been turned up, the room was still very dim because there was no longer any daylight entering by the opening high on the wall. And the second thing was that her ladies were gone, leaving only her, and now Meriel.

"They've all gone to their chambers, My Lady," Meriel told her when she inquired. "About an hour ago. And you can go to yours as soon as... as this is over. The servants have put things right as best they could. I let you sleep because I didn't want to wake you twice."

The older woman held up a little cloth bag. "I've brought your comb and brush and a hand mirror, so you can at least straighten your hair."

Nevien thanked her and took the bag, though it seemed a bit foolish. Elyan was dying. What did it matter how she looked?

Still, she tugged out the worst of the tangles and smoothed her hair with the brush while Meriel held the mirror. She finished quickly and returned the articles to the bag.

"All right," she said calmly. "I'm ready."

***

Nagaro did not go directly to have his wounds tended after leaving the princess in the Audience Chamber. He went first to make sure that those who were searching the grounds for her were told that they could cease their efforts. Only then did he go to the Palace Guards' infirmary, where he sat on a stool while Tredhold bathed the side of his head and his forearm with cool water.

As Tredhold worked, he talked without really saying anything. It was Tred's way of distracting the patient's attention from his wounds while they were being tended. Nagaro knew this, and he therefore wasn't listening.

The truth was that he was beginning to feel somewhat overwhelmed by the day's events, both the battle— with the amount of killing he had done— and the things that had happened afterwards.

He had learned long ago that prolonged battles in which he used his gift for swordsmanship gave him a feeling of confidence and control that lingered for some time afterwards. Today had been one of those times, and the feeling was only now finally ebbing. He was reflecting that, under other circumstances, he might not have had the courage to stand before Elgurn, or to venture alone into the royal chambers in search of the princess. He was glad, however, that he had done those things.

The meeting with Elgurn had not been exactly comfortable, but it was good to have faced the man on his own terms— and to have found that he was not recognized. It had also done him good to see the transformation of the little room, there on the third floor, that he had previously remembered only as a kind of torture chamber. And, as shocking as it had been to discover Kale Fendred's true fate, it was still something that was better to know than not.

And then there was the princess.

The day would have been worth it for that alone— for walking and talking with her as himself. *For having her look at him with eyes that saw him as a whole man instead of something broken.* But he worried that he had spent too long with her. She had not recognized him, no, but she had begun to grow curious about his history, and that wasn't good. He could only hope that she would have something of greater concern to think about once she learned the full gravity of her husband's condition.

"Are ye all right, Nagaro?"

"What?" He was startled out of his thoughts by the question. Tredhold was looking at him with some concern.

"I've asked ye twice if the bandage was too tight."

"Oh." Nagaro glanced down at his bandaged forearm. He flexed the fingers, making a fist. "No, it's fine."

Still the concern in the healer's blue eyes remained. "*Are* ye all right, though? That sword of yours was busy today."

Nagaro sighed. "Yes, I'm all right, Tred. But I did lose my count— of the men I have killed. There were too many today. I can't picture all the faces."

"I've told ye that I think it's easier that way." Tredhold began to gather up scissors and rolls of bandages.

Nagaro's eyes clouded. "I don't want it to be easy," he said, almost harshly.

"I know. Ye've been an uneasy warrior from the beginning, and I expect ye always will be." The healer paused, then asked, cautiously, "What about... being here... in Lankura?"

Nagaro shifted and looked away. He wasn't sure exactly what speculation lay behind the other man's question. Tredhold knew that he had suffered some very great hurt, and that it had involved the use of bladder-thorns. And Nagaro had admitted to the wiry little Leithian five years ago that there had been powerful people involved in that hurting, and that he hadn't dared, then, to go to Lankura to try to join the Palace Guard.

On that occasion, Nagaro had also obtained the healer's promise not to ask him for the details, and he knew that Tredhold would keep that promise. Still it seemed he owed the man more than to merely have his concerns put off or shrugged aside.

"There have been some… memories… coming back…" he said quietly, still not meeting the healer's eyes. "But it's all right. I can bear it." Then, to change the subject, he asked. "How is Prince Elyan?"

Tredhold picked up the basin and the wet cloth, and rose, frowning.

"He won't live more than a few days at most. I fear the sword stroke pierced a lung and must have severed something close to the heart. He can't breathe properly, and he bleeds… inside."

Nagaro swallowed and nodded. He wasn't really surprised, though he had hoped to hear something different.

"Is he conscious?"

"Yes. In fact, he asked something about you."

Nagaro had risen, intending to move towards the door. He stopped, now, in surprise. "He did? What was it?"

Tredhold gave him a significant look. "He wanted to know whether ye really talk to Vothra."

"Oh." Nagaro nodded. He was embarrassed, but it made sense. "I said something to him about Vothra during the battle," he said. "And it means something to a Vothrin who is facing death to know that Vothra is in the world again."

He went outside after that, out into the air and the late afternoon sunlight, to lend his efforts to those of many others in the sad task of digging three mass graves. It was hard work, and he gave himself up wholly to it, glad to have something on which to focus his mind.

The graves were three long trenches, side by side. One was for the fallen members of the Palace Guard, one for the warriors of the City Garrison, and the last was for Nagaro's followers.

The site was in a part of the garden, close to the Common Wall and beyond the stables. There were spring flowers blooming just a stone's throw away in the sun's lingering glow, their fragrance mingling with the salt tang of the air from the sea, partly masking the smell of death.

As the bodies were being readied, an official-looking man from the palace came with a pen and a piece of parchment on a little board. He came to record the names of the fallen so they could be cut into three marker stones. He was plainly nonplused when Nagaro took the board and the pen from his hands and wrote out the fourteen names himself without having to look at the faces. The man seemed as astonished by the perfection of Nagaro's handwriting as he was by the feat of memory.

Nagaro shrugged. He had known each of those men at least a little, and had already made the effort to fix the names in his mind so that he could carry the sad news back to Pakoa.

He inquired whether he might write some words to be cut into the marker stone in addition to the men's names. The man gestured for him to do so, and then looked impressed again when Nagaro, after only a moment of focused thought, penned the following words:

"*Let it be remembered that men of the coast and from the islands came freely in answer to Edrovir's need, that they fought bravely, and that these fourteen fell defending the people of Lankura from harm.*"

After the graves were filled in, there was the task of hauling the bodies of dead Mautep to a place at the very northeast corner of the garden. There they were piled upon a heap of firewood, and the whole thing was set ablaze.

By the time the pyre was lit, the sun had set and the air was still with the coming of evening. The black plume of smoke rose straight up and fanned out far overhead, a dark smudge against the deepening cobalt sky, dimming the pinprick lights of the first stars.

Nagaro stood, well back from the pyre with the other men, watching it burn and shivering in the rapidly cooling air. No one had any desire to warm themselves by that blaze.

Tira Filora and her kitchen maids came around with food and water, as well as basins and towels so that the men could bathe their hands. The Mistress of the Royal Kitchens stopped beside Nagaro and held the basin for him while he washed.

Like everyone else, her gaze was drawn to the fire. The ruddy light played upon the woman's sharply chiseled features. "I'll be glad to put this day behind me," she said.

Nagaro looked at her with sympathy. "I hope you didn't have to use your kitchen knife this morning, Zirdyn," he said as he wiped his hands dry.

She turned to him, her eyes hard, her mouth set. "But I did, Captain Nagaro," she said grimly. "And I pray that I never have to do anything like that again!"

Nagaro turned to take bread and cheese from a basket carried by one of the kitchen maids. "So do I, Zirdyn," he said fervently.

He was referring as much to his own ordeal as to hers.

She shook her head. "*Battle,*" she said bitterly. "I don't know what men see in it. A lot of shouting, and men cutting each other, and blood all over the place. We'd do a lot better if men would give more thought to what really matters and have some sense."

Nagaro could only nod in agreement. He had no words to add.

It was a little later that Nagaro sought out Taru and they crossed the darkened garden together, leaving the pyre and the graves, to return to the palace.

Nagaro was bone-weary. He longed to lie down and sleep, though it was barely night. There were, however, still things to be done first.

"How long do ye think we'll be staying here?" Taru asked him as they walked.

Nagaro had already given the matter some thought. "Until either some part of the Royal Fleet returns, or some other men are found to guard the palace. It may be a day or two. I hope not longer. I just don't want to leave while the place is barely defended."

"Ye surely don't think Angkat's lot will come back?"

Nagaro sighed. "I'd rather believe they wouldn't dare," he said. "But they aren't the only danger that might be out there. I hope more men can be called up quickly from the city, or from the lands 'round about— or that Kuran will come soon. I put the word out earlier among Lankura's fishermen to look for Lord Kuran's fleet and tell him what has passed."

Once inside the palace, he and Taru set up the watches for the night. Taru and Landros agreed to take charge of the first watch. Nagaro and Rubo would lead the second, and Moraga would lead the third, with Timegar's first mate, a Turowan named Guhanu.

The men who were part of the watches would be bedded down in the palace, either in the Guard Quarters or elsewhere on the first floor. The pirate crewmen were not all needed for the task of guarding the palace, however, so Nagaro sent half of them, under Timegar and Gurd, back to the ships to sleep. He sent Pavo with these.

When the big Hashtep gave him a reproachful look, he explained.

"We left the ships sparsely guarded, and they should have men enough to sail if need be. If it comes to that, you must command the *Sword*." Then, recalling the third floor balcony he had seen earlier that day, he added, "Send someone back to me tonight, though, with my spyglass. I'll want to look for Kuran in the morning, and I know a high place."

Nagaro would have slept among his men by choice, but the Palace Chamberlain had other ideas.

The man, a slight, gray-haired Kelorin, was one of those who had been freed from the palace dungeon after the battle. He insisted upon putting one of the rooms intended for visiting nobility at Nagaro's disposal, and Nagaro was too tired to put up a fight over the matter.

The room that was chosen for him was on the farther side of the central hallway from his men. It was a little farther away than he would have liked, but it was the closet one to be had. It turned out not to be too large, and not excessively grand, being simply and comfortably furnished.

Nagaro scarcely noticed what the room was like, and cared even less. He unbuckled his sword, took off his boots, and stripped off his leather vest. Then he bathed his face and upper body, using the porcelain bowl and cloth on the washstand.

Still feeling none too clean, he turned the coverlet of the ample bed completely down and stretched out on top of the sheet, still half dressed. It was a real feather mattress and it received his aching body in a luxurious embrace.

Yawning, he reached to turn down the lamp on the bedside table before settling his head back onto the pillow.

When was the last time he had lain on a feather mattress? Had it been in his own boyhood bed at Averwin? No... somewhere since then... but not during his time here in the palace. The mattress of the palate bed in that little room upstairs had been stuffed with straw...

Then he remembered. It had been seven years ago, in the little house where Taru had grown up, on the shores of Wotana Bay. The bed in which he had awakened from his fever had been graced with a mattress covered with plain linen— stitched, no doubt, by Taru's mother, Olomi— and filled with feathers plucked from birds that Taru had poached from the lord's forest.

Nagaro smiled at the thought, but his smile turned sad as memory led to memory. Olomi and her husband, Jomo, were gone from the world— murdered by the captain of a Mahuk war galley. He could not be wholly sad, however. The time he had spent in that place, waiting for his memory to return, had been a healing time.

He drifted, awash in those memories, until sleep took him.

***

He was wakened by a hand shaking him.

"Nagaro, wake up!"

The urgent voice belonged to Taru, and for a moment Nagaro felt a disorientation in time and place as half-remembered fragments of a dream fled into the darkness. Then someone lit the lamp and the unfamiliar palace room came into focus, revealed by the sudden light.

"What is it, Taru?" he mumbled, rubbing sleep from his eyes.

"Ye have t' come, Nagaro," Taru said urgently. "The prince is asking for ye!"

Chapter 16

Prince Elyan

It turned out that Delvin had brought the summons from Prince Elyan. The young guardsman crowded in anxiously, close behind Taru.

"Aye, Captain," he said. "They told me to fetch ye straight away! And I found Taru, and he brought me here." Delvin licked nervous lips. "Ye will come, won't ye, Zirda?"

Nagaro sat up. "Of course I'll come. Though I don't know what he wants of me. We barely met." He made a rueful face as he re-donned his battle-soiled vest and pulled on his boots. He would go regardless of the reason. It was ill grace to deny a dying man.

"What time is it, Taru?" he inquired.

"About an hour before second watch."

Nagaro stifled a yawn. That meant he had slept for three hours. He noted that Delvin looked steadier than he had that afternoon, though there was a grimness to the set of his chin that hadn't been there the day before. So it appeared that the young man was not unchanged by what he had witnessed, but was coming to grips with it.

Nagaro gave him a quick smile as they left the room. "Did you get some sleep?" he asked.

Delvin nodded. "Aye, Zirda. After I came back with Master Ambras, they let me lie down for a while. I thought it would be hard, but I never fell asleep so fast in my life! It was dark when I woke up. But I'm used t' the night shift," he added staunchly.

The hallway they walked along was quiet and lamp-lit. There were few folk about, and the three men's boots rang loudly on the polished marble floor. As they turned into the central hall, they passed a jumbled pile of abandoned loot that hadn't yet been cleared away. Nagaro had to step over strewn clothing that had spilled from an overturned chest— a man's clothing, mostly silk shirts in rich colors like gold and burgundy.

One shirt drew his eye, plain white with a little fine, dark embroidery around the collar. *If it's still there in the morning,* he thought, *perhaps I'll borrow it.* He could bathe all he wished, but the leather vest made him feel dirty again.

Delvin led them to a suite of rooms that had been the quarters of Harthred, the slain commander of the Palace Guard. There Taru left them, mumbling that he had something to attend to. Nagaro suspected that his friend actually had no stomach for what might be waiting inside the rooms.

There was a single guard at the door who nodded to Delvin, then opened the door and informed someone inside that Captain Nagaro had come. A muffled voice answered, and the guard ushered Nagaro through the door and closed it behind him. The guard himself remained outside with Delvin.

The room beyond the door was a kind of sitting room, lit by a single lamp that was turned down low. Another guard was there, who gestured for Nagaro to follow him and led the way towards a door on the farther side of the room.

As he followed, Nagaro became aware of two women sitting on a couch at one side of the room, talking to each other in low voices. It wasn't until he was nearly past them that he realized they were the queen and the princess.

Nevien glanced in his direction, frowning as he passed. As the lamplight fell on her face, he could see that she had wept, but there were no tears now. Whether her frown had been meant for him, or was merely a reflection of her thoughts, he couldn't tell. Nor was he given time to ponder the matter, for he was quickly ushered through the second door into yet another room. Again the guard remained behind.

Nagaro came to a halt just inside the door. This was the bedchamber of the suit, and it was as dimly lit as the outer room. Besides the bed against one wall, it contained the usual furnishings one would expect in an officer's room. Nagaro scarcely noticed them however.

Prince Elyan had not been laid on the bed, but rather on a low cot in the center of the room, as if he had been carried in on it and they had feared to move him. The cot was positioned with the prince's feet nearest the door. His head and upper body had been raised a little with pillows so that Nagaro could clearly see that his eyes were closed and his lips parted. Even in the dim light, his face looked pale.

The only other occupant of the room was a lean, graying Kelorin with a small neatly-trimmed beard, grayer than his hair. This man had been seated on a stool at Elyan's left hand, but he rose now and came around the foot of the cot to face Nagaro. He extended his hand in greeting.

"Good evening, Captain," he said, speaking in a low voice. "I am Master Ambras, the healer."

Nagaro shook the proffered hand, then bowed. "Well met, Zirda," he said quietly. "How may I serve my lord, the prince?"

Master Ambras sighed. "You'll have to ask him yourself, Zirda," he replied gravely. "All I know is that he has been very insistent that you should be brought to him. You may sit there—" the healer indicated a second stool, placed at the prince's right hand "—and speak to him. He is conscious, though very weak. He has declined to be given *opa* for the pain, and there's little else I can do for him."

Nagaro moved gingerly to take the seat Ambras had offered him. As the healer returned to the other stool, Nagaro sat down and cleared his throat.

"My Lord Elyan," he said. "You have asked for me, and I have come."

The prince's eyelids fluttered open, and he feebly turned his head until he could fix his eyes fully on Nagaro. "Thank you," he said, his voice low and husky. Almost at once, he had a bout of coughing. Though it sounded strangely weak, it wracked the wounded man. He closed his eyes again until the coughing stopped, and a bit of bloody froth appeared on his lips.

Ambras reached out immediately to wipe the froth away with a cloth that looked as if it had done the same duty a number of times already. The prince swallowed and a spasm crossed his face as he did so.

Nagaro winced inwardly, suspecting the man had just swallowed a mouthful of his own blood. He waited while Elyan lay, looking at him and breathing rapidly and shallowly as if trying to recover his breath. At last the prince spoke again.

"I always thought… I would die… in battle…" he said, gasping weakly between each short utterance. "That it would be… quick. This waiting… is hard."

Nagaro nodded. "Yes," he managed, unable to think of anything else to say.

He always tried to kill men with a quick, clean stroke, no matter who they were or what they had done. The thought that he might ever leave a man to suffer lingeringly, as Elyan was doing, appalled him.

The prince closed his eyes again, it seemed to catch his breath. Nagaro sat, waiting, wondering again why the man had wished to speak to him. He waited so long that Elyan's next utterance caught him by surprise. The man abruptly opened his eyes to fix them upon him, and asked, "Can you… speak to… Vothra?"

Nagaro was aware of Ambras' startled movement, but he kept his eyes on Elyan's face. *So that was it.* Tredhold hadn't said how he had answered the man's question, and the Leithian's own beliefs might have prevented him from speaking unequivocally.

"Yes," he said. "I have done so a number of times."

Ambras was leaning forward on his stool now, and Nagaro could feel the healer's eyes. He didn't look up to meet them however. There was an avidness in Elyan's gaze that held him.

With an effort, the prince gathered himself and spoke again. "Will you... call the Spirit... for me? To help me die?"

At this, Nagaro started in dismay, and this time he did look at the healer, seeking some help. He hardly knew what to say. He knew that Vothra had done such things in the past. But that was all he knew.

Ambras appeared as much surprised as Nagaro. The healer leaned forward and silently mouthed, *Can you?*

Nagaro made no response to Ambras. He knew that Elyan would be able to read his face if he did so. Instead, he looked back into the prince's pleading eyes, and swallowed.

"Any man can call—" he began.

But Elyan shook his head with surprising vehemence, and there was pain in his eyes. "I'm... afraid," he gasped. "I've lied... all my life."

Nagaro frowned. "We all tell lies sometimes," he said. "And Vothra will forgive almost anything."

At this, Elyan shook his head even more violently and attempted to raise it from the pillow. The effort triggered another fit of coughing, requiring further ministrations from the healer with his cloth. In the midst of this, Ambras gave Nagaro a reproachful look.

When at last the prince's coughing subsided and he lay quietly gasping for breath, he returned his eyes to Nagaro beseechingly and murmured, "*Please?*"

Nagaro swallowed. Vothra had been watching him, he knew. The Benevolent Spirit had spoken to him in his mind just the previous day.

"I'll try," he said earnestly. "But Vothra doesn't always come at once. Usually the Spirit comes later, when I'm sleeping, and I've never done it for someone else. I don't know whether this will work."

Elyan nodded to show that he understood. "*Please,*" he managed again.

Nagaro closed his eyes, trying to calm himself and to clear his mind. "Vothra, lord of my choosing," he said aloud, "will you come for Elyan— my friend— who is dying?"

I am here.

The words rang in Nagaro's mind, and the response had been so immediate that his eyes snapped open in astonishment. His mind told him the direction, and the distance, from which those words had seemed to come, and his eyes automatically sought the spot at the foot of Elyan's cot.

The figure that stood there was by this time familiar to him. Robed in silver and shadowed in night, it was neither old nor young, neither male nor female. The face that smiled at him was smooth and silver-pale, the shoulder-length hair was silver and black, the eyes that regarded him so gently were dark and starlit.

"*Vothra!*" Nagaro breathed the name aloud, but then he remembered Elyan and Ambras. He turned hurriedly to look at them. Both men were gazing at the place at the foot of the prince's cot, but their looks were puzzled and uncertain. Nagaro turned back to the silver figure. "Can't they see you?" he asked aloud.

Not yet. But I think they should.

The silver figure shrugged itself. It was a motion that had nothing to do with muscles or bones or joints. It was more a kind of shimmering, as of an image seen through heated air.

Instantly both Elyan and Ambras gasped in unison.

"*By the Eyes!*" the healer murmured, and stopped, looking mortified.

Vothra's laughter rippled like cool water across Nagaro's mind, an ineffably gentle sound, in no way akin to mockery. The figure's midnight eyes turned upon the healer. *Spirit that calls itself Ambras*, it said. *Do not berate yourself on my account.*

The eyes turned next to Elyan. The prince was staring, his face contorted as he struggled to summon strength to speak. The figure seemed to take a single step forward and bent to briefly lay an ethereal hand on the bedclothes where they were draped over the prince's feet. Again it spoke:

Peace, Spirit called Elyan. Do not spend what little breath you have in trying to explain yourself, or begging for my pardon. I know all that is in your mind and heart, and there is nothing that you need apologize for to me.

Nagaro was relieved to see that Elyan grew visibly calmer and looked relieved in response to Vothra's words and touch. But still the prince stirred himself to speak. "Spirit..." he murmured. "Help me die."

Are you ready now then? This time the voice was at once stern and gentle, steel clothed in velvet.

"*Yes!*" Elyan's answer was spoken in a whisper, but came without hesitation.

Very well then. We will try.

Abruptly the silver figure turned back to Nagaro. *There is more than one way to do this*, it said. *But the way that is most certain requires your help, Spirit called Nagaro.*

Nagaro shifted on his stool. "Whatever is needed, I will do it."

But the figure raised its hand.

First hear, then answer. I must be allowed to enter into you, to in-dwell in you, and through you, in Elyan. Ambras may be included as well, if he wishes. Indeed it would be better to have another witness to this. But anyone who chooses to be part of the chain will feel my presence in a new way—from within. And he will witness all that occurs and all that is revealed. The full nature of the hurt to Elyan's body, the quality of his pain, and the moment of passing of his spirit should all be witnessed. This may require some strength, and if you falter more than a little, our effort will fail. What do you say now?"

Nagaro swallowed. "I think I understand," he said. "And I am willing to try."

Compared to what Elyan was suffering, what was being asked of him didn't seem like very much.

And you, Spirit called Ambras?

The healer had sat through what had preceded in silent awe, but now he frowned under the gaze of the starlit eyes and found his voice.

"I... I'm honored to be witness to your presence, Gentle Spirit," he said. "But understand that I am trained to heal men's bodies and save their lives... when I can." He hesitated, then asked, still frowning, "Are you asking me to assist in causing this man's death?"

The spirit shook it's head. *No, Spirit called Ambras. Only Elyan's spirit can choose to relinquish its hold upon his flesh. Nothing you can do in the task we undertake could cause or hasten that.*

Ambras nodded then, apparently reassured. "Very well," he said. "I am willing."

Once more, then, Vothra turned to Nagaro. *This begins with you. Are you ready?*

Nagaro nodded. "Yes."

In truth he had no idea what being ready might mean in this circumstance, but he didn't want to keep Elyan waiting when he knew the man was in so much pain.

Very well. I shall enter you now, and in-dwell in you.

Nagaro had time only to take a deep breath as the silvery figure seemed to approach him. Then abruptly, it vanished from his vision, and in the same instant, he felt a presence burst into being within him and spread outward through his body and along his limbs with a strange tingling sensation.

Involuntarily he gasped aloud and shook himself. As the tingling settled, he was aware that he was somehow sharing his body's space with a warm and gentle spirit, possessed of a deeply understanding love, that extended into every corner of his mind and touched upon every fiber of his being.

"*Oh Vothra!*" he murmured. And the words were a pure exclamation of astonishment, not an effort to address the spirit that now seemed to be inside of him. The answering wave of gentle laughter that washed across his mind was indescribably strange, and at the same time, oddly reassuring.

He turned to look at Elyan and at Ambras. Both were staring at him. "It feels strange," he told them. "And wonderful."

Take Elyan's right hand with your left, and I will be able to enter him also, through you.

The words had formed themselves inside Nagaro's head, and he knew without asking that only he had heard them. Reflexively he nodded. There was no compulsion to do as Vothra instructed. He was entirely free, his actions completely under his own control.

He reached out to Elyan. "Take my hand," he said. "And be ready to feel Vothra's spirit enter you."

Elyan made no answer, but raised a trembling hand from where it lay on the bedclothes. He reached out, apprehension in his eyes. As the two men's hands met and clasped, the prince started, and his breathing became ragged. He seemed to be listening, however, and at length he sighed and his breathing eased. His eyes met Nagaro's, and he nodded.

The look in those eyes spoke volumes.

This much is good. Vothra's voice came once again into Nagaro's mind, though he knew that Elyan heard it as well. *Ambras must now take Elyan's other hand with his right, and Nagaro's free hand with his left. Nagaro, tell him that when he does so he will be included in this in-dwelling.*

Again Nagaro nodded reflexively and spoke to Ambras, relaying Vothra's words.

The healer appeared even more reluctant than Elyan. He raised his hands hesitantly.

Nagaro gave the man an encouraging smile as he reached across the cot. "It's all right," he said. "I'm certain that there is no harm in this." An instant later their hands met as Ambras took Elyan's hand as well. Nagaro watched the succession of expressions play across Ambras' face— shock, relief, then wonder.

Very good. Welcome all, and let us begin.

Nagaro didn't need to be told that the other two men had heard the words in their minds, just as he had. In any case, he could read it in their faces.

Thus far I have held you separate in awareness, each from the other. Now let me open the book of Elyan's flesh to all, so those who will remain may bear witness that the wounds are such that life cannot long continue. This may be difficult to bear. Hold steady.

What happened next, Nagaro was never able to forget, though he would have liked to.

He suddenly seemed to see the prince's body from the inside with the eyes of his mind. It would have been extraordinary to have seen it whole and intact, for he seemed to know how all the pieces worked, even though he knew no names for some of them. But to see some of those pieces torn open— violated by the passage of a sword blade— was a dreadful thing.

He had done similar damage with a blade, himself, and he wondered if he would ever again be able to put a sword through a man's heart without visualizing the fist-sized organ, pulsing as it was impaled. He shuddered, and involuntarily his grip on the hands of the other two men began to slip.

Steady!

The word reverberated through his mind, spoken to him alone. He caught his breath and re-tightened his grip. At the same time, he heard Ambras' voice— this time with his ears— speaking in wonder.

"I never knew it could be like this—"

Witnesses! Vothra's voice in their minds silenced both thought and speech. *Are you satisfied that these are mortal wounds?*

"Yes." Nagaro and Ambras spoke aloud in unison.

Very well. Spirit that has called itself Elyan, are you finished with this life and ready to pass with me into the void? The choice is yours alone.

Elyan had closed his eyes. He didn't speak aloud, but he nodded.

There was a pause, then, during which Nagaro somehow knew that the spirits of Elyan and of Vothra were having private speech together.

As he waited, he became aware that he could also "see" what he knew was Elyan's pain. It appeared to him as a throbbing scarlet shaft, sharp and hot, that transfixed the man's body, and it waxed and waned with every labored cycle of the man's breath. It had been there all along, Nagaro realized, though other things had drawn his attention from it. He was not at all glad to have noticed it now, this signature of the wounded man's suffering.

And then he was thankfully distracted from it again as he heard the prince's voice, though not, it seemed, with his ears. Indeed it couldn't have been the man speaking aloud, for the words were not labored, but came in easy, natural cadence.

I am ready now. Farewell, Master Ambras, and thank you for your ministrations. Farewell, Captain Nagaro, and thank you for your service also. My passing will be easier knowing that Edrovir has such a defender. The Spirit has told me what to do. When you feel my hands let go, you will know that my spirit has gone with Vothra.

There followed the tense interval of a dozen heartbeats, and then, finally, Nagaro felt Elyan's grip on his left hand go slack. At the same instant, he felt Vothra's presence leave his mind and body, like the dispersing of a mist before a breath of wind. And he was only himself again— alone, single, empty— achingly bereft of that wonderful and intimate communion.

At least the unwelcome visions were also gone, vanishing from his mind in the same instant. He let out his breath in a shuddering sigh and realized that he was trembling.

With an inarticulate cry, Ambras let go of Nagaro's hand and bent over Elyan's body, checking frantically for a pulse or any sign of breath. He looked up with wonder in his eyes.

"It's true!" he said. "He's gone."

Nagaro looked at the prince's still face. The eyes were closed, and the expression on his features was one of peace. Shakily, Nagaro laid Elyan's hand upon the dead man's chest. "Yes," he said numbly.

"Is that all you can say, man?" the healer exclaimed. "With all that you've done here? A Presence, an In-dwelling, and the Passing of a spirit? By the Eyes of Vothra's Mind, I don't understand you!"

Nagaro blinked at him. "I only called for Vothra. And then I did what I was bidden after the Spirit came, just as you did."

Ambras shook his head at him. "But, what *are* you?" he wanted to know. "That when you call, Vothra comes so—"

"—quickly?" Nagaro finished for him. He shook his head in turn. "I am nothing. Our spirits are joined— Vothra's and mine— that's all. And it's only because the spirit of the woman who raised me became part of Vothra after she died. It wasn't any of my doing. I'm just a man who kills other men with a sword., and I would rather not have seen some of what I saw tonight— though I don't begrudge it, for Elyan's sake."

He stopped, realizing there had been a bitter note in his voice.

It was a long time since he had felt unworthy of his connection to the Benevolent Spirit, but he felt so now, sitting opposite a man whose profession was to heal men's wounds while his seemed to be to inflict them.

He had tried to become a healer once. Tredhold had tried to teach him. But healers sometimes needed to use bladder-thorns, and he'd been unable to do that... Over the last four years, he had forgotten how much he regretted his failure in pursuit of that calling, but he remembered it now.

Ambras was staring at him, and shook his head yet again in apparent bemusement.

Nagaro stood up, grateful that he could manage to do so without shaking visibly. He felt as if his nerves had all been stretched taught and were still quivering.

"If you have no further need of me here," he said rather formally, "I will go back to my bed, to see if I can sleep."

The healer, for his part, still seemed rather excited, but he made haste to assure Nagaro that nothing more was required of him.

So Nagaro left, passing out into the sitting room. The guard in that room took one look at his face and stepped hastily away from him.

The queen and the princess were still there, seated on the couch. They turned worried, expectant faces towards him as he emerged from the bedchamber, and the queen rose, a little stiffly, and approached him. He gave her a quick bow.

"It is over, My Lady Queen," he said, knowing she was Vothrin and should understand. "His spirit has gone with Vothra into the void." Then, because he was after all reporting a death, he added, "I am sorry. It was what he wanted— why he called for me." He stopped speaking, aware that the strain must be audible in his voice.

The queen's face was very pale, but it struck him that it was due to her illness. She did not appear to be distressed by his words. Instead she gave him a formal nod. "Yes," she said calmly. "I know. May the Spirit bring you peace."

He gave her another bow, wondering how much she knew about Elyan and his request. He managed to say, "May the Spirit bring you peace also."

It was a ritual phrase among Vothrin people in such circumstances, and he was grateful for it. It spared him the need to think of any other words. All this time, he carefully avoided looking at Nevien, who had risen but remained standing beside the couch. He didn't want to see the look on her face. "I... bid you goodnight," he murmured, without meeting the eyes of either woman.

Then he fled— through the outer door and into the corridor beyond.

There were three men standing in the corridor. Two of them were Delvin and the other guard, as Nagaro expected, but it took a moment for his mind to register, as he brushed past, that the third was Elgurn.

Belatedly he looked back, long enough to catch the king's darkly frowning look. His mind was numb. He had no mental energy left to deal with the question of what he ought to say to the King Elgurn regarding the death of his son in law.

He had just enough presence of mind to manage the words, "My Lord King," by way of acknowledgment. Without waiting for a response, he strode away blindly down the corridor.

✳✳✳

Although he had said he was going to bed, Nagaro couldn't possibly have slept, as tense as he was. It was time for his watch in any case. So he paced the halls of the palace, blindly at first, but with progressively more purpose as his mind began to settle.

Weariness eventually caught up with him, however, and by the time his watch was over, he was ready to lay himself down on the bed in his chamber and actually fall asleep.

Sometime during his sleep, Vothra came to him.

It wasn't a Presence this time, of course. Just a voice speaking gently in his mind, and the glowing sign of the circle-within-a-circle-joined, floating before his eyes.

"Peace, Spirit called Nagaro, and I beg your pardon. I should have warned you better of what you would see. I have felt your distress these three hours past."

"You did warn me. I just didn't think about what it would be like. The fault was mine," Nagaro answered, uncomfortable at having the Benevolent Spirit ask his forgiveness. "And I would have done it anyway, for Elyan's sake."

Ah. The sound was very gentle, and a little sad, like a sigh. *You think that because I have much wisdom, everything I do must be wise. But I can forget how shocking the sight of the inside of a man can be to one who is accustomed to seeing only the outside.* There was a little pause.

I thought there ought to be no uncertainty concerning the manner of Elyan's death, particularly because of his high position, and so I sought witnesses. But I have made your work— already difficult— more difficult still, and I regret it. The more so because it was unnecessary. I could have entered through you, without letting you see. A Passing can be done with one witness, or with none.

"Oh. Well then, of course you have my pardon." What else could he possibly have said?

It was unnecessary to use you at all, even as my point of entry. There was another sound like a sigh. *But in-dwelling requires effort just to sustain, and more effort to initiate. It is very much easier to begin in a familiar place— and you are very familiar to me, spirit called Nagaro.*

"It's all right. Really." In his dream, he frowned, feeling strange that he should be reassuring Vothra, rather than the other way around.

"Perhaps it wouldn't have been so hard if it hadn't come at the end of a day with too much killing in it," he added, and then the feelings engendered by the all of day's events came welling up in his mind.

"When the day began, I had the blood of seventeen men on my hands," he said bitterly. "And by the end of it the number must have been at least twenty five— maybe even thirty! Sometimes I don't like what I do— not the *work* I've chosen, I mean, but what I have to *do*, to do the work. And today we didn't even free a single slave! We came too late to prevent the sinking of those two ships... the drowning of those men..."

That is true, The voice spoke calmly. *But you have helped put to flight a pack of wolves who brought violence to this place and who cared not what havoc they wrought in the search for gold. If some of them died in the process, that is not unjust. And your power to do good in the world can only increase with the more the world knows of you.*

But Nagaro's thoughts, once set in motion, had gone spinning on. Although he had heard the Spirit's words with his mind, he hadn't really felt their meaning.

"The Mautep wouldn't even surrender!" He groaned. "Except for the six we found in the palace dungeon! We had to kill so many—"

Peace, Nagaro-spirit, peace!

The sudden firmness in the Spirit's voice this time brought him to a halt.

Do not count your consequences too soon, the Spirit continued. *You have not, I think, done ill. Trust me in this.*

"I... I'll try..."

Vothra's laughter rolled through Nagaro's mind like an arpeggio of harp notes. *You will try to trust me, after what I have done? That is good!*

"I meant—"

Yes, I know what you meant, spirit called Nagaro. There was another pause, then, *Coming here has given you some fairer memories of this place than those that have darkened your soul. That also is not ill.*

This subject made Nagaro uneasy, and he reflexively changed it. "Elyan said that you told him what to do— in order to die. I wondered what you told him."

You wish to know that? The voice sounded surprised. *Most would pray they never need to know. It was a quick lesson in the art of letting go. That is one way to describe it.*

"That doesn't sound hard."

It may not sound hard, but not every spirit can do it in the end. And my part is not easy either. Rather like trying to catch something dropped, before it even begins to fall.

"Oh." Nagaro didn't really understand, but the Spirit's words gave him as much of a hint as he really wanted. "Has Elyan's spirit begun a new life?"

Not yet. His spirit chose to tread the void for a time, remembering past lives. That one is an old spirit, with much to remember. But the call of onam, that you call flesh, is strong. The spirit will answer it soon enough.

"He said he was afraid to call you himself. Because he felt unworthy. Sometimes I feel that way."

Ah, spirit called Nagaro, The voice became gently chiding. *Many think themselves unworthy. But as Elyan's spirit came to understand before the end, there is really no way to be unworthy of my help.*

Nagaro's mind caught at the last words. "...no way to be unworthy..." he murmured.

Yes.

"I'll try to remember that."

I hope you will. Peace, now, spirit that calls itself Nagaro. Peace, and a very good night to you.

Nagaro sighed as peace stole over him, and he slept easily until the pale light of dawn crept in at the window. If any more dreams came to him that night, he did not afterwards remember what they were.

Chapter 17

A New Day

Nevien stood beside her bed and stretched luxuriously like a cat. The windows glowed with early morning sunlight and the room felt altogether different than it had the night before.

Still, she stepped cautiously as she went to her dressing table to get her hairbrush, in case the servants had missed any slivers of broken china. Quickly she smoothed the tangles from her hair, glad that today she wouldn't have to do anything more than brush it. Passing around the end of the bed, she padded across the bare wood floor on the way to her wardrobes. The absence of the carpet was tangible evidence that the previous day's events had been quite real. The servants had removed the blood-stained carpet, and they had re-hung all of her scattered clothing in the two wardrobes as well.

The latter she would have rather done herself. It mystified her why being a princess should mean that other people constantly did things for you that you were quite capable of doing for yourself.

She sighed as she opened the doors of the right-hand wardrobe. The events of last night had been real too of course. Elyan was dead. She had gone in to see for herself so that she would know it was really true. She had even laid her hand on his still body to see what death felt like. Then, late though it was, she had gone to the royal bath chamber and taken a bath, trying to wash away the sweat and the grime, and the memory of the touch of her fingers on skin that was no longer warm with life.

She frowned slightly as she exchanged her nightdress for a long cotton shift and closed the first wardrobe. She had to go to the other one for a gown, because her mourning clothes were in it. They hung all pushed together at one side— three gray gowns.

Nevien chose the oldest one. It was dove-gray, and of a very modest cut, with only narrow bands of black embroidery around neck and hem for decoration. She liked it the best, if for no other reason than that she associated the other two with Gill Marchent, her second husband.

The dove-gray gown was one she had originally worn for her first husband, Leyel Virden. It had needed to be let out a bit for her second mourning, but this time she found that it still fit.

At least this time there was something to bury, she thought, as she reached for the black sash and began to wrap it around her waist. Not like the first time, when they'd never found the body. And what they were going to bury would bear a public viewing, as well— unlike what had been left of Gill after his fall from the balcony.

She shuddered, trying to shake off the memory.

She finished tying the sash of the gown, and on an impulse, went to one of the windows. The curtains had been left open all night because Nevien liked to have the sunlight tell her when it was morning. The window was made up of a large number of small leaded panes, and the world seen through it was therefore broken into fragments. Seeking a clearer view, she unfastened the latch and swung both halves of the window wide.

Cool morning air fanned her face.

There was no mist this morning, and the sky was a flawless blue. The garden lay spread out below. Every tree, bush, and fountain looking fresh and clean and new. If she leaned out a little, she could see Castle Rock off to the left and the rising slope of Kel Lankura to the right. Right in the middle, directly across from her, she saw the tips of several ships' masts sticking up beyond the wall at the far side of the garden.

This puzzled her only until she noticed the black and white of the banners flying from them and realized that she must be seeing the masts of the pirate ships. Captain Nagaro and his men must have anchored there and come over the wall, or in by the back gate. So they had come in the same way the Mahuk had that first time, all those years ago. That struck her as mildly amusing and she smiled a little, though with a touch of sadness. The Mahuk had also gone *out* that way, all those years ago, with their hostages.

Nevien was in a strange mood this morning. Another book in the tale of her life had just been closed, and it was as if she stood, poised, hesitating to open the next volume— balanced between past and future, between relief and apprehension, disappointment and hope.

Did she dare to hope that she might get something better this time? She had wished for it—fervently—the last time, and had gotten her wish, after a fashion. It would have been hard for anything to have been worse than being married to Gillard Marchent.

A part of her had actually hoped that her marriage to Elyan would last long enough for her to grow too old for anyone to want to marry her— sparing her from going through all of *that* again. But Elyan was dead, and she was only twenty-four. In three months' time, she could expect the courtships to begin again.

She sighed, then told herself that *yes*, that was true, but for the moment at least she stood safe in the secluded bastion of new widowhood. So she leaned on the window sill, savoring the morning air, brisk with the scent of the sea. On a whim, she closed her eyes and spoke aloud, reciting:

"Sweet Lady Lissafel, Queen of the Night,
Shadow of moon, and bright starlight,
Over the mountains, and over the sea,
Send me a man who will love only me."

There was the sound of a small, polite cough somewhere behind her.

Startled, Nevien opened her eyes and spun around to see Lady Meriel standing by the foot of the bed.

"Meriel! I didn't hear you come in."

"Well, I did knock rather softly." Meriel was apologetic. She came closer, stopping in the place where the ruined carpet had been. "When you didn't answer, I thought you were likely still asleep— or already gone out, and I thought I would just take a peep to see which it was. But you should have a care with the old prayers, child," she added, with unconvincing severity. "You know what they say: Be careful what you ask of the gods, lest they give you what you ask, but not what you desire."

Nevien laughed. "I didn't mean it seriously, Meriel." She closed the window and went to the dresser to find a pair of black stockings. "And, don't tell me you never said that rhyme yourself."

Lady Meriel smiled faintly. "I don't suppose there's a Leithian maid that hasn't. And most of them never came to grief. Still," she added, "in my grandmother's day, that rhyme was considered a powerful invocation of the Maiden Goddess, whenever Talebra was in the sky. And there's nothing worse than having the wrong man fall in love with you – one you don't want. Or one that you can't have."

Nevien was frowning at the stockings in her hand. She glanced back towards the window. That rhyme, she knew, was supposed to be said at night.

"I'd forgotten the part about Talebra," she said. "But it's daylight, and I think the bright moon has set by now. And I don't believe in Lissafel's kiss, anyway— that silly notion that people fall in love because Lissafel whispers the name of the person they're supposed to fall in love with in their ear while they're asleep, and then kisses them on the brow to seal it. You don't believe it either, do you, Meriel?"

Meriel sighed. "No," she said. "Though I did when I was a girl. If it were true, then everyone would fall in love all of a sudden, wouldn't they? And it wasn't that way for me with Grovern, or he with me either. Our marriage was arranged. We hardly knew each other before. But by the time I lost him, we loved each other dearly, and I couldn't say for the life of me when it started to be that way."

The older woman stopped speaking. Her expression had become abstracted, and her bright blue eyes a little misty.

"I'm sorry, Meriel," Nevien said quickly. "I didn't mean to upset you."

Lady Meriel shook her head. "Don't be silly, dear," she said with a little too much cheerfulness. "It's more than five years since the plague took him. All that's left now is a kind of fondness. If only Kuran Kel would look at me with favor, I'd marry again in a heartbeat."

Nevien decided to turn the subject. "Did you come to my room for a reason, Meriel? It must be too early for breakfast."

Lady Meriel sighed. "I came to see how you were, dear child, after yesterday— and last night. It was a lot for you to suffer through. And such a shock at the end of it."

"I'm all right, Meriel. Really." Nevien gave the small Leithian woman a rueful smile. She crossed to the bed and sat down on it to pull on her stockings. Choosing her words carefully, she said, "Elyan and I were never really very dear to one another."

Meriel sighed again. "I know," she said. "But I always hoped that you would come to love each other in time, the way it happened with Grovern and me. And now there's no more time."

Nevien became very busy with her stockings. "We had three years, Meriel."

"With him away at the war for most of it!" Meriel checked herself as Nevien looked up, startled by her tone. "I know I shouldn't speak ill of the dead," the older woman continued apologetically. "He was a fine man. He just could have spent more time at home, that's all."

Nevien had her left stocking on and now gave meticulous attention to the right one. "It wouldn't have made any difference," she said quietly. "And I'd rather not talk about it. There really isn't anything there to talk about."

Meriel straightened her shoulders. "Well, all right then, we won't. And you were right about breakfast. It won't be ready for an hour at least. Would you like me to send your ladies up to keep you company until then?"

Nevien gave the older woman a smile that was as sincere as she could manage. "No, thank you, Meriel," she said, slipping on her shoes. "I'm not in the mood for idle chatter. I thought I might go out onto the balcony to get some air."

After Meriel had gone, Nevien found her black veil and put it on. She had several veils of different colors which she rarely wore— but they were traditional for mourning. And being able to hide behind one had certain advantages. For now, however, she left the part of the veil that could be used to cover her face raised, while the longer part in back covered her hair.

She slipped quietly out into the hall. Lady Meriel must have gone downstairs again, for there seemed to be no one about— until she got to the top of the stairs. There she found one of the Palace Guard at his post,. He was a tall, well-built Leithian in his mid twenties with his right arm in a sling.

"Good morning, Lieutenant Brandle! I'm glad to see you here."

Nevien's greeting was heartfelt. The man was the chief of her own special guard— and he was Lady Meriel's nephew besides. Knowing that a large number of the Palace Guard had been slain, she was genuinely relieved to find that this one, whom she knew well, was merely one of the wounded.

"My Lady Princess." The man answered her formally, with a nod and a salute, then flashed her a wink and a smile.

"I am going out onto the balcony for a little fresh air," she informed him.

Part of the man's duty as a member of the Princess's Guard was to be aware of her whereabouts at all times while he was on duty, but she and Brandle had reached an understanding that allowed Nevien a degree of freedom while making sure that Brandle wasn't dismissed for dereliction of duty. It was quite simple. She would volunteer whatever she wished to have reported, and he wouldn't ask for any further details. In the event that there were any complications, he knew he could count on Nevien to produce an explanation that would exonerate him.

The lieutenant saluted again, and said, "Very good, My Lady."

Nevien continued past the guard post and made her way along the south corridor to a pair of double doors with large windows. They opened onto a long balcony running for nearly sixty feet along the outside of the building's south-facing wall. Opening one of the doors, she stepped out and was momentarily dazzled by the sun, which was very bright there on the south side of the building.

A sea breeze tugged at her veil and pressed her skirts against her legs. She stood for several seconds, breathing the salt air and shading her eyes, before she grew accustomed to the intensity of the light. Then her gaze took in the emerald waters of the river mouth below, the pale sand of the shore on the farther side, and the broad expanse of blue-gray sea to the south and westward. After a moment of admiring the view she realized, to her surprise, that she was not alone.

There was a man at the far west end of the balcony, to her right, about twenty-five feet from where she stood. He was standing at the railing with what looked like a ship's spyglass to his eye, apparently scanning the horizon. It took Nevien two more seconds to realize that the man was Captain Nagaro.

He had altered his appearance since the last time she had seen him. His brown skin and black beard were the same, and he still wore his sword at his hip and the same flowing black pants thrust into his black boots that he had worn the day before. But the deep red leather vest had been exchanged for a white shirt of a rather elegant cut. It also appeared that he had availed himself of the palace bath house, for his black hair was wet. Perhaps for that reason, he hadn't tied it at the nape of his neck, and it hung loose to shoulders.

When she looked closely, she could see a fine red line on his temple—the cut she had commented on, looking much more benign now that it was no longer bleeding. A slight bulge under his right sleeve marked the presence of a bandage. He was so intent on searching the sea with his spyglass that he had not yet noticed her arrival.

Nevien hesitated. There were a number of doors opening onto the balcony at various points along its length. She supposed that the captain must have come through one of the other doors, and that Brandle was unaware of his presence. Otherwise, the lieutenant would surely have warned her.

Properly speaking, she knew she ought to turn around at once and go back through the double doors to wait until the pirate captain was gone. The previous day's encounter had been a highly unusual circumstance. Normal propriety dictated that she shouldn't be alone in the presence of a man other than a family member, a close family friend, or a trusted guard such as Brandle.

Nevien, however, had never been a slave to propriety, especially not when she was convinced that such a precaution was unnecessary.

She had, in fact, decided within a minute of meeting him that Captain Nagaro was a safe man to be alone with. And it wasn't just that he had clearly been instructed in how a gentleman should behave. Nevien had met men before who had been so instructed, but who, while capable of behaving like gentlemen when they chose, were anything but gentlemen at the core.

Captain Nagaro was, she felt certain, rather the opposite. He wore his pirate persona like a mantle— somewhat reluctantly, it seemed— while the respect he had shown to her seemed as natural to him as the color of his eyes or the lithe grace with which he moved. Therefore, she hesitated only for a second before moving quietly nearer so that she might study him more closely.

People were the princess's favorite pastime. She found that exploring their personalities, their individual histories, and the different ways they thought about the world, was much more fun than the more ladylike activities she was supposed to engage in— such as sewing and embroidery, at both of which Nevien nevertheless excelled. Her pursuit of her hobby was, however, frequently frustrated by a lack of interesting people to study.

There was a fair amount of turnover among her ladies— as one left to marry and another took her place— but young women of the privileged classes usually led very sheltered lives and tended to be depressingly dull. And as a princess, Nevien was strongly discouraged from talking to strangers even if she could find one.

Doubtless she would have been discouraged from talking to Captain Nagaro had there been anyone there to do the discouraging. Fortunately, she reflected, there was not.

It was a still morning, and very quiet on the balcony, but Nevien's soft leather shoes made almost no sound on the tiling. This allowed her to approach to within a few feet of the man without him becoming aware. There she stopped, to critically consider his appearance in light of the discussion among her ladies on the previous afternoon.

She had to acknowledge that she found him handsome— just the way he was, as Kendira had put it. That fact hadn't escaped her the day before, but it wasn't a thing she would say in front of her ladies. Not when those young women could make a five-course dinner out of such a juicy tidbit.

The truth was that Nevien found everything about the pirate captain appealing. Beyond the perfection of his face, there was his lean muscular build, and a coiled-spring grace in his movements that suggested strength and power, exquisitely controlled. And more important than any physical attribute, there was the directness of his gaze, his courtesy, his earnestness, and the concern he had shown both for her and for the man he had found locked in north tower.

Very deliberately, Nevien banished these thoughts. While she surely wouldn't complain if Lissafel were to send her a man like this one, it was quite impossible for the goddess to send her this *particular* man. She was a princess. Her marriage would be dictated by the needs of Edrovir, and it was inconceivable that the pirate captain would ever be allowed among her suitors.

She frowned as she considered the other question that her ladies had debated. Was the pirate captain part Turowan? Rianine was right that his skin was darker than it should be for someone of pure Kelorin blood, even if he had been much in the sun. That had led both Rianine and Brendet to conclude that he must be part Turowan, but his profile belied the notion. He had the Kelorin high forehead and narrow, slightly aquiline nose. And he appeared to have a stronger chin than was common among Turowan folk as well, though it was hard to be sure because of the beard.

She frowned harder. His eyes, she had already noted, were Kelorin gray. That left his hair. It was as nearly black as that of any Turowan, but this proved nothing since Kelorin folk with hair of that color were not so very rare. There was one more clue, however: Turowan hair was always quite straight, while she could now see that Captain Nagaro's had a tendency to curl. The cut ends of it were lying in damp ringlets against the white collar of his shirt...

Nevien started slightly, and she looked harder at the shirt collar. Then she stepped forward a pace to see more clearly. There was a narrow band of embroidery on the collar, a simple but elegant tracery of intertwining black and brown threads. And it was repeated on the shirt's cuffs...

A little smile played about her lips.

Just at that moment the pirate captain lowered the spyglass, though he continued staring intently out to sea. Nevien decided it was time to speak.

"Good morning, Captain Nagaro," she said primly.

Nagaro had risen early, refreshed in mind and spirit, and had visited the palace baths to similarly refresh his body before going to the third-floor balcony to do some reconnaissance. He had become completely engrossed in the task, and the sudden sound of a woman's voice, so close to him, therefore caused him to start and turn quickly about.

He froze. Finding himself confronted by the apparition of a lady in gray, he experienced an instant of dislocation.

But this could not be his Lady in Gray. The Lady Maramine was, after all, long dead.

And then he recognized the green eyes that calmly regarded him, and the honey-colored hair peeking from under the black veil, and realized that he was looking at the princess, dressed, as his Lady Maramine had always been, for mourning.

Inwardly he swore. He had no idea how long she had been standing there— scarcely half a dozen feet away— and she was considering him with far too much interest. He resisted the temptation to pull the cord from his pocket and tie his hair, to complete his disguise. She had already seen it untied, and the gesture would only draw attention to itself.

He covered his confusion as best he could by bowing to her and saying, "Good morning, My Lady Princess."

Even as he did so, he was thinking that it was very bad luck for her to find him here. He had hoped that his path wouldn't cross hers again before he was could manage to make his escape, once more, from Lankura. He was considering making some excuse and taking his leave as quickly as possible, but before he could think of anything to say, the princess approached another pace and spoke again.

"I'm sorry if I startled you," she said, speaking formally. "And I want to thank you for what you did last night. For easing Elyan's passing."

Nagaro frowned. The princess didn't seem very much distressed. Last night he had seen evidence of tears on her cheeks. Today there was no sign of them.

"All I did was call Vothra," he said. "The Spirit and Elyan did the rest. And I'm sorry for not speaking to you afterwards. I didn't mean to be rude."

"Don't be silly," she said with a fleeting smile. "Anyone could see you were upset. I don't imagine it was an easy thing, helping a man to die— even if it *was* what Elyan wanted."

There was a marble bench near at hand, one of several set at intervals along the palace wall, and Nevien now went to it and sat down, settling herself demurely as if she meant to stay for a while. The bench was only five feet from where Nagaro stood, too close for her movement to suggest an end to the conversation, even had her eyes not returned to him as soon as she was seated.

"I think even Father understood, in the end, that it was what Elyan wanted," she added.

Nagaro shifted his weight, nervously fingering the spyglass. There was space beside her on the bench, but he knew better than to take advantage of it. Remaining standing in front of her served to emphasize the difference in their stations.

"Your father understood?" he managed. He was more than a little incredulous. Elgurn had not looked very understanding in the hallway outside the door, after the deed was done.

Nevien sighed and folded her hands in her lap. "Well he did say at first that Elyan had lost his chance to ride forever with Kroneg, the Lord of War, because he didn't wait for his time. But I explained to him that Elyan didn't want any part of that. He'd always said that it sounded like Hel to him— to spend eternity on some battlefield in the sky."

Nagaro nodded. This at least he could understand. "I know it always sounded like Hel to me," he ventured.

To his surprise, he thought he saw mischief in her eyes as she put her head on one side and studied him.

"Now that doesn't sound very much like a pirate," she said. "And just when I'd begun to think that you *were* a pirate, after all."

Nagaro didn't know what to make of this. "What do you mean?" he asked.

"That shirt you're wearing... isn't it pirate plunder?"

"This shirt?" he glanced down guiltily, and then hurried to explain. "I found it downstairs, dumped out of a chest onto the floor with some others. I only meant to borrow it until I could get one of my own from my ship. With all the confusion, I confess I didn't think that anyone would notice."

"Well," she said, "In that case, you picked the wrong shirt, or else the wrong place to wear it. I could scarcely fail to notice, since I made it myself. It belonged to Elyan, you see—"

"*Keshaal!*"

Nagaro was completely horrified. *This woman's husband wasn't even buried, and he was wearing the dead man's shirt!*

"I... I beg your pardon," he stammered. "I had no idea! You shall have it back at once!"

His fingers flew to the shirt's top button to unfasten it, but then he stopped dead as the absurdity of what he had been about to do dawned upon him. He stood frozen, feeling the blood in his face. Not for the first time, he hoped fervently that the kuma stain was covering his blush.

To his utter dismay, the princess burst out laughing.

"Lady," he cried, mortified. "Please don't mock me!"

Nevien's laughter died instantly. "I would never do that," she told him quickly. "I never mock people because it's always hurtful. But I *was* teasing you, and I'm sorry, since you plainly didn't understand if. It's a compliment, really," she added. "Because I only tease my friends. It means that I like you, Captain Nagaro."

She gave him a winning smile.

And Nagaro's embarrassment instantly evaporated in the radiant warmth of that smile. He responded with one of his own— not his wicked, feral, pirate smile, but one that was spontaneous and entirely genuine. She couldn't possibly have guessed how much it meant to him to hear her say that she liked him— this woman who had lain beside him so many nights and wept.

He bowed again to conceal his emotion. "You honor me, My Lady," he said, trying to keep his voice steady. "And I *will* return the shirt— as soon as I have an opportunity to exchange it for another."

At this Nevien leaned back against the wall, unfolding her hands and letting them stray to the bench seat on either side of her. "No," she said thoughtfully, "I want you to keep it. Let it be a gift, in gratitude for your service to us."

Now Nagaro was taken aback. "I... I couldn't possibly do that," he stammered. "You made it for your husband—"

"Who surely has no further use for it," she replied calmly. "As his widow, I may dispose of his things as I see fit, and it pleases me for you to have that shirt. I believe it would have pleased Elyan as well."

"But," he protested desperately, "Won't people notice and wonder? They'll think me presumptuous, surely."

But she shook her head. "I doubt anyone will notice," she said. "I gave it to Elyan almost three years ago, and he only wore it once—just to please me—before he put it away in his trunk. It had too little color for his liking. I made him another one— a red one— which he wore often. If this one pleased you enough to pick it out from among his things, then I think you were meant to have it. Besides," she added, considering him critically, "it becomes you."

Chapter 18

The Princess And The Pirate

Nagaro opened his mouth, and closed it again. He had run out of arguments, and the truth was that the idea of having something that Nevien had made held some attraction. He recalled that she had made a shirt, years ago, for him— or rather for Leyel Virden. It had been made of cream-colored silk with blue and gold embroidery so that it matched one of her gowns. He had felt like a dressed-up doll in it. He liked the one he was wearing now much better. Besides, Nevien seemed determined that he should have it.

He managed a smile. "In that case," he said, "I am honored to accept."

"Good," she said. "And I see that I was mistaken in what I said before," she added archly. "You're not really a pirate at all, are you?"

Nagaro's smile turned grim. "I am when I have to be," he told her. It made him nervous to have her guessing at what he was or was not. He knew that he really ought to find a way to take his leave of her. Yet he lingered. He had discovered that he enjoyed talking to her.

He just didn't like to be the topic of the conversation, so he changed it. "I am thinking that you must be very strong, My Lady," he said, "to bear your grief so well."

Nevien dropped her eyes at that, bending her head, and for a moment she hesitated. But then she raised her chin and met his gaze. "No," she said, "It takes no great strength if the burden isn't heavy. If I were truly grieving, the world would know it. I am sorry that Elyan is gone, for the country's sake. He was a warrior who lived for battle and the defense of Edrovir. But we were never more than friends... and that in a distant sort of way. He was crossed, you see."

"Oh—"

Nagaro hardly knew what to say. *Here he had thought that she must be happy, when all the while she'd been married to a crossed man!* The information at least made clear what Elyan's secret had been. And why, after three years, there was no child... but...

"Should you be telling me this?" he asked.

"It's all right," she said. "You're Vothrin, so I know you won't hold it against him. And you won't spread it about if I ask you not to. Elyan kept it a secret for the sake of his career— while he was alive. But he told me he didn't care what happened after he was dead. He believed he would go on to another life, and it wouldn't matter then what people thought of him in this one."

Nagaro nodded. "I understand. I've seen how some men treat a crossed man. I've been taken for one myself."

"But you... aren't?" She seemed to hang a little on the question.

He shook his head. "Not this time. But the Writings say that all spirits come to all things in time." He was quoting from memory. "So we should show equal respect to every person, whether it be a man or a woman, fair or ill-favored, wise or foolish, weak or strong, highborn or low. And however great your gifts may be, they are not yours by right, but only by the whim of Lokundas."

"Oh!" She exclaimed. "That's almost the opposite of what most Leithians believe."

"So I've noticed," he answered dryly, but then stopped. He had been thinking of how rudely the king had treated him, but he realized that Nevien was half Leithian, and he wasn't sure what she believed.

Nevien frowned a little and scuffed at the decorative tile paving of the balcony with the toe of one shoe.

"I remember Elyan talking about living many lives," she said. "He talked as if he were only passing through this life on his way to the next— as if he were looking forward to the change. In this life, he said, he was made to be a warrior. He said he couldn't be the man that folk wished him to be in any other way, but he could at least fight and make himself useful as a warrior, until his time came. He expected to die in battle too— or hoped to anyway. So he got what he wanted... or close to it."

Again Nagaro nodded. All of this made sense, but he was more concerned about the princess, who was very much alive, than about the prince, who was dead. "How could your father have allowed you to marry a crossed man?" he asked.

She laughed shortly. "Father didn't know. He still doesn't."

"Did... *you* know? Before you married Elyan?"

"It was the first thing he told me at the beginning of the courtship— that he would never be able to really love me."

"Then why did you marry each other?" Nagaro wondered. "Why did he even court you?"

She brushed away the words with a wave of her hand. "He was pressed to do it. We both were. Because it was 'the best thing for Edrovir.'

I suppose that to everyone else it must have seemed a perfect match. Besides, there are worse things…" Her voice trailed.

Nagaro turned hastily away, towards the end of the balcony, facing the view of the sunlit sea. He couldn't meet her eyes. He supposed that marriage to him had been one of those "worse things".

"It must be a hard thing, to be a princess," he said quietly, trying to keep the emotion out of his voice.

Her response surprised him.

"Surely not as hard as what *you* do, Captain."

"What do you mean?" his eyes snapped back to her to find that she was studying him again with that hint of mischief. "Do you mean being a pirate? That's not nearly as difficult. Not in the way that I meant. A princess has little choice about anything— no freedom at all, really— while I and my men can do very much what we please. We sail wherever we wish. Nothing hinders us but the weather and the tide."

"But it's very dangerous." Though she spoke lightly, she was still watching him closely.

Nagaro shrugged. "There is danger, certainly, when we fight. But we only fight when we choose, and when we can be fairly certain of victory. I have a covenant with my men that I will try to keep them safe, you see. It only makes sense, since we need to survive so we can continue our work."

"Oh. I see." She appeared to be digesting this.

Nagaro was encouraged to continue. "I'd very much rather be a pirate than a prince. And even a prince would be better than a princess."

Nevien laughed. "What man ever wants to be a woman?"

"You misunderstand me," he said. "I say it because men have so much more freedom. If my spirit hasn't already lived lives as a woman, it surely will. But although the Second Corner of Kelorin Law says that men and women should be equal, even Kelorin men sometimes keep that law very badly in these days."

He was thinking of the Lady Maramine's father, who hadn't allowed her to wed the man she loved.

"Men and women *equal?*" Now Nevien was grinning. "I like that! I have heard of the Four Corners of Kelorin Law, of course, and I think I know what one or two of them are— though not by their numbers. But *that* one I'd never heard before."

"Well of course." Nagaro thought he understood. "Your father is a Leithian, so he wouldn't have taught it to you, since Leithian men think they own their women."

Nevien stiffened and her eyes flashed. "That may have been the old belief," she said curtly. "But my father surely doesn't think he owns *me*. It's only that I know my duty. If he tells me I should wed this man or that, for the sake of Edrovir, he knows I will do it!"

"I beg your pardon, My Lady." Nagaro had actually backed up a step, dismayed by the sharpness of her tone.

With the ears of memory, he could hear the king's voice saying to him years ago, *"I've given you my daughter, the most precious thing I possess..."* But he wouldn't have dreamed of contradicting her. Not with that fire in her eyes.

"Perhaps your father just is not very familiar with Kelorin law," he suggested.

This earned him back her smile, but her eyes narrowed slightly. "And being of Kelorin blood, you *are?*"

His wariness returned. "It happens that I've read some Kelorin law," he said carefully.

"And you know all four of the Corners?" She had her head a little on one side. "I'd very much like to hear them."

Nagaro could see no harm in this, so he willingly recited them.

"The First Corner says that no person shall own another, because all folk are equal under the sun. The Second Corner says that men and women shall walk side by side in all things, and neither shall have dominion over the other. The Third says that folk shall choose those who lead them, and that leaders shall hold their place only so long as they serve those they lead. And the Fourth Corner says that no one shall own anything save by the labor of his hands, service to others, through honest trade, or as a gift freely given."

Nevien's brow furrowed. "The ones that I've heard are the first and third," she said. "But most of them go against Leithian ideas, don't they? Especially against the Right of Birth, which says that men are born unequal. Things like property and lordship over other folk are all inherited according to Leithian tradition. It's little wonder that the Leithians and Kelorin don't get along very well."

"That is certainly so." Her assessment was quite astute, and Nagaro found himself wondering again exactly what Nevien personally believed. He was afraid to probe the subject, however, not wanting to find any reason to dislike her.

"Your Four Corners don't seem to leave much room for piracy, either," she observed significantly after a pause.

Nagaro frowned. "The work we do is freeing galley slaves," he said. "Which is covered by the First Corner. Their need is great, but they have nothing with which to pay us for our service. Since we must live, we take our payment from the men who enslave them. And since those men often act like pirates too, it's hard to see any harm in it."

"It's just as I said then. You're no pirate at all!" She was looking at him now with frank admiration.

He straightened his shoulders under that gaze. "I like to think I'm not. But as you see, I've become rather accustomed to seeing something I need and taking it— or borrowing it without asking." He gestured at the shirt he wore. "Here I'd told my men that they should touch nothing, and look what I've done."

She waved this aside. "It's only a shirt, Captain! I'm sure you wouldn't have taken anything of great value."

He acknowledged this generous assessment with a bow, though to him the value was not the issue. There was a principle involved. *I've been a pirate too long*, he thought.

Abruptly she stood up, leaving her place on the marble bench and moving to the railing beside him, where she stood staring out to sea. There was a little silence that began to lengthen.

Nagaro was just thinking once again that he really ought to take his leave, when Nevien spoke.

"Were you looking for enemies with your spyglass, Captain?"

At least this was a safe subject.

"Yes," he replied, returning his own attention to the south-facing view. "And also for Lord Kuran's ships. It seems that the Mautep have quite gone, but there is still no sign of Kuran. He bade me watch his back garden, and we've done our best, but I'll be glad to return the task to him."

Nevien turned him a startled glance. "You were following Kuran's orders?"

"Kuran Kel does not command me," he answered rather cooly. "He asked it as a favor, and I doubt he thought we would have to fight. If he would only come, we could be on our way. But I'm afraid he may have spied those fleeing ships and given chase. It might be some days, then, before we can leave, and that pleases me not at all."

He had spoken without much thought, and Nevien took immediate exception to his last words.

"You're in such a hurry to leave us?" she cried. "When we haven't had a chance to show our gratitude? There'll be Elyan's funeral first, of course, but after that we'll have a banquet where we can put aside our grief for the fallen and celebrate our deliverance. We wanted all of your men to be our guests at the feast, and you would be the most honored guest of all!"

Nagaro stared. When he realized that his mouth was open, he closed it. This was unexpected. "If I may ask without giving offense, My Lady," he ventured after a stunned several seconds. "In whose name does this invitation come?"

"In the name of my father, my mother, and myself. Why, is something wrong? You will stay and attend, won't you?"

"I..." He floundered. "That is, there's nothing *wrong*..." His words trailed. The princess was studying him with an open and questioning gaze. He decided to simply make a clean breast of it. "It's only that—and I beg your pardon for saying this, My Lady— but I had the distinct impression that our presence here was not entirely welcome."

"Ah," she said knowingly. "It's my father, you mean. You and he didn't understand one another, that's plain."

Nagaro drew himself up. His eyes became hard. "I think I understood *him* quite well, My Lady. And I wouldn't mind so much if I thought he had merely failed to understand me. The truth is that he didn't try. He judged me before I spoke a word!"

Nevien didn't flinch, though a little shadow passed behind her eyes. "I know," she said. "He mistook you for a pirate, didn't he?"

Nagaro frowned. "For a different kind of pirate than I am, at least."

Nevien sighed. "Yes, and he *was* mistaken. But so are you, if you think you understand him entirely."

Nagaro shifted uncomfortably. "It was plain that he didn't want my men in control of *his* palace."

Her chin came up. "My father is charged with the safety of the palace," she said indignantly. "And of Lankura— of all Edrovir, in fact— and he takes the charge very seriously! He's been king for twenty-five years, and it's been a terrible strain on him. He's seen so much ugliness that he forgets sometimes that there is anything fair, or true, or honest in the world— except for Mother, of course— and he fears that death is stalking her."

The shadow came into her eyes again, but she rallied. "In the past two days he has had the control of the palace taken from him twice— first by the Mahuk, and then by you. I regret that, as a result, you didn't see him at his best."

"What would you have had me do?" he demanded. "Bow down to him and offer him my service?"

She inclined her head. "That would have been a gracious gesture on your part."

Nagaro swallowed. He had reasons for disliking Nevien's father of which she had no inkling. If the king had seen too much ugliness, the man had surely engendered some of it himself. Still, it wasn't Nagaro's nature to assume that he was always entirely in the right. Belatedly, he remembered that he had, in fact, offered his service to Kuran Kel.

"Can you tell me, then," he inquired stiffly, "that this invitation was your father's idea?"

Nevien sagged a little. "It was my mother's," she admitted. "She brought it up last night after you had gone. But Father approved of it at once. He has begun to see that he has erred, Captain, and he will come to see it more clearly if you show him the best that you are, rather than otherwise."

Nagaro sighed. "Do not judge others," he murmured under his breath, "nor use them as you think they deserve. Use them, rather, according to your own best nature." It was one of Vothra's admonitions— one of the more difficult ones to live by. It was also one of the reasons why he never liked to kill a man under any circumstances.

He looked down at the tile paving, then back up to meet her eyes. "For your sake, My Lady," he said, "I will try."

"And you will come, with all your men, to the feast?" she asked, eagerness apparent in her voice as well as in her eyes.

He sighed. "I'll have to put it to my men. I don't know how long they will wish to stay, and I've made a promise to them. But perhaps Lord Kuran will be delayed and we will have no choice but to remain."

"Well," she said, with a rueful smile. "I suppose I can't ask for more than that. But perhaps you should look again with that spyglass," she added, looking past him. "Is that a warship?"

"Where?" Nagaro's attention was instantly fully focused on the waters of the channel.

"There! See? Over by the nearest of the islands."

Nagaro brought the spyglass to his eye, and stared hard. She had sharp eyes. There *was* a two-masted craft. "It's only a merchant ship," he informed her after a moment, as he relaxed.

"Oh. May I look, Captain? I've never used a spyglass."

"Of course, My Lady," he said, handing her the glass.

After several long seconds of squinting through it, she said, "It's hard to find the thing I'm looking for. I can see such a little bit of the world through it."

He laughed. "Yes, it is hard. Look for the outline of the island against the sky and follow it until you find a little cleft. Then down a little and to the right."

"Oh! Yes! There it is." She stood, studying the merchant vessel intently through the spyglass.

And just at that moment there was a sudden thud at the other end of the balcony as the door from one of the hallways was roughly flung open, followed by the sound of booted steps.

"Nagaro! There ye are!" It was Taru's voice. "They're bringing the ships 'round into the river mouth, as ye ordered, and the Garrison men are going to— oh! I'm sorry... I thought ye were alone. I didn't see that ye'd found a—" Taru broke off.

Nagaro had turned around in his place beside Nevien at the sound of his friend's voice. His body must have at first hidden the princess from Taru's view until Taru's approach and Nagaro's movement revealed her.

Nevien now lowered the spyglass and turned, regarding the young Turo with interest and a raised eyebrow.

Taru had clearly spoken his last words before realizing the identity of the green-eyed woman in widow's gray with a spyglass in her hand. Though his complection was too dark to show his blush, his face radiated embarrassment.

Nagaro could guess very well what path his friend's mind had been taking, but he knew he was secure in the propriety of his own actions. Taru wasn't often embarrassed and Nagaro thought the experience might do the young Turo some good. So he smiled innocently at his friend and spoke with impeccable formality.

"Taru, this is the Princess Nevien. My Lady Princess, this is my friend and first mate, Taru Nareyo."

"Ah," she said, with a grave smile. "I am very pleased to make your acquaintance, Tor Taru."

Taru gaped. "I... I... My Lady..." he stammered helplessly, then finally managed something that was not entirely unlike a bow and followed it with an echo of her greeting: "I'm pleased to meet ye, too, My Lady Princess."

Nevien accepted Taru's greeting with a polite inclination of her head. Then she turned to Nagaro and handed back the spyglass. "Thank you for letting me try it, Captain," she said serenely. "And now I must leave you. I've taken quite enough of your time, and breakfast is probably ready. Good morning to you both— Captain... Zirda." She gave each of them a nod in turn.

Nagaro responded with an elegant bow. "Good morning, My Lady. This has been a pleasure."

Taru made an awkward imitation of Nagaro's bow, and mumbled something unintelligible. His gaze lingered on the princess's departing figure.

Nagaro noted the lingering look. The truth was that the princess had a very pleasing figure, and the gray gown, for all it's modesty, did nothing to conceal the fact. He coughed. "What was it you started to say, Taru? About the men of the Garrison?"

"Hmm? Oh." Taru shook himself and pulled his eyes away. He shot Nagaro a probing look before focusing on his friend's question. "They're going to try to raise those two Mautep ships," he explained. "They've brought in teams o' horses and they'll be working with the tide t' drag 'em up onto the sandbank along the shore on this side. Commander Korenthel would like some of our men to help bring the bodies to land."

Nagaro nodded grimly. "That won't be pleasant work. I'll ask for volunteers, of course, but I'll do it all with my own hands if I have to." He started to move in the direction of the door through which Taru had come onto the balcony.

Taru glanced furtively along the balcony, making sure that the princess was no longer in view. Then he stepped hastily to Nagaro's side. He lowered his voice to a tense, disapproving mutter.

"Whatever did ye think ye were doing, Nagaro? With *her*, I mean."

"What?" Nagaro stopped with his hand on the handle of the door. He turned a frowning look on his first mate. "She wanted to try looking through the spyglass— that's all."

"That's *all?* Nothing else?"

Nagaro was still frowning. "We were talking some before that," he admitted. "What of it?"

Taru's dark eyes remained fixed on his friend's face. "I don't believe this, Nagaro!" he said, shaking his head. "Prince Elyan is scarcely cold, and already she's flirting with ye!"

Nagaro released the door handle and faced his friend squarely.

"Nevien is a princess, Taru," he said coldly. "And a dutiful Leithian daughter as well, who puts the good of Edrovir before everything else. She's probably never flirted in her life."

"Ye think a princess can't flirt with a man?"

"I suppose some princesses might," Nagaro conceded. "But not this one." Turning again, he pulled the door open and strode through into the hallway beyond.

Taru followed on his heels. "What makes ye so sure?"

Nagaro stopped short, to glance hurriedly along the hall, making certain there was no one in sight. Even so, he lowered his voice.

"She didn't do that sort of thing when I knew her seven years ago, and she wasn't doing it now," he said through his teeth. "Don't you think I can tell when a woman is flirting?"

"I'm not so sure, Nagaro. Ye're so high-minded, and ye seem t' think that everyone else in the world must be too!"

Nagaro didn't care for the look Taru was giving him. "Well if I *did* do that," he retorted. "I'd certainly be wrong about *you*, wouldn't I? You assume a woman is flirting if she so much as looks at man!" And he started off again along the hall in the direction of the nearest stair that led to the lower floors.

Taru had to almost run to keep up. "How long were ye talking to her, Nagaro? Have ye forgotten how dangerous that is for ye?"

Nagaro came to a halt for the second time. He had reached the landing at the top of the stairs, where two hallways crossed. Fortunately there was no one to be seen in any direction, but it struck him that the vertical shaft of the stairway might carry sound to the floor below. He turned to Taru, frowning and holding up a finger for silence. "Not so loud," he muttered.

Taru looked guilty and lowered his voice. "Well, it *is* dangerous."

Nagaro was still frowning. It had been a rather long conversation—longer possibly than was prudent— but it hadn't felt dangerous. And he had rather enjoyed it. Being already annoyed with Taru's uncharitable judgement of the princess, he was more inclined to defend his own actions than he might otherwise have been.

"No I haven't forgotten," he said with some heat. "I didn't set out to talk to her. She happened to find me, and I couldn't very well be rude. Besides, I'm sure she hasn't recognized me, Taru— neither yesterday, *nor* today. And if she hasn't by now, I don't think she will."

He stopped, realizing that his own voice had risen. "But, enough of this," he said quickly. "Come on. There's work to be done."

Taru gave him an uncertain glance but then shrugged, conceding that they both had tasks to do.

They started down the stairs, Nagaro in the lead. As they turned the corner at the first landing, they saw Tredhold at the bottom of the flight, looking up at them.

Nagaro felt a quick stab of alarm. *Might the healer have overheard his words?* But then he supposed that if the man had, at least it was only Tred.

Reasoning that there was nothing to be done about it now in any case, Nagaro decided it was best to act as if nothing were amiss. Accordingly, he greeted the Leithian.

"Hello, Tred. What are you about?"

Tredhold stood still, waiting for them to descend. The man's face, when Nagaro could see it clearly, betrayed nothing untoward.

"As it happens, I was just looking for ye, Captain," the healer said. "Commander Worling is awake and talking, and he'd like to speak with ye."

Nagaro's long strides had brought him quickly down to Tredhold's side.

"Good," he said. "I'd like to speak to him as well. I think that most of us will sleep aboard our ships tonight," he added. "And leave the securing of the palace to the Palace Guard. They may be a little short-handed for it, but if our men take the River Wall and the wall at the back of the garden, everything should be well covered. It should please the commander to have his command back— and it will sit better with the king, as well."

It was his conversation with the princess that had put this idea in his head, but he felt no need to mention that fact.

***

After bidding the two men good morning, Nevien moved briskly away along the balcony, bent on re-entering the palace hallway through the double doors by which she had exited.

Just as she reached the door, she happened to glance westward past the balcony's parapet and noticed that Naru, the dark moon, was there, low in the western sky, his gibbous disk just barely visible by daylight. And there also, lower still— so low on the horizon in fact that she was almost dipping into the sea—was the pale ghost of Talebra. The bright moon was running ahead of the dark one, as she had been for months now. She was also just past full, her trailing edge a little ragged.

Sweet Lissafel, Nevien thought. *Talebra was still in the sky, after all, when I said that rhyme!* She frowned in momentary concern as she opened the door and slipped through into the hallway. But then she shook her head. It was only an old superstition. The Maiden Goddess was surely not so easily commanded.

Moving along the hall in the direction of the guard post and the stairs, she turned her thoughts back to the interview she had just completed. The conversation with the pirate captain had gone very well, she thought. The picture she had begun to form of him at their first meeting the previous day was coming into sharper focus— and he was proving to be *very* interesting indeed. She sighed as she ran over what she had learned about the man.

He had avoided admitting to being of Kelorin blood, though he plainly was, primarily, at least. He surely wasn't half Turowan— he couldn't be more than one quarter part at most. He was well-educated, but surprisingly free of typical male conceit. Even when she had given him a golden opportunity to boast, he hadn't taken it. Instead he had dismissed the hazards of his own occupation compared to the difficulty of her situation, of all things!

She shook her head. *Imagine him understanding how hard it was to be a princess!* That simple insight quite escaped most of the men she encountered. She wondered fleetingly who the fortunate woman was who had given him the green-eyed salamander ring he wore on his little finger, but quickly brushed the matter aside as not really being important. A man like that could hardly fail to have found himself a woman.

What *was* important was that he had shown himself ready and willing to act in the service of Edrovir. He and her father had not so far seen eye to eye, but surely that could be remedied.

She nodded to herself. *Perhaps just a few more well-placed words to each...*

Chapter 19

Kuran's Charge

Kuran was in the king's study, making his report and pacing the carpet in front of the room's large oak desk as he did so. Light from the room's single window illuminated the desk, the carpet, and King Elgurn, who was seated behind the desk. The king had his elbows on the desk's polished surface and his head bowed as he listened. His steepled fingers concealed the expression in his eyes.

"It wasn't until we had just finished our activities in southern waters, My Lord," Kuran continued. "—which is to say, a week and a half ago— that we first got word from the fishermen about the large Mahuk fleet that had been seen sailing north, by way of the Sea Passage."

Elgurn spoke from behind his fingers. "Word from the *fishermen?* When did fishermen start bearing news?"

Kuran paused in his pacing. "Apparently Captain Nagaro has been getting news from them for years. He'd advised me at our meeting to take heed of them also."

"Ah." Elgurn lowered his fingers just long enough to give the Lord of the Fleet a piercing glance. "Continue."

Kuran resumed his pacing. "I, of course, feared that these ships were making for the gold ports, so we turned north at once, and came up the Inside Passage, through the islands. We must have been well behind them, however, for we saw no sign of the craft until six days ago when we surprised six galleys just off of Boka Omei. They were making for the Sea Passage, and their colors matched those of the fleet we'd been warned about. Word from the fishermen later confirmed that they were some of those who made the attack on Lankura— but we knew nothing of the attack when we first sighted them."

Kuran paused to wipe his brow, then continued.

"We engaged them, and slew quite a number of the raiders before four of the ships broke away and fled south. The other two ships had taken damage and lost so many men that the Mahuk chose to abandon them. We rescued the slaves from those two ships before sinking them, and put the poor souls ashore. We then chased their masters as far as Haru Island, but the devils had too much lead. It was only then that I learned of the attack on the palace and the city— and how costly it had been. I immediately abandoned pursuit of the four galleys and returned to Lankura with all speed."

King Elgurn gave a small grunt of approval. Then he lowered his hands to regard the Lord of the Fleet with his pale blue eyes. "Why did you take time to rescue slaves from the Mahuk ships? That's not your usual practice."

Kuran stopped, facing the desk. His expression was grave. "Captain Nagaro told me that a large number of the slaves are captive men of Edrovir, My Lord."

"I see." Elgurn leaned back in his chair. "The pirate captain, again. You seem to set great store by this man's words."

Kuran kept his face impassive. He was aware that the first meeting between the king and the pirate captain had been less than cordial, having made certain to acquaint himself with the course of local events immediately upon his arrival at the Fleet Compound the previous evening. When next he spoke, his tone was carefully mild.

"When I met with him at Lapoa, My Lord, we discussed a number of things. As I mentioned earlier, we reached an understanding on some matters, while others I felt needed investigation. Since you had charged me— when last I stood in this room— with learning all I could about the man, I pursued my investigations quite vigorously and I can report that I have yet to find that Captain Nagaro has deceived me in any detail."

Kuran paused, then asked, "Hasn't he told you any of what he and I discussed?"

"As a matter of fact, he hasn't." The king's glance remained level, though his voice carried a distinct trace of sourness. "Since our first encounter, in which we spoke of the... outcomes... of the battle, he hasn't deigned to honor me again with his presence. It doesn't surprise me, however, to learn that he told you there were Edroviran men among the Mahuk slaves. Your noble pirate makes a great show of being more concerned with slaves than with gold."

Kuran permitted himself just the slightest frown. "The description 'noble pirate' is apt, My Lord, but you seem to have little enthusiasm for the man, even though you style him so."

Elgurn sighed with a grimace of annoyance. "It's how all the world sees him," he said with audible bitterness. "I seem to have been the only one blind to his virtue, and my error has been pointed out to me— *repeatedly*. The commanders of both the Palace Guard and the City Garrison have spoken well of him. Elyan— may the Gods welcome his spirit into Seralind— spent some of his last precious breaths in praising the man. 'A fine fighter and commander', he called him. 'An exceptional swordsman. A true defender of Edrovir'."

The king grimaced again and ran his fingers through his close-cropped hair before continuing.

"Master Ambras seems to believe him to be some sort of emissary of Vothra." The king sighed. "And I think my wife believes that as well. Even before... whatever it was... that happened with Elyan, she was calling him *'that gallant young man'* who had rescued her daughter. And of course let's not forget the man himself, who first berated me for showing him too little courtesy, and then proceeded to quote me the words of Darion— *right out there*!" Elgurn stabbed a finger at the door that led from the study to the royal Audience Chamber. "In the presence of two of the Signers of the Pact of Lankura!"

Kuran winced in spite of himself. "I did find him to be rather a *bold* man, My Lord—" he began.

The king's brow turned thunderous. "Other words come to mind," he growled. "*Insolent*, for one. *Arrogant*, for another. What does he know of Darion? He couldn't have been more than a babe in his mother's arms when the Great King died. While *I* have stood with Darion, *fought* at his side, and struggled every day for the past twenty-five years to fill his shoes! What does this young upstart know of such things? *Nothing!*"

Elgurn stopped speaking. His face had grown flushed, and he had half risen from his chair. Now he sank back into it.

Kuran waited for the storm to pass and then waited several seconds more for the blood to recede from the king's face. He knew Elgurn's moods. Such an outburst was not common. It revealed the extent of the strain the man was feeling. And the pirate captain had apparently struck a raw nerve.

"You are right about one thing, My Lord," he said, when the king had regained his composure. "Captain Nagaro is young and has much to learn— including, it seems, how to speak to a king. Yet he has endured things that are beyond our experience. If you will permit me, I will tell you some of what I have learned of him in Pakoa and elsewhere."

Elgurn sagged visibly, and passed a hand over his eyes. "Of course," he murmured. "Say on, old friend."

Kuran paused, considering where to begin. "Have you any idea what we found when we took the slaves from those ships, My Lord?"

The king gave a short, mirthless laugh. "I think I do," he said, and reached for a sheet of paper that lay among many others on the desk top. Picking it up, he read from it. "We found seventy four men in all. Twenty-six of that number were Turowan, fifteen Kelorin, two Leithian, and thirty-one… '*Hashtep*' —if I can make out the last word, which, I'm told, refers to the people of the Mahuk Baar."

Elgurn returned the paper to the desk with a scowl and an ironic flourish. "That," he said, "is the accounting of the corpses taken from the two Mahuk galleys that were sunk in the river by the brave efforts of the City Garrison."

Kuran cleared his throat. "Indeed, the numbers we found were similar— and 'Hashtep' is the word for the common folk of the Baar, 'Mautep' being the word for the warlord class. But that is not what I was getting at."

The king raised an eyebrow. "What, then?"

"The condition of these men, My Lord. It was deplorable. To begin with, the oar decks were stinking holes, and the slaves were ragged and filthy beyond description. More than that, they were so beaten and cowed that no more than a quarter of them would hold up their heads and look us in the eye. Most flung themselves weeping at our feet. And it is certain that Captain Nagaro was once a slave himself. Can you imagine that man in such a place? I confess I find it difficult. Yet he spent a year and a half as a slave, during which time he managed to foster comradery among the other slaves— Edroviran and Hashtep. And when by sheerest chance a sword came into his hands, he led them in a successful slave mutiny. They captured the ship in the midst of a battle, and sailed away in it! I had heard that there were Fleet warriors among the slaves on that ship, but it turns out there were only four, and *they* followed *him!*"

Kuran paused at this point, and noted with satisfaction that Elgurn was sitting bolt upright in his chair, looking rather stunned.

"But there is another part of the tale, perhaps more telling in its way, My Lord," he continued. "It seems that the plague struck during his first season of captivity on the oar deck. And this man we know as Captain Nagaro, seeing that their masters were leaving the slaves to die without water or food, called to one of the Mautep— who was the nephew of the warlord who owned the ship. Called the man by name, over and over, until the man came! And when the Mautep lordling came, Nagaro asked him for water, so that the slaves might live. And the young Mautep gave them water."

The king was leaning forward now. "But why?" he asked. "Why would a warlord's nephew listen to a slave?"

Kuran spread his hands. "That, I cannot say. Maybe he only saw the sense of not wasting a stable-full of horseflesh. But it doesn't end there. The stricken ship put in at the deserted island of Chitaopa because they had plague above decks and below. The slaves were taken off and chained to a tree— as I've had it described. And *then* our Captain Nagaro persuaded the same warlord's nephew to hobble his ankles instead of chaining him with the rest— so that he could tend his fellows. And tend them he did— Turowan, Kelorin, and Hashtep alike— going back and forth to the stream to fetch water with his hobbled feet, and crawling on his hands and knees while dragging the water skin from one fevered man to the next.”

"And he didn't try to escape?” Elgurn inquired, incredulous.

Kuran shook his head. "No, My Lord, because he'd given the Mautep his word. And when the plague passed, and the ship was about to leave Chitaopa, the warlord's nephew offered to set him free. But our future pirate captain's answer was, 'I will not leave my friends.' I tell you, My Lord, this sounds like a friend I would like to have!"

The king shook his head. "And you *believe* this improbable tale, Kuran?”

"My Lord, I do believe it,” Kuran replied earnestly. "For one thing, the character it displays matches what I saw in him. But also, I've heard the tale too many times from too many witnesses. My favorite is the candlemaker in Kel Tierna who rolled up his sleeve to show me his slave brand and then told me the story I've just told to you, in such plain and simple words, and with such manifest sincerity, that it was impossible to doubt him.”

"I see.” Elgurn sat frowning in thought.

"Just so, My Lord. He is a leader of men who wins followers by showing that he cares about them. And he hasn't gotten where he is by being meek. I think it fair to say that he respects men for their deeds, rather than their titles— which on the whole shows good sense. And, yes, I believe he truly does care more about slaves than gold.”

Elgurn chewed his lip. "It's clear that I made a mistake with him,” he said wearily. "But there were those reports we had of his attacks on merchant ships. And you didn't see him, Kuran, standing there with his sword at his hip, looking as if he thought he owned the palace. And being coolly tight-lipped while that unfortunate young guardsman— scarcely old enough to use a razor— stumbled through his report. I thought he was using the boy. And I assumed that a pirate would act like a pirate! Surely by now the man should be accustomed to such errors—”

The king cut himself short, and sighed. "But what did you learn about the reports we had that he'd taken merchant ships? I suppose there was no truth to them?”

Kuran shook his head. "Most were simple lies, My Lord, told by dishonest men to cover their own theft of goods, or to avoid paying the tax they rightfully owed. A few were acts perpetrated by others. But as for Captain Nagaro's manner, there was a time when you used to like a bold man. Didn't you once tell me that you were only willing to trust me so much with your plans because I was brazen enough to tell you exactly what I thought of them?"

At this, Elgurn actually laughed. "That I did, old friend. But at least you always left your sword at the palace door— before I granted you your title."

"There are some who would have me leave it there still," Kuran said darkly. "And it's likely that Captain Nagaro isn't aware of the law that allows only men of the noble Houses to wear their swords inside the palace. Seeing that he had just used that sword to help drive out the invaders, I doubt that anyone was inclined press the point— much less to take the weapon from him."

Elgurn drew a long sigh. "I expect that you are right," he said. "But who *is* he, Kuran? Which of Edrovir's bickering, jockeying, noble Houses has spawned this... *paragon?* Is he some Kelorin lord's bastard, got of a Turowan wench and using the name of his mother's family?"

At this, Kuran frowned deeply. "I'm afraid I haven't been able to trace his history back further than an obscure fishing village, somewhere north of here. He was apparently living with a Turowan fisherman's family at the time the sea raiders took him."

"He's no fisherman!" Elgurn again picked up the paper, from which he had read, and brandished it before the Lord of the Fleet. "This is written in the pirate's own hand, I am told— though my clerk and the Garrison Commander both confirmed the figures. It's a very fine hand. And the language is much too graceful for any fisherman's son."

Kuran took the paper and read:

"We have laid all of them to rest in a common grave on the southern side of the river, giving them what reverence we could, though the water had worked ill upon their bodies. We will never know who they were, but I am grateful to have been permitted to do this much for them. With respect and gratitude, Nagaro Nareyo."

He handed the paper back. "Well," he said, "*that*'s gracious enough, certainly. And you're right, My Lord, he is clearly an educated man. But why must he be from a noble House? The wealthier merchant families are quite able to educate their sons to this degree."

"Ah, yes. Quite so." Elgurn was apologetic. "You are right to remind me of it. Have you asked among your father's friends? Do any of them recognize the name?"

Kuran sighed. "His name is of little help, My Lord. He freely admits that it isn't the name of his birth, though he would give me no other."

A scowl immediately darkened the king's brow. "I don't like a man who conceals his parentage. What has he got to hide?"

"I couldn't say." Kuran spoke cautiously. "But if he was gotten out of wedlock, as you suggested, it could explain much. That unfortunate accident is often deemed a disgrace to the child— though it's properly the parents' fault. In any case, I intend to make further inquiries."

"Mmm." Elgurn was still frowning, but he dismissed his thoughts, whatever they had been, with a gesture. "Yes, continue your inquiries, my friend, and tell me anything you discover. And for this evening's feast, I hope you will take that young whip in charge. See if you can find an opportunity to give him some lessons in manners, eh? We will all do our duty tonight— honor the man and his followers, and show them how our fair city expresses her gratitude."

***

Nagaro stood in the great cabin of the *Sword of Freedom* buttoning his shirt— for the third time. He had begun dressing for the banquet by putting on the shirt the princess had given to him, then changed his mind. Despite what Nevien had told him, he was afraid someone would recognize it. Besides, he didn't want to set himself apart from his men with an elegant embroidered shirt. He had next begun to put back on the shirt that he had worn all morning, then decided that a fresh one would be better. So he had fished the last clean shirt he owned from his trunk, and was in the process of donning it.

A knock sounded at the cabin door.

"Come in," he said distractedly.

It was Taru who entered, with Pavo close behind him.

"Aren't ye ready yet, Nagaro? There's folk starting to gather out there. I saw Lord Kuran, and a pack o' Fleet men. And there's a crowd o' townsfolk around the city gate."

Nagaro's hands stopped moving and he gave his friend a startled glance. "Townsfolk? What are *they* doing here?"

"They've come to see us pass by, I expect. To see *you* pass by, I should say. I don't expect they care that they'll be seeing the likes o' me or Pavo."

"*Bishka!*" Nagaro frowned as he fastened the last button. "I hope you're wrong. And I don't much care for a crowd regardless of what they think they've come for."

"What is this, Nagaro?" Pavo had moved to the cabin's small table and picked up a folded piece of stiff parchment that was lying on it.

Nagaro glanced at it. "The invitation. I think I'm supposed to bring it, in case I'm asked to present it, to... ah... prove we've really been invited," he said vaguely, pushing the tails of his buttoned shirt into the waist of his flowing black sailor's pants.

Pavo looked puzzled. "Surely king knows he have invited us."

Nagaro smiled weakly. "I imagine he does," he said dryly. "But I read somewhere that it's wise to bring the invitation in case you encounter someone who hasn't been correctly informed."

Pavo shrugged his broad shoulders and reached out to replace the invitation on the table. As he did so, a small slip of paper fell out of it and fluttered to the floor.

Taru bent to pick it up. The young Turo straightened, holding the paper before his eyes. "*Cap-tain Na-ga-ro*," he read aloud, sounding out the words. Nagaro had taught him to read, years before, but he didn't get much practice. "*I look for-ward to the plea-sure of your com-pa-ny. Nev-i-en Har-lind.*"

His brows knit together in a frown. "What's this, Nagaro?" he asked. "I thought ye said the *king* invited us."

Nagaro winced. "He did," he said, with mild annoyance. "Which you would see if you read the invitation." He waved his hand at the folded parchment.

"*That* is the invitation. Whereas *this*..." He pointedly plucked the slip of paper from Taru's fingers. "Is just something the princess must have put inside it. I'm sure there's no need for me to bring it as well," he added, turning and dropping the little note into the open trunk, where it landed, on top of the elegant embroidered shirt.

Taru put his fists on his hips. "Now will ye tell me, Nagaro," he said, insinuatingly, "exactly what ye think she meant by, '*I'm looking forward t' the pleasure o' your company.*'"

Nagaro was more than a little annoyed by this time. "It's just a personal touch! The queen used to do that sort of thing. Since she is plainly ailing, the princess must have taken over the duty."

"Nothing to do with that long talk ye had... *alone*.... on the balcony?"

Nagaro frowned. "There will be at least two hundred people at this banquet. She can't expect to have that kind of conversation with me, or with anyone else. The note is a bit of extra politeness, that's all."

Pavo spoke then. "Nagaro, do you *like* princess?"

Nagaro turned to his Hashtep friend, feeling the probing glance of the man's narrow dark eyes. "I suppose so," he said. "There's nothing to *dislike* about her, certainly."

At this, Taru exploded. "Except that she'd be poison for ye, Nagaro! Ye mustn't let yourself get interested in her! Ye know ye can't have her!"

Taru's heat surprised Nagaro. "Of course not," he said. "And I don't *want* her, Taru. I never did. It's just that I never *disliked* her, because none of it was her fault... and besides that, she was kind—"

"—and she has a shape t' make a man's head turn!"

"*Taru!*" Nagaro found he was scowling at his friend and with an effort he unfurrowed his brow. "I don't know what you're so worried about," he said seriously. "It's not as if I could ever fall in love with her. She's too much wrapped up in... all those... those *bad memories...*

He faltered to a halt as a shadow passed across his face.

"Nagaro, I'm sorry..." Taru began.

But Nagaro shook himself and waved the words aside. "It's all right," he said, reaching for his sword belt and absent-mindedly buckling it around his waist. He picked up the invitation, and thrust it into his shirt. "Come on," he said. "If Kuran is already out there, we had best join him. I want to get this over with."

He made for the door.

Taru remained, staring at the floor. "I don't know," he muttered as Nagaro's boots echoed in the passage beyond the doorway. He glanced at Pavo, who also lingered. "I suppose I'm being foolish, thinking that she got her hook into him years ago. Nagaro's a strange man sometimes— especially when it comes t' women."

Pavo abruptly pointed at the open chest. "Is that shirt not one that Nagaro said he will give back? Why does he still have it?"

Taru glanced at the shirt. "Aye, that's it," he said. "He told me she *gave* it to him. That it was an old one o' Prince Elyan's."

Pavo made a startled movement, his eyes suddenly wide. "When Hashtep woman give shirt of dead husband to another man," he said portentously, "it mean she want him for her new husband!"

Alarm flashed across Taru's face, but he shook it off. "Well, *we* don't have any such custom," he said. "So it doesn't mean anything."

***

They caught up with Nagaro on the main deck. He was standing just outside the door of the stern castle, waiting for them. Other members of the crew were also gathered there, but they were crowded against the port rail where they could watch whatever was happening on the wharf. There was a general babble of voices from the group, and no one seemed to have noticed their captain's arrival.

The *Sword of Freedom* was moored at one of a dozen berths spaced along a wharf on the River Edro's northern bank. The wharf was normally used by ships of the Royal Fleet, but Kuran had given permission for the pirate ships to moor there. The *Tiger* and the *North Wind* lay at berths on the *Sword's* port side, and the *Sea Eagle* lay to starboard.

Lord Kuran's ships lay just beyond that, nearest to the walled compound that housed the men of the Fleet when they were in port. The Fleet Compound was squeezed into the space between the city wall and the riverbank, accommodated by a bend in the river, which angled sharply away from the city at that point and swept back again in a long arc. A broad roadway ran between the wall of the Fleet Compound and the city wall, passing through a massive arch that linked the two.

Directly in front of the pirate ships, the wharf closely adjoined the roadway, with the walls of the city rising on the farther side. On this fine spring afternoon, the walls of Lankura were hung with festive blue and white banners, and the nearest gate leading into the city stood open and welcoming. It was still several hours before sunset and sunlight washed the scene, picking out the brightest hues.

There might have been more to see besides the walls and banners, but the rest of the view was obscured by a gathering throng of people, including about twenty in the dark blue tirkas of the Royal Fleet.

Taru came to stand beside Nagaro.

"I don't know what ye mean by gettin' it over with," he said, "I can't wait t' see what they've cooked up in those kitchens we saw!"

Nagaro knew that Taru wasn't alone in that sentiment. The decision among the pirates to attend the feast had been very nearly unanimous and the fact that the men had entered the palace through the royal kitchens undoubtedly had a great deal to do with it.

He gave his friend a look of acute pain. "I can't tell you how many dinners and banquets I had to sit through in that Great Hall," he muttered between his teeth. "Sitting there like a wooden doll... being *stared* at... and *laughed* at—"

"It won't be like that tonight," Taru interrupted hastily. "At least I'm sure that no one will be laughing."

Someone among the crowd of seamen at the ship's rail must have noticed them at this point, for a voice was raised.

"Hoy, mates! It's the Capt'n!"

"Capt'n Nagaro! Capt'n Nagaro!" Other voices echoed.

Nagaro squared his shoulders, and rearranged the muscles of his face into a smile that he hoped didn't look too unnatural. When the princess had first spoken to him of the banquet, the idea had surprised rather than alarmed him. As the event had approached, however, thinking about it had begun to dredge up buried memories.

Though he didn't really think that anyone would recognize him, he expected the event to be an unpleasant ordeal. As he prepared to advance, he sought within himself for the strand of steel that served him when facing battle, and grasped it. He had to think of this as just another task to complete.

And everyone was waiting for him.

He stepped forward, making for the gang plank with Taru and Pavo flanking him. The little crowd parted and closed behind the three young men, and then followed them across the gang plank, pressing eagerly behind.

Once on the wharf, Nagaro soon located Lord Kuran, surrounded by a group of Fleet officers. All were in full uniform.

The Lord of the Fleet stepped forward and extended his hand.

"Well met again, Captain," he said with a quick smile. His sharp black eyes measured Nagaro from head to foot, taking in the plain white shirt, the black pants and boots, and lingering just fractionally on the hilt of the Mautep sword.

Nagaro took the Fleet Lord's hand and shook it, bending his head respectfully. "I give you greeting, My Lord," he said.

This was proper etiquette. If the other man offered his hand, he didn't expect a bow.

Kuran released Nagaro's hand and stepped back. "Do you ride, Captain?" he inquired. "Besides our own mounts, I had the grooms bring a dozen extra horses from the Fleet stables. I thought you and your officers might ride, if you wish— and are able." He gestured to his left along the wharf and a number of the Fleet officers stepped aside to allow a clearer view in that direction.

Horses! Nagaro's heart leapt. This development promised some compensation for whatever else he was going to have to endure in the evening ahead.

"Yes, I do ride," he said. "Thank you, My Lord."

Without waiting for Taru or Pavo's reaction, he eagerly turned to look at the animals, about a dozen yards away along the wharf, standing in a row with grooms holding their lead reins. His eyes swept over them and were instantly drawn to one that wasn't standing quietly like the others. This one was a big steel-gray whose crested neck identified him as a stallion. The animal was tossing his head and swiveling this way and that, pulling on the lead rein.

Nagaro drew in his breath. *"Magnificent!"* he murmured under his breath, and without further ado, he struck off across the flagstones.

Kuran stared after him with an amused expression, which quickly changed to a frown. "By the Eyes!" he muttered. "He's making for the gray stallion. I should have warned him."

Captain Ruald, standing beside him, laughed indulgently. "If he tries *that* one, he'll soon learn his lesson!"

Kuran gave Ruald a sharp glance. "I didn't set out to embarrass him. What was the Stable Master thinking, sending that one? If it's another one of his jokes, I'll have the man's hide."

Taru had been standing close enough to overhear. Intimidated though he was by the presence of so many members of the Royal Fleet, he couldn't resist speaking. The fact that he had survived an earlier interview with Kuran made it easier.

"Just watch him, My Lord," he said. "Nagaro knows what he's doing."

Kuran's brow relaxed just slightly. "Well," he said. "He's talking to the groom. That man should tell him about the horse's reputation."

Nagaro was indeed talking to the man who held the gray stallion's rein. The groom was gesturing and the horse was dancing, but Nagaro stood confidently, apparently at his ease. Now he pointed with unhurried movements from the rein in the man's hand to the ground. A moment later he repeated the gesture. At this point the groom let go of the rein and threw up his hands, as if to absolve himself of responsibility.

Kuran and Ruald both sucked in their breaths when they saw the groom step away, leaving Nagaro facing the untethered horse. They clearly both expected the worst, but oddly enough all that happened was that the stallion stopped dancing.

The two Fleet officers continued to watch as Nagaro took a step towards the animal.

By this time, many of the folk who weren't too distant were also watching, and the general buzz of voices among the nearer onlookers had stilled. They all saw Nagaro take another step. The horse continued to stand still, its head turned to regard Nagaro with one of its large, dark eyes, its ears pricked in his direction.

One more step brought Nagaro to a position beside the animal's head. He extended his hand to stroke the gray muzzle, then to pat the creature's neck. Then he reached for the hook that attached the lead rein to the nose band of the bridle. Unhooking the lead rein, he tossed it aside so that it fell a half dozen feet away. The stallion tossed his head once at this, turning to see where the strip of leather had fallen.

Nagaro went back to rubbing the horse's neck, however, and the big gray quieted. A moment more, and then Nagaro moved confidently to a place at the stallion's shoulder. Taking up the loop of the reins that lay on the horse's withers, he placed his left boot firmly in the stirrup and swung lightly into the saddle. The stallion shook his head so that the bridle jingled in the hush and stamped his hoof once, but that was all.

An audible sigh was heard from the crowd.

Nagaro, sitting comfortably astride the big gray, glanced about him and became aware for the first time of the attention of the crowd. He felt an instant of incipient panic to find so many eyes upon him, until he realized that there was amazement on the people's faces and that no one was laughing.

"What's this?" he inquired in a conversational tone, but still one that carried far in the nearby silence. "Has no one in Lankura ever seen a man mount a horse before?"

The spell was broken. The babble of many voices resumed and the gray stallion began to dance again. This time, however, the animal's movements suggested eagerness rather than agitation. Nagaro kept his seat on the animal's back without apparent effort.

"By the Mark!" Captain Ruald exclaimed. "I'd like to know how the man did *that*. In all the months that we've had that beast in the Fleet stables, no one's been able to ride him!"

Kuran shook his head. "I think we would all like to know how to work such magic," he said. He turned to Taru. "Can you enlighten us, Zirda?"

Taru spread his hands. "I expect he just talked t' the beast," he said smugly. "That's all he does. He talks to 'em. But I could ha' told ye, My Lord. Nagaro was a landsman before ever he was a seaman, and I don't think the horse was ever born that Nagaro couldn't ride!"

Kuran looked as if he wished to say something but restrained himself as he became aware that the gray stallion was approaching at a prancing trot.

Nagaro was firmly astride, beaming, and in complete control. He reined in the stallion in front of the Lord of the Fleet and swung to the ground as easily as he had mounted. Moving to stand beside the horse's head, he once again stroked the creature's neck.

"Stand easy, brother of the wind," he murmured softly, and the horse's ears swivelled around to the sound of his voice. "I will speak to my friends a little, and then we will ride again."

The stallion tossed his head, for all the world as if he understood, and then stood quietly mouthing the bit.

Smiling broadly, Nagaro turned to Kuran and the others standing with him. "I'd like to introduce my new friend. I'm told that his name is Thunder-Heels, though he answers to Thunder quite willingly, it seems. Isn't he marvelous?"

"Ah, yes. *Marvelous.*" Kuran nodded, but he wasn't looking at the horse. "Tell me," he added, "Why were you so insistent that the groom should let go of the lead rein?"

Nagaro's expression became immediately earnest. "The rein seemed to be bothering Thunder," he replied, glancing at the horse and rubbing the beast's muzzle. "And the groom was making matters worse by jerking on it— and by speaking with anger in his voice."

"Ah." This time Kuran smiled indulgently. "And here your friend very nearly had me convinced that, among your other talents, you are able to speak to horses."

Nagaro gave Taru a reproachful look, then laughed when Taru looked indignant and muttered, "*I never!*" under his breath.

"What Taru meant, I'm sure," Nagaro said quickly, "is that I use a gentle tone with horses that wins their confidence. It's the tone they understand, not the words."

Kuran smiled. "Ah yes, quite so," he said. "I must commend you all the same. We've had nothing but trouble with this horse since he came into the hands of the Fleet a month ago. The grooms have been able to saddle and bridle him, as you can see, but few have managed to mount him, and those that have didn't stay astride for long."

Nagaro shrugged. "He must have had some bad experience—presumably involving a lead rein. His previous owner might tell you something."

"As it happens, the previous owner is dead," Kuran informed him gravely. "Lord Bron Sobring died last summer of wounds suffered in the border war. His brother, Grimbold, made a gift of the horse to the men of the Fleet, since Bron was in the service in his youth."

Nagaro had started slightly at the name of Bron Sobring. He covered it by running his hand through his hair. *Lord Bron was dead! And* this *had been the man's horse?* Well, he told himself, he wouldn't hold that against the poor beast.

"Perhaps Grimbold could tell you something then," he said easily.

"Perhaps." Kuran's thoughts already seemed to have moved on. "We should be on our way. If any of your men would like to choose mounts, I assure you they will find the other horses more amiable of disposition."

A quarter of an hour later they set out. Kuran and Nagaro rode side by side at the head of the procession. Immediately behind them, in two parallel ranks, came the Fleet officers on one side, and the pirate officers on the other. The remaining host of the pirate crewmen brought up the rear. The majority of the Nagaro's officers were mounted, though Moraga and Guhanu had never learned to ride.

"Nor am I likely t' start now," Moraga had gruffly declared, eyeing the horse that was offered to him suspiciously. "'Taint no place for a proper seaman, sitting up there on one o' them four-legged demon-beasts."

Taru had laughed at his fellow Turo, and proudly swung up onto a small roan.

Pavo, however, had declined to ride. When Nagaro had approached him, the big Hashtep had meaningfully returned his gaze, then glanced significantly at some of the watching crowd who were staring at him with frowns on their faces. "I think I maybe walk," was all he had said. Nagaro had glanced at the crowd and nodded. He thought he understood.

The procession quickly passed through the gate in the city wall and turned left into one of the city streets that led in the direction of the palace. Throngs of people lined the street on both sides. Even sitting high astride the gray stallion, Nagaro felt his stomach tighten anew at finding himself the focus of so many eyes. Before his fears could do their work on his mood, however, Kuran distracted him by speaking.

The Lord of the Fleet had maneuvered his mount until he and Nagaro were stirrup to stirrup. He was riding a long-legged bay, and the height of the horse made up somewhat for what the rider lacked in stature. "Some of your men look familiar, Captain," he said. "There's two of them riding together, like mates— the leather-faced old Kelorin salt dog on the sorrel, and the little grasshopper of a Leithian on the dun."

Nagaro didn't need to turn around and look to know who the other man meant.

"That would be Landros Torenin and Tredhold Ferth," he said with a faint smile.

Kuran nodded. "Ah," he said. "Second mate and ship's doctor on the *Fairwind*, if I recall. Good men. I thought we had lost them both when the *Fairwind* went down off Pakoa during the plague summer. When I learned they had both answered the Amnesty by resigning their posts, I was glad to know they were alive, but sorry not to have them back under my command."

Nagaro frowned. He was gazing straight ahead and trying to ignore the people along the sides of the street who were waving at him.

He knew about the Amnesty of course. A great many men in service to the Crown had disappeared during the plague. Some had died, unheeded, but many others had deserted their posts, either fleeing from the contagion in fear or flying home to learn the fate of their loved ones. When the disease had run its course, the king had declared a general amnesty under which any man might either return to his post or resign it, with no questions asked. Nagaro knew which choice Landros and Trehold had made, obviously, but he had never thought about how the Lord of the Fleet might view the matter. Now he felt that Kuran deserved some explanation.

"Five crewmen from the *Fairwind* were pulled from the sea by the Mautep aboard the ship on which I was a slave, My Lord. One was thrown overboard the next day when it was found that he had the plague. The other four survived and later helped in our escape. Three of them are with me still— Landros and Tred, whom you noticed, and a young Leithian named Gurd. The fourth decided he wasn't suited to be a warrior."

Kuran was regarding him narrowly. "How fortunate that you had these men with you when you made your move to escape," he ventured.

Nagaro nodded soberly, looking at Kuran rather than the crowd. "I won't say that we couldn't have escaped without them. We outnumbered the remaining Mautep by three to one— but the fight would have surely been much more bloody."

"Ah. Yes." Kuran's expression was inscrutable. "Do you know why they chose to remain with you, instead of returning to my service?"

Nagaro continued to meet the other man's eyes. "Landros and Tredhold didn't wish to sink more ships with slaves aboard. Gurd, I think, believed in the beginning that he would grow rich as a pirate. He hasn't, of course, but now he is Landros' first mate, and he seems to find that reward enough— since he couldn't have risen so quickly in the Fleet. There are other former Fleet men among those who follow me as well. Most come out of the islands and were never slaves themselves, but they all knew men who were taken."

It was Kuran who looked away. "I see," he said. Several long seconds passed as the horses continued up the street, before the Lord of the Fleet turned back to him and spoke again.

"Landros is one of your captains?"

Nagaro nodded. "Yes. He commands the *Sea Eagle*."

Kuran raised an eyebrow. "I seem to recall," he drawled, "that the name of Landros Torenin was put up for advancement to first mate several times, and the man turned it down. How did you persuade him to become a captain?"

Nagaro kept his eyes straight before him, frowning. He wasn't aware of the crowds anymore, his gaze being turned inward.

"I told him it would only be until I found someone more suitable," he said after a moment. "That was three years ago. I think he doesn't like to make the big decisions— where to sail to next, or whether to attack or not. I put those choices before all the captains— or even before all of the men, sometimes, because the consequences affect us all. Landros is happy to give his council when I do that. But if there's no agreement, or the choice must be made swiftly, he knows that I will choose."

Nagaro stopped speaking and glanced at the Lord of the Fleet.

Kuran was studying him intently. "Interesting," was all that the older man said, however, and then he seemed to turn his attention back to the road that lay before them.

The street had grown wider and the crowd thicker while they talked. Nagaro was astonished, and more than a little unnerved, by the number of people who had turned out to see them pass.

They were folk of all sorts— young and old, rich and poor, Kelorin, Leithian, and Turo— a great motley mass of pressing bodies. The mingled jabber of their voices filled the air. Some were calling, "Kuran! Kuran!" Clearly the Lord of the fleet was popular among the common folk of Lankura. Others were crying, "The pirates! Look at the pirates!"

Nagaro had experienced the attentions of such crowds before— from the seat of an open carriage *...where he had sat, waving stiffly, his face frozen in a wooden smile, as the people jeered.* In his mind, he could hear them. "Useless pretty-faced boy", they had called him. And other things: *simple-minded... painted doll... empty-headed princeling...*"

With a wrench he pulled his thoughts away. If any of these folk had done such things, it had been years ago, he told himself. They couldn't possibly recognize him. No one in Lankura could even have known that Leyel Virden knew how to ride a horse, since he had never been permitted to demonstrate the skill.

He smiled grimly to himself. Doubtless his keepers had feared that they wouldn't be able to catch him had the puppet part of him chanced to interpret a careless phrase as an order to let the horse run. He wished he could turn back time and erase from people's minds the memory of Leyel Virden, sitting in a carriage as a helpless, simple-minded boy, or a pretty but useless doll in fancy clothes.

He couldn't do that, of course. But, he realized, he could do the next best thing. He could set beside that memory a new one— of Nagaro, emphatically a man, on horseback, and anything but helpless, useless, or simple-minded.

Both Thunder-Heels and Kuran's bay were tossing their heads and prancing, excited by the noise of the crowd. Lord Kuran held his horse in check with a tight rein. Nagaro used a looser one, and now he gave the big gray his head as he leaned forward to speak to the animal.

"Come, my friend," he murmured. "Let's show these folk what a beauty you are!" The stallion's ears swivelled to listen. Then the horse tossed his proud head, arched his neck, and surged forward in a graceful, high-stepping trot. The stallion seemed to float over the cobbles while Nagaro sat effortlessly erect in the saddle, as secure as if he were rooted there.

Kuran, caught by surprise, muttered, "*What now?*" and let out his own reins, pressing his horse forward so he wouldn't be left behind.

Nagaro, however, had no intention of outdistancing the rest of the procession. Guiding Thunder-Heels as much with the pressure of his calves as with the reins, which he held lightly in his left hand, he steered the big gray first to the right, and then the left, in long sweeping arcs across the width of the street.

"Look at that! That must be Captain Nagaro!"

"Captain Nagaro!"

"Nagaro the Pirate!"

The cries suddenly arose on either side— and there was such cheering! Nagaro reined in the gray, surprised. He raised his free right hand to acknowledge the cries of the crowd.

Lord Kuran was able at last to bring his horse alongside. The Lord of the Fleet raised his hand to the crowd as well.

"Lord Kuran!"

"Captain Nagaro!"

The crowd cheered them both as their horses pranced on, together, along the street.

But not quite everyone was cheering. A well-dressed Leithian man on the right-hand side of the street suddenly raised his voice.

"I remember this man," he cried. "This Captain Nagaro! He was in my shop this morning, selling some of his pirate plunder. Selling it for silver and gold! What do ye do with your gold, *Nagaro the Pirate?*"

Hearing the man, Nagaro reined Thunder in. He remembered this shopkeeper— one of several with whom he had done business that morning— and he was suddenly aware of the weight of the purse in his pocket. He had meant to transfer the coins from it to his cash box aboard the *Sword of Freedom*, but he had forgotten to in his preoccupation with preparing for the banquet.

Kuran slowed his own mount and leaned over to speak in a low voice. "Pay him no heed, Captain," he advised. "You will always find one malcontent."

Nagaro shook his head. "No," he said. "Where there is one who is bold enough to speak, there are others who timidly keep silent. This should be answered."

Turning the stallion's head to the side, and squeezing the animal's flanks, he rode towards the man who had spoken, bringing his horse to a halt a pace in front of the shopkeeper.

A hush fell over the crowd as the entire procession came to a halt behind him.

Chapter 20

Most Honored Guest

The man looked up at Nagaro, startled but defiant. "Have ye come to frighten me then?" he inquired with a show of bravado.

"No, Zirda." Nagaro's tone was mild, but he spoke loudly enough to be heard widely in the sudden hush. "I mean to give you an answer. What do we do with pirate gold? I call it finder's gold. That means unexpected wealth, un-earned— riches that come by chance. By Kelorin law, a man may not own such gold, but only use it. And only to meet his need. If he has more than enough, he must find another in need and pass the rest along. That's what we do with whatever riches we find aboard the Mautep ships when we set their slaves free."

The shopkeeper squinted up at Nagaro, speculatively. He was a stout man, in a velvet vest, with a well-fed look.

"So, ye give it to folk that have need?" he said, unabashed. "Then I'll put ye to the test. I believe your purse is full, and I need a new writing desk!"

There was a ripple of laughter from the onlookers.

Nagaro ignored it. "What kind of a *need* is this?" he asked in a conversational tone. "Are you likely to starve for want of a writing desk? Would it keep you from suffering in the winter wind, or keep the rain from soaking you? Do you need it to carry your grain to market? Besides," he added. "You look like a man who can afford to buy his own writing desk. And why did you trade me your gold for a handful of baubles this morning, if your need was so great?"

This time the ripple of laughter was distinctly louder.

The Leithian smiled grimly. "Aye," he drawled. "Ye're not a fool, Captain. I can see that. But ye still look like a pirate to me!"

Nagaro backed his horse a pace or two and swept the crowd with his eyes. He raised his voice.

"Is there anyone here who is suffering?" he cried. "Who truly has a need, and no means to fill it?"

For a long moment there was only an uncertain rustling among the crowd and a low murmur of whispered voices.

Kuran, where he sat on his bay a little distance away, was watching with a frown, his sharp, black eyes flicking this way and that as he measured Nagaro and studied the faces of the townspeople.

Suddenly a Turowan woman stepped forward, pressing her way through the throng. She looked to be in her middle thirties, though her face held great weariness and she might have been younger. Her black hair hung limply, neither braided nor bound, and she pushed three young children ahead of her. She looked up at Nagaro.

"My children need shoes, Zirda," she said simply. "Since their father died, there's money for food, but not much else."

Nagaro looked down at the children, and they looked up at him, their dark eyes wide. The oldest, a boy of about seven, was barefoot. The two little girls wore the remains of shoes, tattered and split, the soles all but dropping off. Nagaro saw also that the clothes worn by the children and their mother were old, but clean and neatly patched.

"Yes," he said. "This is a need I can see." Without hesitation, he drew out his purse, reached into it, and pulled out a half dokan coin. Leaning down from his horse, he held out the coin to the woman. "Take this, Zirdyn," he said. "Buy your children shoes, and maybe some clothes for them and for yourself, for I think I see a need there also."

Reaching up, the woman took the coin. She stared at it as if she had never held gold in her hand before. Indeed it was likely that she hadn't.

"*Hakura!* she exclaimed. Thank ye, Zirda! And may the Spirits bless ye!"

Nagaro straightened in the saddle, but he shook his head. "You needn't thank me for passing on finder's gold, Zirdyn," he told her. "They say it burns the hand that holds it too long." He wheeled the big gray about, and raised his voice. "Is there anyone else here who has such a need?"

There were general murmurings, and then individuals among the crowd began to raise their hands and their voices in turn:

"I need money to buy medicine for my old mother!"

"I need a hundred and fifty rins t' pay the rent!"

"If I don't pay Sortas the three hundred rins I owe him, he'll take my carthorse, and then how shall I earn my keep?"

Kuran had smiled a little at how Nagaro had dealt with the Turowan woman, but now he was frowning. Abruptly he swung his horse around and found Taru, who had ridden up close behind him.

"What does the man think he's doing?" he demanded. "Giving the woman money to buy shoes was clever enough, but if he lets these folk see that he's giving away money to all takers, there'll be no end of it!"

Taru returned the Lord of the Fleet a look that was more amused than exasperated. "Oh, there will be an end of it, My Lord," he said. "When the money runs out."

Kuran gaped for a moment, then his eyes swept the ranks of the pirates, who seemed to be patiently waiting. Kuran's eyes narrowed. He turned back to the scene in the street.

Nagaro, in the meantime, had guided the gray stallion to a halt in front of a Kelorin man. He was holding up his hand for silence. "Where is your mother now, Zirda?" he inquired.

"At home, o' course, Capt'n. Sick in bed!"

Nagaro studied the man. "Can you give me details?" he asked earnestly. "What ails her? What has the healer told you? The cost of the medicine? And is there anyone here who can bear witness to the truth of your words? I beg your pardon for asking, but this isn't a need I can see."

Kuran backed his horse until the beast stood beside Taru's mount so he could speak to the young Turo without taking his eyes off Nagaro.

He watched as Nagaro questioned the man. In the end, a witness did indeed come forward. Apparently satisfied, Nagaro reached into his purse again and handed the man some silver coins. Nagaro moved on then, to the man who had claimed to need money for rent. This second man had witnessed the interrogation of the first. As soon as Nagaro turned in his direction, he spoke up to withdraw his claim, confessing that he had enough silver after all to pay without the need of charity. So Nagaro moved on to the third man, who had claimed he would lose his carthorse if he didn't pay his debt.

At this point, Lord Kuran leaned over, and asked Taru in a low voice: "Does your captain do this sort of thing *often?*"

Taru shrugged. "He's never done this before, *exactly*, My Lord," he conceded. "I mean... not with such a great crowd o' folk. But it's the sort o' thing he does."

"And the other crewmen don't mind that he's spending gold that should have been theirs?"

Taru shook his head. "They might have in the beginning, Zirda, but not any more," he said seriously. "I mean, it's not *our* gold really, is it? And Nagaro always seems t' see that there's enough, somehow. Once we came up short, trying to outfit the ships in the spring, and he went to the Town Council and they took up a collection—"

"*A collection?*" Kuran shook his head and sat his horse in silence as he watched Nagaro work his way along one side of the street, then cross to the other, calling once again for any to come forward who had needs that they had no means to meet.

There were half a dozen more requests, all together, but they were made more cautiously. Some were denied, but in other cases Nagaro's hand disappeared into his purse and emerged with coins of gold or silver that were passed into upraised hands. Finally, he held up the empty purse, turning it upside down for all to see.

"That is all I have, good people," he told the crowd. "And I am sorry that I don't have enough for all who are in need. But remember," he cried. "Those of you who have received gifts today, it is finder's gold that has come into your hands. If it is more than enough for your needs, seek out some other who has suffered a misfortune, and pass on any that remains."

There was a cheer from the crowd in answer.

Nagaro acknowledged it by bowing low over his horse's neck. Then he straightened in the saddle. Turning the gray stallion about, he rode back across the street to the Leithian shopkeeper who had first spoken and halted in front of the man.

"Zirda," he said, "Has your question been answered?"

The man was staring at him, plainly impressed. He nodded. "Aye, Captain Nagaro," he said, and there was respect in his voice. "Ye've more than answered it."

Nagaro inclined his head to the man. Then he turned the gray stallion about once more and began to ride back to the head of the procession where Kuran waited on his long-legged bay next to Taru on his little roan.

He hadn't gotten very far, however, when the voice of a woman was heard, suddenly, above the general murmur of the assembled folk.

"Why do ye let this pirate go so easily?" she cried. "Why do ye cheer for him? Because he has bought your good will with gold and silver? How do we know that he won't come back another day with his ships and his men to rob our homes and slay us in our beds?"

Her words were followed by several seconds of silence and then a hushed murmur arose. Nagaro had reined in his horse upon hearing the woman's first words, and now he turned the big gray around yet again and rode back along the front of the crowd, seeking for the woman who had spoken.

It wasn't hard to find her. She stood out at the front of the crowd, head belligerently raised, hands on hips. She was Kelorin, perhaps forty years of age, with narrowly-chiseled features and traces of gray in her hair.

As Nagaro approached on the stallion, the nearest members of the crowd stepped back, looking apprehensive. The woman stood her ground, however, meeting his glance with bold defiance.

Nagaro pulled Thunder-Heels to a halt in front of her and gazed down with an expression of sorrow rather than anger.

"What has happened, Zirdyn?" he asked in a mild voice that carried far in the hush. "Or what do you think you know, that you would say such a thing?"

"Do ye dare to ask?" The woman tossed her head. "Let me ask ye *this*, Captain Pirate: *Where is my son?* My fine, strong lad that was a merchant seaman on the *Morning Tide?* The ship sailed out o' Lankura last Sedrin with all hands and a full cargo, but only half the men came home— with an empty ship! They were attacked by pirates. The cargo taken. The crew slain! Can ye give me back my son, Captain? Or will ye try to make me forget my pain with your finder's gold?"

Nagaro sat on the gray stallion, stricken, not hearing the low rumble of the crowd.

"*Oh, Zirdyn!*" he said, emotion catching in his voice. "I know better than to think that all the gold in all the kingdoms of the world could ever buy your pain— any more than it could bring your son back to you, if he is slain as you say. But I swear to you in Vothra's name, that this was none of my doing! No ship of mine has ever attacked any ship of Edrovir, nor any merchant ship of any kind. Nor have I, nor any of my men, ever slain a man of Edrovir. If you were told differently, it is slander!"

One could have heard a pebble drop half a mile away in the silence that followed. The woman stood, her back straight and her head up, still challenging. Yet there was uncertainty in her face and she made no immediate answer.

Nagaro turned, his eyes sweeping the faces of the assembled folk. "People of Lankura!" he cried, raising his voice so that it carried far along the street. "I thought I had already given away all the finder's gold that I carried, but I was wrong. I still carry *this!*"

Reaching for the hilt of his sword, he drew the blade out and held it aloft, pointed at the sky. The late afternoon sun caught the blade, flashing golden light.

"I took this sword from the hand of a fallen sea warrior of the Mahuk Baar, and it too is finder's gold!" Nagaro's voice rang along the street, from wall to wall.

"It came to me in my need. And I took it! And I used it to help save myself and my friends. My own need is past, but I keep it still. I use it to serve the needs of others— to help free other men from slavery in the galleys of the Mahuk Baar. What do you say, people of Lankura? Shall I keep this sword— this finder's gold— yet a while? Or shall I pass it to another who might serve you better?"

"*Keep it!*"

"*Keep it!*"

The cry echoed on every side.

Nagaro bowed his head in acknowledgment, still holding the sword aloft. When he raised his head he spoke again.

"In Vothra's name, good people, I swear to you that while it is in my hand, this sword will never be raised against any of the innocent folk of Edrovir! By the Eyes and Ears of Vothra's Mind, I swear it!"

Then he gathered the reins with his left hand, and spun the gray stallion around to face the host of his gathered followers, the sword still raised.

"What do you say, my friends?" he cried. "Are you with me? Do you also swear as I have done, by whatever powers you revere?"

A hundred voices answered as one.

"*Aye, Capt'n! We swear it!*"

Once more Nagaro turned his horse back to face the crowd. The sword swept down and to the side in a shining arc as he bowed low over his horse's neck. As he straightened, he sheathed the blade, and it was as if a light had gone out. Addressing the woman, who still stood there a little apart from the crowd, he said in a gentle voice, "Are you answered, Zirdyn?"

She seemed to shake herself. "Yes, Zirda," she whispered. "*Oh, yes.* I am answered!"

He saluted her with his empty hand. "May Vothra give you peace," he said, and lifting the reins, he turned the gray about one last time and trotted back to where Lord Kuran still sat on his tall bay with Taru by his side.

Taking up his former position on the right hand of the Lord of the Fleet, he said simply, "Let us ride on, My Lord."

Kuran had managed to get his mouth shut before the pirate captain could notice that it was open. He leaned over and said in a low voice, "Don't you wish to stay a little and savor the moment, Captain?"

Nagaro frowned. "A woman's pain is not to be savored," he said. "And I don't think we should keep the men from their dinner."

At this, Lord Kuran laughed outright. "Especially when so many of them are Turo, eh?" He raised his hand in a commanding gesture that signaled the column behind him to advance.

As they started forward, the murmur of the crowd around them began rising into a chant.

"*Nagaro!... Nagaro!... Nagaro!...*"

Kuran leaned over to speak. "I see that you have some skill in dispensing charity, Captain."

"The finder's gold?" Nagaro asked distractedly. He was eyeing the chanting crowd. "I've had quite a lot of it pass through my hands, I guess."

"*Nagaro!... Nagaro!... Nagaro!...*"

"A pity you had to give so much of it away today."

Nagaro was still frowning. He shrugged in annoyance. "There's always more," he said. "And it isn't good to keep it too long. It doesn't really burn your hand, but if you get used to having it, you begin to forget that it isn't yours, and—" He broke off. "Why are the folk in *this* part of the street chanting? Surely they were too far away to hear what I said."

Lord Kuran crooked an eyebrow and smiled. "News travels quickly in a crowd. We're moving too slowly to outrun it."

"Oh." Nagaro paused uncomfortably. "I hope it isn't much farther to the palace."

It wasn't far, as it turned out. The great gate that opened into the courtyard in front of the palace soon loomed ahead of them.

The chanting continued all the way to the gate. Beyond the gate, however, the folk lining their way took on a different character. They were not common townspeople, but wealthier folk, or men and women in the palace livery. Members of the City Garrison made a kind of honor guard, spaced at intervals in two lines along either side.

Even here, however, Nagaro found himself being loudly cheered. There were more voices here calling Lord Kuran's name than there had been in the city, but the cheers were still dominated by cries of, "Captain Nagaro!"

Nagaro was relieved when they finally reached the foot of the steps leading up to the front portico of the palace. A row of grooms waited there to take their horses.

Nagaro swung lightly down from the saddle and moved to the stallion's head. "Be easy, friend," he murmured to the horse. "These are good people." One of the grooms moved to take the horse's bridle. The big gray blew wetly, and stamped a foot once, but then allowed himself to be led quietly away.

"Amazing," murmured Kuran at Nagaro's elbow.

Nagaro shrugged. "Not really," he said. "The man expects a gentle horse, because he sees a gentle horse. And, being treated gently, the horse has no reason not to be."

"Ah." Kuran nodded appreciatively.

They mounted the steps and were ushered through the doors by members of the Palace Guard. In the vestibule, Delvin approached them. He addressed Nagaro, hesitantly and with obvious discomfort.

"I... I'm afraid ye must remove your sword, Zirda, within these walls."

"I must?" Nagaro's tone revealed his surprise.

Beside him Kuran spoke, his voice level and his face completely deadpan. "I'm afraid so, Captain," he said, "unless you can claim the blood of a noble House. And of course, you would have to present at least one credible witness to the truth of such a claim."

Nagaro sighed. "I can make no such claim," he said, unbuckling his sword, and handing both sword and belt to the waiting guardsman. "But I think there might be some here who are glad that I was wearing my sword within these walls a week ago."

Delvin took the sword almost reverently, bowing apologetically.

Lord Kuran coughed. "Necessity sometimes requires an exception," he observed. "And we *are* grateful." He turned to Delvin.

"My station, of course, permits me to keep my blade," he said, "but on this occasion I choose to relinquish it. I deem it an honor that it should lie beside the sword of Captain Nagaro while we are at table. I trust you will guard them both well."

So saying, the Lord of the Fleet unbuckled his own sword, and handed it to the stunned Delvin. The youth took it, gaping, then belatedly remembered to bow.

"Aye, My Lord. Of course, My Lord," he mumbled.

The majority of the other pirates hadn't troubled to bring their swords. Those who had, surrendered theirs without objection, seeing that Nagaro had surrendered his.

So they were duly ushered through the vestibule, and the Compass Room, and arrived at the double doors that opened into the Great Hall. The pirates, of course, didn't really need ushering, since they had been this way before, but they dutifully followed the lead of the liveried servants.

Nagaro distracted himself from the new knot of apprehension that was growing in his stomach by noting that the blood stains had been scrubbed from the marble floors. The debris of battle had been cleared away as well, and some of the damage had even been repaired. The Audience Chamber still lacked proper doors, but carefully patched wood on the doors to the Great Hall, and the gleam of new brass, revealed that the locks had been replaced.

Those doors were currently flung wide. A pair of Palace Guards flanked the open doorway.

Through that doorway, Nagaro could see flower-garlanded walls and festively appointed tables. It was a scene so cruelly familiar that it struck him like a physical blow. In a moment, he would be expected to enter that hall and sit at one of those tables, under the gaze of several hundred pairs of curious eyes.

At least he would be with his friends...

The servant who had conducted them stepped aside, motioning him forward with a sweeping gesture. Nagaro forced himself to keep walking, conscious of Lord Kuran moving beside him. Just inside the Hall, a woman stepped up to greet them. With a shock, he saw that it was Nevien, still dressed in widow's gray and with a black veil flowing over her hair. Her eyes fastened on his face, and instantly she *smiled*.

It was a smile of such dazzling radiance— filled with such obvious pleasure— that his anxiety fled to the edge of consciousness, where it hung like a waiting shadow.

"Ah, Captain Nagaro! Welcome, Zirda!"

"My Lady Princess." He managed a bow. The gesture was perhaps a little stiff, but still quite serviceable.

"And My Lord Kuran."

"My Lady." Kuran also bowed.

The smile the princess bestowed upon Kuran was also extremely cordial, and the Lord of the Fleet answered it in kind. Nevien then looked past the two men she had just greeted, and said, "And it appears that you have brought all of your men, as we hoped, Captain. And Lord Kuran has brought a contingent of his officers as well."

She turned to gesture towards the foot-end of the hall, farthest from the raised dais where the king would sit. "We have set half a dozen tables for your men there, Captain. I thought they would be most comfortable all together."

Relieved, Nagaro managed a more fluid bow. "Thank you, My Lady," he said, then turned to the men behind him. "We are to be seated there," he said, pointing. "All together, at those six tables. I think you may choose your seats in any way you like."

So saying, he moved to lead the way, only to feel Nevien's hand on his arm.

"I beg your pardon, Captain," she said. "But since you are the most honored guest, we've prepared a place for you with Lord Kuran's officers at one of the high tables."

Nagaro stared at her. "What?" he exclaimed, more sharply than he intended. "Am I not to be with my men?"

The lurking shadow of his panic began to rush in upon him once again, and he couldn't keep the alarm out of his voice.

"Now, don't ye worry, Capt'n," Landros put in, as he stepped forward to lead the pirates. "I'll look after the lads and make sure they don't get into mischief. Ye just go on and enjoy your place of honor. It's only fitting."

"But... I... I should be with my men!" Nagaro felt as if the floor were being pulled from under his feet. "I *belong* with my men—"

Nevien leaned closer and lowered her voice. "Nonsense, Captain," she said, with an encouraging smile. "Anyone can see that you've had a gentleman's education. You will do fine, I'm sure."

She turned to Kuran, who had been watching narrowly. "You will show him where to sit, won't you, My Lord?" she asked. "At your usual table. He's to be placed on your right hand."

"I'd be happy to, My Lady." Kuran bowed to her, then gave Nagaro a conspiratorial wink. "Come along, mate," he said, in a fair imitation of

Landros' nautical drawl. "I'll show ye where to sit, and see that ye don't get into mischief!"

Nagaro saw that he had no choice but to surrender to his fate.

He was grateful to Lord Kuran for covering his distress with a jest, and thankful also that Nevien apparently only thought he was uncomfortable with the grandness of the hall and the company of so many highborn folk. He gave the princess a parting smile that he hoped didn't look as painful as it felt.

As he moved to follow Kuran, he caught a glimpse of Tredhold, watching him keenly, with a frown on his face. Taru, who was closer, gave him a mock punch on the shoulder, accompanied by a quick, tight grin, and a shrug that was clearly intended to be nonchalant. Pavo was somewhere farther back, still trying to make himself inconspicuous— a difficult feat, since the young Hashtep stood well over six feet tall.

It seemed a very long way to the other end of the Great Hall. Nagaro scarcely noticed that he passed three tables arranged along the hall's center aisle, each bearing a whole roasted boar. Liveried men stood by with long forks and knives in their hands, prepared to carve the meat.

Lord Kuran's usual table turned out not to be right in front of the dais, but rather to one side, and not quite at the end of the hall. Kuran took his seat, at the center of one of the long sides, with his back to the wall so that he had a good view of the rest of the Great Hall. Nagaro sank onto the chair immediately to Kuran's right, and the most senior of the Fleet officers arranged themselves in the remaining chairs. The less senior officers were placed at an adjacent table.

As soon as they were all seated, half a dozen conversations sprang up at Lord Kuran's table. Since none of the speakers addressed themselves to Nagaro, however, he was left momentarily to the turmoil of his own thoughts.

It wasn't, he told himself, as bad as it might have been. The place where he was seated was widely visible, to be sure, but as Leyel Virden, he had been made to sit at the table on the dais on such festive occasions. That position was far more conspicuous.

On this occasion, the table on the dais was as yet empty. The arrival there and seating of the king would signal the beginning of the meal.

Nagaro gazed tensely across the width of the Great Hall. A space immediately in front of him, stretching across most of the width of the hall, was clear of tables. He hoped fervently that there would not be dancing. It appeared that there would at least be music, for there was a little semi-circle of empty chairs, arranged in front of the dais, facing towards the foot end of the hall.

Beyond the open space, there were a number of tables arranged along the farther wall, in front of the tall windows. Those tables, Nagaro noted, were rapidly filling up with men and women whose fine clothes and elegant manners would have identified them as members of the noble class even if he hadn't thought he recognized several of them. A number of the lords were staring at him.

"Frightfully rude of them, really— staring like that."

Nagaro started at the voice. It was Kuran who had spoken.

"Ah... who?" he managed.

"*Them*. Kuran gestured with his head. "The lords across the way. They fancy themselves our superiors, and since they believe us to be inferior, they seem to think that the rules of courtesy do not apply."

Nagaro frowned thoughtfully, glad of the distraction. "But you are a lord," he ventured after a moment. "Elgurn made you one, and he gave you a Wared."

"So he did." Kuran's laugh was bitterly ironic. "But the Leithians say that a lord is born, not made, and even the Kelorin believe a lord should be chosen by the people of his own Wared. I was made a Lord first, and handed a piece of what used to be Loros Wared afterwards."

"I thought the folk of Kel Wared were pleased to have you as their lord."

"Well, yes, they are," Kuran admitted. "The first chance that they had to agree to the choice, they were glad to do it, but they weren't my own people, originally. I come out of Oranil Wared on the other side of the river."

"Oh. I see." Nagaro chewed his lip. "I think," he said after a moment, "that you shouldn't have left your sword at the door— My Lord." He added the title belatedly, realizing guiltily that he had been omitting it.

Kuran frowned. "What do you mean?"

"Only that the folk of your Wared *did* agree, which makes you their Lord. And since you have their choosing, you shouldn't let other folk forget it."

Kuran considered him narrowly. "I yielded up my sword to honor you," he said. "True nobility has no need for titles."

Nagaro levelly met the older man's gaze. "I know," he said. "But only a handful of people heard what you said when you handed over your blade. And when you walked into this room, everyone could see that you're not wearing it."

The Lord of the Fleet looked as if he were about to say something, but Captain Ruald, who was sitting on his other side, leaned forward and addressed Nagaro.

"I still can't believe that you gave all your money away in the street, Zirda," he said. "It was such a waste! You don't really believe that all those folk you gave it to were honest, do you?"

Nagaro frowned at the Leithian. "I thought I explained, Captain, that it wasn't *my* money," he said. "And of course I can't be certain that they're all honest. There can always be a few who find clever ways to deceive. But knowing that a part of one's charity might go astray seems a poor excuse for not trying to help people."

Ruald blinked. "I believe you mean that."

"Yes, I do."

The officer seated on Nagaro's other side spoke next. "I don't see why you don't think it's your money, Captain. You and your men risked your necks for it. Why shouldn't you keep it all?"

Nagaro sighed. "We don't *keep* it all, because we don't *need* it all—" he began, but he was interrupted by the sounding of three bells that signaled the arrival of the King of Edrovir.

All eyes turned towards the dais and the nearby door that led to the foot of the stairs descending from the royal chambers on the third floor.

Elgurn entered through the doorway with Queen Semorel on his arm, accompanied by two other lords whom Nagaro instantly recognized. One was Kelorin, and one Leithian. They were both older men, close in age to Elgurn. The musicians suddenly appeared, instruments in hand, and preceded the royal party to the steps of the dais, playing a lively little march and then standing to one side as the king and his party were seated before taking their own seats in the chairs provided for them.

Nevien also appeared from somewhere to take her seat beside her mother, two chairs to her father's right. The two lords sat at the other end of the table, on the king's left hand. One more chair, beside the princess, remained conspicuously empty.

Kuran leaned over as the two senior lords seated themselves, to speak low into Nagaro's ear. "Those two lords are Anduar Tyronin and Pendrik Glenmark, Signers of the Pact."

Nagaro nodded, trying to look as if this was something he hadn't already known.

"Lord Anduar has been impressed with your forthrightness," Kuran continued, still in an undertone. "Lord Pendrik, on the other hand, finds you disrespectful and impertinent."

Nagaro turned a startled glance upon the Lord of the Fleet. "But I haven't spoken to either one of them!"

Kuran crooked an eyebrow. "They were sitting in the gallery of the Audience Chamber when you spoke to the king there a week ago."

"Oh Vothra!" Nagaro swallowed hard. "I noticed there were men there, but I confess I didn't pay them a great deal of heed."

Kuran gave him a stern look. "You may find that a dangerous kind of omission," he murmured, then coughed and pointedly returned his attention to the table on the dais.

King Elgurn had begun to speak.

Nagaro listened distractedly to Elgurn's words of general welcome, while at the same time wondering just how much he ought to worry about what the Pact Signers thought of him. He didn't intend to stay in Lankura. But he did intend to continue to make his home in Edrovir. It was disconcerting to realize that he had no idea who *else* had been sitting in the gallery on that day.

"...and, of course, Captain Nagaro, of Pakoa, who bravely came to our aid..."

Nagaro's attention was jerked abruptly back to the king's speech by the sound of his own name.

Kuran elbowed him sharply. "Stand *up*, man!" he hissed.

Nagaro stood up so hastily that his chair nearly overbalanced. He was vaguely aware of Kuran catching hold of it before his own attention was caught and held by all of the *eyes*. Every pair of eyes in the Great Hall seemed to be on him!

Nagaro felt his heart start to pound. Blood thudded in his ears. He could no longer hear what Elgurn was saying.

"Now *thank him!*"

Kuran's muttered words, punctuated by a poke in the thigh, barely penetrated the fog of Nagaro's panic. Somehow he found his voice and managed to say, "Thank you, My Lord King," before gratefully sinking into his chair in response to Kuran's emphatic tug on his pants leg. There he sat, staring stonily at the air. His panic was ebbing, only to be replaced by acute embarrassment.

"There now, mate! Didn't I say I'd keep ye out o' trouble?"

Kuran's drawl was much kinder than Nagaro had expected.

"I'm sorry, My Lord," he muttered. "I should have been paying better attention."

"Now, now. There's been no harm done." Kuran was almost jovial. "Besides, *I* should have warned you of what to expect. You're so easy about so many things that I forgot that you probably wouldn't know your way around a banquet hall."

Nagaro gave the older man a grateful glance, but said nothing. If Kuran believed that, it was for the best.

Already someone had set bottles of wine and pitchers of sothiril on the table, and the musicians had begun to play an accompaniment to the feast. Soon the food began to arrive as well, sparing Nagaro the immediate need to make further conversation.

Kuran picked up one of the pitchers and poured golden sothiril into the crystal goblet set at Nagaro's place. "I know you won't touch the wine, so I won't either," he said, pouring himself a glass as well. "You're a good influence on me, Captain."

The food was excellent, as always, for the royal cooks of Edrovir were carefully selected for their skill.

There was a delicate salad of spring greens, followed quickly by the other courses. Besides the roast boar, there were roasted pheasants, ducks, and geese, served with a choice of several different fruit sauces. There were also several varieties of steaming fresh bread, a savory pilaf topped with chopped green onions, and mounds of tiny new spring potatoes garnished with herbs. Everything was passed around on platters, allowing the diners to help themselves to whatever they wished. The dessert was a crumbly kind of cake, topped with sugared pecans.

Nagaro, his nerves still on edge, began by eating sparingly. But before the meal was over, he had calmed down enough that he was able to enjoy the food.

The conversation of the other officers at the table helped, for a number of them were curious about relatively trivial things and asked him questions that were easily and safely answered.

Ruald, for example, wished to know what sort of things Nagaro said to horses, and the man to his right had further questions regarding his notions about money and wealth. The man was obviously a bit shocked to learn that Nagaro did not have a great store of riches laid by at his home on Pakoa.

"I have a house with five rooms," Nagaro explained, "which I share with two friends. There's also a little pasture, and three horses. Two of the horses we purchased. They weren't really a *need*, I confess, but rather something of an indulgence— though they are very ordinary animals."

Kuran had been content to listen for a time, but now he spoke. "I have seen the house," he said, "which is just as the Captain describes it. And the horses. Two of them are indeed ordinary, but the third— the mare— is another matter."

Nagaro turned to him. "The mare— my Farusia— was a gift," he explained. "One of the men who was with us when we made our escape gave her to me to show his gratitude. He was clever enough to choose a gift I couldn't bring myself to refuse. But I think he valued my service too highly."

Kuran eyed him. "What price is too high for a man's life and freedom?" he asked. "But he must have been a man of some means. That horse is worth nearly as much as the house."

Nagaro was a bit stunned. "So much as that? I didn't realize. But then he wasn't a sailor or a fisherman. He was a merchant's agent."

He decided to leave it at that. It was best not to mention that the man was Jinari. Then he frowned as something struck him. "When were you on Pakoa, My Lord?" he asked. "And how did you happen to see my house?"

Kuran's face became inscrutable. "I was there some two weeks ago—making inquiries."

"About... *me?*"

"Of course. I had orders."

Nagaro's eyes narrowed. "Is that why you asked me to keep watch in the islands for Mahuk ships? Not to keep those waters safe, but to keep me away from Pakoa?"

The corner of Kuran's mouth twitched. "Let us say that it served both purposes. Rather cleverly, I thought." There was a suggestion of a twinkle in the older man's black eyes.

Nagaro regarded the Lord of the Fleet severely for several seconds before his brow relaxed. "I confess I had thought it likely that you had more in mind than testing my trustworthiness, My Lord," he said. "And Landros *did* say you're an old fox."

This drew gasps from several of the other men at the table, but Kuran threw back his head and laughed loud and long.

Kuran's mirth was interrupted by another sounding of bells.

The Lord of the Fleet immediately sobered.

"Ah," he observed. "It's time for the toasts. You may expect to receive one," he added, winking at Nagaro. "For that you do not stand up. Everyone else does. And of course, you stand when toasting any other person."

Nagaro nodded seriously. He knew this already, but he didn't wish it to be apparent.

In fact, the very first toast was offered in his honor. It was Elgurn who stood up and raised his glass, calling on all of those assembled to drink to the health of "Captain Nagaro, a brave and gallant friend of Edrovir who came to the aid of our fair city in her hour of need."

As Nagaro listened to the king's words, he began to frown. All the eyes in the room were on him again. He felt those stares acutely, and again, his heart began to thud more heavily in his chest. But it wasn't this that troubled him. Elgurn's praise was gracious, but it was for him alone, and that wasn't right.

He ought to say something...

The king finished speaking, and all around Nagaro, folk began to rise.

Nagaro made a decision.

He stood up. There was a rushing in his ears, and sweat prickled along his sides.

Kuran, standing beside him, put a hand on his shoulder, trying to gently press him back into his seat, but Nagaro ignored it. He raised his hand, though he already had the full attention of all those present. There was a murmur running through the hall. There might even have been some laughter. Nagaro had to raise his voice to be heard.

"Good people of Edrovir!"

His throat felt uncomfortably tight in the sudden silence that followed his first four words, but there were other words that demanded to be said. He swallowed, and spoke into the silence. His voice rang clearly across the hall.

"If you would drink to me, you must drink also to the men who sailed with me, for alone I could have done nothing. I put the choice to them, and they chose to fight for Edrovir. Drink to all of us together, or to none!"

Nagaro sat down amid a muted muttering of voices. The eyes were on him still.

Desperate for a friendly glance, his eyes sought the high table where Nevien sat beside the queen, her mother. In the process, his gaze met the king's. Elgurn was still standing with his glass in his hand, regarding Nagaro with his cool blue stare. Now the king turned his gaze back to the room in general. He raised his glass, and his voice.

"Let us drink, my friends!" he cried in a commanding voice. "To Captain Nagaro and to his men!"

All around, the glasses clinked together and a chorus of voices murmured, "*To Captain Nagaro and his men.*"

After a moment there was a rustle as folk began to sit down. Before they were even all in their seats, however, there came a voice from the farther end of the hall. It was Landros, speaking loudly enough to be sure of being heard from one end of the huge room to the other.

"What do ye say, lads? Shall we give three cheers for the Captain?"

"*Aye! Aye!*" came the shouted reply.

So Landros led the cheer, the men thundering their response.

"Hai! Hai!" "*Hurrah!*" "Hai! Hai!" "*Hurrah!*" "Hai! Hai!" "*Hurrah!*"

There followed several seconds of astonished silence after the men's last shout died away. Then someone began to clap. Another joined in, and a wave of applause swept the Great Hall.

Kuran leaned towards Nagaro, who was sitting, staring straight ahead. "Well," he observed. "There's nothing like a little praise to keep the men loyal, eh?"

Nagaro shot Kuran a look. "It wasn't right," he said quietly. "To honor me without honoring them. We all fought for Edrovir together, and fourteen of them died for it."

Kuran crooked an eyebrow and studied Nagaro's profile for a long moment before he frowned and shook his head.

There were more toasts after that. Glasses were raised for the City Garrison, the Palace Guard, and to the honor of Prince Elyan and the others who had fallen.

Afterwards Nagaro wasn't sure how many times he had risen and the glasses had clinked together. He was grateful at least that attention was no longer focused on him exclusively, though every time he looked around it still seemed there were eyes turned his way.

One pair of eyes began, after a while, to disturb him.

There was a man— a Kelorin— sitting at a table on the other side of the hall, who seemed to be studying him rather keenly. Nagaro tried not to look at this man, but it was hard not to make surreptitious glances at intervals to see whether the man was still looking at *him*. He had to keep making the effort to turn his eyes elsewhere.

The toasts eventually came to an end, and the musicians picked up their instruments once more. The murmur of conversation rose, mingling with the music.

Some folk rose from their seats and began to move about, seeking friends or acquaintances who had been seated at other tables. Nagaro was vaguely aware that Ruald had left the table. He responded politely, if somewhat distractedly, when the officer on his right rose and murmured, "Good evening, Zirda."

He caught himself looking across the room at the unknown Kelorin again and jerked his eyes away, turning his glance very deliberately to the table on the dais.

He saw that Princess Nevien was deep in conversation with her mother, and that the king was conversing earnestly with the two Signers of the Pact. The latter observation would have been quite innocuous if all three men had not paused in their discourse at that very moment to look directly at *him*.

Nagaro hastily drew his eyes away, and reached for the nearest pitcher to pour himself some more sothiril. He wasn't thirsty, but sipping the drink at least gave him something to do. He barely noticed that there was no one left at the table besides himself and Kuran. And since he hadn't been paying attention to what the Lord of the Fleet was doing, he was startled when the older man cleared his throat and spoke to him.

"You have set me a difficult problem, Captain, by opening my eyes to the number of Edroviran citizens there are among the galley slaves of the Mahuk Baar. Once, already, I have had a chance to ram and found that I couldn't give the order."

Forgetting the watching eyes, Nagaro set down his glass.

"My Lord," he faltered, "I am truly sorry to have made your work more difficult."

Kuran cocked his head a little to one side. "It seems I must find some new approach," he said, "If we are not to find ourselves very often beaten. I thought you might be of some assistance."

"I would help in any way that I could, My Lord," Nagaro responded earnestly.

"Would you indeed?" Kuran's black eyes were watching him intently. "In that case, I have a proposition for you, Captain."

Nagaro returned the older man a questioning look. "My Lord?"

Kuran again cleared his throat. "I would like to offer you a king's commission," he said, "in the Royal Fleet of Edrovir. At the rank of Captain. I would prefer to make it higher, but it is beyond my power to do so."

Chapter 21

The King's Commission

For several seconds Nagaro could only stare at the Lord of the Fleet, scarcely believing that he had heard correctly. This was the very last thing he had expected.

"*A king's commission...?*" he murmured at last. "As a captain?"

"I realize that it would be a step down." Kuran sounded apologetic. "You are accustomed to commanding four ships and three other captains, which is more consistent with the rank of commander."

Nagaro shook his head. "It isn't that, My Lord."

His thoughts were spinning. He had thought for such a long time that the Fleet was an impossibility. He had thought that Lankura was far too dangerous a place for him— had feared that he would be recognized if he returned to the scene of his torment.

And of course, he had wanted no part of sinking galleys with slaves on board.

Now here he was in Lankura, and no one— not even the king or the princess— had recognized him! And here was Lord Kuran, saying that he couldn't go on sinking ships, and asking for *his* help in dealing with the Mautep.

Was it possible that he could do this?

Nagaro frowned. "When I was seventeen, I wanted nothing so much in the world as to join the Royal Fleet," he said with perfect honesty. "But... *other things*... intervened. A lot has happened since then. And I've been a pirate for the last four years."

He paused, then asked, "Have you discussed this with the king, My Lord?"

Kuran waved a hand dismissively. "Not yet. But he generally grants me considerable latitude in such matters. I am sure I can persuade him of the wisdom of this."

"You *are?*" Nagaro was so astonished he forgot to be polite. "I... I mean, I'm *surprised*, My Lord," he added hastily. "Forgive me for being blunt, but I didn't think the king liked me very much."

Lord Kuran studied him, his eyes unreadable. "The king need not *like* you, to be impressed with you," he said carefully. "If it would make you feel better, I will go right now and speak with him. But first I'd like to hear that you're interested— that you would seriously consider this offer. If I'm going to speak to Elgurn I don't wish to waste my breath."

Nagaro swallowed, his throat suddenly dry as dust, and he took a swallow from his glass of sothiril. "I *am* interested," he managed, cautiously. "But I can see some... *obstacles*. I have made a home on Pakoa. And then there are the men who sail with me. What would they do?"

Kuran looked thoughtful. "I could probably make places for some of them as well, if they wished to join the Fleet. But not too many. I haven't the ships."

Nagaro's brow furrowed. "I don't know how many it would be," he said seriously. "But if there were a large enough number, I suppose we could bring one of the ships..."

"A *ship*? Of Mahuk manufacture?" There was a glint in Kuran's eye. "We could certainly use one of those."

Nagaro was still frowning, still thinking. "There are a number who are accustomed to being officers," he said. "Some of them might look favorably upon joining the Fleet, but not as common seamen."

This time Kuran's black eyes narrowed. "You drive a hard bargain, Captain."

Nagaro gave him a startled look. "I'm not trying to bargain, My Lord. I'm only telling you the difficulties as I see them."

"Ah. Yes. Of course." Kuran coughed. "I believe that I could offer commissions to any of your officers who would be interested," he ventured after a moment, "provided there were enough ships. Such commissions would be provisional, of course. I'd have to see how the men performed under Fleet command. It might not be at their present rank, either, depending on their experience. I'm not prepared to immediately offer the rank of captain to anyone but you."

Nagaro nodded. "That sounds reasonable, My Lord."

"Good enough!" Kuran stood up, pushing back his chair. The glint had returned to his eye. "I will speak to Elgurn at once. This shouldn't take long, Captain, and then we can discuss any other *obstacles* that you may see."

As the Lord of the Fleet strode away in the direction of the dais, Nagaro took another hasty gulp of sothiril. What had he just done? How could he even consider this offer without first speaking to the men? What would Taru think of it? And Pavo? What if Kuran wanted an immediate answer? Then another thought struck him. *What about Narei?*

His wildly spinning thoughts were interrupted when he became aware that there was someone standing quite close beside him on his right.

He hastily glanced up— into the face of the Kelorin man who had been watching him from across the room.

The man was of average height, and spare, though broad in the shoulders. He appeared to be in his fifties. He had graying dark brown hair, and very pale gray eyes that were at that moment fixed upon Nagaro's face with a disconcertingly intense stare. Apparently sure that he now had Nagaro's attention, he spoke.

"Greetings, Zirda," he said, extending his hand.

Nagaro hesitated, having been startled.

The man made a slight bow, then almost as an afterthought, gestured to himself and added what Nagaro assumed was his name: "Rastyl Korven."

Nagaro stood up hastily. He reached for the man's hand. "Nagaro Nareyo," he said, imitating the abbreviated form of the other man's courtesy, and adding a small bow of his own.

The eyes remained fixed upon him, and Nagaro now saw that the irises were so light in color that they were barely darker than the surrounding whites of the man's eyes. The pupils stood out sharply in contrast, and perhaps it was only this unusual feature that made the eyes seem to stare so.

There seemed to be a responding flicker in those eyes. "Yes," the man said. "I have heard what name you go by."

Nagaro felt a sudden chill. *What did the man mean?*

But the tone of the words had been flat, without insinuation. *Perhaps he was over-reacting.*

The man seemed to be waiting for Nagaro to say something. His expression appeared to be neutral, but those strange, pale eyes were impossible to read.

"I'm sorry if you think I ought to be familiar with your face or your name, Zirda," Nagaro ventured with complete honesty. "I must confess that I am not."

Something immediately shifted in the man's face. Nagaro thought he might have seen disappointment there.

"Your pardon, Zirda." There was a quick, brittle smile that didn't quite seem to include the man's eyes— though with those eyes it was hard to tell. "I have often been told that I am abrupt, and lack grace. I only wished to make the acquaintance of the night's most honored guest. Good evening, Zirda."

The man bowed again, then turned and was gone.

There were so many folk on their feet and walking about in the hall by this time that Nagaro quickly lost sight of the man in the throng. Feeling a surge of relief, he turned back to his seat and sat down.

He felt suddenly foolish. What had he been afraid of? That the pale-eyed man would suddenly point at him and shout, "Look! This man is Leyel Virden!" aloud, for everyone to hear? Most likely, the man had mistaken him for someone else from across the room. Then, upon discovering that Nagaro plainly didn't know him, he had been too embarrassed to admit his error.

Smiling wryly to himself, Nagaro picked up his glass yet again and lifted it to his lips. Over the rim of the glass he beheld a richly dressed, elderly man bearing down on him with a beaming smile and a woman of similar age and attire upon his arm. Nagaro recognized the man as the lord of a minor house. He had just enough time to set his glass down and stand up again before the couple reached the table.

The man stuck out his hand. "Ah, Captain Nagaro!" he boomed. "Allow me to introduce myself and my dear wife—"

***

Kuran stood behind the table on the dais, frowning slightly. Elgurn was deep in conversation with the lords Pendrik and Anduar, and Kuran didn't like to interrupt that consultation. As he waited, Nevien turned around in her chair and caught his eye. The queen had already retired, so the princess was sitting alone. She motioned for Kuran to take Elyan's empty seat.

Kuran raised an eyebrow at the symbolism, then shrugged and pulled out the chair. Turning it around, he sat on it backwards, straddling the seat and crossing his arms on top of the chair back.

Nevien turned her own chair halfway around and leaned over to address him.

"Well, My Lord," she said. "What do you think of my pirate captain?"

Again the eyebrow arched. "*Your* pirate captain, My Lady? I thought he was *my* pirate captain."

Nevien affected a pout. "I saw him first!"

"I think not, My Lady. I encountered him off of Lapoa nearly a month ago."

Nevien laughed at Kuran's perfect deadpan. "All right: You saw him first. Now, what do you think of him?"

Kuran frowned. "An unusual and impressive young man. And quite an enigma. I thought at first that he must come from one of our merchant families, but the more I see of him, the less he seems like a merchant's son. His words and actions fairly scream nobility, yet when he was asked to leave his sword at the door, he denied any claim to noble blood."

Nevien frowned in her turn. "Have you tried asking him about his origins?"

Kuran shrugged. "Not outright. He wouldn't give me his birth name at Lapoa, and I have assumed that he wouldn't answer other questions of a similar kind."

"Then how do you know that Nagaro Nareyo isn't his true name?"

Kuran gave her a significant look. "The name is in the Turowan tongue, which I am quite able to interpret. Roughly translated, it means 'Nameless Man of the Sea.'"

Nevien gave a low whistle, then hastily put her hand to her lips. "There *is* a pretty mystery," she said. "And *I've* been puzzling over exactly how much Turowan blood he might have, and where he learned the Four Corners of Kelorin Law. He quoted them to me— in order. I looked them up afterwards and he had them almost word for word!"

Her eyes danced. "This Captain Nagaro is the most intriguing person to cross my path in many a weary day. You simply *must* find a way to keep him in Lankura!"

A smile tugged at Kuran's lips, and was expertly suppressed. "Well then, I must see what I can do," he said with mock severity. "I can't permit My Lady Princess to be bored. Should I, perhaps, offer him a commission in the Royal Fleet?"

Nevien laughed merrily. "That would be perfect, My Lord. You must do it at once!"

Kuran turned grave. "As a matter of fact I already have, though not for the sake of relieving your boredom, My Lady. And it's anything but certain that he will accept. He immediately spoke of obstacles, and I am here to put the matter to your father because the pirate captain fears it won't meet with the king's approval."

Nevien arched a slender eyebrow. "I know how persuasive you can be, My Lord," she said. "And I hope that you can work your wiles— on both of them. But while you are working on my father, I think that *I* will go down and see if I can uncover any of the pirate's history."

It was Kuran's turn to laugh. "I expect that you'll have better luck than I," he said. "When it comes to wiles, I'm sure I can't hold a candle to you."

He stood up, for he had noticed that Anduar and Pendrik were departing. As if it were an afterthought, he leaned down and said in a conspiratorial whisper, "But as for Turowan blood, I would ask him how he gets his kuma stain so perfectly applied."

"Kuma stain? What is that?"

Kuran lowered his voice even further. "Many pale-skinned Kelorin sailors color their skin brown with kuma to ward off sunburn." He gave her a wink as he straightened, then turned and stepped away to address her father, leaving the princess to stare after him with a look of wide-eyed revelation.

***

Kuran began with, "My Lord King, I have a small matter that requires your attention." Then he elaborated.

Elgurn listened, his face impassive. "A king's commission?" he said, when Kuran had finished. "I can't see why you wish to make trouble for yourself, Kuran. This man is plainly very capable, and of high... ah... *integrity*, in his way... but he has no experience of submitting himself to command. What makes you think that he'll be ruled by you?"

Kuran frowned. "I will grant you that it's a matter of some concern, My Lord. But he isn't actually an arrogant man— and I believe that he respects me. He is also a very sincere man. If he were to take the oath, he would intend to uphold it in every particular. And I would very much rather have him here under our eyes than away in the islands, steering his own course."

"Steering his own course? What do you mean?"

Kuran dropped into the chair that had been vacated by Lord Anduar. He leaned an elbow on the table and lowered his voice. "You didn't see him, My Lord, this afternoon as we rode through the town together." He proceeded to describe the distribution of the finder's gold, and the events that had followed.

"He had them in his hand, My Lord! If he had taken it into his head to tell them that they would be best served by storming the palace and casting you into the street, I believe you would have had them at your door."

Elgurn scowled darkly. "This is surely a simple trick— a common conceit— throwing money to a crowd and making idle promises—"

Kuran emphatically shook his head. "You are mistaken, My Lord. It was no conceit. He was entirely sincere. And from the way he went about handing out the gold, it was plain that he had done it before—" Kuran broke off and straightened a little to glance surreptitiously about. Then he leaned closer and spoke lower still.

"My Lord— if I may inquire. What were you discussing with Anduar and Pendrik?"

Elgurn's face became carefully expressionless. "You can guess well enough," he said, in a low mutter. "The Brothers of the Blood are getting bolder— and more persuasive. I fear that some others among the Leithian Faction may go over to them. And of course, the members of the Kelorin Faction are aware of the situation. But what has this to do with your noble pirate?"

Kuran answered in the lowest of whispers.

"Only this, My Lord. If the worst comes to pass— if there is civil war— this Captain Nagaro is not a man to sit idly by, waiting for the dust to clear. He will do *something*— whatever he believes is the *right* thing. If he is left to himself, I can only guess at what that thing might be. We could easily lose the allegiance of the islands to him. The folk of the Lomoas would follow him in an instant, and his name is respected in the Faranos as well. *But*, if we bind him with an oath to the service of Edrovir, we will be certain of where he stands. He is the very soul of honor."

The king was frowning again. "If he is plotting any such thing as you suggest, he surely won't take your commission."

Kuran shook his head emphatically. "He has no such ambition, My Lord— at least not *yet*. But that's a thing that could change according to circumstances—"

"But he has only four ships!"

"I believe he could double that number in a season, My Lord, if he saw the need. He has no trouble taking Mahuk craft, and there are plenty of men in the islands willing to follow him. And he commands men's loyalty. You heard how they cheered him tonight."

The king's angry frown turned pensive. "You argue your point well, my old friend. And I can see that you wish to have him." He sighed. "Since experience has taught me the wisdom of giving Kuran Kel what he wants, I will say, very well. Offer him this commission. Let's see if he takes it."

"I may also have to offer commissions to some of his officers, as well as positions in the common ranks to some of his men."

Elgurn laughed a short, barking laugh. "So he comes dear, does he?"

Kuran shrugged. "It's that loyalty of which I spoke, My Lord. But he might bring us a ship into the bargain."

"One of these ships that you say are swifter than ours?" Elgurn crooked an eyebrow, then laughed, and waved his hand as if sweeping the matter aside. "I leave the details to you, my friend. You have full latitude. But stay here a moment. There's another matter to discuss..."

***

Nagaro was sitting in his seat at the deserted officer's table, swirling the remaining sothiril in his glass. There had been a brief succession of noble folk— coming to make the acquaintance of the evening's most honored guest. In between smiling, bowing, and saying politely innocuous things, he had turned his glance from time to time towards the dais.

He had seen Kuran stop to talk to the princess, and he knew the Lord of the Fleet was now speaking to the king. Since he had finally been left alone again, he would have liked to join his men— who were still having a boisterous time at the other end of the Hall— but he was waiting for Kuran to return.

Not wishing to seem to be watching Kuran and Elgurn, he was being careful to appear to give his attention to the glass and its contents. Still, he was not entirely surprised when there came a rustle of skirts and the Princess Nevien unceremoniously took possession of the chair that had been Kuran's.

She wasted no time in being demure, but immediately addressed him. "Good evening, Captain Nagaro," she said. "How have you been enjoying our celebration?"

He turned to regard her, and found that she was studying him keenly. "I've found it... *instructive*, My Lady," he said, cautiously. Then, because he feared that must sound ungracious, he added, "I appreciate the honor, and the food was certainly very good."

Nevien gave him a kindhearted smile. "I am sorry if you've found it trying," she said. "Too much formality, I imagine. You don't seem like a man who thrives on formality. Still, I think that you have made a very good impression. At least you needn't fear the contrary."

"Ah... thank you, My Lady," he ventured, uncertainly. She was altogether too perceptive concerning his discomfort, even if she was wrong about its cause. "It's good of you to take the trouble to come and offer me that reassurance."

She smiled again. "You are more than welcome, Zirda. But the truth is, I had another motive."

"Oh?" He thought warily of her conversation with Lord Kuran.

"I was hoping you might resolve a question, and so settle a wager."

At this he was frankly astonished. "A *wager*, My Lady?"

"Yes," she went on brightly. "You see, one of my ladies— Brendet— is of the opinion that you must surely be at least half of Turowan blood, while I feel just as certain that it can't be more than one quarter. I hope you don't find it too personal a question," she finished earnestly as Nagaro bridled.

"Do you and your ladies often make wagers on men's parentage?" he asked.

Nevien was instantly contrite. "I'm sorry," she said. "I've offended you. And it *is* terribly foolish, I know. I usually don't get involved in such childish games, but this time I was so *very* sure I was right, that I couldn't resist."

"Oh. I see..." Nagaro was not at all comfortable knowing that the princess's ladies were taking such an interest in his heritage. They might be only a handful of foolish young women, but if they found the matter so interesting, others might as well. And the princess's interest was even more alarming— both because she was anything but foolish and because she was almost certainly correct.

"But... what are the stakes?" he asked, to buy time. "Surely ladies don't wager gold or silver?"

"Of course not!" Nevien was indignant. "If I am right, Brendet must give me her best pearl-handled comb, and if she is right, she shall have this little ring that my mother gave to me." Nevien fingered a ring that she wore on her little finger. The stone was a fire opal, and very striking. "I confess that I would hate to give it up, but I didn't think I would have to, you see." She gave him a pleading look.

Inwardly Nagaro squirmed, but then inspiration struck. "As it happens," he said, "no one will have to give up anything, because I can't answer your question."

"You *can't?* But why not? —If it won't offend you, Captain, I mean."

"Because I don't know the answer, My Lady," he told her seriously. "I was a foundling. I have no idea who my parents were, or how much Turowan blood I might carry in my veins."

Her eyes went wide with shock, and her hand flew to her mouth. "Oh dear! I *am* sorry, Captain. I didn't mean to—"

"It's quite all right," he made haste to assure her. "It's nothing I have ever tried to hide, nor anything I need be ashamed of."

She shook her head emphatically. "No, of course not! But it must be hard... not knowing, I mean." The princess seemed to have entirely forgotten her wager. Her green eyes welled with sympathy, and the concern that rang in her voice was quite touching.

"I'm really quite used to it," he told her. "After so many years."

"Oh." Her distress appeared to ease. "Yes, I suppose you would be," she said after a moment. Then she frowned, and he noticed that it made a little line between her perfect eyebrows. "But... if you were a foundling, how did you come by your education?"

Nagaro heaved a mental sigh. He had been afraid that this was coming as soon as she started asking about his lineage. It was time to tell her his story— the one he was prepared to tell the world.

Over the years, he had gotten rather good at it, having come to understand that folk would generally allow him to keep what appeared to be a few small secrets as long as they believed they'd been told the truth regarding larger matters.

"I was raised by a noble lady who found me on her doorstep," he told her. "My lady guardian was Kelorin, and a Vothrin as you may have guessed, and she saw to it that I had some education— even lessons in swordsmanship. But when she died, her family would have none of me, so I decided I would have none of them. I took a new name, and I went my own way."

It was a story that was made up of six parts truth, three parts artful omission, and perhaps one part of outright deception. He had never actually sought out any member of the House of Virden to see what kind of reception he would receive. He felt justified in his version of the story, however, since the Lord of the House of Virden, Maramine's father, had made every effort to disavow any blood relationship between the family and Leyel Virden during the nine months he had spent in Lankura under the sway of heskial.

"But why a Turowan name? And why do you wear your hair in the Turowan fashion?" The princess's sea-green eyes were wide, under her dark lashes.

Bishka!

Nagaro winced and tried not show it. *Kuran must have told her the linguistic origin of his name.*

"My friend Taru, and his family, took me in when I was in need, My Lady," he explained. "I use their family name, and I honor them in other ways as well."

"*Ah,*" she breathed, "*I see.* But you told me, before, that you were a fisherman."

"Taru and his father were fishermen. I was learning the trade from them, until the day the Mautep sea warriors came and took us away—"

"—and made you slaves!" She triumphantly finished his sentence. "Yes. I see now how it all fits together!"

She had accepted it!

Nagaro was at pains not to let his face reveal anything. He was vastly relieved, of course, though underneath his triumph he felt a little guilty for having deceived her.

But Nevien was considering him closely again, and the thoughtful expression had returned to her face. "Do you think that your parents could have been fishermen then?" she asked.

"More likely farmers. But I really don't know."

"I still think you must be *mostly* Kelorin," she said, regarding him critically. "The features of your face are quite Kelorin, and you are taller, and more lightly built than is usual for Turowan folk."

Nagaro shrugged, and struggled not to frown. She probably thought she was helping him.

The princes's dark lashes descended a little then, and a teasing sparkle appeared in her eyes. "I'm sure it's only the color of your skin that makes Brendet think otherwise, Captain" she went on. "But then I understand that Kelorin sailors sometimes paint their skin…" Her words trailed suggestively.

Keshaal! How much had Kuran told her? Nagaro dipped his finger into his sothiril and rubbed the back of his hand to show that the color remained.

"Not paint—"

She still held him with that teasing look. "*No…*" she said archly, "…not *paint*. That isn't the right word. No, it was *stain*, I think…"

And inwardly Nagaro sagged. He couldn't tell her an outright lie, especially not when there were so many folk who knew that he used kuma stain. If he had wanted to keep it a secret, he would have had to swear to secrecy every man who had been a slave with him on that Mautep oar deck.

So he looked the princess straight in the eye, and said, "As it happens, you are right, My Lady." He tried to make it sound as if it were a trivial matter. "It's called kuma stain, and I am in danger of burning rather badly in the sun without it. But I hope you won't spread the fact about too widely. There are some among the darker-skinned folk who look upon pale skin as a kind of weakness."

It wasn't false, although it wasn't his real reason, but it was the best he could do.

"Oh! I hadn't thought of that!" She was instantly contrite again, and all hint of teasing vanished. "But I needn't tell anyone. If I say that you don't know how much Turowan blood you carry, it will be enough for the wager. And no one will have to give up anything, just as you said."

A movement on the dais drew Nagaro's attention. "I think Kuran may be coming back," he ventured.

The princess turned around to look. "No," she said, after a moment, "I think he meant to, but Father just called him back." She turned back to face him and asked, "Will you take the commission that Kuran has offered you?"

He stared at her. "Does Lord Kuran always tell you everything, My Lady?"

For an instant her eyes widened, but then she gave a merry little laugh. "I don't believe that Kuran ever tells anyone *everything*," she said. "But he tells *me* a great deal. We're very good friends, Kuran and I. And, now, Captain," she added, "*Do* you mean to take the commission?"

"I don't know," he said quite honestly. "Would it please you, My Lady, if I did?" He bit his tongue, quite amazed at himself, but she answered him very seriously.

"Yes, of course it would. I believe that Edrovir would benefit greatly from your service. Besides which, didn't I say that I liked you? There are so few people here worth talking to— people with anything interesting to say."

"Oh... ah... thank you." He had no idea what else he ought to say to that. *Had he asked the question just to hear her say again that she liked him?* It seemed to him that perhaps he had, and that embarrassed him. Fortunately she didn't seem to have noticed.

She put her head on one side. "What is there to keep a man like you on Pakoa, Captain? Are there many educated people there?"

"Educated people?" He laughed. "No, there are scarcely any, but there are many people I count as friends and who I would miss very much if I came to live in Lankura. I've made a home on Pakoa. And the hardest thing would be to leave Narei—"

"*Narei!*" The princess pounced triumphantly on the name. "I *knew* there had to be a woman!"

"A *woman?*" Nagaro was startled, but then he laughed again. "Well, she *will* be a woman, one day. But as yet she's not quite four years old. Narei is my daughter."

Your... *daughter?*" Nevien's eyes widened in shock. This, at last, was clearly a complete surprise.

So, he thought, there was *something* Kuran didn't know... or hadn't told the princess...

"But can't you bring her with you?" she asked, recovering. "Or don't you mean to bring your wife?"

The word hit him like a blow.

"I... have no wife," he said, his voice catching a little. He found it a more difficult thing to say than he had expected, sitting here, next to the princess.

His memory was conjuring a vivid— and exquisitely painful—image of the two of them standing side by side between the rows of deep pink roses and white farusia blossoms in the palace garden, reciting marriage vows. Reading the question in Nevien's eyes, he shook off the memory with an effort.

"Narei lives with her aunt— her mother's sister— and her family," he said hurriedly. "It's the only home she has ever known. I couldn't take her from it."

"But what happened to her mother then? Is she... dead?"

It was the obvious question— and the obvious guess. And Nagaro had determined long ago that he wouldn't try to hide Narei's existence from the world, nor try to cover up the manner of her begetting. But to tell *that* story to the princess, of all people…

"I have no idea where her mother is," he said quickly, without meeting Nevien's gaze.

He was looking past the princess to the dais, hoping to find a means of cutting short the conversation. And as luck would have it, he saw that Kuran had at last risen, and was stepping away from Elgurn.

He gestured in the direction of the king's table. "This time it looks as if Kuran is really coming," he said lightly. He brought his eyes back to the princess's startled face. "If you wish to make your report to him before he gets here, My Lady, you had best hurry," he added, giving her a less sinister version of his pirate smile, to show that he was teasing.

His answer to her question had plainly surprised her, but he had succeeded in distracting her with the jest. A little color now rose in her cheeks.

"You are really very clever, Captain," she said. Then she smiled apologetically. "I shall have to be much more careful in the future if I try to play at cat and mouse with you."

He shook his head at her. "I'm not half so clever as your friend Kuran," he told her seriously. He was thinking rapidly, and he realized that, if he took the commission and came to dwell in Lankura, it wouldn't do to have her trying to uncover all his secrets.

If she truly wished to be his friend…

She had risen, and on an impulse, he plunged ahead before she could depart. "Instead of being more careful with your questions, My Lady, I would rather that you were more *honest*," he said pointedly. "There are a few secrets I prefer to keep, and you'll only lose my good will if you keep trying to uncover them."

Nevien stood looking down at him for a moment, her face wearing that thoughtful frown that made the little line appear between her delicately arched brows. At that moment, her sea-green eyes were fairly brimming with the clear light of honesty.

"I will remember that," she said quietly. "And I hope I may have the pleasure of seeing you again— soon— in Lankura. I bid you good evening, Nagaro Nareyo."

He made haste to rise, but she was gone before he had a chance to give her a proper bow. As he stood staring after her, he saw her intercept Lord Kuran and engage him in conversation. He frowned. *Was she indeed giving the Lord of the Fleet her report?*

He hadn't long to contemplate this question, however, because a rather pointed clearing of the throat caused him to turn around.

Lord Pendrik was standing a few feet from him, fixing him with a piercing glance. More than six feet tall, with a breadth of shoulders to match, Lord Pendrik was an imposing man. Somewhere past sixty years, his hair was silvered gold and his eyes pale blue. His face was rather flushed.

The other Signer of the Pact, Lord Anduar, stood to one side and slightly behind the Leithian Lord. Nearly as tall as Pendrik, Anduar was much leaner. He was close in years to Pendrik, but the gray in his hair was more like iron than silver, and there was steel in his gray eyes.

Pendric spoke. "Well now, at least he sees me, even if I must approach to within an arm's length before he takes notice," he observed, his voice a low rumble.

Though the Leithian had continued to stare hard at Nagaro, his words were apparently addressed to Anduar.

The Kelorin lord stepped forward, bringing himself abreast of his fellow Pact Signer. His gaze shifted from Nagaro to Pendrik. "Come now, My Lord," he said smoothly. "You surely don't expect to compete with the Lady Nevien for a young man's attention."

Nagaro could feel the blood in his face. "My Lord Pendrik— My Lord Anduar—" he said quickly, bowing to each of them in turn. "I beg your pardons for any past slights. And to what do I owe the honor of your present attention?"

"And he even knows our names!" Pendrik observed pointedly. Again it seemed he addressed Anduar, though his eyes were on Nagaro.

Nagaro smiled wanly. He was glad that Kuran had given him some feeling for these two men. "My Lord Kuran has been instructing me—" he began.

"Has he now?" Pendrik's words were finally directed to Nagaro. "And you've been listening to Elgurn's little half-breed bulldog, have you?"

Nagaro stiffened. "I wonder what things *you* may be called by other men when you're not present, My Lord," he replied. "Perhaps I should ask Lord Kuran."

He winced, inwardly, as he finished speaking. He should possibly have curbed his tongue, though he had found Pendrik really quite rude.

Pendrik's face now registered undisguised annoyance. He turned to Anduar. "Now will you *still* tell me that this man isn't insolent?" he demanded.

Lord Anduar's expression had not changed, though something flickered in his eyes. "Actually I thought it rather a gentle rebuke," he said blandly. "Your words in reference to Lord Kuran were rather *ill-chosen*."

Lord Pendrik flushed. "But must I endure this... from a *pirate?*"

"There you are right, my friend." Anduar's voice was satin-smooth. "I should have said rebuked you myself."

Lord Pendrik began to frown, but Anduar turned his penetrating glance on Nagaro and spoke before the Leithian could muster a response.

"My Lord Pendrik and I wished to make the acquaintance of the man of the hour— or should I say one of the *men* of the hour, Captain? Your phrase 'drink to all of us, or to none,' has a certain ring to it."

"*Ha!*" Lord Pendrik muttered. "He was correcting his king— again!"

"I only meant to set something right." Nagaro interjected.

Anduar had ignored Pendrik's remark. He was regarding Nagaro keenly, but when he spoke his tone was surprisingly mild.

"Is that how you secure the loyalty of your men?"

Nagaro was nonplused. "I'm afraid I don't understand, My Lord."

"Don't you?" Anduar raised an eyebrow.

"Ah well, Anduar," Pendrik interrupted, "You shouldn't be surprised that the man defends his own kind—"

Pendrik broke off. He seemed to have forgotten his annoyance, but his tone was dismissive as he turned to Nagaro. "By the way," he inquired, looking Nagaro up and down, "Just what exactly *is* your kind, Zirda?"

Nagaro's eyes grew hard. "That would be the *human* kind, My Lord," he said coldly.

The man's rudeness was scarcely to be believed!

Once more he caught a flicker in Anduar's eyes, and there was the slightest twitch at the corner of the Kelorin's mouth.

Lord Pendrik stared at Nagaro for several seconds. Then, abruptly, the Leithian lord threw back his head and laughed a great booming laugh. "Ha, ha! *Human kind!* How droll. Ha ha ha! How very droll!"

Nagaro opened his mouth to make some retort, but closed it again when Anduar caught his eye, and very subtly shook his head.

Pendrik was still laughing, though it had become a low rumble. Abruptly he stopped laughing and stepped closer. "Well met, Zirda!" he declared heartily, extending his hand. "I like a man who enjoys a good jest at his own expense."

Nagaro considered for one second refusing to take the hand, and thought better of it. Even if he hadn't caught the warning glint in Lord Anduar's eye, it was evident that he wasn't going to change Pendrik's settled opinions with one or two barbs. And incurring the man's enmity could serve no good purpose.

He reached out and took the hand. "Well met, My Lord," he said, making an effort to at least sound sincere.

Lord Pendrik pumped his hand vigorously, and then took his leave with a perfunctory, "Good evening, Zirda."

As the Leithian ambled away, Nagaro could hear him rumbling to himself: "*Human kind! Ha, ha! A good joke...*"

Lord Anduar immediately stepped forward to offer his hand as well. Nagaro took it with rather more enthusiasm.

As the Kelorin shook hands, he leaned close. "Well met, Captain," he said, speaking low. His glance darted sideways in the direction of the dais, and he lowered his voice still further. "The 'bulldog' is coming," he murmured. "And you are well-advised to listen to him. Good evening, Captain."

Then he too was gone, striding off after Lord Pendrik.

Nagaro stood and stared after Anduar's retreating figure. Presently a voice spoke at his elbow.

"I hope that didn't go too badly, Captain, without me here to keep you out of trouble."

It was Kuran's voice. Nagaro turned to regard the Lord of the Fleet. "I'm not sure," he said. "Though I think that it would have gone rather differently if you *had* been here."

"How so?" Kuran's black eyes were questioning.

Nagaro smiled a brief, tight smile. "For one thing, I don't think Lord Pendrik would have referred to you as a 'half-breed bulldog' in your presence."

The black eyes didn't waver. "Ah, well, if that's the worst of it—"

"Actually, what he said was, 'Elgurn's *little* half-breed bulldog'."

This time the black eyes flashed. *"That bloody, bodjering son of a she-ass!"* Kuran bit off his words, mastering himself with a visible effort. "You didn't hear me say that, Captain," he muttered. "And I hope you were more discrete."

"Somewhat." Nagaro smiled wryly. "Although Pendrik didn't call me anything so offensive. He just asked me what my 'kind' was. When I told him 'the human kind', he took it for a jest. Lord Anduar was also trying to keep me from angering Lord Pendrik, I think."

Kuran sighed. "To be honest, Pendrik has not the sharpest wit, but he can be a half-way decent sort when he's at his best. Right now he'll be full of food and wine and feeling so comfortable with himself that he doesn't think before speaking. Anduar, on the other hand, has a mind like a knife, and he never does anything to dull the edge of it. If he learns that you keep the ban, you will go up in his estimation. But sit down, Zirda, we have matters to discuss."

They both reseated themselves at the table.

Nagaro cleared his throat. "What did the king say?"

"He gave me leave to do as I see fit, as I expected. He did have some concerns, however. For one thing, he asked whether you could take orders."

Nagaro's brow furrowed in thought. "I don't really know," he confessed. "I've never had to— except from Mautep slave handlers, and those are orders one doesn't have much choice about obeying. I certainly can take advice— good advice, at least."

Kuran studied him narrowly. "Being a Fleet man generally means following orders— even if you think they're *not* good orders."

Nagaro steadily returned the other man's gaze. "I understand, My Lord."

Kuran nodded fractionally but continued to study him. "I hope you do," he said pointedly, then added, "There's another matter that is also of some concern to both the king and myself."

"What is that, My Lord?"

"We would be more comfortable if we knew something more of your history." The black eyes were steady, though it seemed there was a hint of apology in Kuran's voice.

Nagaro gave him a probing look. "Didn't the Lady Nevien tell you what you wished to know, My Lord?" he inquired mildly. "I thought perhaps that was the reason she came down to speak to me."

The Lord of the Fleet didn't so much as blink. "I learned some details from her, yes. Others are still missing. Such as the name you were given at your birth."

Nagaro's glance remained steady. "I don't know, myself, what name my parents gave me, My Lord— if either of them gave me any name at all. So why not Nagaro?"

"Mmm." There was a flicker of acknowledgment. "Why not, indeed? But the name of the House that was involved.... and of the lady...?"

Nagaro briefly flashed his pirate smile. "Those are secrets I keep."

Kuran frowned. "I would have you understand, Captain," he said with evident discomfort, "that for my part, I would be content with that. But if there was a...*falling out*— shall we say— in the past, with the lord of a noble house over something, and I now grant you a commission— at no less a rank than *captain*..." He cleared his throat. "There could well be repercussions: for me, for the Fleet, and even for the king. Lords do not like being thwarted."

Now Nagaro frowned. He had not thought of this. "My Lord," he said earnestly after a moment, "I have no intention of making any claim on that House— nor of even acknowledging the connection. I never met the Lord of the House, and the lady who cared for me is dead. I don't actually believe there is anyone of that House who would care what becomes of me, one way or the other."

It was perhaps an exaggeration, but it was better than saying that he had no intention of being recognized.

Kuran was regarding him with sympathy. "The more fools, they," he murmured, then added, "I shall consider that sufficient, Captain. I trust, at least, that it was not a *major* House?

"No, My Lord. A very minor one."

Kuran nodded. "That is well. May I conclude that you intend to accept the commission?"

Nagaro immediately shook his head. "I didn't mean to give you that impression, My Lord. As I have said, I will consider it. But I must discuss the matter with the men who follow me. We have a covenant, and they have certain expectations of me. If I did accept... when would you wish me to report for duty?"

Kuran considered. "Normally we take new recruits in Dunrel, around midsummer's day. That would give you more than two months to return to Pakoa and make whatever arrangements you require."

Nagaro's frown returned. "That may not be sufficient, My Lord, since the men may not be willing to release me from my pledge. The season is still very young, and we have lost time minding your back garden. The finder's gold we take is the only means of livelihood for these men, and some of them have chosen to sail with me for just one season, to earn what they need to buy a boat, or a house, or a shop, so they can return to an honest trade."

"Mmm." Kuran was frowning now as well. "I can afford to give you some leeway, Captain. But I would require a commitment. The offer stands right now, and Elgurn's view is favorable at the moment, but I can't promise that will not change."

"I see." Nagaro picked up his long-forgotten glass of sothiril, and studied the inch of golden liquid remaining in it. He set the glass down again, returning his gaze to Kuran's face. "How much time will you allow me to give you my answer?"

The Lord of the Fleet's black eyes glinted. "I'll give you two days, Captain, for I must sail again myself. Let's say until sundown of the day after tomorrow?"

Nagaro swallowed, and moistened his lips. "Very good, My Lord," he said in a voice that was as firm as he could manage.

Two days! It wasn't unreasonable, but if some of the men were eager to sail, they might not even allow him those two days.

Kuran rose to his feet. "Good enough, Captain! I look forward to hearing your decision, and I hope it will be favorable." He extended his hand.

Nagaro rose as well, but he didn't immediately take the older man's hand, for something else was troubling him.

"My Lord," he said on an impulse, "May I ask you a very candid question?"

Kuran crooked an eyebrow. "Of course you may *ask*."

"Did you send the princess down to try to get information from me, or was it her idea?"

Lord Kuran didn't blink or flinch. His expression was opaque. "You don't altogether trust me, do you Captain?"

Nagaro shook his head. "No," he confessed, quite honestly. "But I have no evidence so far that you mean me any harm."

Kuran regarded him for several more seconds as if reading his eyes. Then he appeared to relax a little and he heaved a sigh. "You are wise in that, Captain," he said. "I'm not always open about my purposes. In fact, I *don't* mean you any harm. I see that you may be of use to me— to Edrovir, I should say. And I hope that, in the process, I may be of help to you as well— in advancing your career."

Nagaro's brows came together in a sharp line. "I am very glad to know this, My Lord," he said seriously. "But you haven't answered my question."

This time the Lord of the Fleet appeared genuinely surprised. His brow creased as if he were trying to remember what Nagaro's question had been. "Ah," he said at length, then frowned a little harder. "It is not for me to command the Lady Nevien," he said at last, speaking carefully. "She has her own reasons for the things she does."

"I see." Nagaro was still regarding Lord Kuran narrowly. This answer seemed to him less honest than the previous one. "It's only this, My Lord," he added. "It appears that the princess considers you a friend. I would rather believe she is not mistaken."

Kuran stared at him. "I assure you, Captain, that the Lady Nevien has no better friend than Kuran Kel."

"Good." This time Nagaro put out his hand. "Princesses have need of friends."

Kuran took the hand with a firm grasp. He shook his head, even as he shook the hand. "You continue to surprise me, Captain Nagaro. I assumed you were worried about yourself— not about the lady."

Nagaro's teeth flashed in a quick smile. "You surprise me, also, My Lord. With all of the inquiries you made on Pakoa, I'm surprised that you hadn't learned my history. You do business with the merchant Gedras, and he has known my tale for years."

At this, Kuran laughed outright. "Has he indeed? But he wasn't there, you see, when I was in that port. It seems that *he* was in Kel Tierna, from whence I had just come! Something about having finally found a husband for that eldest daughter of his."

"*Berenil...*" Nagaro suppressed a shudder.

Kuran looked at him sharply. "Don't tell me that chilly vixen had her sights set on *you*?"

Nagaro winced. "Not after she'd spoken with me for five minutes."

"Ha!" Kuran laughed. "It took me a little longer than that. But not much."

The Lord of the Fleet sobered.

"And now I have other matters to attend to. Good evening, Captain," he said formally. "I will await your word." He started to turn away, then turned back. "Oh, and Captain... I advise you to pay your respects to the king before you leave the hall tonight..."

Chapter 22

Decisions

"**K**uran wants to make ye a captain in the Fleet?" Taru spoke excitedly. "*Hakura!* And he must want ye very badly, if he's willing t' take some o' the rest of us just to get ye!"

Nagaro and Taru were riding side by side, back through the streets of Lankura, with Pavo walking beside them this time, keeping up easily with the walking horses and staying close to Nagaro's stirrup. The streets were now dark and empty, and Nagaro had made sure that the three of them were far enough in front of the other men that their conversation would not be overheard. He had wanted his two closest friends to be the first to hear the news of Lord Kuran's offer.

Nagaro frowned. "I don't know about that," he said. "Usually he must get nothing but green recruits in Dunrel, while those who follow me are all trained men. And I offered him a ship, as well, if enough of the men wanted to come. It doesn't seem to me that he would be put out so very much to take on a ship-full of men, all trained to the sword and ready to sail her."

"Well aye, Nagaro, but ye said he'd be willing to make me an officer. *Me*— that's a fisherman's son from Wotana Bay— an *officer* in the Royal Fleet!"

"But probably not a first mate, Taru. More likely just a third mate— and they're not much more than officers-in-training, unless of course something happens to the first or second mate. Then they're moved up."

"I don't care!" Taru gestured expansively, and the excited gleam of his eyes caught the moonlight. "If ye think it's safe for ye to be here now in Lankura— and there won't be any sinking o' ships— I say ye should *take* the offer! And I'm coming with ye!"

"What about you, Pavo?" Nagaro asked, turning to his other friend. "I saw some of the looks that were coming your way today. Folk here don't even know what 'Hashtep' means. To them you're a 'Mahuk.' One of the enemy. If I were to do this, what would you do?"

Pavo walked on without turning his head for several paces before he answered. When he did turn his face up to meet Nagaro's eyes, his expression was unreadable in the darkness.

"I will go where you go, Nagaro," he said quietly.

"I can't ask you to do that, Pavo."

But Pavo shook his head. "No," he said, "you did not ask me to do it. You asked me what would I do. Always I choose to go where you go."

***

Nagaro said nothing to any of the other men until the entire party arrived at the wharf, where they handed back the horses to the waiting grooms.

He then surprised his three captains by calling them to a meeting in his cabin aboard the *Sword of Freedom*. There he laid out all the details of Lord Kuran's offer.

Landros' reaction was immediate and emphatic.

"Didn't I tell ye that Kuran knows quality when he sees it?"

Nagaro sighed. "He told me that he believes I could be useful to him, Landros. And he said he hoped he could help me advance my career at the same time, whatever that means."

Landros grinned, and his teeth flashed in the light of the lantern that hung above the table they were all seated around. "Oh, laddie," he said, shaking his head. "It'll be a pleasure to see *your* career advance. It will indeed— whether ye know what it means or not!"

Nagaro shifted uncomfortably. "Does that mean that you would choose to come too, Landros? If I were to do this?"

"I'll be one step behind ye all the way, mate! Of course, if ye decide *not* to do it, I'd still follow ye to the end o' the earth as a pirate— even if I *did* think ye were a bloody fool for turning it down. The only thing that was stopping me from going back to the Fleet was sinking ships. If there's to be no more o' that, then I'm in if ye're in. Tred 'll say the same too. Ye can count on it."

Nagaro frowned, but nodded, and turned to the captain of the *Tiger*. "What about you, Moraga? You were never a Fleet man."

Moraga shook his head emphatically. "Count me out, Capt'n," he said gruffly. "I can't see meself takin' orders from a pack o' high-flown Fleet lubbers. Pirating's good enough for me. I figure I can keep it up, even without ye— though it won't be the same, an' that's a fact."

"Timegar?" Nagaro turned to the last of his captains.

The veteran sea warrior rubbed his narrow, graying beard. "I'm afraid I'm with Moraga," he said. "This is a fine opportunity for a young man like you, Nagaro. Landros is right on that score. Ye'd be a fool to turn this down. I've never heard o' anyone getting a commission at the rank of captain. It's just not done. But I retired from the Fleet years ago, and I've no desire t' go back. Ye showed me a way to do a bit o' good work, and I've a few more years of pirating in me, I think. I'll just keep on working with Moraga."

Nagaro drew a long breath. "There's still the men," he said.

There followed some discussion, to which Nagaro listened with one ear. Each captain knew the men under him fairly well— their hopes and plans. And Nagaro knew his three captains well too. He hadn't really been surprised by their reactions. The strength of Taru's enthusiasm had surprised him more, and he had been both relieved and disturbed by Pavo's choice.

All together, the longer he thought about it, the clearer his course seemed to be. He could feel his life turning around him, pivoting on this hour, this moment in time. He wondered whether Lokundas was smiling— and if so, what kind of smile it might be.

The talk eventually began to wane.

Nagaro stood up, and spoke into a little pause.

"The exact numbers and the names don't matter right now. It's enough to know that there are some who would be likely to come, and some who wouldn't."

He sighed. "Lord Kuran asked for a commitment from me, but not from any other man. Everyone else will have ample time to think about it. That leaves only one other thing that I want you each to put before your men tonight— and send me back the answer: When must I tell the Lord of the Fleet to expect me? Will they all release me to return to Lankura in Dunrel? I won't promise Kuran anything earlier than mid Sedrin if there's even one man who wishes to hold me to my pledge."

***

Elgurn looked up from his desk as Kuran entered the study. The king's lips curled in the hint of a smile, even as his brow furrowed in a frown. "Well, Kuran," he said. "It seems your bird has flown."

"My... *bird*, My Lord?"

"Your noble pirate."

"Ah." Kuran nodded. "Yes, it appears that the pirates all sailed before dawn. Out with the ebbing tide."

Elgurn's frown deepened. "You don't seem greatly distressed. Here you gave him two days to make up his mind, and it seems he needed less than one night to decide to show you his back."

Kuran's face continued to show no strong emotion as he drew a folded paper from his dark blue uniform tirka.

"He came to his decision more quickly than I expected," he admitted mildly. "But I am not displeased with the result. Before he left, Captain Nagaro delivered this with his own hands to the guard at the gate of the Fleet compound."

Kuran unfolded the paper and held it out to the king.

Elgurn took the paper, looking slightly sour. "He gave you his answer in a *letter?*" He held the paper so the light from the window fell on it, and read:

"*My Lord Kuran Kel, Lord of the Royal Fleet of Edrovir. I hope you will be pleased with this, my acceptance of your offer of an officer's commission in the Royal Fleet, at the rank of captain. I cannot, at present, tell you how many others to expect, who may return with me to avail themselves of your other generous offer. Whether I can bring a ship, will depend upon the number of men. I further regret that I cannot come in Dunrel, as you wished. The covenant I make with those who follow me obliges them to conform to the rule of honor as I set it forth, and in exchange, I do all I can to protect their lives and bring them safely home at summer's end. To this covenant, we have added a pledge that, in exchange for their service throughout the length of the season, each man can expect a share of what we take. I am bound by honor to this covenant and to this pledge, and for this reason, I cannot promise that you will see me again in Lankura before mid Sedrin. If you do not see me before the winter comes, it will mean I have missed the last merchant craft out of Pakoa and cannot bring my own ship. In that event, you must look for me in the spring. I will, in any case, come as soon as honor and practicality allow. I sign this, with respect and gratitude, Nagaro Nareyo.*"

The king's countenance had become progressively more thunderous as he read, and when he finished, he angrily thrust the letter back at Kuran.

"What is this impudence?" he demanded. "What is this talk of covenants and pledges but an excuse to delay his coming while he further enriches himself by his piracy? And how dare he presume to dictate to you— to *us*— the time and manner of his coming?"

Kuran had recovered the letter and now held it carefully.

"My Lord," he said, with equal care, "You have misjudged this man once, and you are now in danger of doing so again. His purpose in discussing covenants and pledges is to explain exactly how he feels himself constrained by what he has promised to his men. That promise precedes any that he gave to me, and for my part, I wouldn't have him break it. That he honors his word to his men speaks highly of him. It further explains how he wins their loyalty. As for the time of his coming, it happens that I had told him he might come later than Dunrel, if necessary— and we didn't agree upon how much later it might be."

"Yes, but... *not until next spring?*" Elgurn's scowl had relaxed only fractionally.

"Or mid Sedrin. I think he rather expects it will be then."

"You think he means to come at all?"

Kuran tapped the paper in his hand. "I have his word here, in writing, and he is a man who keeps his word, My Lord. So yes, I believe he means to come."

Elgurn heaved a sigh, and glanced down at his desk. He toyed with some of the papers there. "I find it troubling that he won't say how many other men will come, or whether there will be a ship," he ventured after a moment in a slightly less belligerent tone.

Kuran sighed as well. "Since he *is* a man who keeps his promises, and also not a fool, he is cautious with his words. He promises only what he is certain he can deliver. In this case, that is himself. For the rest we will have to wait and see."

Elgurn fixed Kuran with his pale blue gaze. "Yes, and I don't like it, Kuran," he said sharply. "That the King of Edrovir, and the Lord of the Royal Fleet, must sit and wait to see what this man will bring us. Nor do I like the free and easy tone he takes with you. One would almost suppose that he fancies himself the lord of some foreign country, rather than a mere pirate captain from the southern isles."

Kuran carefully refolded the letter, and slipped it back into his tirka.

"His tone reflects the way we have come to speak to each other. I didn't begin life as one of the noble class, and he, though he started so, is no longer. So we understand one another. But his upbringing *has* left its mark upon him. The merchants of the coast call him the Prince of Pakoa, and not because he has been good for trade— although he has. He moves in Pakoa and among the southern isles very much like a lord in his Wared."

The king's scowl returned. "I am sure I don't need to remind you, Kuran, that *I* and the lord of Pakoa, and of all the southern isles. The folk dwelling there owe direct allegiance to the Crown."

Kuran bowed slightly. "Of course, My Lord," he said soothingly. "And I didn't mean to suggest that he tries to *rule* those islands— although it seems that the members of the Pakoa Town Council value his opinion so much that they scarcely do anything without consulting him. What I meant was that he takes *care* of the land and the people, as a Kelorin lord of old used to serve his Wared. And he's been a good steward for you, My Lord."

Elgurn's eyes narrowed fractionally. "If that is so," he said sourly, "Perhaps we should leave him there— tell him he comes too late if he doesn't come in Dunrel."

At this, Kuran went to the door, which had been standing open, and closed it.

Returning, he brought a chair that had been standing against the wall. He placed the chair squarely in front of Elgurn's desk and sat down upon it. Leaning forward, he said in a low tone, "My Lord, my council is that we should take him whenever he comes. There is one more argument that I have so far neglected to mention."

The king's eyes narrowed a little further. "One argument you have saved in case of need, I think you mean," he observed dryly. "But let me hear it."

"You have heard that Captain Nagaro is a good swordsman, My Lord?"

Elgurn's glance was cool. "I have— though I haven't seen the proof of it. I was at the *other* door of the Audience Chamber during the Mahuk attack, you see, since we were beset on both sides."

Kuran lowered his voice a notch, despite the closed door. "He is beyond good, My Lord. He is truly exceptional. 'Not since Darion has there been such a swordsman' —that is what they are saying in the isles, and all up and down the southern coast."

Elgurn laughed derisively. "What do the folk there know of such things?"

Kuran smiled. "That is what *I* said, when first I heard it. The man who said it had surely never set eyes on Darion, much less seen him wield a blade. I, on the other hand, *have done both*."

The king's laughter died.

"Have *you* seen the pirate captain fight?"

Kuran nodded. "It was only a demonstration bout, fought with practice swords— and against Captain Ruald, whose skill surely didn't stretch my noble pirate to his limit. But I saw enough to tell you that the comparison to Darion is apt. Captain Nagaro has great skill, and exceptional speed, and there is a certain... *grace*... that recalls Darion, as I remember him."

Elgurn's pale blue eyes were locked upon Kuran's face. "Are you thinking that he might be able to stand against Lothard Hurn?"

Again, Kuran nodded. "That is *exactly* what I am thinking, My Lord. I saw to it that he got the worst of our practice blades, and Ruald the best, and yet he made that clumsy thing look like the finest product of the swordsmith's art. Ruald did his best, but he couldn't touch the man. Our pirate does not have Lothard's reach, being not so tall, but I think he has the speed to overcome that disadvantage."

The king's expression had suddenly become thoughtful.

"But could he be persuaded to fight a challenge for the Crown? Any man may serve as a King's Champion, of course, regardless of birth, but even as a Fleet officer, he couldn't be *compelled* to do so. Would this pirate captain fight for *me?*"

Kuran smiled grimly. "I believe he would fight for the good of Edrovir."

"*Ah…*" The shrewd blue eyes grew more thoughtful still. "Then we need only find a way to convince him that Edrovir would not be well served by seeing Lothard take the crown. *That* should not be difficult…"

***

Nagaro sat at the kitchen table in the Bay Tree Inn, nursing a cup of hot sothiril. It was a crisp day in early Sedrin, on the cusp of autumn, and the four ships of the pirate fleet lay at anchor in Pakoa Harbor after a successful summer spent hunting Mautep galleys among the southern isles and in the northern waters of the Mahuk Baar.

Nagaro and Taru had come ashore the previous evening to sleep in their shared house, and had come to the Bay Tree rather late for breakfast. Yuli had lured them into the kitchen with promises of pancakes cooked just for them, with extra helpings of her justifiably famous stewed apples with cinnamon and sugar. Taru had just finished his breakfast and had gone about some business of his own, while Nagaro lingered.

Yuli had been kneading bread, but she had just set the last loaf aside under a towel to rise, and now brought her own mug to the table to join him.

"Taru said ye actually *talked* to the princess," she said eagerly. "Ye must tell me about her, Tor Nagaro. What is she like? Is she as beautiful as they say?"

Nagaro shrugged. "I find her beautiful," he said. "Although beauty isn't really what matters."

Yuli gave him a sly look. "What do ye think matters, then?" she asked, over her cup.

He fingered the handle of his own cup and frowned, realizing he had set a trap for himself. "What matters is how she treats people," he said. "She treats them with respect, no matter who they are. She's clever, too, and a little mischievous, but always kind underneath. If you could meet her, Yuli, you'd like her, I'm sure. And I think she would like you too."

Yuli flung up her hands. "Ai! Tor Nagaro! As if a princess would take any notice of the likes o' me!"

Nagaro's frown only became more earnest. "But she *would*, Yuli," he insisted. "She spoke to both Pavo and Taru. And she said she liked me, so why wouldn't she like you?"

Yuli shook her head at him. "Tor Nagaro," she said. "Ye're a very fine gentleman, and I'm an innkeeper's wife!"

He sighed. "I'm a pirate captain, Yuli. And I *may* become a captain in the Royal Fleet— if I don't keep Lord Kuran waiting too long.

Yuli's expression turned somber. "I still can't believe ye're going away. I'm going t' miss ye."

"Don't start talking like that, Yuli," he said quickly. "Or you'll have us both weeping into our sothiril. I don't much like the idea of going, myself, when I think about what I'm leaving behind. But I gave Lord Kuran my word, and I have to keep it."

Yuli had finished her sothiril and now she stood up, pushing back her chair.

"But ye *should* go, Tor Nagaro," she said with an effort at cheerfulness. "It's a grand chance, and ye deserve it."

She crossed to the wash stand, and began to transfer dirty dishes from it to the washtub. "And I'm sure that Lord Kuran 'll wait for ye. He's no fool, they say. And he did come here to Pakoa Harbor, ye'll remember, just t' ask about the truth o' everything ye told him. It's got me beat, though, how he learned so much about ye, without doin' the askin' himself," she added. "I suppose it must ha' been from talkin' to his sea warriors. There was one o' them in here that asked me a peck o' questions."

Nagaro sat up straighter and his brows knit. "What did this Fleet warrior look like, Yuli?"

"Oh, he was a small man, with a neatly trimmed beard. And he looked like he was half Turowan..." Her voice trailed, and she suddenly turned around, her hands dripping soapy water, her eyes wide. "Now, ye don't think—" she began.

Nagaro's mouth was set in a line. "That sounds to me like a pretty fair description of Kuran Kel."

"But he talked like a common seaman!"

"He can do that, Yuli. I've heard him do it."

"*Hamanei mata noa!*" Yuli put her hands to her mouth, heedless of the soapsuds. "And there I was gabbin' on like an old woman! What must he ha' thought o' me!"

Nagaro sighed. "I expect that he thought you were just what he was looking for."

"*Merciful Spirits!*" Yuli looked mortified. "I do beg your pardon, Tor Nagaro! I hope I didn't tell him anything ye wouldn't ha' wanted me to tell!"

"Probably not," Nagaro told her kindly. "I can't imagine you'd say anything bad about me, Yuli." Then he shrugged. "He offered me the commission after all."

He actually suspected that Yuli had, if anything, painted too glowing a picture. And there was no point in asking her for the details. She would only give him a version that was meant for his ears.

Yuli was shaking her head. "Well, I'll know him if ever he comes in here again. And I might have a thing or two to say t' him besides. Playin' tricks on poor honest folk!" She turned back to her dishwater. "The Lord o' the Fleet," she muttered to herself. "Playin' me for a fool in my own kitchen!"

Nagaro sighed and finished his sothiril. Rising, he crossed the kitchen to drop his cup into the washtub. Then he picked up his cloak and pulled it about his shoulders. It was chilly and damp outside.

"How long will ye be in port?" Yuli asked over her shoulder.

He paused in the doorway. "A week, maybe a little longer. There are some things that need to be seen to."

As he passed through the door into the inn's common room, Nagaro abruptly came to a halt. Tulara was there, at the other end of the long room, sweeping the floor. The room was otherwise empty.

He drew a long breath. Should he speak to her?

The suggestion Taru had made to him on the evening after Pavo's wedding— that he ought to court Tulara— had been on his mind in the past several weeks. He hadn't thought much of the idea to begin with because he didn't have what he thought were the right kind of feelings for Tulara. Now, however, as he thought about moving to Lankura and leaving Narei behind, his thoughts kept coming back to one thing Taru had said that night. Tulara would make a good mother for Narei.

In the old tales he couldn't remember anyone ever *deciding* to fall in love— or *trying* to fall in love. Still, if two people gave something a chance to happen... well... might it not?

Nagaro stood, hesitating. Tulara was still sweeping. She was moving closer, but she had yet to notice him. He wasn't likely to get a better chance than this to speak to her when there was no one else around. But he wasn't at all certain how to put it to her, and there was the awkward fact that he would be leaving the island in a week. Maybe she would be willing to come to Lankura. And then... in a year, perhaps... if the right things happened, he might be able to bring Narei.

He took a few steps into the room.

Tulara must have caught the movement, for she looked up and saw him. "Oh hello, Nagaro," she said, smiling warmly.

A little encouraged, he said, "Hello, Tulara." Then he took a deep breath and crossed the distance to where she stood. "There is something I wished to ask you."

"Yes? What is it?" Her deep brown eyes were wide with the innocent question.

Nagaro swallowed hard, and plunged ahead. "We've been friends for a long time, Tulara... and I thought... maybe we could try to see whether it could become, well, more than that. If we spent some time getting to know each other better, I mean. We could sit together and talk anywhere you like—"

He stopped because of the expression on her face. It was something between shock and embarrassment. He was suddenly very glad he had decided not to mention anything about Narei at first. If it had sounded as if he was only looking for a mother for his daughter, it would surely have made things worse.

Tulara's expression turned into a troubled frown. "Oh, Tor Nagaro," she said earnestly, and his heart sank at the formality. She *never* called him 'Tor Nagaro', unless it was for the benefit of other folk who were likely to overhear.

"Ye're very kind to think o' me that way," she went on hurriedly. "But it was surely never meant t' be so. Not a great hero like you, and a simple kitchen maid like me."

He frowned then, not liking to hear her belittle herself. "Tulara, you shouldn't say such things—" he began, but she held up her hand to stop him.

"I didn't mean it like that," she said quickly. "I know, now, that I'm just as good as any woman on this island. And ye helped me t' see that, Tor Nagaro. Ye taught me how to do sums, and ye always treated me like I was as good as anybody else." She gave him a small, quick smile, that was grateful, but nothing more. "If Captain Nagaro did that, how could anyone else do any different? It's just that, well..."

She cast her eyes down and toyed uncertainly with the broom handle, as if she were trying to find the right words. After a moment, she said. "It's just that this island is fine for me. I don't want any more than what's right here. But ye're going away to Lankura, and I believe ye belong there. The Spirits have surely marked ye for bigger things. Anyone can see that." She looked up, straight into his eyes, with a slightly pleading, slightly worried gaze.

He couldn't escape the sense that she was desperately hoping he would accept this explanation, and so, what else could he do?

"Oh. Well. All right, then," he stammered. "If you're that sure."

Somehow he managed to take his leave of her and get out of the door onto the inn's broad front porch. There he stopped and stood, overwhelmed by a strange mixture of relief and disappointment— relief that the ordeal of asking her was over, and disappointment that her rejection of his overture had been so swift and unequivocal. A sudden wave of bitterness rose within him as Yuli's words and Tulara's words ran together in his mind.

You're a very fine gentleman... A great hero like you... The Spirits have marked you for better things...

Why did they all say things like that? Why did they treat him as if he were so different from everybody else? Both Yuli and Tulara liked him, he was sure of it, and yet...

Perhaps it was just as well that he was going away.

A movement in the common room caused him to glance at the inn's large front window. He could see Tulara inside. She had resumed her sweeping, and it had brought her into easy view from where he stood.

So it was that Nagaro saw the young man approach her from behind and reach up playfully to put his hands over her eyes. He saw Tulara drop the broom... saw her joyful smile... could almost hear her laughter as she started to turn around. The young man moved around to face her then, and Nagaro saw that it was Habu, Yuli's son. The young Turo bent to kiss Tulara, even as she threw her arms around his neck.

Nagaro turned and fled from the porch.

Tulara and Habu!

Well, why not? Habu was a kind-hearted young man, just a year older than Tulara. It was years since Habu had been sweet on the girl named Sulani— who had married someone else— and he and Tulara had been working under the same roof all that time.

But why, Nagaro wondered, hadn't she just told him she had already found someone else? Had her experience with Taru that past spring made her wary of mentioning another man's name when telling a man she wasn't interested? She had given him a hint, though, hadn't she? *"I don't want anything more than what's right here."*

He felt like a perfect fool for having imagined that she might look favorably upon his suggestion— for failing to consider the possibility that a sweet, clever, pretty young woman like Tulara would surely have attracted other suitors after all this time.

He tried to tell himself there was no reason to let the conversation with Tulara upset him. It wasn't as if he'd had feelings for her, after all. Habu was a good match for her, and Tulara would make a good innkeeper's wife. He was truly glad for her.

And she was still his friend. The smile she had given him at his first appearance had been quite genuine. After some reflection, he realized that the way she had given him her answer had been calculated to hurt him as little as possible. She had surly meant well, even if she *had* made him feel as if he didn't belong on the island. He still felt a fool, but he knew he would get over it.

By the time his whirling thoughts had slowed enough for him to notice where he was, he found that he was halfway to Gedras' house. Since he had business with the merchant anyway, he decided to go the rest of the distance.

***

It turned out that Gedras was at home and immediately made himself available, explaining that nothing had been sold yet from the goods the pirates had taken during the summer. This news was hardly unexpected, and it wasn't what Nagaro had come about in any case.

"I'm afraid I have another service to ask," he told the merchant. "I'd like you to help Timegar with the bookkeeping— for determining the men's shares, and the refitting of the ships, and so on— if you can spare the time. I tried to explain to him how I do it all, but he gave me the kind of look I imagine you might give me if I tried to teach you swordsmanship. I'd expect you to charge a fee of course."

Gedras polished his spectacles and replaced them on his narrow, high-bridged nose. "Well, I have no objection to taking on a bit more work," the dapper middle-age Kelorin said cautiously. "You would have to explain it all to *me* of course. I confess I've never been quite sure how your system works. And I have half a notion that it only works at all because your men trust you implicitly. I'm not sure I shall enjoy the same high regard."

Nagaro frowned a little. "I'm sure they all know that you're honest, Gedras," he said seriously. "But it is true that it isn't quite the same, having someone involved who isn't one of them. That's why I want Timegar to be in charge of it, in name at least. You can work out the numbers, and he can present them to the men. Perhaps in time, he will master the whole process. I've thought about bringing Gurd in as well so everyone can see that they agree on the figures. Moraga would have been better, being the other captain, but he's never learned more arithmetic than he can do on his fingers and toes."

Gedras smiled a little, but nodded. "It's a good plan. I think a second man is an excellent idea, and Gurd is a fair choice. His family are shopkeepers in Harmoth, I understand. He may not have taken to the trade, but I'll wager he knows his sums."

"Could I bring them around this afternoon?"

Gedras frowned. "Tomorrow morning would be better, to sit down together with your men, but if you could bring your books today for me to look over, I'd be glad of it."

Nagaro was apologetic. "I should have thought to bring them with me this morning. I've scarcely started the book for this year, but I could let you look at last year's books to see how I do things. I start with the estimate of what will be needed to refit the ships in the spring. And I take your estimate for the value of all the last season's cargo— less one tenth part for the tax, and another fifth part because the estimate may be high, or everything may not be sold in good time—"

"Whoa there!" Gedras raised his hands in mock distress. "Best bring me the books first, and then we'll talk about it. I suppose you know how many men there are who each need to be paid a share?"

Nagaro looked uncomfortable. "If it were any normal year, I'd be able to tell you that right now. But this year I don't yet have a final count of how many will be going to Lankura with me. Those that do will take a smaller share, since they expect to be drawing Fleet pay. I hope to be able to give you an answer by the end of the week."

There was some further discussion, after which Nagaro took his leave of the merchant, promising to return with the last year's ledgers before dinnertime.

As he was taking down his cloak from one of the hooks in the hall, he heard an unexpected crackle of paper. Puzzled, he examined the garment and discovered a small note, folded in half and pinned to the inside of it. Frowning, he unpinned the little scrap of paper and unfolded it. Written on the inner surface in neat, small letters, he read:

I have need to speak with you. —L

Nagaro stiffened and turned around, scanning the entry hall, half expecting to catch sight of someone on the second floor landing of the stairs, or to hear the rustle of retreating skirts. Under this roof, 'L' could only mean Lissel, Gedras' youngest daughter. There was, however, no one to be seen, nor any sound to be heard.

He stood uncertainly, still holding the paper. What could Lissel want with him? The same thing her eldest sister, Berenil, had wanted years before?

Berenil had dropped a note for him to pick up, intending that he ask Gedras if he might sit with her. They hadn't seen eye to eye at all. In fact, he had found her mercenary way of looking at the world completely unappealing. The memory of the episode with Berenil inevitably dragged after it an even less happy recollection involving the middle sister, Gesrin. That incident had occurred about a year after the first, and only a few days before Gesrin was to be married to the son of a local shopkeeper.

Nagaro had come to the house on business and made the mistake of going to investigate when he had heard someone weeping in the side hall beside the stairs. The weeper had turned out to be Gesrin, and the tears not the least bit genuine. She had tried to persuade him to kiss her, on the grounds that it was her last chance to do so before she was wed. When he'd told her that she should save her kisses for her future husband, the frustrated young woman had stamped her foot and shouted at him. Just when he had thought the situation couldn't get any worse, a sudden eruption of giggles from the nearby closet under the stairs had revealed the presence of Lissel, who had overheard every word.

And now Lissel wanted to talk to him.

With an effort he thrust the embarrassing memory aside. Lissel had changed since then. When he'd first seen her, she had been a giggling fifteen-year-old with her hair in braids. She had ceased to wear braids some time ago, and more importantly, she had also ceased to giggle.

In fact, she had somehow gotten to be twenty without his having noticed, and he had lately become aware of her as a rather serious and thoughtful young woman. He didn't know her at all of course. The Pakoan custom of restricting all contact between marriageable young men and women to parentally sanctioned 'sittings' had made sure of that. Still, if she was interested in sitting with him, he wouldn't mind learning more.

He looked at the note again and frowned. It plainly said, "I need to speak with you," *not*, "I wish to sit with you." The wording might well be significant. The only way to find out what she meant was to ask her, and there was only one way to do that. Nor did he have time to dither about it since he would very soon be leaving Pakoa.

He took a deep breath, turned around, and knocked for the second time that morning on the door of Tor Gedras' study.

A few minutes later, he was outside, striding up the street with his hood pulled down low against what had become a fine drizzle. He had an appointment to sit with Lissel on the following day. Gedras had looked distinctly surprised at the request, but, with the unerring instinct of an experienced father of young girls, he hadn't asked what had sparked Nagaro's sudden interest.

Nagaro buried the little note deep in one of his pockets and attempted to bury all thought of the next day's interview in some back recess of his mind.

He had a great many other things to think about. First, he must stop and speak to Ulapa, the caretaker, regarding long term maintenance of the house, since he and Taru had decided they were not ready yet to part with it. He frowned as another thought intruded. He really should arrange to have the horses ridden every week. Perhaps, he thought, Ulapa would know someone who would to do that for a few rins.

***

It was on the way to Ulapa's house that he encountered Tira Zomora. She stepped out of the shadow of a garden wall with a suddenness that nearly made his heart stop. Nor did she waste any time in getting to her point.

"Ye're going back to Lankura," she said accusingly as she confronted him with her hand on her piebald pony's bridle. "And taking island men with ye. The last time ye took men there, some o' them didn't come home."

Nagaro didn't flinch under her dark gaze.

"There were fourteen who died helping to retake the palace and the city from the sea warriors," he said. "I laid some of them out, myself, and helped dig their grave. I wrote down the list of their names— and the words that will honor them— all to be cut into the stone that will stand as their memorial. All of these things I will carry with me until the end of my days. I don't think there's anything you can say, Zirdyn, to make it weigh more heavily. And Vothra— who sees my heart— knows there is no need for it."

Zomora's nostrils flared slightly, but she gave no other evidence of emotion. "These things you say you have done are of little comfort to those who grieve," she said.

Nagaro held her gaze. "I know that," he said wearily. "I witnessed that grief earlier in the summer when I carried the sad news to the families, here on Pakoa, and elsewhere. Nor is it any comfort to them to know that these men were buried, with equal honor, beside men of the Palace Guard, and the City Garrison. But I believe it means something to the folk of Lankura. And every king of Edrovir, from now on, will see the grave and read what is written there— and in reading their names will see that more than half of them were Turowan."

The medicine woman reared her head. "Ye think that will make a difference?"

"I hope it will," he told her. "It gives a small crumb of *purpose* to their deaths— that their sacrifice may move our kings to have more care for the island folk, and for the Turo. But I would far rather that men hadn't had to die to achieve that end."

Zomora appeared to relax, just fractionally. She sniffed. "Is your name also to be carved on the marker? As the one who led them?"

Nagaro straightened his shoulders. "At the top it will say only, 'Men Under Command of Captain Nagaro', where the other markers will say 'Men of the Palace Guard', or 'Men of the City Garrison', and also list the commanders. They had to put something there, and I suppose they found it awkward to call our men 'pirates'. I led them, but I didn't order those men into that fight, Zomora. I let them choose, and they went willingly into what they knew would likely be a very hard fight." He paused, his face clouding. "But I'm sure they didn't expect to die."

Zomora shifted. For the first time, her gaze softened perceptibly. "Men rarely do," she said. "The ones who are about to follow ye back to Lankura don't expect to, I'm sure."

"I don't know what they expect," he told her honestly. "I am going because Lord Kuran asked me to help him do his work without sinking ships. I've told the men that, and those who will come have chosen to come. They won't necessarily be serving under me in Lankura, either, I expect. They will be serving under Lord Kuran."

Zomora's lip curled. "Which means I may have to take him to task as well," she said sourly, and with that, she pulled at her pony's bridle and moved on along the narrow street.

For a long moment, Nagaro watched her go. Then he sighed again and resumed his interrupted journey to Ulapa's house. Zomora, he supposed, would always remain Zomora.

Chapter 23

Ending And Beginning

When Nagaro arrived at the house on the hill after speaking with Ulapa, he was surprised to find Pavo there as well as Taru. Both men were in the modest dining room, seated at the plain wooden table. Pavo stood up in obvious agitation when Nagaro entered the room.

"Nagaro! At last you have come!" he exclaimed. "Now you must tell me what to do!"

"Why?" Nagaro asked, alarmed. "What's wrong? Has something happened?"

"Oh yes, something have happened. Tenepti have told me she is carrying my baby inside. Nagaro, I do not know how to be father! You must tell me how to do it."

Nagaro barely restrained himself from laughing out of sheer relief. The panic in Pavo's eyes stopped him. "But this is wonderful news, Pavo," he said instead. "Really. Congratulations! And as for being a father, I think you will do fine. Just figure it out as you go along— that's all I do. Now please try to relax." He motioned for Pavo to sit down again, then pulled out one of the remaining chairs and sat down himself.

Pavo sank back into his own seat, looking a bit sheepish.

"Huh! Is that the best ye can do, Nagaro?" Taru inquired a bit stiffly. "*I* say it's bloody bad luck having it happen so fast."

Nagaro's expression turned sober. "It only takes one night, Taru. I found that out—"

Taru threw up his hands. "It doesn't take *half an hour*, if that's what ye mean! I'm just saying that a man ought to have time to get properly used t' being married, afore the Spirits send him a baby to feed!"

Nagaro sighed. "Men don't feed babies," he said patiently. "Women feed babies— for the first eight or nine months, at any rate." He met Pavo's eyes. "Don't *worry*, Pavo, it will be all right. All the changes come pretty slowly— after the first one. There are *some* men I might worry about," he added, giving Taru a quick, sharp, glance. "But I think *you* will do just fine."

Pavo managed a considerably less panic-stricken smile. "I feel better because you say so, Nagaro."

Nagaro's frown suddenly returned. "But this means you shouldn't come to Lankura when we sail," he said. "I know Tenepti said you should go, when we stopped here in the spring, and she would follow in a year if all went well. But if she's expecting a baby, that changes things."

Nagaro was re-opening a contentious issue.

Pavo's insistence on coming with him to Lankura had worried Nagaro from the beginning— despite the fact that he appreciated the other man's loyalty, and not withstanding how much he would miss Pavo if the young Hashtep stayed behind. He had tried to explain to Pavo just how difficult things might be for him in Lankura. There was no community of other Hashtep there. Pavo would be alone in a place where men with faces like his were known only as enemies.

Pavo, however, had remained adamant— and had originally thought to bring Tenepti with him from the beginning.

The only concession Nagaro had been able to win from his friend had been to go alone at first and wait a year before bringing Tenepti— a year to see how one Hashtep would be received in Lankura, and among the men of the Fleet— a year before bringing his wife into what might well prove to be a hostile place. Pavo had made even that concession grudgingly, but if his young bride was with child, surely the young Hashtep would see the wisdom of his remaining in Pakoa to see her through this time?

Pavo, however, shook his head. "Oh no," he said. "It does not make difference. Tenepti have explained to me. She can go to stay with her sister. She say Matahi will take very good care of her— and of baby!"

Nagaro frowned a little harder. "I'm sure she would," he said. Matahi was married, with two children of her own, and very protective of her younger sister. "But don't you think you should be here on Pakoa when the baby comes?"

Pavo's broad forehead furrowed. "But baby will not come until six or seven more month. If I do not go to Lankura, in six month I must sail with Timegar and Moraga if I am to have work to do. So still I will not be here."

"Oh. I see." Such was the life of a sea warrior.

Nagaro had imagined the baby being born in the winter, which would have been the case if it had been conceived in Medrin when they had first stopped at Pakoa with the news of the battle of Lankura. The conception must have occurred in Duleyin when they had stopped again to re-provisioned the ship. He sighed and rubbed his forehead. He knew better than to argue further with Pavo, having no other persuasions to offer.

Pavo had continued to regard him seriously, and now the young Hashtep spoke again with unusual hesitancy. "Nagaro... do you not *want* to have me in Lankura with you?"

Nagaro felt an immediate stab of guilt. "Of *course* I want to you there, Pavo! You and Taru are both like brothers to me. But it would be horrible if you came to harm because you're a Hashtep. Most people are good, and most of the folk in Lankura will at least wait to see what you're like before they act. But it only takes one bad person..."

Nagaro left the rest to Pavo's imagination.

Pavo, however, only shook his head, and said, "I do not think harm will come to me if I am with *you*— and with Taru."

Nagaro glanced at Taru and saw his other friend wince. Taru had for the most part kept out of the discussions of this issue. He was almost as worried as Nagaro, but had confessed that he thought it was useless to argue with Pavo.

Nagaro sighed again. "Even if Taru and I could be with you every minute—" he began, and stopped. He was watching Pavo's eyes, and what he read there was unfailing trust. He swallowed. "I know you are doing this because you choose to, Pavo," he said carefully. "And I know I can't protect you from every possible harm. But I swear that if it's in my power to prevent it, I will not let any harm come to you because you were born in the Mahuk Baar."

Pavo simply nodded. "And I also swear that no man will hurt *you*, Nagaro, if I can stop him," he said seriously. Then he smiled broadly. "But I think maybe nothing bad will happen. Sheptuum have always keep you safe, and Sheptuum knows I am your friend."

Nagaro made an effort to return the smile. "I don't know about Sheptuum, he said, "but I hope you are right that nothing bad will happen."

Taru coughed. "I'll just make another pot o' sothiril," he said, standing up and making for the kitchen with the tea pot in hand.

While Taru was seeing to the sothiril, Nagaro fetched a stack of bound ledgers from a chest in the corner. He brought the books back to the table, sat down, and opened one of them to the first blank page, thinking he might as well start the lists.

It didn't take him long to set up two pages, one simply saying, 'Men Bound for Lankura,' and the other 'Men Remaining on Pakoa.' He then entered his own name and those of Taru and Pavo on the first page, and those of Moraga, Timegar, and Gurd on the second.

When Taru returned with a fresh pot of sothiril, they each had a cup.

Pavo stayed long enough to politely finish his sothiril, then stood up. "Now I will go home to Tenepti," he declared. After a moment's thought, he added, "Both of you can come to my house for lunch today. Tenepti will be very glad to see you."

Taru grinned and said, "O' course I'll come."

Nagaro begged off. "Thank you, he said, "but I'm going back into town to collect the names for these lists. And then I'll visit Narei and have lunch at Ani's house. I'm going to be leaving Narei for quite a long time, after all."

Taru shook his head. "Ye shouldn't worry so much about that child o' yours," he said. "Ye know Ani 'll take good care of her."

***

Nagaro stopped first at the barracks where many of the men were staying. Once there, he called a muster and took down the names of as many of the men as were prepared to tell him their decision. He was surprised at the number who said they would go to Lankura.

The barracks also housed a number of former slaves who had been freed during that summer's voyages and Nagaro was further surprised when a handful of these approached him as well, asking whether they might also take passage to Lankura to see whether they could join the Royal Fleet. Nagaro duly recorded their names, though he had to tell them that Lord Kuran's offer didn't include men in their position. They were untrained and would quite possibly face rejection, since it was long past the date for taking on new recruits.

His second stop was the inn, where some of his men were rooming. Others who had more far-flung lodgings could be expected to congregate there as well, since enough of the morning had fled that it was nearly time for lunch. Nagaro announced what he was doing and sat at one of the tables in the common room, taking down names as men approached him, one by one.

Presently, he looked up from recording a name to find that Sindar was standing on the other side of the table.

Sindar flashed a broad smile. "I want go Lankura," he said eagerly. "I want go with you!"

Nagaro felt a sinking in the pit of his stomach. He had feared this would happen. "I don't think that would be a good idea, Sindar," he said cautiously.

Sindar's brow furrowed. "I *want* go Lankura!" he repeated more emphatically, and added, "I *want* be Fleet man!"

From the young Kelorin's emphasis, Nagaro suspected that Sindar hadn't understood him correctly. He sighed and switched to Hashti.

"I am sorry, Sindar" he said as kindly as he could. "In Droviri Fleet, all order will be in Droviri. You do not know yet enough Droviri word. If you do not understand order, you will not know what to do."

Sindar stood up straighter. "I know, 'see ship.' I know, 'see boat.' I know, 'go up.' I know, 'come down,'" he declared stoutly in the Common Speech.

Nagaro sighed again. "There will be other order than those," he explained in Hashti. "Many other order. Some order you do not know—"

"*Tell* me! You teach. I learn!" Sindar's eyes were pleading.

Nagaro shook his head. He felt terribly cruel, but there was no help for it.

"I know you will learn *in time*, Sindar, but it will take too much time. Lord Kuran wants us to come very soon and he will not wait."

Sindar frowned, obviously struggling with the words. At last he resorted to speaking Hashti, as Nagaro had.

"There will be too many order? Lord of Droviri Fleet will not wait for me to learn?"

Nagaro nodded. "I am very sorry, Sindar, but you should not come this time. For now, you should stay with Timegar. You sail with Timegar. You learn from him. Maybe in a year, or two year, you can come to Lankura."

Sindar's shoulders sagged dejectedly. "Stay..." he murmured. "Learn from Timegar..." He turned away, his head down.

Nagaro looked after Sindar's retreating figure. He felt as if he had just kicked a puppy. Finally he turned to the next man. It was Gurd, who had also watched Sindar walk away.

"Don't worry, Capt'n," the Leithian said with a shrug. "He's much better off sailing with us. And he'll soon get over the disappointment."

Nagaro sighed. "I hope so," he said doubtfully. "I know *you're* staying," he added. "I've already put you on the list of those staying here."

He put down the pen, "I'd like to ask you to help Timegar and Gedras with the books, Gurd. What do you think of the idea?"

***

When he left the books with Gedras half an hour later, he told the merchant that Gurd had agreed to help with the bookkeeping. After outlining how the records were laid out, he showed Gedras the partial lists of the men who were going and who were staying.

"About a third of them haven't yet made up their minds," he explained. "I've told them the lists will be here, and that they must come to you to record their choices."

Gedras stared at the pages. "But there are as many going as staying!" he exclaimed. "Why, you already have more than enough to fill a ship! If half of the remainder decide to go with you as well, what do you intend to do?"

Nagaro ran a hand through his hair. "I hadn't meant to take two of the ships," he said, "but it looks as if I may have to."

***

Two ships. That would leave only two behind to continue working out of Pakoa. He would have to see how Timegar and Moraga felt about that. At least it would spare them the need choose a new man to serve as a third captain…

These thoughts ran around and around in his head as he wended his way around the edge of the harbor, past the kuma mills at the southern end of the town, and started up the steep trail that ran over the top of a high ridge and down into the valley where Animara lived with her family. When he reached the top of the ridge, he paused to admire the view of the small ravine-like valley. Cut by a swift-flowing stream, it sloped sharply southward to meet the sea where it ended in a narrow cove. The valley looked very much as it had the first time he had stood on that ridge, four years before.

The branch of the trail leading to Ani's house zig-zagged down through the terraced rows of kuma bushes and disappeared into the small stand of cedar, pine, and juniper at the bottom. He knew that it crossed the stream there, under the trees, and emerged on the other side of the ravine, where he could see the comfortable three-room stone house that he would always think of simply as Ani's house.

He smiled, putting aside all thoughts of ships and numbers of men and potential captains, and struck off down the zig-zag trail.

Emerging from under the trees, he followed the path through the remains of the summer's vegetable garden and knocked on the sturdy cedar-wood door. Even before the door opened, he could hear the merry laughter of children from within, and as soon as Ani opened the door, he was greeted by an enthusiastic chorus of, *"Uncle Nagaro! Uncle Nagaro!"* punctuated by cries of, *"Papa, Papa!"*

He had caught the family at their lunch as he had hoped.

Ani greeted him with her familiar smile. "Nagaro! Come in!," she cried. "And sit ye down. I'll fetch ye some bread and a bowl o' soup."

She opened her strong arms to give him a quick embrace. Her husband, Sudano, immediately fetched another chair, and Nagaroe gladly took a seat at the table.

Narei had already finished her soup. She immediately slid off of her high stool and ran around the table to climb into his lap. She twisted about to look up into his face. "I missed you, Papa!"

"I've missed you, too, Ginger Pie."

"Why, Papa, why?" Narei recited, "Why do you call me Ginger Pie?"

The name and the question were a ritual between them. So was the answer:

"Because you're spicy and sweet, and good enough to eat!" Nagaro leaned down and pretended to take a bite of her, while Narei squealed in make-believe terror.

He kissed her on the forehead, then, and settled down to eat his bread and soup while Narei snuggled contentedly into the hollow his shoulder. Around the table the happy voices rose.

Nagaro sighed contentedly. *Always room under Ani's roof, and a place at her table*, he thought as he basked in the warmth of her domain.

The thought took him back to that awkward day when he had first come to meet Animara— the sister of Jila, the woman who had tricked him into begetting Narei. On that day, Ani had welcomed him into her family with warmth and kindness and an absolute conviction that it was the right thing to do.

Although he couldn't quite call Ani his sister-in-law— since he had declined to marry Jila— she still felt like a sister to him. And, had he been allowed to choose any woman in the world for an older sister, he couldn't possibly have chosen better than Animara.

***

The meal was done. Narei and the other three children had run outside to play, and Sudano had gone off about some task that was waiting for him. Nagaro still sat at the table while Ani gathered up the dishes.

She glanced at his pensive face. "What are ye thinking?" she asked. "Is it about leaving?"

Mutely, he nodded.

"Are ye still thinking it's the right choice?"

Now he frowned. "Yes," he said. "I've been going over it in my mind all summer, and there's still more on the side of the balance that favors

going than on the other side. But most of the things on the other side—
the really important things— are right here in this house."

"Ye'll be comin' back," she said quietly. "From time to time."

Nagaro winced. "The Fleet may stop in Pakoa once or twice a year, for
a day or two, Ani. That's all.."

And then his words tumbled out. "Ani, I wish Narei were *older!* I've
explained it to her, but she doesn't really understand how long it will be
before she sees me again."

Ani sat down across from him, the dishes momentarily forgotten. She
reached across the table to place her strong, brown hand on top of his.

"Don't ye fret," she said firmly. "We'll see her through it— Bahiri an'
the boys and me. We'll see that she knows ye *are* coming back."

"But it won't be *often* enough! And you'll never know when it might
be. It's going to be just like it was with your father, years ago."

Ani's luminous dark eyes gazed gently at him. "Not quite the same,"
she said. "Ye know how t' write a letter, Nagaro. And I know how to find
folk that can read one."

"That's true..."

His sense of gloom lifted fractionally, but there was still something
he needed to say. It was something he hadn't mentioned to her when the
ships had stopped at Pakoa in the spring and he had first told everyone
of his intent. Nor had he brought it up when the ships had come again in
Duleyin.

He turned over the hand that she had covered, and closed his fingers
on hers.

"Ani," he said, watching her face. "I know it's best that Narei should
be here for now. But I've been thinking that, one day— if everything goes
well and I stay in Lankura, I mean— I'd like to bring Narei there to live
with me."

He faltered. He had seen the shadow pass behind her eyes.

"Not for a year or two," he added hastily. "And only if she wants to. I...
I know you love her too, Ani, and it's you who've worked so hard to care
for her these last four years."

Animara gave him her quiet smile. "She's *your* daughter," she said
simply. "And I think the most important thing ye said was, 'If she wants
to.' But how would ye manage it? Ye 'd still be away a lot o' the time."

"I'd have to find a house to rent, and hire a governess— a woman to
look after her— and a tutor to teach her lessons."

She shook her head at him.

"Well, ye understand such things better than I," she said with a little
sigh. "Though it seems there's some if's an' and's to it. And it's too soon
t' guess what Narei will want to do in a year or two. So there's surely no
need to decide right now. Still, I'm glad ye told me what's in your mind."

She gave his hand a squeeze before retrieving hers.

He gave her an apologetic smile. "Thank you, Ani."

The door burst open and ten-year-old Pilo stuck in his head. "Uncle Nagaro! Ye've got t' come an' see the castle we've built. Out by the woodshed!"

"All right, Pilo, I'll come." Nagaro rose and gave Ani one last grateful glance as he made for the door.

Animara smiled, and nodded.

"Don't ye fret about it, Nagaro," she said knowingly. "Ye'll never go far wrong if ye go where your heart leads."

***

The clock in the hall was striking eleven.

It was the next day, and Nagaro was sitting for the second time in his life on the window seat in the elegantly appointed parlor in the house of Gedras the merchant. As on the first occasion, one of Gedras' daughters was sitting beside him. The first time, it had been the eldest daughter, Berenil. This time, it was Lissel, the youngest. The striking of the clock only served to emphasize the awkwardness of the silence the lay between them.

Nagaro glanced surreptitiously at the young woman beside him. She was nervously studying her clasped hands. The heavy curtains were drawn across the window behind them, and Lissel's face and form were illuminated by the light of a pair of decoratively painted oil lamps that graced the opposite wall of the room.

It was a flattering light. Not, he thought, that Lissel needed flattering. She had delicately sculpted features, soft gray eyes, and gently wavy black hair that fell softly about her shoulders. The pale violet gown she wore suited her well.

Nagaro knew he should speak first, being the man, not to mention the elder. He cleared his throat. "I wasn't sure what to do when I saw your note," he ventured. "This was the surest way I could think of to get a chance for us to speak together."

Lissel twisted her fingers together. "I don't know what you must think of me, Tor Nagaro," she said quickly without looking at him. "Writing a note like that."

"Actually, I thought it was a clever way of getting around the fact that young men and women aren't simply permitted to speak to one another."

She did look at him then, nervous and wide-eyed. "You didn't think it forward of me?"

"No, I didn't."

"Oh." She looked back down at her hands. "You're much easier to talk to than I thought you'd be." She paused, twisting her fingers again, then seemed to become aware that she was doing it and stopped.

"I... I've been so afraid of doing this," she began. She gave him a quick glance, then rushed on. "Especially when I think of that horrid little affair in the back hall... with Gesrin. I... I want you to know that I was laughing at Gesrin, not at *you*. She was so *very* angry, I couldn't help myself! I know I shouldn't have let her talk me into hiding and listening like that. It was quite horrid! But she was so sure she could get you to kiss her, and she wanted to be able to boast about it. I *knew* you wouldn't do it. Anyone could see you never liked her a bit... and you're... not that kind of man anyway." She stopped, blushing scarlet, and not looking at him.

Nagaro sat, momentarily stunned "That was a long time ago," he managed, when he found his tongue. "I hadn't thought about it for years."

That wasn't quite true, but he certainly hadn't thought about it very *much* for quite a long time— until reading her note. "Please don't worry about it," he added.

"Oh. You're very kind, Tor Nagaro."

The clock in the hall ticked on. Nagaro could hear it through the open door. "Is that all you wanted to tell me?" he asked at last, feeling a bit let down.

"Oh, no," Lissel said quickly. "That's not it at all." There was another pause as if she were trying to collect her courage.

"I really didn't know what you would think I wanted," she said at last, apparently addressing her hands, tightly clasped in her lap. "I... I hoped you wouldn't think it was anything like with Gezrin. I guess you wouldn't have come if you had. And I hoped you wouldn't think it was anything like with Berenil either." She gave him a questioning glance.

"I, ah, didn't assume anything, really," he said, as his heart sank.

"Oh, good!" she exclaimed with evident relief. "I mean, you're so famous that there must be dozens girls who would give anything to be married to you. But that's not for me. I just hoped you'd be willing to... to... do something for me..." Her voice trailed off.

"What is it then?" he made himself ask. He was trying hard not to feel as if he had just been kicked.

Dozens of girls who would give anything... but not her...

"Would you please... talk to Sindar? Tell him I'd like it very much if he would ask to sit with me?"

"*Sindar?*" Nagaro was so surprised that the name came out sounding as if he were rather shocked.

Her head came up at once, and she turned to face him, her gray eyes earnest and intense. "Yes," she said firmly. "Sindar."

"I... ah, well..." he floundered, trying to come to grips with this unexpected development. "I can try to tell him, certainly. And if I can't explain it to him so that he understands, I'm sure that Pavo Maat will be able to. But, even if he *understands*, I'm not sure what he'll *say*."

"Oh." The change in her expression was painful to see. "You're trying to say that he doesn't like me."

"No! I mean, not *exactly*." Nagaro struggled to explain. "It's just that he grew up in a little village in the Mahuk Baar. All of his life, before coming here, he saw only Hashtep women. He finds Kelorin women... well, ugly. I tried to tell him that you are beautiful, not ugly, but I don't think he sees it that way."

Lissel was blushing again. "Oh," she said. "You told him... *that?* About... me?"

"It happened at Pavo's wedding feast," he told her quickly. "We were talking about the young women at the maiden table. And we were speaking in Hashti— using Hashti words. I'm not sure that the words meant 'beautiful' and 'ugly'— but something like that." He paused. "Do you find Sindar handsome?"

"Oh yes!" Her eyes glowed. "I think he's very handsome. But it wouldn't matter if he wasn't," she added. "He's so lost... and alone... There's so much he doesn't understand. I want to help him."

Nagaro was thinking that this could actually be a good thing for Sindar. The young man certainly had a great deal to learn, and having a young woman take an interest in him might make staying on the island more attractive. But there were serious potential difficulties.

He frowned. "You would have a hard time talking to him. He speaks very little of the Common Speech."

"Oh, I know! But I can teach him. I'll find a way."

Nagaro nodded, but still he frowned. "I... don't suppose you've mentioned this to your father? I don't like to say that he might not approve— or might not say yes to the sitting— but I know that he'll be thinking of your future. Right now, all Sindar seems to want to do is become a sea warrior."

"I don't care what he wants to do!" Lissel declared defiantly. "And I know my father wants me to be happy!"

"Well, all right. That's good then."

Nagaro sat for several long seconds. "I will talk to Sindar," he said at length. "And I'll have Pavo talk to him. I'll see whether he wants to do this, and I'll come with him to speak to your father if he wants me to."

"Oh, thank you, Tor Nagaro!" Lissel beamed at him. "You're *such* a kind man."

There didn't seem to anything more to say after that, so he rose to go.

Outside, he strode away up the street, passing folk who nodded and smiled. Once again, he was intensely grateful that Gedras' house had a parlor for sitting, instead of the more traditional front porch. No one need ever know that he had sat with Lissel. No one need speculate, or guess, perhaps, that Captain Nagaro had been disappointed— again.

Not that he had really been *hoping* of course... But still... *There was Tulara for Habu... Lissel for Sindar... But Nagaro is too fine... too famous...*

There might indeed be a dozen young women on the island who would be glad to marry him because he was famous, but that wasn't what he wanted at all.

He caught himself then and thrust the thoughts aside. After a few more strides, he sighed. It was going to be a genuine relief to become just another captain in the Royal Fleet. Lord Kuran must have more than a dozen of them.

***

Sindar's reaction, when Nagaro attempted to explain to him about Lissel, was rather ambivalent. Even in Hashti, it was hard to make him understand.

"This woman— she is one who said good afternoon? When Pavo made his marriage?"

"Yes."

Sindar scowled. "That woman I do not like so much. Why I can not have one of Hashtep woman that is more beautiful?"

Nagaro frowned, trying to think how to answer. "Hashtep woman you talked to did not like *you* so much. Lissel does like you. So it is better to try with Lissel. *I* think she is beautiful, and maybe you will like her if you try."

"You think she is beautiful?"

"Yes."

"Then why you do not make marriage with her?" Sindar sounded suspicious.

Nagaro ran an exasperated hand through his hair. "Because she does not like *me*. She likes *you*. She thinks you are *handsome*." He used the Common Speech word. "She wants to sit and talk to you, to see if you like her."

"She wants to sit and talk only? But she does not want to—" Here Sindar gestured, pantomiming a passionate embrace. Even his Hashti vocabulary wasn't adequate to the purpose.

Nagaro sighed. "The way it is done on Pakoa, is this," he explained carefully, "First you sit and talk. Then— if you both want to— you ask her father for marriage. After marriage, then you do... the other thing." On this subject, his Hashti vocabulary was no better than Sindar's.

Sindar almost pouted. "I do not like to wait so long."

In the end Nagaro resorted to sending Sindar to talk to Pavo.

This resulted in a kind of grudging acquiescence. Sindar agreed that he would try this thing.

So Nagaro went with him to speak to Gedras. The merchant didn't exactly seem pleased with the idea, but gave his consent with superficially good grace. So Nagaro was able to feel that he had fulfilled his promise to Lissel. Secretly, he hoped that the sittings would go better than he feared they might.

***

The remainder of Nagaro's time on Pakoa fled too quickly. Whenever he could, he stole away to Ani's house, or went riding with his friends.

The latter activity was bittersweet. Once he had found the small size of the island confining. Now he found that the familiarity of all the roads and paths tugged at his heart. He kept being reminded of how much he loved all the little bits of the island— a zigzag path where it climbed past rocks on a hillside, a cluster of ironwood trees silhouetted against the sky, a sudden view of the sea.

It wasn't as bad as it might have been. Having Taru and Pavo with him, he was often distracted from other thoughts by his friends' company, and he was glad that he would be taking them with him.

The other two young men had both learned to ride under Nagaro's tutelage, but he could still literally ride circles around them if he chose. This was particularly true since their mounts were not as swift as his, though each was well-suited to its master. Pavo's steed was a big-boned chestnut plow horse, already named Basil when the friends had purchased him. Pavo had shrugged and accepted the name. Taru's horse was a black pony with a mischievous disposition whom Taru had gleefully christened Onions.

Sometimes when riding with his friends, Nagaro gave Farusia her head and went for a wild, headlong run down some quiet stretch of road, or along the packed, damp sand just short of where the waves came rolling in. Then he would rein the mare in and hold her, snorting and dancing, until his friends caught up. But on their final ride, on the morning of the day before they were to sail, he was content go at his friends' pace.

It was during a brief rest period that Taru raised the subject of Tulara. They had stopped to dismount while the horses drank from a stream and did a little grazing, and the three young men were sitting on the grass. With a forced attempt at casualness, the young Turo inquired whether Nagaro had spoken to her.

Nagaro felt immediately guilty. He had meant to tell Taru what had happened, but he just hadn't seemed to find an appropriate opportunity. He proceeded, with some embarrassment, to sketch the tale of his encounter with Yuli's kitchen maid— and of what he had witnessed afterwards.

Taru was shocked and incensed.

"*Habu?* That great lumbering lout? What can she be thinking— taking up with *him?* Ye shouldn't ha' let her do it, Nagaro!"

Nagaro was taken aback. "What would you have had me do?" he demanded. "I'm not going to try to stop her from doing what she wants!"

"But she can't really want this! Not when she could have had *you!*"

Nagaro felt the blood in his face. "She doesn't want me, Taru. She made that plain."

"Maybe she was playing with ye."

Nagaro sighed. "No," he said. "You didn't see the look on her face when she knew it was Habu that had come up behind her. And I'm quite sure she didn't know I was watching through the window."

Taru subsided after that into shaking his head, and muttering, "*Habu!*" under his breath. It wasn't until they resumed their ride that he seemed to shake off the bad mood. By the time they arrived back at the house on Hill Road, he appeared to be his usual cheerful self once again— much to Nagaro's relief.

***

Late that afternoon, Nagaro made his final visit to Ani's house. He held Narei so long in his embrace that the little girl began to squirm. Then he released her and stood watching her run and play with her cousins until the shadows lengthened and he knew he had to go.

That night he couldn't sleep. In the end, he got up and lit a candle and paced the bare wood floor of his bedroom.

Did he really know what he was doing? Going to dwell in Lankura? If only he could see what the future held! He toyed with the idea of calling upon Vothra, but he knew that the Benevolent Spirit couldn't see the future any more than he could. And as for advice, the time for that was long past. He had already given Lord Kuran his word.

He heaved a long sigh.

Vothra wouldn't tell him what to do in any case. Vothra only gave the most general kind of advice— like telling him that it was a worthy goal to find a way to keep the Royal Fleet from sinking ships. And Nagaro already knew that it was. He sighed again. When he had written that letter to Kuran, he had felt quite sure of himself. Everyone had told him it was the right thing to do. And no one else seemed to have changed their views on the subject.

Nagaro paused at one end of the track that his feet were describing on the floorboards. Moving to the window, he drew the curtain aside and stared out into the cloud-shrouded night. Not a single star offered him the guidance of its light.

Few of Nagaro's advisors had any inkling of the dangers that Lankura might hold for him. Only Taru and Pavo really knew.

Taru was all for the enterprise. Of course, Nagaro knew that Taru's view was colored by his own ambition, but he was also sure that his Turowan friend would have put that ambition aside in an instant if he thought there was any real risk involved. And Pavo went forward with a total confidence that Nagaro found unnerving.

Amongst all the others, only Tredhold had withheld his council. The healer had said nothing, but he had seemed to be watching Nagaro very closely with his thoughtful blue eyes.

Nagaro released the curtain and went to sit on the edge of his bed. He reviewed the risks, one more time— though he'd gone through them all with Taru and Pavo in the privacy of his cabin on the *Sword* the night before they had left Lankura.

He wasn't afraid that he would be recognized by the common folk, who had only seen him passing in the street during his captivity in the capital city. The queen had known nothing of the heskial, but had seen rather more of him. Yet she hadn't known him. And of course, the princess had seen more of him than anyone— he blushed painfully in the darkness at the memory of the more intimate moments before jerking his thoughts away. It was very reassuring that Nevien had shown no sign of seeing through his disguise.

The five men who had known about the heskial presented a greater risk because they had seen the huge difference between his natural behavior and his drugged behavior. Of the five, Gillard Marchent and Bron Sobring were already dead, and Kale Fendred was mad.

Nagaro had hesitated before telling Taru and Pavo about Kale's strange fate, but he had decided that telling his two friends didn't seriously violate his promise to the princess to 'keep the matter close' because they were his closest friends, and they knew his secret. To serve as his friends, they needed to know everything, and they would keep this second secret as closely as they kept the first.

Then there was the king, and of course Nagaro already knew that his disguise and fooled Elgurn— possibly in part because the king believed that Leyel Virden must be dead.

And finally there was *Dreigen*. Even sitting secure in the familiar warmth of his room, Nagaro felt a chill and shuddered involuntarily.

Dreigen, the hated Lore Master, the originator of the monstrous plot and wielder of the bladder thorns...

No! Don't think about that.

With an effort, he focused on the facts that mattered.

Dreigen also must be sure that Leyel was dead. He was the one, after all, who had told Elgurn about the fatal effect of withholding the heskial. While it was conceivable that the Lore Master might recognize his victim despite this conviction if he were to see him, their paths were unlikely to cross. Dreigen's absence from the victory celebration had been typical. He was a solitary man by nature, reclusive, and deeply immersed in his work. The man had always been disinclined to attend events in the Great Hall, and he didn't stay long when he deigned to make an appearance.

And in any case, Nagaro didn't expect to be a frequent visitor to the palace as a mere member of the Royal Fleet.

Nagaro let out the breath he hadn't realized he was holding. He should really be quite safe, as Taru had pointed out. He drew another long breath and let it out slowly. Then he snuffed the candle on the night stand. Stretching out on the bed and closing his eyes, he let his weariness carry him into slumber.

***

The ships sailed the next morning at the second hour after dawn. There were two of them, the *Sword of Freedom* and the *Sea Eagle*, each with a full crew pulling at the oars. Moving to the rhythmic rise and fall of the long sweeps, the two craft slipped out of the narrow entrance of Pakoa harbor. Once clear of the headlands, the ships took a northerly course. The oars were shipped and the sails unfurled to catch a stiff, steady wind out of the west.

The sky was a flawless blue and the dark green sea, ruffled by the wind, threw back the rays of the mounting sun with glittering brilliance. Close by on the ships' port side, the green hills and white beaches of Pakoa slipped quickly past. To starboard, the distant coast of the mainland was a long, low, purple silhouette that slid by more slowly.

As the two ships came abreast of the watchtower on the rocky spit that was Pakoa's northernmost extremity, the horn of the watcher sounded a single long note of farewell. Aloft in the crow's seat, Kunoa raised a hand in answer. At the foot of the tower, a dark-haired figure in a yellow skirt, sitting sidesaddle atop a black-and-white pony, silently watched the ships go past.

Nagaro, standing on the captain's platform at the forward rail of the stern castle of the *Sword of Freedom*, took no notice of either watcher. His gaze was resolutely fixed upon the broad expanse of the Great Channel and the chosen course that lay before him.

Glossary of Names and Terms

Alam Shufa (Ah-lahm SHOO-fah): Location on the northern coast of the Mahuk Baar, convenient for putting men ashore unobtrusively.

Alisset (Al-ih-seht): A young Leithian woman. One of the princess's ladies.

Ambras (AHM-brahs): Master Ambras, a Kelorin healer, personal physician to Queen Semorel.

Anduar Tyronin (AHN-doo-ar teer-O-nihn): A Kelorin lord. One of the six Signers of the Pact of Lankura, which ended the civil war that followed the killing of King Tevren.

Angkat (AHNG-kaht): A Mahuk warlord. Chief rival of Baalkir.

Animara (ah-nee-MAR-ah): A Turowan woman. Sister of Jila, and Narei's aunt, called 'Ani' for short. Mother of Bahiri, Tavo, and Pilo. Wife of Sudano.

Averwin (AV-er-wihn): Small country estate that was Nagaro's boyhood home.

Baalkir jir-Akaan (BAHL-keer jeer-ah-KAHN): A Mahuk warlord, now Emperor of the Mahuk Baar, to whom the *Fist of Death* belonged. Uncle of Roheed.

Bahiri (bah-HEER-ee): A young Turowan girl, daughter of Animara and Sudano. Nagaro's niece.

Berenil (BEHR-ehn-ihl): A young Kelorin woman, oldest daughter of the merchant Gedras.

bishka (BIHSH-kah): A relatively mild but expressive expletive in Hashti, the language of the Mahuk Baar.

bodjer (BAH-jer): Epithet derived from a Leithian expression that was originally much cruder, "bodjer" means roughly "to do an injury to" as commonly used in the Common Speech.

Boka Omei (BO-kah O-may): Largest island at the northern end of the seaward side of the Lomoas. It has two large harbors on its leeward side: the Bay of Omei to the north, and Boka Bay to the south.

Bona Farana (BO-nah far-AH-nah): A gold port located towards the southern end of Big Farano Island.

Borobai (BO-ro-bahy): An island near the southern end of the Inner Faranos, south of Tobai.

Bouno (bo-OO-no): A Turowan former galley slave and one of Nagaro's followers. Formerly a merchant seaman.

Brandle (BRAND'l): A young Leithian, one of the princess's guards and nephew to Lady Merriel.

Brendet (BREHN-deht): A young Leithian woman. One of the princess's ladies.

Bron Sobring (brahn SO-bring): A Leithian lord, one of Leyel Virden's "keepers".

Chaheel (chah-HEEL): A Hashtep former galley slave and one of Nagaro's followers. A "crossed" man, partnered with Nanu.

Chitaopa (chih-TAOW-pah): A small uninhabited island off the northern coast of Jinara.

Clarimel (CLAR-ih-mehl): A young Leithian woman. One of the princess's ladies.

crossed: English translation of a word in the Common Speech used as a term for homosexual.

Darion Loros (DEHR-ee-ahn LOR-ose): Half Kelorin, half Turowan, first king of Edrovir, called Darion the Great.

daashu (DAH-shoo): Hashti for "thank you."

Delmanei (del-MAH-nay): A Kelorin woman, wife of the merchant Gedras.

Delvin (DEHL-vihn): A Kelorin youth, a member of the Palace Guard in Lankura.

dokan (DOE-kahn): An Edroviran gold coin. Equivalent to ten trokins or one thousand rins.

Dreigen (DRAY-gehn) (The "g" is hard as in "get"): Half Jinari, half Kelorin. King Elgurn's Lore Master and an expert on poisons.

Droviri (dro-VEER-ee): Hashti word for the Edroviran language (called the Common Speech by its speakers). Also used as an adjective meaning "Edroviran", or to mean an inhabitant of Edrovir.

Duani (doo-AH-nee): An island in the middle of the seaward side of the Lomoas. The South Duani Channel separates it from the Lomoan islands immediately to the south of it.

Duleyin (doo-Lay-ihn): Seventh month of the Edroviran calendar, equivalent to July.

Dunrel (DOON-rehl): Sixth month of the Edroviran calendar, equivalent to June.

Edro (EHD-ro): The River Edro, longest river in Edrovir, flowing northeast to southwest and emptying into the sea at Lankura.

Edrovir (EHD-ro-veer): A kingdom inhabited by the Kelorin, Leithian, and Turowan peoples, stretching from the Gorietha mountains on the east to the western sea, and from the Kor Vaskol mountains in the north to the borders of Hran and Jinara in the south.

Elgurn Harlind (EHL-gurn HAR-lihnd): A Leithian, third king of Edrovir.

Elyan (EHL-ee-ahn): Prince Elyan. A high-born Kelorin, third husband of the Princess Nevien.

Emril (EHM-rihl): A Kelorin woman who raised Roheed jir-Akaan, while kept as a slave by Baalkir's brother Notep.

Erantil (EHR-ahn-tihl): Erantil Crimson, an expensive, highly favored variety of sothiril berry, producing sothiril that is unique in flavor and blood-red in color.

Evrel (EHV-rehl): Fourth month of the Edroviran calendar, equivalent to April.

Farano (FAR-ah-no) Islands: The Faranos. The Farano Islands, inner and outer chains, lie off the northern coast of Edrovir, north of the mouth of the River Edro.

Farano's Mouth: The gap, roughly opposite the River Edro, between the Farano Islands and the Lomoas.

Farano Passage: North-south channel separating the island chains of the Inner and Outer Faranos.

farusia (fah-ROO-see-ah): a small shrub bearing large white trumpet-shaped flowers, also the flower of this plant. (Also the name of Nagaro's bay mare that he keeps on Pakoa.)

Filora (fih-LOR-ah): Tira Filora. An older Kelorin woman, Mistress of the Royal Kitchens in the palace of Lankura.

Finorel (FIHN-or-ehl): Twelfth month of the Edroviran calendar, equivalent to December.

Gedras (GEHD-rahs) (The "G" is hard): A Kelorin merchant living in Pakoa Town.

Geldoran Finrad (GEHL-dor-ahn FIHN-rahd): Commander Geldoran. A Kelorin officer in the Royal Fleet of Edrovir, second in command to Kuran Kel.

Genorel (GEHN-or-elh) (The "G" is hard): First month of the Edroviran calendar, equivalent to January

Gesrin (GEHS-rihn) (The "G" is hard): A young Kelorin woman, second daughter of the merchant Gedras.

Gillard Marchent (GIHL-ard MAR-chent) (The "G" is hard as in "give"): A high-born Leithian, also called Gill. One of Leyel Virden's "keepers" and Princess Nevien's second husband. Deceased.

Great Channel: The channel separating the various island chains from the mainland. While variable in width, it is generally broader than any of the north-south channels separating the various islands and island chains from one another— hence the name.

Grimbold Sobring (GRIHM-bold SO-bring): A Leithian lord. Brother and
successor of Bron Sobring as lord of Sobring Hold.

Grovern (GRO-vurn): A Leithian man, husband of Lady Meriel. Deceased,
of the plague.

Guhanu (Goo-HA-noo): A Turowan man. A follower of Nagaro, Timegar's
first mate.

Gurd (gurd): A young Leithian sea warrior, formerly with the Royal Fleet
of Edrovir, a follower of Nagaro, once a slave freed from the Mahuk
war galley *Fist of Death*.

Habu (HAH-boo): A young Turowan, son of Yuli and Ramu, keepers of the
Bay Tree Inn on Pakoa.

Hakesh (HAH-hehsh): A Mautep sea warrior serving under Captain
Taokep.

Hakura Kili (hah-KOOR-ah KEE-lee): Guiding Spirit of the Turowan
people. The exclamation "Hakura!" generally expresses awe or
excitement.

hamanei mata noa (hah-MAH-nay MAH-tah NO-wah): Turowan words
to ward off evil, or misfortune (roughly translated, "spirits protect
us"). Sometimes shortened to "hamanei!" meaning "spirits!", which
can be used as an exclamation in any distressing situation.

hanuk (HAHN-ook): Hashti word for "sword".

Hanuroa (HAH-noo-RO-ah): The spirit world in the Turowan belief
system, where the spirits of the dead are believed to dwell.

Haofa (HAU-fah): A Hashtep former slave, a follower of Nagaro, translator
of Hashti for Timegar.

Harl Sobring (HARL SO-bring): A Leithian lord, father of Bron. Deceased.

Harmoth (HAR-mahth): Southern-most major coastal city in Edrovir,
Tredhold's home town.

Harthred (HARTH-red): Commander Harthred. A Leithian officer in
command of the Palace Guard at the royal palace in Lankura.

Haruda (hah-ROO-dah): A Turowan merchant seaman from Pakoa
Island, a follower of Nagaro.

Hashtep (HAHSH-tehp): Name the common people of the Mahuk Baar
use for their race. Also used as an adjective to describe anything
pertaining to that race (except the language, which is Hashti).

Hashti (HAHSH-tee): The language of the people of the Mahuk Baar
(spoken by Hashtep and Mautep).

Hel (hehl): In Leithian belief, a place of punishment after death for the
spirits of those who have transgressed. Roughly equivalent to the
Christian concept of Hell.

heskial (hehs-kee-AHL): a will-controlling "spirit magic" drug distilled
from the flowers of a variety of the heskia vine grown in Jinara.

Idrin (IHD-rihn): Thirteenth and final month of the Edroviran calendar, a seven-day period surrounding the winter solstice. Considered an ill-omened time.

Ilsafeth (IHL-sah-fehth): A Leithian woman, Tredhold's wife, a "Fleet widow" with two children by her previous husband.

inan pash (EE-nan pash): Hashti phrase for "you are welcome." Literally, "not (an) obligation".

Inside Passage: The irregular channel running north-south between the islands of the Lomoa chain, from Pakoa northwards.

Jaamra (JAHM-rah): Strait of Jaamra. A passage between two islands of the Mahuk Baar, site of the sea battle during which Nagaro and his fellow slaves took the Mahuk war galley *Fist of Death* and won their freedom.

Jila (JEE-lah): A beautiful and notorious Turowan woman. Sister of Animara and mother of Narei.

Jinara (jih-NAR-ah): A coastal country lying between Edrovir and the Mahuk Baar, involved in a long-running border dispute with Edrovir.

Jinari (jih-NAR-ee): Edroviran name for the inhabitants of Jinara. Also their language and an adjective meaning "pertaining to Jinara".

Jomo Nareyo (JO-mo nar-EHY-o): A Turowan fisherman of Wotana, father of Taru. Deceased.

Judaba (joo-DAH-bah): Northernmost of the Jinari islands and closest island to Chitaopa.

judili hanuktar (joo-DEE-lee HAHN-ook-tar): Hashti for "demon swordsman."

Kale Fendred (kayl FEHN-drehd): A Leithian lord, boyhood friend of King Elgurn and one of Leyel Virden's "keepers."

kajadeem (kah-jah-DEEM): Hashti word for "honor."

Kapala (kah-PAHL-ah): One of the outer, seaward islands in the southern Lomoas.

Kasadrin (KAH-sah-drihn): A board game of Kelorin origin, also called "King's Men" but literally translating as "lord's people."

Katuk (ka-TOOK): A young Hashtep man from the Mahuk Baar, Pavo Maat's younger brother.

Kel Lankura (kel lahn-KOOR-ah): A low mountain near the mouth of the River Edro, on its northern shore and adjacent to Edrovir's capital city, Lankura.

Kel Tierna (kel tee-EHR-nah): A coastal city in Edrovir, south of Lankura.

Kelorin (KEL-or-in): The fair-skinned, dark-haired people originally from the isles of Kelor (the land of Kelornas) in the far western sea. It is their own name for themselves or their language. Also used as an adjective to mean "pertaining to Kelor or the Kelorin people."

Kendira (kehn-DEER-ah): A young Kelorin woman. One of the princess's ladies.

keshaal (keh-SHAHL): A Hashti expletive, stronger than *bishka*.

kia kaar hanuk-tak (KEE-ah kahr HAHN-ook-tahk): Hashti phrase: "Put down (the) sword belonging (to you)."

Kiraam Shaku-Tal (KEER-ahm shah-koo-TAHL): Name given to Nagaro by Roheed. In Hashti it means "thief of slaves".

Kormine (kor-MEEN): A Kelorin woman, wife of Timegar.

Kroneg (KRO-nehg): Leithian god of war. Arbiter of the outcome of armed conflict, and ruler of the dark moon, Naru.

kuma (KOO-mah): Kuma stain, a brown stain for fair skin used for sun-protection. Kuma ointment is made from the meat of the nuts of the kuma plant and serves as a carrier for the stain that is derived from their shells.

Kunoa (koo-NO-ah)A: A young Turowan man from Pakoa, a former slave freed from the Mahuk war galley *Fist of Death* and a follower of Nagaro.

Kuran Kel (KOOR-ahn KEHL): Half Kelorin, half Turowan, the lord of Kel Wared and Lord of the Royal Fleet of Edrovir.

Lankura (LAHN-koor-ah): Capital city of Edrovir, located at the mouth of the River Edro.

Landros Torenin (LAN-drose tor-EHN-ihn): An older Kelorin sea warrior who served in the Royal Fleet of Edrovir as second mate of the *Fairwind*. A former slave freed from the *Fist of Death* and a follower of Nagaro, serving as captain of the pirate ship *Sea Eagle*.

Lapoa (lah-PO-ah): An island near the northern end of the leeward side of the Lomoas. The Lapoa Channel separates it from Oapa, the island immediately to the south.

Leithian (LAY-thee-en): A fair-skinned, blond or red-haired people originally from a land called Leith, lying in the east beyond Arlinas. Also their original language, largely lost in Edrovir, or an adjective for anything relating to Leithian people.

Leyel Virden (LAY-ehl VER-dehn): Name given to Nagaro by the Lady Maramine, also known as the "idiot prince" and first husband of Princess Nevien.

Lissel (lih-SEHL): A young Kelorin woman, youngest daughter of the merchant Gedras.

Lissafel (LIHS-ah-fehl): "The Lady", maiden goddess of the Leithians. Ruler of the hearts of men and women, and of the pale moon Talebra.

Lokundas (lo-KOON-dahs): The "Turner of Worlds", Kelorin personification of fate. One of the old gods of the Cloud Mountain People.

Lomoas (lo-MO-ahs): A group of islands off the southern coast of Edrovir. The Lomoa Islands lie south of the Inner and Outer Faranos and south of the mouth of the River Edro.

Long Harbor: The most southernly gold port, located at the northern end of Little Farano Island, at the harbor formed by the channel that incompletely separates Big Farano from Little Farano.

Lothard Hurn (LO-thard hurn): A Leithian lord, son of Reith Hurn who killed King Tevren and became one of the Signers of the Pact of Lankura. (Reith is deceased.)

Luweda (loo-WAY-da): A Turowan woman, younger daughter of Yuli and Ramu, the keepers of the Bay Tree Inn on Pakoa.

Madrel (MAH-drehl): Third month of the Edrovirin calendar, equivalent to March.

Mahuk (MAH-hook): Used as an adjective to identify things from the Mahuk Baar, such as ships. Used in Edrovir to refer to the tawny-skinned, black-haired people from the Mahuk Baar who are properly called Hashtep, or Mautep in the case of the warlord class.

Mahuk Baar (MAH-hook bar): A coastal country and islands to the south of Edrovir, beyond Jinara. Inhabited by the Hashtep people and their Mautep warlord class.

Maramine Virden (mar-ah-MEEN VER-dehn): A Kelorin lady, guardian of Leyel Virden, and victim of a fatal plot by King Elgurn, his Lore Master Dreigen, and others. Deceased.

Matahi (mah-TAH-hee): A young Hashtep woman on Pakoa Island, older sister of Tenepti.

Matapili (MAH-tah-PEE-lee): A Jinari fisherman and courier for the Jinari merchant's agent Utabala.

Mautep (MAOW-tehp): Hasthi word for the Hashtep warlord class of the Mahik Baar.

Medrin (MEHD-rihn): Fifth month of the Edroviran calendar, equivalent to May.

Mendorel (MEHN-dor-ehl): A Kelorin shopkeeper and candle-maker in Kel Tierna. Also a former slave freed from the Mahuk war galley *Fist of Death* and one-time follower of Ngaro.

Meriel (MEHR-ee-ehl): Lady Meriel. A high-born Leithian woman, one of Queen Semorel's ladies, and chaperon to Princess Nevien and her ladies.

Minowei (mih-NO-way): Princess Minowei to the Turowan people. A Turowan chief's daughter, known from the story of her romance with the Kelorin lord Nevrath who founded the house of Loros. She became Nevrath's wife, first Lady of Loros, and mother of Darion.

Moluaro (mo-loo-AR-o): A large, long island in the middle Lomoas, immediately south of Oapa.

Moraga (mor-AH-gah): A Turowan merchant seaman and former slave freed from the *Fist of Death* who follows Nagaro and is captain of the pirate ship *Tiger*.

Morberk (MOR-burk): A member of the Palace Guard in Lankura. (Leithian, judging by his name)

Mundata Punda (moon-DAH-tah POON-dah): A Jinari merchant for whom Utabala serves as a merchant's agent and bookkeeper.

Muwabei (moo-WAH-bay): A Turowan fisherman of the Lomoas.

Nagaro (nah-GAR-o): Name taken by Leyel Virden after his escape from Lankura. It means "nameless man" in the old Turowan tongue.

Nanu (NAH-noo): A Turowan man, a former slave freed from the Mahuk war galley *Fist of Death*, and a follower of Nagaro. A "crossed" man partnered with Chaheel.

Narei (NAR-ay): A little girl, Nagaro's daughter by Jila, of mixed Turowan and Kelorin blood. Her name means "sea" in the Turowan language.

Naru (NAR-oo): The smaller and dimmer of the world's two moons, often called simply "the dark moon." It travels a little faster than the bright moon, Talebra, at times overtaking the larger moon and crossing in front of it. In Kelorin legend, Naru is a "ship that sailed between the stars", carrying the various human races and the "seeds" of the different kinds of animals and plants.

Nevien (NEHV-ee-ehn): Princess Nevien, daughter of King Elgurn and Queen Semorel of Edrovir. A young woman of mixed Leithian and Kelorin blood.

Nevrath (NEHV-rahth): A high-born Kelorin man (son of a Wared lord), who courted and married Princess Minowei. Founder of the house or Loros and father of Darion.

Nondorin (NOEN-dor-ihn): Eleventh month of the Edrovirin calendar, equivalent to November.

Notep (NO-tehp): A Mautep lord, younger brother of the Emperor Baalkir jir-Akaan and father of Roheed.

Oapa (o-AH-pah): A small island in the northern end of the Lomoa chain, on the leeward side, immediately south of Lapoa.

Obai (o-BAHY): An island of the Inner Faranos, closest island to Wotana Bay.

Obiari (o-bee-AR-ee): Master Obiari, a Jinari lore master whose works are much favored by King Elgurn's sinister Lore Master, Dreigen.

Olomi (o-LO-mee): A Turowan woman of Wotana. Wife of Jomo and mother of Taru, killed by Captain Urchak.

onam (O-nahm): Kelorin word for the substance of which the material world is composed: matter, flesh.

opa (O-pah): A narcotic drug given in extreme cases for pain, but known for causing strange dreams or hallucinations. Probably opium or something related.

Oran (OR-ahn): A Kelorin member of the Palace Guard in Lankura.

Osfaraad (ose-far-AHD): An island of the Mahuk Baar where Nagaro and his followers put rescued Hashtep slaves ashore, near the northern border of Mahuk waters.

Oteyin (o-TAY- ihn): Eigth month of the Edrovirin calendar, equivalent to August.

Pakoa (pah-KO-ah): An island off the southern coast of Edrovir, southern-most isle of the Lomoas and Nagaro's home port. Pakoa Town is the island's only real town and its port, located on Pakoa Harbor.

Panila (pah-NEE-lah): A young Turowan woman, wife of Moraga.

Patamtala (pah-tahm-TAH-lah): A Jinari port on the island of Judaba.

Pavo Maat (PAH-vo MAHT): A young Hashtep, Nagaro's Hashtep friend with whom he escaped from slavery on the Mahuk war galley *Fist of Death*. Pavo is now second mate on Nagaro's flagship, the *Sword of Freedom*.

Pendrik Glenmark (PEHN-drihk GLEHN-mark): A Leithian lord, one of the Signers of the Pact of Lankura, which ended the civil war that followed the killing of King Tevren.

Perenil (PEHR-ehn-ihl): Captain Perenil. An officer of the Palace Guard in Lankura. (Kelorin, judging by his name).

Pilo (PEE-lo): A young Turowan boy, younger son of Animara and Sudano.

Ramu (RAH-moo): A Turowan man, keeper of the Bay Tree Inn on Pakoa. Husband of Yuli and father of Habu and Luweda.

Rastyl Korven (rahs-TEEL KOR-vehn): A Kelorin lord with pale gray eyes.

Rianine (REE-ah-neen): A young Kelorin woman, one of the princess's ladies.

rin (rihn): A small copper coin that is the basic unit of the Edroviran system of currency. There are one hundred rins to a trokin and one thousand rins to a dokan.

Roheed jir-Akaan (ro-HEED jeer-ah-KAHN): A young Mautep sea warrior who tried to help Nagaro during his time as a galley slave because of a "blood debt" charging him to help men who were orphaned in infancy. Nephew of Emperor Baalkir and son of Notep.

Ruald Grinard (roo-AHLD GRIHN-ard): Captain Ruald. A Leithian officer in the Royal Fleet of Edrovir, captain of Kuran Kel's flag ship, the *Pride of Lankura*.

Rubo (ROO-bo): A Turowan former Fleet warrior and ship's cook, a follower of Nagaro.

Sar Tipaal (SAHR tih-PAHL): A port city of the Mahuk Baar. Emperor Balkeer's capital and site of his great shipyard.

Sea Passage: Taking the Sea Passage means sailing north or south on the seaward side of any of the island chains. (Not a channel, as such, but a course easily taken by seamen who lack the skill to navigate in the open ocean out of sight of land.)

Sedrin (SEHD-rihn): Ninth month of the Edroviran calendar, equivalent to September.

Seftep (SEHF-tehp): A young Hashtep, a former slave freed from a Mahuk war galley and a follower of Nagaro.

Semorel (SEHM-or-ehl): King Elgurn's Kelorin queen. Mother of Princess Nevien.

Seralind (sehr-ah-LIHND): Name for the place of reward after death in Leithian belief, paradise or heaven.

shaku (SHAH-koo): Hashti word for "slave."

shaku raal (SHAH-koo RAHL): Hashti for "slave dog."

Sheptuum (shehp-TOOM): God of the Hashtep and Mautep people of the Mahuk Baar.

Shofeer (sho-FEER): Name of a Mautep warrior family and their House. The Mautep call Nagaro's sword the "Sword of Shofeer" because it belonged to a warrior of that House.

Simion (SIH-mee-ahn): A young Kelorin, formerly a sea warrior of the Royal Fleet and also a former slave freed from the Mahuk war galley *Fist of Death*. A "crossed" man.

Sindar (SIHN-dahr): Infant son of the Kelorin woman Emril. She was kept as a slave by Notep to care for his son Roheed after the latter's mother died in childbirth. Name given by Nagaro to a young Kelorin man, an escaped slave who speaks only Hashti.

Soku (SO-koo): A small island at the northern end of the Lomoas, immediately adjacent to the Bay of Omei on the large island of Boka Omei.

Solbrid (SOL-brihd): The Leithian mother goddess. Ruler of earth and giver of life.

sothiril (SO-thur-ihl): A tea-like infusion made from the berries of the plant of the same name. Also used to refer to the dried berries.

Sudano (soo-DAH-no): A Turowan kuma farmer, husband of Animara.

Sulani (soo-LAH-nee): A young Turowan woman, once adored by Habu.

Taan (TAHN): A Hasthep man from the Mahuk Baar, Pavo Maat's older brother.

Tambali (tahm-BAH-lee): A port city near the northern border of Jimara, Utabala's home.

Talebra (tah-LAY-brah): Name of the larger and brighter of the world's two moons. Often called simply, "the bright moon."

Taokep jir-Muktaar (TAU-kehp jeer mook-TAR): Captain Taokep, a Mautep warship captain serving the warlord Tuluptak.

Taru Nareyo (TAR-roo nar-AY-o): A young Turowan fisherman's son from Wotana. Nagaro's Turowan friend with whom he escaped from slavery on the Mahuk war galley *Fist of Death*. Taru is now first mate on Nagaro's flagship, the *Sword of Freedom*.

Tavo (TAH-vo): A young Turowan boy, older son of Animara and Sudano.

Tenepti (tehn-EHP-tee): A young Hashtep woman of Pakoa, Pavo's true love.

Tibo (TEE-bo): A Turowan fisherman of the Lomoas.

Timegar (TIH-may-gar): A Kelorin man from Pakoa. A former Fleet warrior and a follower of Nagaro, serving as captain of the pirate ship *North Wind*.

Tira (TEER-rah): Respectful form of feminine address, roughly equivalent to "Mrs'" or "Ms." without implication regarding marital status. Used preceding a given name.

tirka (TUR-kah): A short-sleeved outer garment, opening down the front and cut long enough to cover the hips. Generally worn over a long-sleeved shirt and usually belted.

Tirobo (tih-RO-bo): Southernmost island in the Inner Faranos of any significant size.

Tobai (to-BAHY): An island in the Inner Faranos, immediately south of Obai.

Todrin (TOE-drihn): Tenth month of the Edrovirin calendar, equivalent to October.

Tor (tor): Respectful form of masculine address, roughly equivalent to "Mr". Used preceding a given name.

Tosmataak (Tose-mah-TAHK): Place where Tuul came from, presumably in the Mahuk Baar.

Tredhold Ferth (TRED-hold FURTH): A Leithian former ship's doctor in the Royal Fleet of Edrovir, and a former slave freed from the *Fist of Death*, now serving as a ship's doctor for Nagaro.

trokin (TRO-kihn): A silver coin worth one hundred rins. There are ten trokins in one dokan.

Tulara (too-LAR-ah): A young Turowan woman, formerly a tavern woman but now employed at the Bay Tree Inn in Pakoa Town. A romantic interest of Taru.

Tulevien (too-LEHV-ee-ehn): A young Kelorin woman, one of the princess's ladies.

Tuluptak (TOO-loop-tahk): A Mautep warlord.

Tunapa (too-NAH-pah): A Lomoan island on the leeward side of the north end of the Inside Passage.

Turo (TOOR-o): "The Turo" is the Turowan name for their own people. It also means a Turowan man. Turowa is the female equivalent.

Turowan (toor-O-ahn): A member of a brown-skinned, dark-haired people native to the coastal region of Edrovir, also called the Turo. Also their language and an adjective used to describe things relating to the Turowan people.

Ulapa (oo-LAH-pah): An aging Turowan man and former sailor, caretaker of Nagaro and Taru's house on Pakoa Island when they are absent.

Urchak tok-Faar (UR-chahk toke-FAHR): A Mautep sea warrior under Emperor Baalkir, former captain of the *Fist of Death*.

Utabala (OO-tah-BAH-lah): A Jinari merchant's agent and interpreter, a former slave freed from the Mahuk war galley *Fist of Death* who returned to the service of his master, Mundata Punda.

Vedorel (VEHD-or-ehl): Second month of the Edroviran calendar, equivalent to February.

Vothra (VO-thrah): The Benevolent Spirit of the Kelorin people, teacher of the Path as set forth in the Vothrin Writings. Not a god, but a joining of many human spirits, Vothra offers council and guides a spirit after death through the void and into a new life.

Wared (WAH-rehd): Kelorin word for the territory ruled by a Kelorin lord.

Wotana (wo-TAH-nah): A fishing village in Galenor Wared, twenty miles north of Lankura, on Wotana Bay. Taru's original home.

Worling (WOR-lihng): Captain Worling. A Leithian officer of the Palace Guard in Lankura.

Yuli (YOO-lee): A Turowan woman, wife of Ramu. They keep of the Bay Tree Inn on Pakoa Island. Mother of Habu and Luweda.

Zirda (ZUR-dah): Respectful masculine form of address, roughly equivalent to "sir." Used without an accompanying name.

Zirdyn (zur-DEEN): Respectful feminine form of address, roughly equivalent to "madame." Used without an accompanying name.

Zomora (zo-MOR-ah): Tira Zomora. The Turowan medicine woman on Pakoa Island.

Notes on Nagaro's World

Titles and Forms of Address in Edrovir

The titles **Lord** and **Lady** in Kelorin tradition were borne only by the chosen leader of a house and his/her immediate family, and only during the period of the person's service. In the Leithian tradition, the equivalent titles denoted hereditary status and were borne by all members of what were perceived as "noble" families. After these two cultures became enmeshed, Kelorin usage became a bit more relaxed, extending often as a kind of courtesy to previous living leaders and members of families that had included lords and ladies in the past to more closely resemble the Leithian usage. The Kelorin wished to remain on equal footing with the Leithians, and broadening their own definition was easier than persuading the Leithians to narrow theirs. These titles are always placed before the given name (or given plus family name), not before family name alone.

Addressing someone as "My Lord" only indicates the other person's status, not that the person speaking is under the other person's jurisdiction. Proper formal forms of address for royalty are: "My Lord King," "My Lady Queen," "My Lord Prince," and "My Lady Princess." Simple "My Lord," or "My Lady" can be substituted in less formal situations.

Zirda and **Zirdyn** are roughly equivalent to the modern American usage of "Sir" and "Madame," respectively. They always substitute for a person's name, rather than preceding it. They are of Kelorin origin and their purpose was to show respect for the person being addressed. The Leithians had to adopt the terms to avoid insulting people, but some individuals can manage to make the words sound insulting by the way they are spoken. A subtle rebuke or insult may be implied by using "Zirda" to address someone entitled to use some other title, such as "Captain."

Tor and **Tira** are most similar to our "Mr." and "Ms." They always precede a given name, not a surname or family name. Family names are used primarily when a more precise identification is required, or possibly to boast if the family is a "noble" one. Tor and Tira are Kelorin in origin and used to show respect. They are used only for adults, not children ,and their use shows a perception that the person addressed is an adult. They are not used between friends and family members, being for more formal situations.

Edroviran Calendar

Months of the year: The Edrovirin calendar has thirteen months. In order, they are: **Genorel, Vedorel, Madrel, Evrel, Medrin, Dunrel, Duleyin, Oteyin, Sedrin, Todrin, Nondorin, Finorel,** and **Idrin.** Each month has exactly four eight-day weeks (therefore thirty-two days), except Idrin, which has only seven days and therefore only one seven-day week. The winter solstice (referred to as the "turning of the year") falls on the fourth of Idrin.

Days of the week: There are eight days in a week, referred to by their numbers: **First Day, Second Day,** and so forth. If a person says, "on Third Day" or "on next Third Day," they mean the third day of the current week or of the following week, respectively. If a person says, "the third of Medrin," they mean the third day of the month of Medrin.

Edroviran Currency

The **rin,** a copper coin, is the base of the Edrovirin currency, rather like the dollar. There are half-rin and quarter-rin coins, as well as ten-rin pieces. The **trokin** is a silver coin worth 100 rins, and the **dokan** is a gold coin worth ten trokins, or 1000 rins. There are also half-trokin coins and half-dokan coins. People will often state larger amounts in rins, even though they could be stated in round numbers of trokins and/or dokans. For example, people are more likely to say, "450 rins" than "four and a half trokins."

Edroviran Military Organization

Edrovir is a young nation with relatively rudimentary military institutions. The words I've chosen to represent their military ranks do not reflect the usage in any current branch of the armed forces. For the **City Guard** or **Palace Guard**, I use "commander" for someone who is in command, and "lieutenant" for someone who is a step below that. I have used "sergeant" when I wanted something a bit lower still, and the rank and file are just "guardsman."

The **Royal Fleet** is more clearly defined. The Lord of the Fleet is in charge of the entire Fleet. He has some small number of "commanders," each of whom is in charge of a number of "captains." On board an individual ship, the captain is in charge and the other officers consist of "first mate," "second mate," and "third mate." The first mate in usually in charge of the oar deck crew while the second mate is in charge of the main deck crew and therefore the sails. The third mate is there to add depth to the chain of command in the event that something happens to one of the other officers. There would also be a steersman manning the tiller, a drummer to beat time on the oar deck, a ship's doctor, and a cook – but none of these are officers. All crew members on a war galley are fighters, regardless of rank or other function served.

History of Edrovir

The **Turowan** people had lived for multiple generations as loosely organized clans along the coast and in the islands of the region that became the nation of Edrovir. The hinterland had previously been inhabited as indicated by some ruins, but was unpopulated at the time of the cataclysm known as the **Time of Fire and Water** which precipitated the arrival of the Kelorin and Leithian peoples from **Arlinas** to the east.

The **Kelorin** people, under the leadership of **Atheran** and the guidance of Vothra, had come by ship from the western islands of **Kelornas** several generations before and settled in the north of the land they named Arlinas, which they found unpeopled but marked by scattered ruins left by a vanished race. Those vanished people also left caches of crystals known as **rithrals** whose power-channeling properties seduced the Kelorin people away from the wisdom of Vothra's Path. **Leithian** people began arriving from Leith (lying still farther east) after the Kelorin were already well established throughout much of the northern, middle, and western parts of Arlinas and the rithral lords were rising to power. The Leithians settled in the southern and southeastern parts of Arlinas and coexisted with the Kelorin in a state of uneasy equality for perhaps a generation prior to the cataclysm. The cataclysm (caused by multiple meteorite strikes) coincided (not coincidentally) with the catastrophic ending of the **Age of the Rithral Lords** and descending of a "**shadow**" on the land of Arlinas. These latter events, associated with a mysterious figure known as **Naibarad the Destroyer**, possibly the most powerful of the rithral lords, were what truly drove the Kelorin and Leithian peoples to abandon Arlinas, crossing the Goreitha Mountains into the valley of the River Edro and its surrounding lands.

With the rithal lords dead and the rithrals either destroyed or left behind in a shadowed land, the Kelorin and Leithian people were forced to make a new beginning. In the power vacuum of the unpopulated region of Edrovir, they spread rapidly across the land as their rival lords staked out territories, some of which included areas inhabited by Turowan folk. The Turo, technologically less advanced and peaceable by nature, offered little resistance. Over the next twenty to thirty years, friction between Kelorin and Leithians grew and armed conflicts escalated, (as did border disputes with the neighboring nations of Jinara and Hran, to the south). Finally, a man named **Darion Loros**, the son of a Kelorin lord, **Nevrath**, and a Turowan chief's daughter, **Minowei**, emerged as a unifying figure. He pushed for the establishment of a **Council of Lords** made up of all the Kelorin and Leithian lords, and three Turowan chiefs, to provide common governance for a unified nation of **Edrovir**, with its capitol at **Lankura**. The Council of Lords, in turn, overwhelmingly chose Darion to be the new nation's king.

As Edrovir's first king, Darion wrote a **charter** to establish the basic legal framework for the new kingdom. He had married a Kelorin woman, **Selfira**, and they had a son, **Tevren Loros**. After eighteen years of rule, Darion's unexpected and untimely death was widely blamed on his Lore Master, **Dreigen**, a man of mixed Kelorin/Jinari ancestry who had been presented to Darion by a Leithian lord, **Harl Sobring**. A badly divided Council of Lords narrowly chose the twenty-six-year-old Tevern to be Edrovir's second king. Tevren lacked his father's even temper and diplomatic skill. Pressed to marry a Leithian woman, he instead chose a Kelorin, **Lindra of Irvenen**, and his brief reign was marred by increasing tension between the more militant factions of Kelorin and Leithian lords. When Lindra bore Tevren a son at his ancestral home of Loros Hall, a group of Leithians lead by Lord **Reith Hurn** waylaid the young couple as they sought to return to Lankura leaving both Tevren and Lindra dead and their infant son missing.

Outrage over what was widely considered to have been a double murder lead to serious internal strife, culminating in an incipient civil war which was prevented from coalescing when the six strongest lords, three Kelorin (**Anduar Tyronin**, **Berinar Sundorin**, & **Devral Sedras**) and three Leithian (**Reith Hurn**, **Pendrik Glenmark**, & **Odus Morbern**), called a truce. They met at Lankura and signed a document known as the **Pact of Lankura** The pact stipulated that none of the six signers could serve as king but that they would choose the king, thus abrogating the authority of the Council of Lords. The **Pact Signers** chose a Leithian, **Elgurn Harlind**, to be the third king of Edrovir. Elgurn had been one of Darion's most loyal supporters and he had a Keloring wife, **Semorel**, who in due course bore him a daughter, **Nevien**. The six Pact Signers continued to contribute to the rule of Edrovir by advising Elgurn as the **King's Council**.

Religions

Kelorin: The Kelorin people originally had a pantheon of deities of whom two are mentioned: **Lokundas**, the "Turner of Worlds," who is basically a personification of fate, and **Nomemduran**, the "Maker of All Things." **Vothra**, the Benevolent Spirit of the Kelorin, and Vothrin teachings, (the Vothrin Path), were superimposed on these older beliefs. The older deities have been largely abandoned, but the habit of worrying about tempting Lokundas lingers. Vothra is spirit being made up of multiple human spirits that have joined together. Since each of those spirits has lived multiple lives, Vothra is possessed of great wisdom, but is not a god and not all-knowing or all-powerful.

The Vothrin Writings: The *First Book of Vothra* is nattributed to the spirit that first brought to the living world an awareness of the nature of the "void" and the existence of spirits in the state between lives. That spirit called itself Uona and came to dwell in the body of a man named Luzan who found a way for his spirit to leave his body before that body was at the point of death. Luzan lived on one of the Kelorin isles, was blind from early childhood, and later suffered a crippling injury to both legs. Because the body Uona inhabited was blind, the *First Book of Vothra* was set down on paper by Luzan's sister Ilira. Vothra came into being after the death of Uona/Luzan. The spirit of Uona was able to maintain communication from the void with Ilira during her continued life. Uona became the founding spirit of Vothra and was gradually joined by other spirits,making Vothra stronger and more able to contact the spirits of the living. The *Second Book of Vothra* is a compilationof writings by living people who were in close communication with Vothra.

Turowan: The Turo have a guiding spirit named **Hakura Kili**, who is benign. There are also unnamed **World Spirits** that have power to affect men's lives and are generally described as "wayward" in the sense of being unpredictable.

Leithian: The Leithian pantheon consists of four deities. **Hrothgard**, is the patriarch, called "King of the Heavens," who controls the weather and is also the patron of rulers. **Solbrid** is the mother goddess (sometimes called "Mother Solbrid" or "Queen Solbrid"). She is the giver and taker of life. **Kroneg** is the god of war and patron of all things male. He is associated with Naru, the dark moon. **Lissafel**, the maiden goddess, is sometimes called "The Lady" and is the patron of lovers. She is associated with Talebra, the bright moon. **Seralind** is the Leithian heaven, and **Hel** is a place of punishment after death.

Mahuk Baar: The Hastep people, including the Mautep warrior class revere a single god, **Sheptuum**. **Hiptatak** is Sheptuum's messenger. **Chofir Naak** is their heaven or afterlife.

Jinara: The Jinari have one god, whose name is not spoken but is referred to by various phrases such as, "The un-named one," or "He whose name we do not speak." **Jembari** is a Jinari prophet.

Acknowledgements

I must first thank those who gave me input on the manuscript during its development. Most significantly this includes my test readers for the final version: Suzanne Coulter, Aubrey Lyons, and Scott Kilburn. In addition, there are the members of ScHoFan, a critique group under the auspices of the Greater Los Angeles Writers Society (GLAWS), who gave me feedback on earlier versions of the critical opening chapters. They include, in alphabetical order: Carol Ann Alves, John Gwinner, Ken Hughes, Scott Kilburn, Katy Mann, Carmen Mendivil, Robin Reed, Taguhi Tavitian, and Garrett Weinstein.

I am also grateful for the support of my husband and the other members of my family who continue to tolerate and even encourage my pursuit of this madness. I owe a special debt of gratitude to my friends Anne Bannon and Suzanne Coulter, who have believed in me and continue to believe in my vision for this ongoing project. And finally, my heartfelt thanks go to Kristie McCue who has been behind me all the way from the very beginning and whose heroic efforts as my editor, book designer, and file format wizard have made everything possible.

Also by Carol Louise Wilde

Books of the Nagaro Chronicle

Gift of Chance (1)

Covenant of the Sword (2)

Return to Lankura (3)

Thief of Slaves (4)

Heir of Darion (5)

Brothers of the Blood (6)

The final title in this series,

Legacy of Loros (7), is forthcoming

About the Author

Carol Louise Wilde is the author of the fantasy adventure series the *Nagaro Chronicle*. She long led a double life: biology research scientist by day, and by night, chief archivist for the nation of Edrovir and its neighboring states. The *Nagaro Chronicle* covers but one brief period in the long and eventful history of this world and its inhabitants. Ms. Wilde lives in Southern California with her husband of forty odd years. They have two sons to carry on the tradition.